NO ONE SAW

Also by Beverly Long

Ten Days Gone

Visit the Author Profile page at Harlequin.com
for more titles or visit the author's website,
www.beverlylong.com.

BEVERLY LONG

NO ONE SAW

mira

mira™

ISBN-13: 978-0-7783-0965-9

No One Saw

Mira
22 Adelaide St. West, 40th Floor
Toronto, Ontario M5H 4E3, Canada
www.Harlequin.com

Printed in U.S.A.

Recycling programs
for this product may
not exist in your area.

For Lydia and Claire. You are loved.

One

With a week's worth of mail in one hand, A.L. McKittridge unlocked his apartment door with the other. Then he dragged his carry-on suitcase inside, almost tripping over Felix, who had uncharacteristically left his spot by the window where the late afternoon sun poured in. He tossed the collection of envelopes and free weekly newspapers onto his kitchen table and bent down to scratch his cat. "You must have missed me," he said. "Wasn't Rena nice to you?"

His partner had sent a text every day. Always a picture. Felix eating. Felix taking a dump. Felix giving himself a bath. No messages. Just visual confirmation that all was well while he was off in sunny California, taking a vacation for the first time in four years.

I can take care of your damn cat, she'd insisted. And while he hadn't wanted to bother her because she'd have plenty to do picking up the slack at work, she was the only one he felt he could ask. His ex-wife Jacqui would have said no. His just turned seventeen-year-old daughter, Traci, would have been willing but he hadn't liked the idea of her coming round to an empty apartment on her own.

Baywood, Wisconsin—population fifty thousand and change—was generally pretty safe but he didn't believe in taking chances. Not with Traci's safety. She'd been back in school for just a week. Her senior year. How the hell was that even possible? College was less than a year away.

No wonder his knees ached. He was getting old.

Or maybe it was flying coach for four hours. But the trip had been worth it. Tess had wanted to see the ocean. Wanted to face her nemesis, she'd claimed. And she'd been a champ. Had stood on the beach where less than a year earlier, she'd almost died after a shark had ripped off a sizable portion of her left arm. Had lifted her pretty face to the wind and stared out into the vast Pacific.

She hadn't surfed. Said she wasn't ready for that yet. But he was pretty confident that she'd gotten the closure that she'd been looking for. She'd slept almost the entire flight home, her head resting on A.L.'s shoulder. On the hour-plus drive from Madison to Baywood, she'd been awake but quiet. When he'd dropped her off at her house, she hadn't asked him in.

He wasn't offended. He'd have said no anyway. After a week together, they could probably both benefit from a little space. Their relationship was just months old and while the sex was great and the conversation even better, neither of them wanted to screw it up by jumping in too fast or too deep.

Now he had groceries to buy and laundry to do. It was back to work tomorrow. He grabbed the handle of his suitcase and was halfway down the hall when his cell rang. He looked at the number. Rena. Probably wanted to make sure he was home and Felix-watch was over. "McKittridge," he answered.

"Where are you?"

"Home."

"Oh, thank God."

He let go of his suitcase handle. Something was wrong. "What's up?" he asked.

"We've got a missing kid. Five-year-old female. Lakeside Learning Center."

Missing kid. Fuck. He glanced at his watch. Just after 6:00. That meant they had less than two hours of daylight left. "I'll be there in ten minutes."

The Lakeside Learning Center on Oak Avenue had a fancier name than building. It was a two-story building with brown clapboard siding on the first floor and tan vinyl siding on the second. There wasn't a lake in sight.

The backyard was fenced with something a bit nicer than chain link but not much. Inside the fence was standard playground equipment: several small plastic playhouses, a sandbox on legs and a swing set. The building was located at the end of the block in a mixed-use zone. Across from the front door and on the left were single-person homes. To the right, directly across Wacker Avenue, was a sandwich shop, and kitty-corner was a psychic who could only see the future on Monday, Wednesday and Friday.

A.L. took all this in as he beached his SUV in a no parking zone. Stepped over the yellow tape and made a quick stop to sign in with the cop who was at the door.

The guy's job was to ensure that there was a record of everybody who entered and exited the crime scene.

Once he was inside, his first impression was that the inside was much better than the outside. The interior had been gutted, erasing all signs that this had once been the downstairs of a 1960s two-story home. There was a large open space to his right. On the far wall hung a big-screen television and on the wall directly opposite the front door were rows of shelves, four high, stacked with books, games and small toys.

It was painted in a cheery yellow and white and the floor was a light gray tile. There was plenty of natural light coming through the front windows. The hallway he was standing in ran the entire length of the building and ended in a back door.

There was a small office area to his left. The door was open and there was a desk with a couple guest chairs. The space looked no bigger than ten feet by ten feet and was currently empty.

He sent Rena a text. Here.

A door at the far end of the hallway opened and Rena and a woman, middle-aged and white, dressed in khaki pants and a dark green button-down shirt, appeared. Rena waved at him and led the woman in his direction. "This is my partner, Detective McKittridge," she said to the woman. She looked at A.L. "Alice Quest. Owner and director of Lakeside Learning Center."

A.L. extended a hand to the woman. She shook it without saying anything.

"If you can excuse us," Rena said to the woman. "I'd like to take a minute and bring Detective McKittridge up to speed."

Alice nodded and stepped into the office. She pulled the door shut but not all the way. Rena motioned for A.L. to follow her. She crossed the big room and stopped under the television.

"What do we have?" he asked.

"Emma Whitman is a five-year-old female who has attended Lakeside Learning Center for the last two years. Her grandmother, Elaine Broadstreet, drops her off on Mondays and Wednesdays between 7:15 and 7:30."

Today was Wednesday. "Did that happen today?"

"I have this secondhand, via her son-in-law who spoke to her minutes before I got here. It did."

The hair on the back of A.L.'s neck stood up. When Traci had been little, she'd gone to day care. Not at Lakeside Learning Center. Her place had been bigger. "How many kids are here?" he asked.

"Forty. No one younger than three. No one older than five. They have two rooms, twenty kids to a room. Threes and early fours in one room. Older fours and fives in the other. Two staff members in each room. So four teachers. And a cook who works a few hours mid-day. And then there's Alice. She fills in when a staff member needs a break or if someone is ill."

Small operation. That didn't mean bad. "Where are the other staff?"

"Majority of the kids get picked up by 5:30. According to Alice, she covers the center by herself from 5:30 to 6:00 most days to save on payroll costs. Emma Whitman is generally one of the last ones to be picked up. Everybody else was gone tonight and she'd already locked the outside door around 5:45 when the father pulled up and pounded on the door. At first, she assumed that somebody else had already picked up Emma. But once Troy called his wife and the grandmother, the only other people allowed to pick her up, she called Kara Wiese, one of Emma's teachers, who said that Emma hadn't been there all day. That was the first time Alice had thought about the fact that the parents had not reported an absence. She'd been covering for an ill staff member in the classroom that Emma is not assigned to."

Perfect fucking storm.

"She quickly called the other two teachers and the cook, everyone who'd worked today, just to verify that nobody had seen Emma. When they hadn't, she called the police," Rena said. "Officers Pink and Taylor responded and secured the scene and began a room-by-room search. I arrived at the same time as Leah Whitman, mother of Emma Whitman."

"When the parent or grandparent or whoever drops off, do they deliver that child to the assigned room?"

"I asked that. Alice said that's what they want to have happen. But there are times, when a parent is in a hurry, that they will leave the child in this general area." She waved her hand toward the front door. "When they do that, they are supposed to do two things. One, sign a clipboard that normally hangs there," she said, pointing to the wall, right outside the office door, "and two, make sure they connect to a staff person, that somebody knows there is a child who needs to be escorted to his or her room."

"What happened with Emma?"

"Again, according to Troy Whitman, Mrs. Broadstreet supposedly arrived around 7:15 this morning.

She walked Emma into the building. There she saw Emma's teacher, Kara Wiese, standing in the doorway of the office, and left Emma with her. Then she went to work at her job at Milo's Motors."

He knew the place. It was a used car dealership on the south side of town. "Did the grandmother sign in?"

"There's no record of it." Rena crossed the room and picked something up from a table. She returned with the clipboard and sign-in sheet, already in a closed and tagged evidence bag. She showed it to A.L. There were two signatures. Neither of them were Elaine Broadstreet.

"I've also already bagged and tagged the sign-in sheets located in the two classrooms," Rena said.

"Mrs. Broadstreet isn't here?"

"No. She's on her way."

"Where are the parents right now?" A.L. asked.

"Troy and Leah are in Classroom 1. They're shook."

It was a parent's worst nightmare. He studied the space. The office was maybe six feet from the front door. "You said that Alice called Kara Wiese to see if Emma was here today."

"Yes. Because Alice already had Mrs. Broadstreet's version of events via Troy, she asked Kara about it."

"And what did Kara say?"

Rena's eyes looked troubled. "That she never saw Mrs. Broadstreet or Emma this morning."

Somebody was lying or had a real shitty memory.

"Height and weight of child?" he asked.

"Three-feet-two-inches and forty-four pounds. They had a well-child visit just three weeks ago," Rena added, to explain the exactness. "She was wearing blue jeans, a pink shirt with a unicorn on it, a gray lightweight hoodie and pink-and-white tennis shoes. And we've got a ton of pictures, off the parents' phones. I had them send me a couple of the best ones." She held out her phone for A.L. to see.

He looked. Sweet kid. Brown hair to her shoulders, more curly than straight. Round face. Big blue eyes.

"Cameras?" A.L. asked, looking around.

"No."

"The whole building has been searched?" A.L. asked.

"Yes. Inside and the immediate perimeter of the building."

It would have been too fucking easy if she'd been hiding in a closet. "So we've got a five-year-old who hasn't been seen for over ten hours?" A.L. said. That had to be their priority. Find the kid. Then figure out what had happened and who was at fault. The temperature in Baywood had been a pleasant seventy-six today, according to the weather app on his phone. He'd checked it at the airport. Tonight it would get down to midfifties. Not great for a kid wearing what Rena had described.

He looked down the long hallway that led to the back door. Behind the center was a parking lot for staff and beyond that was rural Wisconsin—lots of corn and beans that hadn't yet been harvested and even some pastureland for dairy cows. If the child had been dropped off this morning but never found her way to a classroom, was it possible that she'd somehow made her way out the door and wandered off somewhere? Or had someone taken her?

Both were terrifying thoughts.

"I've already reached out to the state police," Rena

added. "And made a request to the state Justice Department to issue an Amber Alert."

That was how it worked. The police couldn't unilaterally issue an Amber Alert. They requested and the Justice Department approved. Most people thought about Amber Alerts in connection to motor vehicles, assuming the purpose was to get as many eyes watching for a particular vehicle on the road. However, it could be used anytime a child seventeen or under was believed to be at risk of serious harm or death and if there was enough information to make it worthwhile. Here they had location and time of disappearance and a good description of the child. More than enough.

The Amber Alert would be broadcast on radio and television every thirty minutes for the first two hours and then every hour for the next three hours.

Also mobile phones would be lighting with a text message and signs on the highway would also share the information.

"Other social media?" he asked.

"Post is getting written right now, asking for volunteers to immediately report to this location, but once I knew you were on the way, I waited. Just wanted to make sure we were on the same page. I let Chief Faster know what was going on and he'll contact the FBI."

She'd accomplished a great deal in less than fifteen minutes. But that was how it worked with missing kids. Balls to the wall from now on out. And while he wasn't a big fan of Faster, their new chief of police who'd been on the job now for about six months, he should be capable of reaching out to the feds. Getting resources quickly from them would be very helpful.

They had experts who could lead the search activities and provide everything from flashlights and snacks to scent-trained dogs.

"The chief said he'd send Ferguson and Blithe," Rena said. "Faster wants us to focus on figuring out what happened this morning and let the two of them coordinate with the FBI on the search."

That would work. They were both solid detectives. A.L. trusted them. Not as much as he trusted Rena, but neither of them had been his partner for five years.

Her phone buzzed and she glanced at it. "Amber Alert is approved," she said, looking up at him.

"Okay." She knew as well as he did that once the social media post and/or the Amber Alert went, the press would be on this story like flies on shit. But it would also bring in the volunteers. And they were going to need them for any substantial search activity.

"I want to talk to the parents before we push both the alert and all other social media. Tell them we need five minutes."

Rena typed as they walked down the art-lined hallway. They'd had a box—hell, Jacqui might still have it—of similar masterpieces that Traci had created. Every night before he'd left for work—he'd been doing nights in those years—he'd made a big deal out of what Traci had produced that day.

What the fuck would he have done if one of those days she simply hadn't come home?

He knocked on the classroom door before pulling it open. Leah Whitman was perched awkwardly on a small plastic chair. Troy was in the far corner of the room, his back to the door, his cell phone at his ear. He turned when he heard the door and ended his conversation. He put his phone in his pocket as he crossed the room. He was wearing matching blue work pants and shirt and he smelled faintly of oil and sweat.

"Any word?" he asked, looking at Rena.

"No, sir," she said. "This is my partner, Detective McKittridge." She turned to A.L. "Troy Whitman."

A.L. stuck out his hand. "I'm sorry for the circumstances, sir. But we're going to do everything we can to find your daughter."

Now the woman stood. "I'm Leah Whitman. This is just terrifying."

"It's crazy," Troy said, in a tone that sounded as if he was correcting his wife.

Terrifying? Crazy? For more than ten hours, a five-year-old had been unaccounted for. It was no time to quibble over words. A.L. flipped open his notebook. He wrote the date and by habit, looked at his watch. Notes were always dated and timed. It was twenty-three minutes after six, or 18:23 in military time. Then he did the math, using seven fifteen that morning as the floor. That's when the clock had started clicking. Didn't matter that they'd just heard about it. What mattered was how long the child hadn't been seen. They were somewhere near the start of hour twelve and that's what he wrote on the second line.

Behind before they'd barely gotten started.

"Can you walk me through your day?" A.L. asked.

"It was just a day, an ordinary day," Troy Whitman said.

"A few details would be helpful," A.L. said, looking up. "Either one of you can start."

"I left the house early," Leah said.

"What do you do, Mrs. Whitman?" Rena asked.

"I'm a paralegal at Bailey Shepherd."

The law firm of Bailey Shepherd was located just down the street from the police station. On the rare days that he took time for lunch, he passed it on his way to his favorite diner. "Why did you leave the house early?"

"I had…a meeting."

"Where?"

"Madison."

"And what time did it start?"

"Why does that matter?"

It wasn't a hard or tricky question. A.L. kept his gaze steady.

"Eight o'clock," Leah said.

"Thank you," A.L. said. "What time did you leave your house?"

"Six thirty. Maybe even a few minutes earlier. Emma was still sleeping when I left. The last thing I did was look into her room." She turned to her husband.

He took the ball. "I woke her up about 6:45. She got dressed and ate a bowl of cereal. She watched a little television while we were waiting for Leah's mom to pick her up."

"She was late?" Rena asked.

"No. We were early. I guess I was anxious to get going. Leah normally takes care of mornings. I do afternoons. Anyway, Leah's mom got there and she brought Emma here."

"Anything odd or off about the pickup?" A.L. asked.

"No. I mean, I saw her pull up and Emma and I

met her at the car. She made a comment about it. That I hadn't even given her a chance to come inside." He looked at his wife.

"My mom…repeats herself," Leah said, almost apologetic. "I guess I'm used to it, but it drives Troy crazy."

"I needed to get to work," Troy said, his tone testy. "I have to work. Especially…" His voice trailed off.

A.L. gave him a minute.

"Especially now. We're busy," he said.

Definitely some tension between Troy and Leah. A.L. had a feeling it wasn't the first time they had argued about her mother. It was the kind of argument he was familiar with. His ex-wife had been a daddy's girl and her dad had been a pompous ass that got in A.L.'s grille whenever possible. But A.L. had generally bit his tongue. Even now, on the rare occasions when the whole family gathered, he tried to remember that whatever immediate pleasure might be derived from going toe-to-toe with the man would quickly dissipate if Traci felt torn between her father and her grandfather.

His ex-wife had never been very good as peacemaker and he wasn't quite sure yet if Leah Whitman was giving it a go. A.L. focused on Troy. "So she and Emma drive off. What do you do?"

"I went to work."

"Where do you work, Mr. Whitman?" A.L. asked.

"Garage on Division. It's my business."

A.L. caught a shift in Rena's eyes. Brief. Nobody else probably saw it. He made a mental note to ask her later. Garage on Division had been a Baywood landmark since the sixties. It had changed hands some years back. That must have been when Troy Whitman had purchased it. "You worked all day?" A.L. asked.

"Yeah. Until I knocked off and drove here. At first, I was just pissed that the door was locked. And then I was told that all the children had been picked up. I figured that Leah had gotten off work early and picked her up. So I called her. She was still at work. Then I called Elaine."

Rena had already told him the next part but he wanted to hear it again. "Walk me through that conversation," he said.

Troy threw a hand up in the air. "I don't know. I think I said something like 'I'm at the day care and Emma isn't here. Do you have her?'"

"And what did Leah's mom say?"

"She said no. That she hadn't seen her since she'd dropped her off this morning at the day care. That she'd walked her inside and handed her off to her teacher by the front door."

"Did she say 'teacher' or was she more specific? Did she say a name?"

Troy closed his eyes briefly. "She said Ms. Wiese. That's what the kids call her. Ms. Wiese."

"Does Emma know your phone numbers?" He remembered drilling that into Traci's head when she'd been about four or five.

"Mine. Maybe," Leah said. "We've been working on it."

"How about your address?"

"I think she would recognize our street and maybe some landmarks along the way to either my mom's house or to Lakeside Learning Center. Those are the two places that she goes to most of the time." Leah paused, then looked straight into A.L.'s eyes. "Do you think she wandered off or was she…taken?"

He'd seen two child abductions in his career. Both had been many years ago, before he'd come to Baywood. One had been a noncustodial parent that had ended well after a tense fourteen hours. The other had been much worse. The eight-year-old boy had been killed by his abductor, who was ultimately shot and killed by the police.

"I don't know," he said.

"We don't have any money to speak of," Leah said. "For a ransom."

Ransom payments were for the movies. The sick bastards who took kids often had other plans. Not that it was common for kids to be taken by strangers. Most missing children were taken by a noncustodial spouse or other family member. "Emma is your biological daughter?" he asked.

"Yes," both answered.

"No previous marriages for either of you?"

"No," Troy said. Leah shook her head.

"Troy, who were you speaking with when we entered the room?" A.L. asked.

"My brother. He lives in Milwaukee."

"Any other siblings for either of you?" Rena asked. They both shook their heads.

"This is a very difficult time, I know," said A.L. "But unfortunately, when we have a missing child, we need to make sure that we've done everything we can to find her. And everything includes the police taking a look at your house and your vehicles. I'd like your permission to do both."

Now the Whitmans looked at each other. Leah spoke first. "You don't think we had anything to do with this." Her tone was incredulous.

"Of course not," Rena said.

It was the right response, regardless of whether they did or didn't. And right now, A.L. had no opinion. He'd hold on to that as long as he could. A good cop had instincts and he followed them. A really good cop did the same but he didn't let his mind settle on one path and discount other options that needed to be examined.

But there was no sense in alienating the parents or adding unnecessary angst to their lives by making them feel as if they were already on trial. Always better if everyone was cooperating.

"I think the time would be better spent looking for my daughter," Troy said.

"We're going to do that, too," A.L. assured him. He looked at his watch. "Right about now, an Amber Alert and some other social media are going to hit. Is there anybody that you need to contact first before they hear the news?" He looked at Troy. He'd already talked to his brother.

"I'd better call my parents," Troy said.

"Where do they live?" Rena asked.

"Milwaukee," he said.

That's where his brother lived. Maybe not in the same place, thought A.L. It still seemed odd that the brother hadn't taken care of letting the grandparents know. But family dynamics were always weird. He watched Troy again step away to the corner of the room.

"Anybody else?" Rena asked gently, looking at Leah.

She shook her head. "I don't want to talk to anybody right now."

That was understandable. But once word got out, people were going to want to reach out to her. Many in comfort. Some in curiosity. Maybe even a couple assholes who were salivating to get a first-person account of someone else's tragedy.

Anything to make their own day better.

"Do you have a home phone or just your mobile phones?" A.L. asked.

"We both just have cell phones," Leah said. "But maybe I'll just turn mine off."

"No. We don't want you to do that. We need to be able to reach you. Can I see your phone?"

She handed it to him. He entered both his and Rena's numbers. "Now you'll know that it's one of us calling." He paused. "If Emma has been taken, and we don't know that, but if, we're going to want to monitor both your and Troy's phones. Is that okay?" He could make it happen one way or another but again, always easier when a person simply agreed. "That way, if a call comes in that is in any way related to Emma's disappearance, we'll have another set of ears and the technology to hone onto anything that might be helpful to us."

"Like?" Leah asked.

"Speech. Regional dialect. Background noises that might give us a clue to where Emma is. And we'd be able to immediately start to identify the location where the call originated."

"Can you let Troy know?" Leah said dully.

"Of course," Rena said. "We know this is tough.

But we're going to do everything we possibly can to find her. I promise."

Troy walked back. "Well, they know," he said. "They were going to jump in the car but I told them to wait…until we knew more."

"What are your parents' names?" A.L. asked.

"Perry and LuAnn Whitman."

"Address and telephone number?"

Troy hesitated but then rattled off an address as well as a cell number for his dad, then his mom. "Are you going to call them?" he asked.

A.L. shrugged. "I'm not sure at this point. You have a good relationship with your parents?"

"Yeah. Of course."

"Both of you?" he asked, looking at Leah.

"Perry and LuAnn are lovely people," she said.

"They'd say the same about you?" A.L. asked.

"I think they would," Leah said.

"Brother's name and number?" A.L. asked.

"This seems like a waste of time," Troy said. But, nevertheless, he pulled up the contact information for a Travis Whitman. It was a different address than the parents. A.L. copied everything down.

"Married? Children?" A.L. asked.

"Divorced. More than ten years now. No children. His ex is remarried with two kids and lives in Montana. And before you ask, there are no issues between us and Travis."

"Great, thanks," A.L. said. "Now let's talk about your cell phone."

When A.L. filled him in on the details, Troy raised an eyebrow. Not unexpected. Who would like the idea of somebody listening to all his or her private cell phone calls? He said nothing, however, until A.L. was finished. Then he asked, "When will that start?"

"As soon as we can make a few phone calls," A.L. said.

"Fine. Do whatever you need to do."

A.L. entered his number and Rena's into Troy's cell. Just as he finished, Rena's cell phone buzzed.

She looked at it quickly. Then at the Whitmans. "Amber Alert is out. Social media requests for volunteers to search are circulating. We've got resources outside that will organize the people who show up."

"I want to search," Troy said.

"That's fine," A.L. said. "But I think one of you needs to be home. In the event that Emma somehow winds up there. Can you do that?" he asked, looking at Leah.

"Of course," she said.

"We'll send an officer with you. You won't be left alone."

Leah simply shrugged. A silent *whatever*.

A.L. understood. She wanted her kid found. Nothing else was really important.

There was a knock on the classroom door. Alice Quest stuck her head inside. "Kara Wiese is here. And I just saw Elaine Broadstreet pull into the parking lot."

Probably better to keep those two apart for now. Their recollection of the morning events appeared to be very different. "Thank you," A.L. said. Alice nodded and shut the door.

He motioned Rena to go outside before turning to the Whitmans. "Excuse us, please."

"I want to talk to my mother," Leah said.

"That's fine," he said. "Just give us a minute."

Once he and Rena were in the hallway, he said, "I'll take Kara Wiese. You've got the grandma. Let's try to figure out what really happened."

Two

Kara Wiese was early thirties, dressed in workout clothes, with her dark shoulder-length hair pulled back into a ponytail.

A.L. stuck out his hand. "I'm Detective McKittridge. Thank you for coming back to the day care so quickly."

"Of course. I just can't believe this," she said. "Emma is so sweet." She paused. "Not that all the kids aren't great. But, you know, some are just really special. Emma is one of those. You know what I mean?"

He did. Traci had been that kind of little kid. She'd sparkled. "Smart?" A.L. asked, motioning for Kara to enter an empty classroom.

"Very. She's already reading."

Maybe she could read street signs. Or signs on buildings. That could be helpful.

"What time did you arrive this morning, Kara?" A.L. asked. He took a seat on one of the small chairs. He knew he probably looked ridiculous but he didn't want to tower over Kara, who was barely five feet. She also sat.

"About 6:15. We open at 6:30 and I always want time to start a pot of coffee."

"Was anybody else here when you arrived?"

Kara nodded. "Alice was in the office. She's usually here when I arrive."

"But she doesn't start the coffee?" A.L. asked.

Kara smiled. "She doesn't drink coffee. I don't get that," she added, laughing nervously but stopping suddenly, as if she was embarrassed that the sound had come from her at a time like this. Her hands were clasped together, so tightly that her fingers were white.

"After you started the coffee, then what?" A.L. prompted.

"I waited until there was enough in the pot to pour a cup and I carried that back to my room. Turned on the lights and started the music."

"Music?"

"I play all kinds of music all day. The kids seem to like it."

When Traci was four, she'd known all the words to Alan Jackson and Jimmy Buffet's "It's Five O'Clock Somewhere." His mother-in-law hadn't thought it was that cute. "Was your music loud this morning?" he asked. "Would you be able to hear it outside the classroom?"

"Maybe if you were standing right outside the door but no farther than that with the door closed."

"Do you keep the door closed all the time, even when there are no kids?"

Kara seemed to consider the question. "I guess I do. Habit, you know."

"What time did children start arriving?" A.L. asked.

"Shortly after 6:30."

A.L. pulled the sign-in sheet from Kara's room. "Can you verify that this is the sign-in sheet from your room today?"

"Why is it…in plastic?" Kara asked, sounding concerned.

"We've started the process of gathering anything that might be evidence," A.L. said.

"Of course," Kara said. She glanced at the sheet. "Yes, that's our sheet."

"Our?" A.L. repeated.

"Claire's and mine. Claire Potter is my co-teacher. She starts an hour after me and stays an hour later. I leave at 4:30 and she stays until 5:30. We need a second staff member once we have more than thirteen kids. Early in the morning and late in the afternoon, the number of kids makes it so that one of us can handle it."

It had worked that way at Traci's day care. "I suppose the math doesn't always work out perfectly. I mean," A.L. clarified, "you might have too many kids arrive before 7:30 or too many stay later than 4:30."

"On rare occasions, but parents are pretty predictable with their drop-off and pickup schedules," Kara said.

"Were Emma Whitman's parents predictable?"

"Usually. Her grandma dropped her off a couple days a week and then her mom the other days. I'm not usually here when she gets picked up."

"What time would you expect Emma in the mornings?"

"By 7:30. She's almost always in the room before Claire is."

"Did you see Emma today?"

"No. I guess I didn't think too much about it. She

has allergies in the fall and had missed a day the prior week because she was sick."

"Did Claire arrive at her usual time?"

"I think so. I mean, I'm pretty busy with the kids. I don't really watch the clock."

"Do you ever leave your room prior to Claire's arrival?"

"Not once kids arrive. I could never leave them alone." She said it fast, decisively. Almost too much so, thought A.L. "Let's take another look at the sign-in sheet. Now, you said that you would not have been able to leave the room after children started to arrive. The sign-in sheet in your room indicates that the first child arrived at 6:42 a.m." He pointed to the first line.

"Yes. Landon is always my first kid."

"And between 6:42 and 7:30, six more children arrived."

Kara nodded.

"Do you specifically recall being in the room when each of these children arrived?" A.L. asked.

"Yes," Kara said. "Has someone said that I wasn't?"

"No," A.L. said. "We're just trying to get a full understanding. Do you recall if Claire Potter was in the room when any of those six children arrived?"

"I don't think so. Maybe for the last one. I don't know."

Now she was sounding frustrated. "Okay, no problem," he said. "Kara, this morning, did you at any time, before or after Claire's arrival, walk to the front of the building and talk briefly to Emma's grandmother, Elaine Broadstreet? Did she hand off Emma to you?"

Something flickered in her dark eyes. More frustration? Anger? "I figured that's what she was saying, based on Alice's questions. But that never happened. I never saw her or Emma."

Whatever emotions were reeling through her, her voice was steady. Confident.

"What kind of relationship do you have with Elaine Broadstreet?"

"I don't really know her. I have responsibility for a bunch of kids. I don't have time to chat with a lot of people."

"What were you doing tonight when Alice Quest contacted you?"

"Getting ready to go to the gym. That's where I go most days of the week after work."

"Anybody else at your house right now?"

Kara shook her head. "My husband works twelve-hour days, 7:00 a.m. to 7:00 p.m. at the hospital. He's a nurse in the Emergency Department."

"He should be getting home soon, then?"

She shook her head. "He's lucky to get out by 8:00 once he finishes charting. Then there's a group of them that go out after work and toss back a few beers. It's a pretty stressful job. He doesn't generally get home until 10:00 or 11:00."

A.L. had seen the inside of more than a few emergency rooms when he'd been a young cop. Lots of interesting characters ended up there. "What's your husband's name?"

"Sam. Sam Wiese."

"Do you have any children?" A.L. asked.

"No. We've only been married for two years," Kara added, maybe a little defensively.

A.L. personally thought people ought to wait a good long time before popping out babies. He and his ex had barely known each other's favorite breakfast cereal when Traci was born. "Okay. Thank you for coming back today. We're committed to pursuing every possible lead. In that regard, we're going to want to search both your car and your house."

"Really?" she asked. Now he clearly heard the irritation. But she quickly recovered and added, in a more neutral tone, "I'll do what needs to be done. I want you to find Emma."

"We will," A.L. said. His phone buzzed and he glanced at the incoming text. It was Tess. *Saw the Amber Alert. Are you working on this?*

Yes, he texted back.

No one better.

He appreciated the confidence. Didn't generally burn up too many brain cells worrying about whether he was the best. But right now he hoped like hell that he was good enough. Emma Whitman needed somebody in her corner.

Rena and Leah Whitman stood in the hallway, waiting for Elaine Broadstreet to enter. She came in the door so fast that it didn't close behind her. The wind caught it and Rena saw the officer positioned outside the door reach over to shut it. Her stomach flipped. Somewhere out there in the wind was a five-year-old.

Mrs. Broadstreet was somewhere between sixty and sixty-five. Her hair was a pretty silver and cut short.

She wore minimal makeup and no jewelry. Her blue pantsuit might have come from any department store but it fit her still-trim figure well enough.

Elaine Broadstreet's eyes immediately went to her daughter. "Have you found her?"

Leah shook her head.

"Oh, God." Elaine extended her arms, as if she meant to hug her daughter. But when Leah didn't step forward into the embrace, Elaine awkwardly pulled her arms back and pressed her fingers to her lips.

"This is Detective Morgan," Leah said.

Elaine lowered her hands, turned toward Rena. "What are you doing to find my granddaughter?"

"We're going to do everything we can," Rena said. "And you can help us by making sure that we've got the very best understanding of what's happened thus far today. Can we step in here for a few questions?" she asked, motioning toward the empty kitchen area.

Mrs. Broadstreet didn't answer but she and Leah followed Rena into the small room. There were no chairs so they stood.

"Can you walk us through your early morning, Mrs. Broadstreet?"

"What?" Her tone was now exasperated. "What does that have to do with anything?"

"Sometimes even small details are very helpful," Rena said.

"Well, I got up about 6:00. I showered, got dressed, and drove to my daughter's house to pick up Emma. There, I never even got out of the car, Troy had her out of the house so fast."

"What time was that?" Rena asked.

"I remember looking at the clock on the dashboard as I pulled away from Leah's house. It was 7:08."

"Then what?"

"Then I drove here."

"What route did you take?"

"Paradise to Main to Second Street to Oak Avenue."

They would be able to verify that with street cameras. Rena ripped a sheet of paper out of her notebook and pulled a second pen from her bag. "Can you write down the make and model of your vehicle as well as your license plate number?"

Elaine sighed but she did it.

"What time did you arrive at the day care?" Rena asked.

"I don't know. I didn't look at the clock. But I've done that drive a hundred times. It takes ten minutes, give or take a minute or two either way."

If that was right, she would have arrived as early as 7:16 or as late as 7:20. "Then what happened?" Rena asked.

"We got here and Emma got out of her car seat. She can unbuckle herself. We walked in. I saw her teacher near the front door and handed Emma off to her."

"What teacher would that be?"

"Kara Wiese."

"Did you talk to her?"

"I think I said good morning."

"And what did she say?"

"Good morning. And then she said hello to Emma. Then I left."

"Did you see her make any other contact with Emma?"

"Contact?" Elaine asked.

"Reach for her hand. Other conversation? Point her towards the classroom? Anything?"

Elaine closed her eyes. She was silent. Finally, she opened them. "No. I didn't see anything like that. Because I wasn't looking. I had turned and I was walking out the door. Because I knew that Emma's teacher was there."

"You and Kara Wiese had no other conversation than 'Good morning'?" Rena asked.

"No."

"Okay. You regularly drop Emma off at day care, right?"

"Several days a week."

"And is this your normal drop-off process?"

Elaine Broadstreet shook her head. "No. I walk her to her classroom."

"But not today. Why not? Were you running late?"

"No. Like I said, I didn't spend any time at my daughter's house. We were early. I didn't walk her to her classroom because her teacher was at the front door. There was no need. What the heck happened here? How did they lose a child?"

"We'll find her, Mom," Leah said. "We…have to. That's the only thing that can happen."

Rena knew that wasn't true. There were any number of bad alternatives to a child missing for over ten hours.

"Mrs. Broadstreet, was there anyone else in the lobby when you handed Emma off to Kara?" Rena asked.

"I… I don't know. I don't think so. I really wasn't here very long."

"But you don't recall talking to anyone else? Greeting anyone else?"

"No."

"Okay. Did you sign Emma in this morning, on the clipboard next to the office?"

"Yes."

She pulled out the evidence bag. Showed Elaine the sign-in sheet. "This is the sign-in sheet from that clipboard. There are two signatures on here. Are either one of these yours?"

"No," Elaine said. "But I signed the sheet. I'm sure I did."

She had not mentioned that until Rena had specifically asked her about it. But that didn't mean she was lying. "Were there any other signatures on the sheet when you did that?" Rena asked.

Again, Elaine closed her eyes as if she was trying to visualize the moment. "I don't know. I really don't remember."

"When you signed the sheet, did you note the time?" Rena asked, pointing to the spot where it would have been entered.

"I…imagine I did."

"But you don't recall specifically?"

"No. Like I said, I don't recall specifically noting the time. But I look at my watch a hundred times a day. It's not a special action that I take. So I wouldn't necessarily remember it. But if there was a spot there for the time, I'm sure I filled it in." She looked at her daughter, as if seeking confirmation.

Leah didn't offer it up. Her face was devoid of emotion. But then again, her kid was missing. She probably felt as if she'd been run over by a train. "Earlier, Elaine, you said that after you saw Kara Wiese, you turned and left. You didn't say anything about signing the sheet?"

"Look, I'm a little rattled here. I wasn't thinking about everything that I did. But I signed the sheet. I turned, signed the sheet and left."

"Okay," Rena said. "Where did you go after you left here?"

"I went…" Elaine Broadstreet's voice trailed off. "I went to work, of course. At Milo's Motors."

"What time did you arrive there?" Rena asked.

"Probably about 7:45," Mrs. Broadstreet said. Her tone had cooled. "Although I don't see what that has to do with anything."

"Again, just trying to get a full understanding of the time lines," Rena said.

Leah was now staring off into the corner. Elaine's eyes were flicking toward the door, as if she might make a run for it.

"Where were you when your son-in-law contacted you this afternoon?" Rena asked.

"Still at work. At first, I didn't understand what he was asking. I mean, I understood the words but it didn't make sense. Why would he think that I had Emma?"

"What happened after the two of you talked?" Rena asked.

"I told him that I would meet him at the day care. I found my boss, told him I was leaving early, and I raced over here. I was sick, just sick, at the thought that Emma was missing. I was shaking so badly I could hardly drive."

"Of course," Rena said. "What's your home address, Mrs. Broadstreet?"

"141 Duncan Avenue."

"Would Emma know that?"

Elaine Broadstreet looked at her daughter.

"I don't think so," Leah said. "We always talk about going to Grammie's house but we don't use the address. We don't say we're going to Duncan Avenue."

"Of course," Rena said again. "Mrs. Broadstreet, do you live alone?"

"Yes."

"Is there a Mr. Broadstreet?"

"There was. He's been dead for many years."

"Okay. We're going to want to take a look at your house and your vehicle. Do we have your permission to do that?"

"I guess. Although I think the time might be better spent searching around the day care."

"We'll be doing that, too," Rena assured her. "Just one more question, Mrs. Broadstreet. You're absolutely sure it was Kara Wiese that you saw in the lobby this morning?"

"I…of course I'm sure. Emma has been in her room for months."

"And what's your relationship with Kara?"

"She's fine. I mean, I think she's good with the kids."

"Then you can't think of any reason why she might not remember this morning's events exactly the same way as you do?"

Mrs. Broadstreet stared at her. "I've told you what

happened. I saw her by the office and I left Emma with her. If she's saying anything else, then she's a liar."

Rena found A.L. alone in Emma Whitman's classroom. "Blithe checked vehicles for Alice Quest, Troy Whitman, Leah Whitman and Elaine Broadstreet. All cleared. Now he's going to accompany Leah Whitman home. He'll search the house while he's there. I've got Officer Taylor following Elaine Broadstreet home and he'll search that property."

"Tell me about your conversation with Elaine," he said.

She did.

"We need to check her route, see if we can place her there," A.L. said.

"Just sent the text asking for someone to check the street cameras. It bothers me that she didn't say anything initially about signing Emma in on the clipboard. I had to prompt it."

"Could be something," he agreed. "Will be less important if we can place her driving here with Emma and then driving away without Emma."

"Agree. Tell me what Kara Wiese had to say?"

He did and finished up with, "Troy Whitman and Kara Wiese are joining the other volunteers. I imagine Alice Quest is in her office, calling her attorney and insurance carrier. I told our guys that we were going to need Alice and her desktop computer to get some information. They've cleared her office and Classroom 1, as well as the hallway bathroom for use. Everything else is off limits for now."

"Fine. You know she told me she has a granddaughter Emma's age," Rena said. "Two granddaughters, in fact. Five and three. I think she's feeling this on all different levels."

"Is she married?" A.L. asked.

Rena flipped a page of her notebook, proving that she'd put the time with Alice to good use. "Divorced for more than fifteen years. Ex-husband died six years ago. Has one adult daughter who lives in Baywood with her husband and two children. That's why she came to Baywood five years ago. To be close to her daughter, who was having a difficult pregnancy. Needed a job. Has a degree in early education and had taught preschool when she was raising her daughter. This business was for sale and she jumped at the chance to buy it. She'd come into some unexpected money when it was discovered that her ex never took her off as a beneficiary on his insurance policy."

"Lucky break for her. So what do you think so far?" A.L. asked.

"I have no idea. A loving grandmother, by all appearances, drops off her five-year-old granddaughter at day care, in the custody of a trusted teacher. Ten hours later, it's discovered that the child is missing and nobody from the day care has seen her and said teacher claims she was never in the lobby and didn't see either the child or grandmother."

"Is the grandmother lying? Is she confused? Is Kara Wiese lying? But why? She's worked here for more than three years. Her boss has never had any reason to be concerned," A.L. said.

"Agree. If we believe one, we can't believe the other. If we believe both of them, then the only logical explanation is that Elaine thought she handed Emma off to her teacher but it was somebody else. And maybe that person didn't even realize what was happening. She's standing there, minding her own business, and somebody says good morning. She responds with good morning like most people do. Then she leaves. Goes to work. To the gym. Wherever. Doesn't matter. What matters is that Emma is alone in the hallway for a few minutes, then maybe she's outside. And then something happens. What, we just don't know."

"What's this *feel* like to you?" A.L. asked.

"You're not the touchy-feely type," Rena said, her tone full of suspicion.

"Missing five-year-old," A.L. said. "I'm willing to pull out all the stops. If I thought it would help, I'd be knocking on the psychic's door right now."

"Well, I'm not psychic but I think there is definitely something not quite right between Troy and Leah Whitman. They're each staying pretty strong, given the circumstances, but they don't seem to be drawing strength from one another."

He'd noticed that. No hugs. No arms around a shoulder. No clasped hands. Didn't mean they were bad people, bad parents, or in any way responsible for Emma's disappearance. "When Troy mentioned Garage on Division, you had a reaction."

She shrugged. "It's probably nothing."

"Missing five-year-old," he said.

"Gabe was having some trouble with his car last week. Needed a tune-up or something. Anyway, the garage we usually use closed down about six months ago so he was looking for someplace new. He asked for recommendations at Sunday dinner at the Morgans'. One of his sisters said that she always took her car to Garage on Division, but then his brother said that he'd heard some bad things about their work. That there was even some talk that the place might be close to shutting down."

"Gabe and his brother are talking again?" Months ago Danny Morgan had made a pass at Rena and things between the two Morgan men had gotten sticky.

"Gabe and Danny are civil to one another. We've had a couple family things this summer and nobody ended up in the emergency room. Always happy and relieved about that."

"Nobody else in the family knows," A.L. said.

"God, no," she said, shaking her head. "It's a secret that Danny, Gabe and I are taking to our graves."

"Another couple years, you'll be laughing about the whole thing."

"A stiff smile, perhaps. I wish it was like it was before."

"Give it time. Jacqui and I can actually do small talk now." He'd been divorced for five years after his wife had decided to warm somebody else's bed. "It doesn't happen overnight."

"I suppose. Anyway, we ended up taking the car to the Volkswagen dealer so I don't really know anything about Garage on Division."

"Interesting that the rumor was they might be closing. Troy said they were busy," A.L. said. "Although being busy and making money in a small business aren't the same thing. Anyway, what else do we know?"

"Tension between Elaine and her son-in-law."

"Not that unusual," A.L. said.

"Perhaps," Rena said. "Hence the abundance of mother-in-law jokes."

"Speaking of family, I think we need to verify that Kara Wiese's husband is at work today," A.L. said.

"Agree. And there are three teachers we haven't talked with yet."

"One of who was ill today. That's why Alice Quest was working in a classroom."

"Right. And there's the cook who comes in for a few hours every day."

He saw a black Suburban pull up and park. Two men got out. Both wore dark suits and white shirts. One had a blue tie and the other a red.

FBI. They might as well be carrying a placard. They stopped at the door, spoke to the officer, flashed some badges and then were through the doorway.

"Detective A.L. McKittridge," he said, extending his hand.

"Special Agents Drew White and Monty Connell." They flashed their IDs.

Drew White had the blue tie. Up close, he was at least ten years older than Monty Connell. A.L. guessed them fifty and forty, respectively. "My partner, Detective Rena Morgan," he said.

Everybody shook hands. "We talked to your boss on the way here. I think we're up to speed, assuming nothing new has happened in the last ten minutes," White said.

"Nope," A.L. said. Other than he'd become pretty convinced that somebody was lying.

"We've got our canine unit en route. They're about fifteen minutes behind us."

"We've got a sweater of Emma Whitman's from her classroom," Rena said.

White nodded. "Good."

Connell was looking around. "These the only two doors in the building?"

"Yes."

"Parents have both checked their phones? What about a home phone?" Connell asked.

A.L. wanted to tell him that this wasn't his first rodeo but he resisted. The FBI had resources that they were going to need. Their heat-signature-seeking drones might be very helpful. "No home phone. They are continually monitoring their cell phones."

"Anybody been to their home, just in case the little girl somehow got back there?" White asked.

"Mother left here about ten minutes ago to sit tight there. Should arrive any minute. We've got an officer with her who will search the property," A.L. said. "Same thing will happen at the grandmother's house and at the day care teacher's house." He saw a white van pull up. "That belong to you?"

White nodded. "Our canine unit."

"Unfortunately, we're losing the daylight," Connell said. "We've got about two hundred flashlights with us but at a certain point, it can simply get too dangerous to have volunteers searching in the dark."

"Volunteers are gathering on the east side of the building," Rena said, looking at her phone. "Detective

Ferguson is in charge of that effort. I can walk you out there and introduce you."

"That's fine," said White. "Bring the kid's sweater."

Three

Volunteers were continuing to pour into the makeshift check-in station that Ferguson had set up. From the big window in the main room, A.L. and Rena watched their fellow detective bring some order to the group. Older people. Teens. Middle-aged. Most of them had likely been getting dinner ready or were already eating when the Amber Alert had hit their phones. By the looks of it, that hadn't slowed them down any. He could practically imagine the wheels churning in their heads. Things like this didn't happen in Baywood. And they were going to do what they could to make it right.

They'd had to beach their cars at either end of the street and walk in because barricades closed the street to everybody but local traffic. On any other day that many people would generate some noise. Now nobody was talking. Just quietly following directions and waiting patiently to be told what to do. Disbelief etched on their faces.

A.L. knocked softly on the office door. Alice was behind her desk. Just sitting. Her hands folded and resting on the lacquered wood. "In my wildest dreams," she said.

She'd never imagined this. He took one chair in front of her desk and Rena took the other. "We have a few more questions," he said.

"It's really just a nightmare," Alice said.

Crazy. Terrifying. Now a nightmare. The descriptors were mounting up. He badly wanted somebody to walk in the front door, saying words like *miracle* or maybe even *dream come true.* Yeah, that would be good. He'd even be happy if it was one of the FBI guys crowing that it was a dream come true to have Emma back safe and sound.

But until that happened, he was going to work the damn case. "I wanted to ask you about the teacher who was absent today." In the ten minutes that he and Rena had strategized before knocking on Alice's door, they'd agreed that talking to that teacher had to be a priority.

"Olivia Blow," Alice said.

"She miss a lot of work?" Rena asked.

Alice shook her head. "None of my staff misses much work, which is a testament to their dedication. Kids come to day care with all kinds of bugs and teachers do catch some of them. But mostly they manage to power through it."

"But Olivia didn't power through today. What was wrong with her?" A.L. asked.

"I don't know. I didn't actually get a chance to talk to her. She sent a text late last night, around midnight. Said she wouldn't be in."

"So she knew last night?" Rena said. "That she'd be sick this morning."

"I do think that's how it works sometimes," Alice said.

She might be right, A.L. thought. But then again. "When's the last time Olivia Blow missed a day of work?"

Alice turned her chair so that she could open the cabinet behind her desk. She pulled out a manila folder. Turned the cover back. Ran her finger down and across what appeared to be a spreadsheet. "Actually, this is the first day that she's missed."

"How long has she worked here?" Rena asked.

"For over two years," Alice said.

"What's her home address?" A.L. asked.

Now Alice tapped on the keyboard on her desk. Then she picked up a pen and scribbled something on a notepad. Tore off the sheet. "Here. But you won't find her there."

"Why not?" A.L. asked.

"Because she called me less than ten minutes ago. Said she was going to come join the search."

"She's suddenly feeling better?" A.L. asked.

Alice shrugged. "I didn't grill her on her health."

Alice already sounded tired. And discouraged. A.L. thought she should buck up. Things could get much worse before they got better. "Would you call her on her cell?" he asked. "Tell her to come inside the building."

Alice picked up the cell phone on her desk. Scrolled through her contacts. "Hey, Olivia. Are you here at Lakeside?" Alice listened. "Could you do me a favor and come to the front door. I'll meet you there and let you in. There are a couple officers who'd like to ask you a few questions."

Alice listened and then put down her phone. "She'll

be right here. I really hate that my staff are going to get treated like common criminals."

"We're just asking questions," Rena said, her voice kind. "We're not making any assumptions."

"I know," Alice said. "But I really think you need to be looking elsewhere."

They were. A.L. already had someone pulling the list of all known sexual predators in the area. Every one of them would receive a visit from an officer. Emma's disappearance was basically all anybody would be working on.

It took Olivia Blow less than two minutes to knock on the front door. Alice and A.L. went to answer it. Olivia was dressed in jeans and a T-shirt and tennis shoes. She had a small backpack over her left shoulder. She looked to be early thirties. Her hair was a short wavy medium brown and she had big dark brown eyes. Attractive. Looked healthy enough.

"I'm Detective McKittridge with the Baywood Police Department," he said.

She stuck out her hand and he returned the shake. Rena had joined them in the hallway. "This is my partner, Detective Morgan," A.L. said. "We'd like to ask you a few questions."

"Of course," she said, not sounding too concerned.

"We can use Classroom 1," he said. He didn't intend to do this in front of Alice.

Rena led the way, Olivia went next, and he brought up the rear. Alice retreated to her office. Once the three of them were inside, both he and Rena pulled out their notebooks.

"May I call you Olivia?" A.L. asked.

"Of course."

"You've been working at the day care full-time for more than two years. Is that right?"

"Yes."

"Where did you work before that?"

"I was in college. A late bloomer you might say. Didn't go anywhere right after high school. But after ten years of waitressing, I'd had enough. I wanted to work with kids."

"No children of your own?" Rena asked.

"No. Hopefully someday. I haven't met Mr. Right yet. I'm just thirty-two so I have a few years."

"Of course," Rena said.

A.L. knew that Rena could tell Olivia a thing or two about waiting and babies. Rena hadn't gotten married until she was thirty-six. They'd tried right away, but it was more than two years later and even though there'd been some gymnastics with an infertility specialist, still no pregnancy.

"Alice tells us you've had a great work record here," A.L. said. "Never missed a day of work until today. But it appears as if you're feeling better."

"Better," she said. "Not great. But I slept most of the day so that was helpful since I was up most of the night. When I heard the news about Emma I couldn't not join the search efforts. We have to find that little girl."

"Anybody else home at your house today?" A.L. asked.

She shook her head.

"Anybody else able to verify that you were at your home today?" A.L. phrased the question just a bit differently.

She stared at him. "Why would that be necessary?" Her voice had cooled. She was starting to get the picture.

Rena leaned forward. "Olivia, you have to admit that it is interesting that you've never missed a day. Suddenly, on the day that Emma Whitman goes missing, you're sick."

"It's not that interesting. I actually got sick the day before. I ate my afternoon snack and within a half hour, I was sick. My stomach hurt." She paused. "I had really bad diarrhea, if you must know. That continued well into the evening and wasn't showing signs of improvement. That's when I sent Alice the text. I wanted to give her as much notice as possible. When I woke up this morning, I knew I'd made the right decision. I was exhausted and no doubt dehydrated. Not to get too graphic."

"We'd like to have an officer search your house and your vehicle. Would you agree to that?" Rena asked.

"Whatever. It won't take long. I live in a one-bedroom, one-bath apartment and I drive a Prius."

"Is this your address?" Rena asked, showing her what Alice had written down.

"Yes. Somebody can look at my car here. And then I can meet them at my apartment."

A.L. stood up. "That'll be fine. If you'll wait outside the front door, I'll have an officer take care of that."

He and Rena walked Olivia to the door. She was pushing it open when she turned. "I get why you need to search my car and my house. I do. And I guess I'm glad that you're being thorough. But just tell me one thing. Do you think that we're going to find her? That she's going to be okay?" Her voice broke.

"I don't know," A.L. said. It was the best he could do. "The weather is working in our favor. Not too cold at night."

"That's if she wandered off. Do you think that's what happened?"

"Do you?" he countered.

She shrugged. "On the drive here, I went over it a hundred times in my head. Five-year-olds are pretty responsible and she would have known not to leave the day care."

A.L. said nothing. He'd had the very same thoughts. He quite clearly remembered Traci at that age. She'd been able to follow directions and certainly knew about stranger-danger.

"There's a lot of people out there," Olivia said. "Searching. Maybe that gives the Whitmans some comfort. Knowing that people care."

The people of Baywood were very caring. Midwest nice. None of that helped explain a missing five-year-old. "Thanks again," he said.

She walked out and he made a few quick calls on his cell. When he was assured that there was an officer who could take care of searching both the car and the apartment, he went to find Rena. She was still sitting in the classroom.

"What do you think?" he asked.

"I don't think we're going to find anything in her apartment or car. Because there's nothing there. We're barking up the wrong tree," Rena added.

"So, she simply had the bad luck to have a case of the ill-timed shits."

Rena closed her eyes and leaned her head back. "Better her than us."

"Indeed. Look, I'm going to request criminal background checks on all four teachers, Alice, the cook, Leah and Troy Whitman, and Elaine Broadstreet."

"They're the main players," Rena said. "Who do you want to talk to next?"

"Let's get contact information from Alice on all staff and all parents. Right now I'm interested in talking to the six parents who signed into Kara Wiese's room between 6:30 and 7:30. I want to make sure that her story that she was in the room checks out."

When they made their request, Alice said it would take her about fifteen minutes to pull the information. She said she'd have first and last names and cell numbers and home phones, if different. She might also have places of employment if they'd provided that. However, the integrity of her data depended on whether the parents had kept their information up to date.

While they were waiting, Rena's cell phone buzzed. She glanced at it. "We have confirmation that Elaine Broadstreet's vehicle was on Paradise, then Main, then Second Street just as she said. There's no cameras on the corner of Second Street and Oak Avenue so we lost her there. But they pick her up again when she's back on Second Street. Child who matches Emma's description in a rear car seat on the way, and seat is empty when she's back on Second Street."

"Seems as if she might be telling the truth," A.L. said.

"At least about getting her to the building."

"Can I see the front office sign-in sheet again?"

Rena handed him the plastic evidence bag. "I estimated Alice's arrival time as somewhere between 7:16 and 7:20. First signature on this form is 7:52 and second is 10:50."

"And Alice says she signed the form but that was only after you prompted her with a question about it," A.L. said.

"Yes. And said that of course she'd have written a time if there was a blank for the time but couldn't remember what time she'd written."

"We need to talk to these parents tonight," A.L. said.

"Okay. That's eight calls, then, that we need to make."

Alice poked her head out of her office and handed them two sheets of the information they'd requested. "I made a copy for each of you."

"Thank you," Rena said.

"Alice, I have a question about the sign-in sheet that is posted by the office," A.L. said. He showed her the plastic bag. "It's dated with today's date. Who wrote that?"

"Kara. She always gets the sheet ready. Does it first thing when she comes in the door."

"Has she always had that responsibility?"

"I guess. Besides me, she's always the first one in. She started getting the sheet ready and I guess it sort of became part of her job. At night, whoever is the last one in the building, which is usually me, is responsible for removing the sheet and putting it in my in-box."

"Okay, thank you."

He walked back to Classroom 1 and Rena followed. A.L. held up the sign-in sheet. "Kara did not tell me about getting this sheet ready. Said that the first thing she did was make coffee."

"Again, like Elaine not mentioning she signed in, perhaps it's so routine that it doesn't bear mentioning."

"Maybe. Let's split up the parents of kids in Kara Wiese's class. I'll take the first three, you take numbers four through six," he said. "Then we'll regroup before we call the two parents from the office sign-in sheet." They set up on opposite sides of the large space.

A.L. dialed his first number. It rang twice.

"Hello."

It was a woman. A.L. checked the name on his sheet. "Sarah Hewin?" he asked.

"Yes."

"This is Detective McKittridge with the Baywood Police Department. I need to ask you a few questions about the Lakeside Learning Center."

"Of course," she said.

He wasn't surprised that she didn't ask why. The news would have spread quickly through the whole of Baywood, but lightning-fast through the parent group.

"Your child's teachers are Kara Wiese and Claire Potter, correct?"

"Yes."

"I have a sign-in sheet in front of me that indicates that you dropped Landon off at 6:42 this morning. Is that correct?"

"Yes."

"Was there a teacher in the room at the time?"

"Of course. Kara Wiese was there."

"Okay, thank you. Just one more question. How did you know what time to write down?"

"Uh… I guess I looked at the clock on the wall."

"Okay, thank you."

His remaining two calls went about the same. Each verified that the time written on the sheet was correct and that Kara Wiese had been in the room. The only difference was how they knew the correct time. One had checked his phone and the other admitted that she'd guessed based on the time her car clock showed when she pulled into the parking lot.

He finished at about the same time Rena got through her calls. "Anything?" he asked.

"I was only able to reach two of the three. Left a message for the other one. But nothing odd with the two that I spoke with. The first one verified that Kara Wiese was the teacher in the room and the second one said that both Kara Wiese and Claire Potter were in the room."

"What time did the parent sign in?" A.L. asked.

"7:27."

"That makes some sense if the second teacher starts at 7:30. She might have been a few minutes early."

"But well after Emma was dropped off," Rena said.

A.L. looked at the classroom sign-in sheet again. "Right. The one you didn't reach is the one who signed in closest to when Elaine Broadstreet supposedly saw Kara in the lobby."

"Yeah. Michael Purifoy. His son's name is Jake. And he noted the time as 7:18. Hopefully he'll call back soon."

"For now, let's call the two who signed the clipboard by the front office. Want to split them?"

"Let's just do it together on Speaker," Rena said.

A.L. matched the first name on the sheet to one on the list that Alice had provided. "Jasmine Opal," he said. "She works at Wiseback Plumbing." He dialed her cell. She answered on the first ring.

"Hello."

"Is this Jasmine Opal?"

"Yes," she said, her voice substantially cooler. Probably thought he was a telemarketer.

"This is Detective McKittridge from the Baywood Police Department. My partner, Detective Morgan, is also on the line." Always better to be truthful if her statement ended up being important. "We have a few questions about Lakeside Learning Center."

"My son isn't in Emma's class," she said quickly, as if she thought that might be her get-out-of-jail-free card. Nobody really liked talking to the police.

"No worries," he said. "What we're interested in is your drop-off this morning. I am looking at a sign-in sheet that shows your signature at 7:52. Does that sound right?"

"Yes."

"And where was that sign-in sheet when you signed it?" he asked.

"On the hook, by the office door, where it always is," she said.

"And do you normally sign in there?" he asked.

"Well, no. I like to walk Nathan to his room. But I was running late. I saw Alice in the hall, she said that she was working in Nathan's room, and I asked her if she could do me a big favor and walk Nathan down. I've already been late to work four times in the last three months. If I'm late again, I'm going to get another warning in my file. I cannot lose my job. It's ridiculous, really. Like, what's the big deal if I'm a few minutes late? I answer phones. Is the world going to end because somebody has to call back for their PVC pipe?"

A.L. rolled his eyes in Rena's direction.

"Maybe," she mouthed.

A.L. turned in his chair so that he couldn't see her. "Do you recall, Ms. Opal, whether there were any other signatures on the form already?"

"No. I know that for sure because when I signed it, I remember thinking that there were no other losers who had to shuffle their child off at the door because they couldn't get up in time."

"Okay, then. We appreciate your time," A.L. said.

"I really hope Emma is found. Every parent I've talked to is so nervous."

"We're doing our best," A.L. said. "Goodbye."

He looked back at Rena. "I'll bet her boss is looking for a reason to fire her."

"Perhaps. But she was pretty confident that she was the first signature."

"At 7:52. Only way that could happen, if Elaine Broadstreet really did sign in around 7:15, is that somebody took that sheet and replaced it with a fresh one," A.L. said.

Rena stared at him. "I don't think Emma Whitman thought to do that before she made a run for the back door."

"Yeah, me either."

"If we only knew if Elaine really had signed the sheet."

"We'll go back at that if we need to," A.L. said.

"Let's call the other one," Rena said. "It's a lot later in the morning."

A.L. pushed the paper her direction. "Your turn."

Rena smiled and dialed. She rang several times and was expecting it to roll over to voice mail when it was answered.

"Hello." The man on the other end sounded a little breathless.

"Devon Bridge?" she asked.

"Yes. Who is this?"

"This is Detective Morgan with the Baywood Police Department. I'm here with my partner, Detective McKittridge. We'd like to ask you a question about your drop-off process at Lakeside Learning Center this morning."

"Sure. I'm in a cornfield right now, looking for Emma."

"Thank you for volunteering to search. Your daughter, Gabrielle, is in Emma's class, right?"

"Yeah. They're friends. Hell of a thing. All I keep thinking is that this was a good day for us to be late. It could have been Gabby."

"You were late?" Rena followed up.

"Yeah. Gabby had a dentist appointment at 10:00. It was probably close to 11:00 before we got there."

"I'm looking at a sign-in sheet that indicates 10:50. Does that sound right?"

"Sure. Close enough."

"Where was this sign-in sheet when you signed it?"

"By the office. I saw Benita and she said that she'd walk Gabby to her classroom. So I signed the sheet and left."

"Benita?"

"Benita Garza. She's my mother-in-law. Gabby's grandmother. She works part-time at the learning center as their cook."

"Okay, thank you. Do you recall, Mr. Bridge, if there was any other signature on the sheet when you signed it?"

"You know, I'm pretty sure there was. I remember looking at it to see if I recognized the name as one of the kids from Emma's room, but I didn't. I wouldn't be able to tell you who it was, though. Can't remember that."

"That's no problem. Thank you very much for your help. And thank you again for being part of the search party."

Rena ended the call. "That's that," she said. "I suppose we should verify with Alice Quest and with Benita Garza that they escorted children back to rooms."

"Odd given that Alice was in a room."

"Yeah. But if it's like everything else tonight, there's probably a perfectly reasonable explanation." Her tone was bitter.

"Don't get discouraged, Morgan. It's early yet."

"It's dark and she's five."

"I know. Let's go talk to Alice."

Four

Alice was in her office. Her back turned to the door. Filing papers into hanging folders in the cabinet behind her desk. She turned when she heard them. "I never get a chance to do this," she said, with no inflection.

A childcare center had a weird feel to it when there were no children there. Likely she felt it even more acutely because she was so used to the noises, the smells, the laughter, the tears. It was probably time for all of them to get out of there for the night.

"Alice, there are two parent signatures on the sign-in sheet that was next to your office door."

"I know. I checked it once Troy relayed to me what his mother-in-law had said about dropping Emma off in the lobby with Kara Wiese. Elaine Broadstreet never signed it."

"Right. For the two parents who did, do you know who escorted them to their rooms?"

"I took Nathan Opal to his room. As I've said, I was filling in for Olivia Blow. Once Tanya Knight arrived at 7:30, I told her that I needed to run down to the office for just a couple minutes. Check my voice mails, my emails, that sort of thing. I was just headed back when Nathan's mom flew in and asked if I'd get Nathan to his room. I wasn't sure who had taken Gabby Bridge to Kara and Claire's room, so when I spoke with Kara, I asked her. She said it was Benita, who happens to be Gabby's grandmother."

Rena had been right. There was a reasonable explanation. It was enough to make anybody crazy. Everything was so fucking reasonable and yet there was a missing five-year-old.

"Okay. I think we're done here tonight. Are you going home?"

"Soon. I've sent an email to every parent and called them, too, letting them know the day care won't be open for business tomorrow. While I'm sure they will understand, some of them will have to scramble to make other arrangements. I had to leave messages for a couple. I asked them to call me here once they got the message. I'll wait a bit."

"Okay. There is an officer posted at both the front and back doors. When you leave, make sure one of them knows it."

"I will. Thank you, Detectives. I really do appreciate everything you've done tonight. Everything that everyone is doing. It's…" She stopped, obviously choked up.

"We know," Rena said, her voice soft. "Good night, Alice."

A.L. knew that Rena wouldn't offer any promises. None of them knew how this was going to turn out. It was already awful and it might just get damn horrific before it was over.

When he and Rena got outside, he stood for a minute, taking in the evening air. It was dry and fairly warm for a Wisconsin fall night. High fifties, maybe even low sixties. There were stars in the sky and a half moon.

"Nice night," he said.

Rena didn't say anything.

"Let's go talk to some neighbors. See if anybody was out and about this morning at around 7:15," he said.

"And saw a five-year-old wandering around?" Rena asked.

"Saw anything."

On their way to the next-door neighbor's house, they detoured through the volunteer setup area. They found Ferguson giving some instructions to a couple retirement-age men on where to set up some food that had been ordered and would be delivered soon.

"How's it going?" A.L. asked.

"It's been a madhouse," Ferguson admitted. "But the FBI guys know how to do this. They'd got everybody who wanted to search organized pretty quickly. Christ, they already got porta potties delivered and set up down the street. They started the search behind the day care."

That made sense. Especially now that they had verification by the street cameras of Elaine Broadstreet's travel. It *was* likely that Emma had indeed arrived at the day care. What had happened after that was the unknown.

If Emma had strolled out of the day care without someone seeing her, it was possible she'd exited via the back door. If somebody had somehow taken her out of the day care, the same was true. Once the searchers got past the parking lot, it was going to get a lot tougher. On open ground, they'd be walking in straight lines, so close that their arms would touch if they extended them, in hopes of stumbling upon something of importance. In the not-yet-harvested fields, they'd each take a row.

There were probably fifteen or twenty more people in the immediate area. "These the searchers who didn't want to traipse through a cornfield?"

"Only a couple. Most of them arrived after the initial group had launched. The FBI is about to get a second group going. They'll walk the immediate area to our right, try to cover as much as a mile in that direction."

"Okay. Did you get a chance to eat something?"

"No. But we've got food and bottled water coming in. I'll grab something. I can get you guys a plate, too."

"No thanks," A.L. said. "We're going to talk to some of the neighbors. We'll hit the panini shop across the street at some point and can get something there if the mood strikes us." Hard to think about food when a child was missing. But people needed to eat and have something to drink. And then someplace to take a piss. Those were the mundane things that had to be considered at a time like this.

He and Rena walked toward the next-door neighbor's house. It had probably been built about the same time and maybe by the same builder as the learning center because it looked very similar with the exception that somebody had added a front porch along the way. It was getting dark but the streetlights were on, giving off enough light that he could see there was an older couple, maybe in their midseventies, sitting in lawn chairs on the porch.

He stopped a couple feet away from the front steps. "Evening," A.L. said. "I'm Detective McKittridge and this is my partner, Detective Morgan. May we have a word?"

"Rena Morgan?" the woman asked, her voice rough.

It wasn't the response he'd been expecting.

"Yes," Rena said.

"Come on up. We know your mother-in-law. She sold us this house more than twenty-five years ago and we've stayed in touch over the years. She's always talking about her daughter-in-law and how proud she is of you."

A.L. moved aside to let Rena take the lead up the steps.

"Why, you're just as pretty as she said you were," Grace said.

"Well, thank you," Rena said. "And you are?"

"Grace and Jim Stern. In all the years we've been here, there's never been nothing like tonight," Grace said. "A child. It's just horrible."

"It is," Rena said. "And given that your house is located right next door to the day care, we wanted to stop by and ask a few questions."

"We're happy enough to help," Jim said. "Considered joining the other people who were going to search but decided it wouldn't be helpful to have a couple of old people falling down and getting in the way. Earlier we had a nice young gentleman and his dog look around our backyard just in case, I guess, that the little girl had come this direction."

"Were you around this morning, say about 7:15?" Rena asked.

"We get up about 5:30," Grace said. "Have coffee and breakfast by 6:00. So, yes, we were here. I made some banana bread this morning so I was probably in the kitchen. What were you doing, Jim, at 7:15?"

"I was downstairs, fixing that old toaster."

"We're just curious if you saw anything unusual at or near the day care?" Rena said.

"Unusual how?" Grace asked.

Rena shrugged. "Anything that might have seemed different. Different people. Different noises. Different smells. Anything that might have struck you as odd."

"I can't think of anything, but then again, we weren't paying attention. The day care has been there for years. It creates some traffic on the street, which we weren't crazy about in the beginning, but we enjoy watching the little ones on the playground, and sometimes they take them for walks right past our house. They got a rope that they have the littler ones hang on to and when they get a little older, the kids hold hands. It reminds us of when our kids were young."

A.L. could easily imagine the scene. Lots of innocence had been lost tonight.

Rena pulled a card from her pocket. "If you think of anything, I'd appreciate a call."

"Will do," Grace said, reaching for it. "Tell your mother-in-law we said hello."

"I will."

They walked down the steps. When they were far enough not to be overheard, A.L. said, "You really can't go anywhere in this town that somebody doesn't know at least one of the Morgans."

"They were sweet. I'm sure Gabe's mom will remember them. I swear she's stayed in touch with every buyer or seller she ever worked with."

"Let's go to the sandwich shop. I doubt he's very busy. Nobody can get down the street."

"His business is called Panini Playground," Rena said, with one eyebrow raised. "You think that maybe affects his business?"

"Yeah, I've heard better. Maybe it's a play off the learning center."

"You're thinking that somebody there might have seen something?"

"I don't know. Doesn't hurt to ask."

"They wouldn't have been open that early," Rena said. "It's a lunch and dinner place."

"You never worked in a restaurant, did you?" A.L. said.

"No. Why?"

"People are in hours earlier than it opens. Prepping for the day. Then they work all day."

"Sort of like police work," she said.

A.L. ordered a panini with salami and pepperoni and Rena chose a chicken and pesto from a tired-looking sixtysomething guy wearing a once-white apron over jeans and a chambray shirt.

"Slow night," she said as she paid for her order. A.L. had hit the bathroom.

He shrugged. "You a cop?"

"Yeah."

"That's about all we've had tonight. Plus a few volunteers. Hell of a thing. A missing kid."

"Anybody from here around this morning?"

"I got in about 9:00."

Early but not early enough, thought Rena. "Are you the owner?"

"Yeah. Going on seven years."

"I'm Detective Morgan. What's your name, sir?"

"Antonio Gibacki."

"How's the neighborhood, Mr. Gibacki?"

"We've been happy. There's a couple apartment buildings two blocks over that occasionally have a few lowlifes, but I know how to protect my place if it comes to that."

She decided to ignore that he probably was insinuating that he kept a gun on the premises.

A cook, partially visible in the kitchen via the pass-through window, placed two baskets on the stainless-steel edge. The man turned and grabbed them. "Just last night," he said, setting the steaming food in front of Rena, "I had two assholes that I needed to show to the door."

"Because?" Rena said.

The man shook his head. "They were a couple of punks. Loud. I had some regulars in here and they were getting irritated."

"So these punks were strangers?" Rena asked. A.L. had returned and now stood silently next to her.

"I hadn't seen them before. Maybe they're new to the apartments. I don't know. I don't think I'll see 'em again."

Strangers in the neighborhood the night before a

five-year-old child went missing. "Mr. Gibacki, this is my partner Detective McKittridge. Can you tell us what these guys looked like?" she asked.

The guy blew out a breath. "White. Skinny. Early to midthirties. Both of them had on pants that they practically had to hold up to keep them on."

"Hair?"

"One brown. The other was a redhead. Had a thick head of hair. To his shoulders. I had a cousin who had that thick, coarse red hair and he hated it."

Rena resisted the urge to pat her own red hair but she could feel some heat creep into her face.

Maybe the guy saw it. Maybe he realized that he'd stepped in it. "Now, you got nice red hair. Real pretty."

"Thank you," she said. Not always. Her husband called her RB for short. Redhead Bedhead. "Scars? Tattoos?" she asked.

The guy frowned at her. "They all got tattoos. Every single one of these idiots. Can't be bothered to buy a bar of soap to clean up but they can afford some six-hundred-dollar ink. These two weren't any different. The redhead had a whole arm full of it and the other had something but I'm not sure what. They really weren't here all that long."

"I understand." Rena picked up the baskets.

"Didn't happen to see what these two might have been driving?" A.L. asked.

The man shook his head. "I watched them walk up the street until they got to the end of the block. They didn't get into a car. I guess that's why I thought maybe they were new to the apartments."

Rena smiled at the man. "Nice meeting you," she said. "Food smells good."

Once she and A.L. were in the plastic booth, she looked at her partner. "What do you think?"

"I think we eat and go find these apartment buildings. Knock on some doors."

Rena picked up her sandwich. Looked out the big window. "It's pretty dark," she said. "How long do you think they'll search?"

"I suspect most everyone will either self-elect to go or be sent home in a couple hours. They won't want some tired civilian tripping over tree roots and breaking a neck. And then back at it at first light."

"Maybe we'll figure out where she is before that?" Rena said.

"Hope so. Eat up. We've got people to talk to."

"It's after 9:00. People are going to bed."

"Then we're going to wake some folks up."

There were two three-story buildings. They started with the closest one. The ten-by-ten-inch window on the unlocked front door was filthy. Inside, the floor of the small lobby was covered with early fall leaves. The walls were a dirty gray and most of the graffiti was something that he wouldn't have wanted his daughter to see. A.L. counted mailboxes. Twelve. That meant four apartments on each floor.

There was no elevator. Just thirteen dirty steps per level. Twenty-six steps later, he knocked on Apartment 312. Waited. Knocked again. Hard enough to shake the door. Nobody answered. Maybe they worked evenings or maybe they were out for a late dinner. Or maybe they didn't want to answer the door. But he didn't think so. There was absolutely no noise to indicate somebody was inside. They moved on. At 310, a middle-aged woman cautiously opened the door, maybe a foot or so.

"Detectives McKittridge and Morgan," A.L. said. He and Rena both held their badges steady. "We'd like to ask you a few questions."

The door opened wider. Behind the woman, sitting on a couch, was a teenage boy with earphones on. When he saw the badges, he took off the earphones and looked a little spooked as if he thought they might have come for his pot stash. Their couch was old and sagged in the middle. The tables were scratched but the kid's drink was sitting on a coaster. There was a healthy-looking red mum in a pot on the windowsill.

"May I have your names, ma'am?" Rena asked.

"Gloria Anderson," she said. "This is my son, Conner Anderson."

"Anybody else live in this apartment?"

The woman shook her head. "I'm divorced. I…hope you're not here about my ex," she added, with a quick glance at her son.

"No," Rena said. "We're investigating the disappearance of a five-year-old child from the Lakeside Learning Center, about two blocks over."

"We both got the alert on our phones," she said.

"Have you seen this child?" A.L. asked, holding out his cell phone.

Gloria looked at the picture. Motioned for her son to get up off the couch and look. Both shook their heads.

"Where were the two of you today?"

"Working," the woman said. "At Price Lumber. I'm a bookkeeper. Conner was in school."

"What school?" A.L. asked.

The woman looked surprised at the question. It was good to get basic details from everybody. They might not run every story down but at least they had it in case it became important later.

"Baywood High. He's a sophomore. I dropped him off on my way to work, around 7:45. He's a good boy, a good student."

"That's great, ma'am," A.L. said. "How long have you lived here?"

"Four years."

He was more interested in newcomers. He passed his card to the woman. "If you see this child or think of anything that might be important, I'd appreciate a call."

"Of course."

"One last question," A.L. said. "We're interested in talking to two young men, both white, one with brown hair, the other with red hair and an arm sleeve of tattoos. Does that description ring a bell?"

"No," Gloria said.

"Mom," Conner said. "I saw those guys. A couple days ago. On the corner."

"Which corner?" A.L. asked.

"The corner of Wake Street and Clayton Avenue. The bus stops there."

Clayton was the next street over. Wake was two blocks down. It was the closest bus stop to this area. And the really good news was that all the city buses were wired with video. "Do you recall what day and time that would have been?"

"I think it was Monday and it was after school. So maybe 4:00, 4:30."

"Anybody with these two men?" Rena asked.

"I don't think so. I mean, I wasn't really paying attention to them but the one guy has really red hair. He's hard to miss."

"Okay. Thanks," A.L. said. "If you happen to see these two men again, give me a call right away."

"I will. Did they take that little girl?" the kid asked.

"We have no reason to believe that," A.L. said. "But we're talking to everybody who might have some information."

Both the mom and the kid nodded, but A.L. didn't think that either of them believed what he was saying. They lived in a world where if the cops were looking for you, it wasn't good.

In the ten remaining apartments in the first building, eight doors were answered. They heard nothing of interest from anybody and nobody had seen the two men. The most recent move-in date was a nineteen-year-old girl who'd left her parents' house nine months earlier. They passed out cards and instructions to call if the two guys happened to show up.

They walked outside and stood for a minute, breathing in the fresh air. A.L. took out his phone. "I'm going to have the video pulled from the city bus that runs this route. Everything from Monday through Wednesday."

"We should get the descriptions to the guys looking at the Perv List."

Otherwise known as the sexual offender registry. "Yeah," A.L. said. "Good idea. I'll take care of that."

He put his phone back into his pocket. "Let's do this other building."

Ten of twelve doors were answered. One couple had moved in less than a month ago, but both had jobs that they'd been at on Wednesday. Nobody had seen the two men.

"You think the kid was right?" Rena asked as they walked to their vehicle.

"Good kid. Good student."

"That was according to his mom. What else is she going to say?"

"Right now, I don't have any reason not to believe him," A.L. said. "What's to be gained from him telling us that he'd seen the guys?"

"Wanted to feel important?" Rena said, sliding in to the passenger side.

"My money is on the kid, that he saw them. And we got Mr. Gibacki putting them near the day care the night before Emma disappears. That's enough that they stay on the radar screen."

"We didn't talk to everybody. There were a total of five doors that didn't get answered," Rena said.

"I made a note. I'll follow up with the landlord tomorrow to see if the apartments are rented. We can come back."

"It's getting late," Rena said. "Too late to be questioning more people."

"You're right." A.L. stifled a yawn. Fucking weird day. He'd had breakfast this morning with Tess in an open-air restaurant overlooking the Pacific Ocean. It had been a real nice way to start the day. Now he was ending it on a low note. A missing five-year-old.

Adults were supposed to make sure that things like this didn't happen to kids.

"Go home. Get some sleep," he said.

"You're not going home," Rena accused.

He shrugged. "I may see where they're at with the search."

Rena sighed. "I'll go with you."

Five

A.L. felt as if somebody had rubbed sandpaper across his eyes. At midnight, all non-law-enforcement volunteers had been sent home. He and Rena had stayed on, ultimately covering miles before it had started to rain about three and the search had been suspended. A.L. had hit his bed around three thirty and his alarm had rung at six. A hot shower and a bucket of coffee later, he was now upright and going over his notes from the previous day. Rena was at her desk, on her phone. Her voice was low and she was turned in her chair, likely in an effort to have a little privacy in a shared office space where there was no real hope for that.

When she hung up, he watched her face. Her jaw was tight and her face flushed with color. He didn't ask. If she wanted to tell him, she would.

"Coffee?" he asked, holding up his cup.

She shook her head. Looked at the watch on her wrist. "Search team has been out for fifteen minutes."

Yeah, pretty much once there was adequate daylight. "Almost twenty-four hours," he said. Way too damn long for a five-year-old to be unaccounted for.

Now Rena was staring at her computer screen. "Confirmation that houses and vehicles of Kara Wiese, Troy and Leah Whitman, and Elaine Broadstreet have been searched. Also, the supervisor of Sam Wiese, Kara's husband, has verified that he was at work as expected."

"And there was no five-year-old hidden in his employee locker?"

Rena rolled her eyes. "I guess not. Is that where your head is going? That Kara Wiese is the one who is lying?"

"As opposed to the grandmother? Hell, I don't know," A.L. said. "We need to talk with the other teachers." Alice might have talked with all of them the day before but now they would have to wade deeper.

"I think we should start with Claire Potter," Rena said. "She's in the same room as Kara Wiese." Rena looked at her watch. "It's pretty early. Maybe we should wait a little while."

"Not waiting. Who's the other teacher?"

"Tanya Knight. And the cook, Benita Garza."

"Okay. I saw Ferguson on my way in. Faster pulled him off the scene. The FBI said they could handle it. So he's an available resource if we need him. I'd say we see if he can do those two interviews this morning. After we talk to Claire Potter, I want to go see Milo at Milo's Motors."

"To verify that Elaine Broadstreet was at work yesterday?" Rena asked.

"Yeah. I know Milo. Not well but he bowls with my

dad and my uncle. He's a good guy and I always got the impression that he ran a pretty good operation. I guess I want his read on whether Elaine could be wrong about something important. In the middle of the night, I remembered the comment Leah made about her mother repeating herself. I guess now I'm wondering if that's an irritating habit that she's had her whole life or maybe the woman's age is catching up to her."

"She didn't repeat herself when I talked with her. She seemed pretty with it, considering she'd just heard that her granddaughter was missing. I didn't get the impression that she's senile."

"I guess that's what we need to ask Milo about."

"Leah and her mom don't seem all that close," Rena said.

"Not everybody is the Morgans." Rena's husband's family was downright clingy in his opinion.

A.L.'s computer dinged. He looked at it. Studied the screen. Motioned for Rena to come have a look. Once she was behind his chair, he pointed to the information that had gotten his attention. "I ordered criminal background checks on Alice Quest, the four teachers, the cook, Troy and Leah Whitman, and Elaine Broadstreet. They all came back clean except this one."

"Elaine Broadstreet," Rena read. "Felony possession of a controlled substance and child endangerment. Ninety days of jail and two years' probation." She kept reading. "It was almost twenty-five years ago," she said. She picked up a pad of paper on A.L.'s desk and scribbled down the case file number. "I'll get somebody to pull this." She took two steps. Turned. "Does this surprise you?"

"Yeah," he admitted. "Might explain the disconnect between Leah and her mom."

"Yeah. That's kind of sad. Seems like a time when they really need to be there for one another. It makes me crazy to think that…something like this can happen so fast. That a child could be…lost…just like that."

"All kinds of dangers in the world," he said, "but most of the time, we're able to keep our kids safe. You'll be able to do that." Last she'd shared, they'd identified a carrier. Gabe's sperm, Rena's eggs. Fertilized in a petri dish and implanted in another woman's body for a hefty fee.

"I'm not crazy about Shannon. She's the one. That's what I was talking to Gabe about earlier."

"Then why did you pick her?" A.L. asked.

"Gabe knows her. She used to work at the same company but left a couple years ago to have her own kid."

"But?" A.L. said.

"I don't like her home life. She's married to a loser. He's done time in County for drug offenses. I'm not sure he has a regular job. Probably why she's willing to do this. She needs the money."

"But she's not using?" A.L. said.

"Oh no. That's all been verified. She's clean. Healthy. Eager to do this."

"But you still don't like it?"

"No. But Gabe thinks I'm being ridiculous. He knows her. He trusts her. And it makes him mad that all that isn't enough for me."

"Stressful situation," A.L. said. "You both probably need to cut each other some slack."

"We're running out of time. This happens in less than three weeks."

"So that gives you a little time to get your head around it," A.L. said.

"I hope so. Because if I back out of this now, after everything we've gone through, I don't think Gabe will forgive me." She pushed her chair away from her desk. "Let's go. We need to figure out where the hell Emma is."

They found Claire Potter at her apartment. She was up and dressed in yoga pants and a T-shirt. She was an attractive black woman in her late thirties who straightened her shoulder-length hair and wore an excessive amount of bracelets that clinked together whenever she moved her arms. She was also almost six feet tall. All that told Rena that even though their names sounded a bit alike, it wasn't likely that Elaine had gotten Claire and Kara mixed up.

"Can you tell us about your day yesterday?" A.L. asked.

They were sitting in Claire's small living room. She'd offered them herbal tea but they'd both turned her down. She sat across from them, her long legs folded under her body, a cup in her hands. "It was a good day. Like most days. The kids are great. For the most part," she said with a smile. "I'm worried about what the parents are doing for day care today. Of course, I understand that we couldn't open. Hard to do that with police tape around the building."

"How long have you worked there?" A.L. asked.

"Almost two years. That's when I moved to Baywood. My son was starting high school and I wanted him to go to a better school."

"Are you married, Claire?" Rena asked.

"Divorced. Six years."

"Then it's just you and your son who live in this apartment."

"Me, my son and two very ugly turtles."

Rena smiled. "What's your relationship with Kara Wiese?"

"Good. She was already at the day care when I started but we've been teaching together since day one. She's really good with the kids. I tower over her so I suspect we look ridiculous when we're together but it's always been a good match. I'm pretty sure that's what she would say, too."

Rena leaned forward. "Elaine Broadstreet, Emma's grandmother, says that she dropped Emma off at the day care yesterday into Kara Wiese's care. Kara is denying that. Would you have any reason to think that she would be lying about that?"

"Of course not. Why would she? If that had happened, she would have brought Emma back to our classroom."

"Have you and Kara had any conversation about this?" A.L. asked.

"We saw each other last night. Both of us volunteered to search. But she didn't tell me what to say, if that's what you're suggesting."

"Not suggesting anything," A.L. said, holding up his hand. "Just trying to get an understanding of the situation. Would you say that you and Kara are friends?"

"Yes. We're coworkers. We're friends. We both like

California rolls and chocolate cake. I'm really not sure what else I can tell you except that we're all just sick about this."

A.L. stood. "We are, too. Can you tell me what time you got to work yesterday morning?"

"I start at 7:30."

"I know that's your start time. But were you early yesterday? On time? Late?"

"I'm not generally late. Not generally much early, either," she added with a quick smile. "I usually arrive about 7:25. I park and walk into the classroom, ready to work."

"No stopping in the break room for a cup of coffee? Or to put away your lunch?" Rena asked.

Claire shook her head. "Don't drink coffee and the cook at the day care is really good. I eat lunch there."

"So you're confident that you were in your classroom by 7:30?" A.L. followed up.

"Yes."

"Was Kara in the room?" he asked.

"Of course."

"Do you remember how many kids?"

Claire's bracelets clinked as she used her fingers to silently count. "Six or seven, I think. That's pretty normal."

"Did you see Emma Whitman?" Rena asked.

"No."

"Did Kara leave the classroom at any time in the morning?" Rena asked.

"I'm sure she did. She probably used the restroom. There's one in the classroom for the kids but we don't generally use that one. There's one for staff in the hallway."

Rena had seen that when they'd searched the building. "Do you recall when she might have used the restroom?"

Claire shook her head.

"When she leaves for the restroom, does somebody come in to cover her absence?" A.L. asked. "So that you maintain the right teacher-to-student ratio."

Claire looked uncomfortable. "It's what we're supposed to do," she said. "But really, it's just such a short absence. We just…do it. I mean, Alice must know but she never says anything."

"You're not aware of any other reason why Kara might leave the room other than these short bathroom breaks?" Rena asked.

"Well, she might have if she needed to make a personal call. Kids can be magpies and you don't necessarily want them repeating parts of your personal business when they go home at the end of the day."

"Does she have lots of personal calls to make?" A.L. asked.

"No. People text mostly now."

"But sometimes she would step out to make a call?" Rena asked.

"To make or take. Like all of us."

Take, as in incoming. "Do you happen to know who called Kara?" Rena followed up.

"I don't really know. I mean, I think she was about to close on a new house so she was talking to her Realtor or maybe her banker a lot."

"Very good. Thank you again," A.L. said.

He and Rena left the apartment building. When they were back in the car, A.L. turned to her. "New houses cost a lot of money."

"I'll get her phone records," Rena said, pulling out her own phone. "Now to Milo's Motors?"

"Yeah, but I don't necessarily want Elaine to know that we're talking to her boss. So I'm going to call Leah Whitman because one, I want to check in with her and two, it might give me a chance to see if her mom is with her. If she is, this is a good day to drive to Milo's Motors."

A.L. dialed and the call was answered on the second ring.

"Hello," Leah said, almost sounding breathless. He had the call on Speaker and Rena gave him a look that needed no explanation. *She thinks you're calling with news.*

A.L. nodded. "It's Detective McKittridge. Just checking in to see how you're doing," he added quickly.

"I'm okay," she said. "I didn't get much sleep."

"That's understandable."

"Is there any news, Detective?" she asked, her tone sharp. She wasn't interested in his platitudes. She wanted her daughter back.

"No, I'm sorry. But know that we will not rest until we find Emma."

"Troy went back to search this morning."

That meant she still had a house of people. Blithe from their department. A couple FBI geeks helping to watch the phone. "Is your mom able to be with you?" A.L. asked.

"Yes. She called in to work. I didn't ask her to.

But they understand…that she wants to be here." She paused, sounding discouraged.

"This is really hard, Leah. We know that. But hang in there. Either my partner, Rena, or I will check in with you later today."

"Fine. Thank you."

"You're welcome. Goodbye, Leah."

A.L. put his phone down. "Christ, that sucked." He sounded weary.

"Yeah," Rena said. "I really want to be able to call her with good news." She looked at her watch. "We need to be back for the ten o'clock meeting in Faster's office."

It was a good news, bad news kind of thing. Good news in that resources were plentiful. It was raining cops. Federal, state and county. Bad news was that resources were plentiful. Keeping everybody on the same page was a substantial undertaking with a case like this and they needed to be careful not to trip over each other.

A.L. likely didn't think Faster would be up to the task. She was willing to reserve judgment.

A.L. keyed an address into his GPS. "Nine minutes to Milo's Motors. Let's see what he has to say."

Twelve minutes later, they were inside Milo's office, sitting in the two guest chairs, while Milo sat behind his paper-laden desk. There was a computer on the desk but Rena didn't think it was turned on.

"Good to see you, A.L.," Milo said. "I haven't seen your dad or your uncle for a while. Bowling doesn't start for another couple weeks. How are they?"

"Good," A.L. said.

Rena wondered if he actually knew. He didn't talk about his family much. Just his sister, Liz, who lived in Madison.

"I was wondering if you could answer a few questions about Elaine Broadstreet," A.L. said.

"Of course. Hell of a situation with her grandchild. I got four of my own and I think I might lose my mind if something like this happened."

"We understand that Elaine has worked for you for a number of years."

"That's correct."

"And how would you characterize her work?"

Milo looked surprised. "She catches mistakes that the sales guys make all the time. Catches some of mine, too." He stopped. "Of course, she isn't perfect. Lately there's been some things that might have been a problem for us."

"Like?"

"Errors in spreadsheets. Documents that promised terms that we quite frankly never promise. That sort of thing. It's okay. We'll get past it but I did tell her she needed to be careful. I don't like to say too much. She's a real nice lady and everybody makes mistakes."

"You said 'lately,'" A.L. pushed. "Does that mean that her work has slipped noticeably in the past few weeks, months?"

"A month or so. But not everything. There's just been a couple things that, quite frankly, surprised the hell out of me. It's things she's done for years without any problem and suddenly we've got a hell of a screw-up going on."

"Any change in her personality?" Rena asked.

Milo shrugged. "She's a good person. Like most good people, she gets frustrated when there are mistakes. Claims that she doesn't know how they happened, that she knows how to do the work."

"Is she dependable?" A.L. asked.

Milo shrugged. "Sure. I mean, she's here every day. Not really a morning person but she stays late and that helps us because we don't have much traffic on our lots until midafternoon usually."

Rena shifted in her seat. "What time does her workday start?"

"I think she's here most days by 9:30 or 10:00. I'm not a clock watcher. I wouldn't want to work for one and I figure most other folks feel the same way. We don't have a time clock or anything like that. People get paid for forty hours. I'm confident that they're going to put the time in."

"Of course," Rena said. "But do you happen to recall what time she arrived for work yesterday?"

"I don't but I suspect Portia knows. She works the service desk and everybody has to walk past her. Want me to call her and ask?"

"That would be helpful," A.L. said.

Milo picked up his phone and they listened in to his side of the conversation. When he hung up, he said, "Portia said it was about 10:00."

"Are you and Elaine friends outside of work?" Rena asked.

Milo looked at A.L. "I think Susie might have something to say about that." He turned toward Rena. "My wife of forty-three years."

"I suspect she would," A.L. said. "But any feel for how Elaine spends her time outside of work?"

"Well, I don't think she bowls. She's always teasing me about that. I guess she spends a lot of time with her family. And a couple times a year, she takes a week off and goes to Vegas."

"She likes to gamble?" A.L. asked, his voice the same tone as if he was asking if she liked chocolate chip cookies.

"Blackjack is her game. From what I've heard, she's pretty good."

"Lucky, then," A.L. said.

"Yeah, well, I hope her luck holds out and they find that little girl."

"We do, too," A.L. said. He stood up and Rena followed suit. "If you don't mind, I'd appreciate you keeping our visit here just between us."

"No problem. Always happy to help Baywood's finest. Tell your dad I bowled a 259 the other night."

Rena waited until they were in the car before speaking. "I specifically asked Elaine Broadstreet what she did after she dropped Emma off at the day care. She said she went to work. If she was at the day care by 7:30 and it's a fifteen-minute drive from there to here, there's more than two hours of time that is unaccounted for."

"We need to ask her about that. And about her criminal record. And try to get a feel for whether she's failing cognitively," A.L. said.

"I want to turn the clock backwards," moaned Rena. "Yesterday, my most pressing issue was Laurie Cannon and a disappearing Volkswagen."

A.L. turned his head. "Your Volkswagen disappeared?"

"Not mine. Mrs. Cannon's. She's a widow in her seventies who has reported her car missing six times this summer."

"She loses her car?" A.L. said.

"Well, that's what responding officers thought. Because they would always find it, within a block or two. They didn't ignore the possibility that it had been moved but it got dusted for prints and there were never any besides Mrs. Cannon's. They evidently suggested to her one too many times that perhaps she forgot where she parked it. She was so furious that she called in and complained. That's when it got kicked over to me."

"This is what I have to look forward to," A.L. said morosely.

"Complaints from irate old women?" Rena asked.

"No. Forgetting where I park my car."

"Cheer up," Rena said. "She didn't forget. Six sophomore boys from Baywood High were arrested early this morning. They were caught picking up, literally, a MINI Cooper four blocks away from Mrs. Cannon's house and admitted that they've also been moving Mrs. Cannon's vehicle. So I get to be a hero and tell Mrs. Cannon that the situation is resolved when I really did nothing."

"That's how it works sometimes. Other times, we bust our hump and we get nowhere. Enjoy the easy ones. Where was this?"

"Mrs. Cannon is on Kingview Street."

She didn't have to say more. A.L. would understand how this could happen six times without any-body being the wiser. The houses on Kingview didn't come equipped with external security cameras. And the city didn't have a street camera within three blocks.

"Never any damage to the vehicle?"

"Nope. Nary a scratch," Rena said.

A.L. snorted. "Kind of refreshing, actually. It's like a prank from a 1970s sitcom."

"I know. Far cry from a missing five-year-old."

A.L. nodded. "We've got enough time to swing by and give her the good news."

The drive to Mrs. Cannon's house took seven min-utes. It was located at the far north side of town, where the houses were small, the yards big and worn-looking, several with rusted swing sets forlornly perched upon a field of thistles.

Rena picked her way across the grass with A.L. a step behind her. She noticed that half of the railing on the small front porch looked freshly painted. Her gaze went up, around. Pre-paint, the railing had been in bet-ter shape than the rest of the porch. Like it had gotten a coat of paint not that long ago.

She suspected Mrs. Cannon wasn't able to reach the other areas as easily. She took care of what she could.

She knocked and a woman opened the door. Mid-seventies, wearing loose jeans and a flannel shirt with a pack of cigarettes in the pocket. She was holding a paintbrush in one hand. "Yes," she said.

"I'm Detective Morgan. We spoke on the phone." She held out her badge. "This is Detective McKit-tridge." A.L. also had his badge out.

Mrs. Cannon didn't look at either. "I recognize your

voice," the woman said. She had a smudge of dark green paint on one wrinkled cheek.

"I wanted to let you know that you shouldn't have any more trouble with your vehicle. We arrested a group of boys who are responsible. They were caught in the act of moving another person's car. They admitted doing the same with your vehicle."

"I knew I hadn't forgotten where I parked my car," the woman said. "Figured it had to be something like this. I tried to catch them. Stayed up all night but nothing happened. You can't do that every night," she added. "Not at my age, anyway."

"Of course not," Rena said.

"I'm grateful to hear something. I didn't figure my concerns might get much attention right now. With that little girl missing."

Rena looked over Mrs. Cannon's shoulder and saw a newspaper spread out on the kitchen table. Knew that below the fold was an article about Emma Whitman, with a picture of her at her recent birthday party. "We're doing everything we can to find her." Rena extended her hand. "I won't take up any more of—"

"It's just like what happened in Dover all those years ago," Mrs. Cannon interrupted.

Rena lowered her hand. Felt the back of her neck get clammy. "Dover, Wisconsin?"

"Yes."

She knew the town. Maybe twelve thousand people, roughly a quarter the size of Baywood. About a hundred miles north. She turned to look at A.L., who shook his head. She turned back to Mrs. Cannon. "I guess I'm not familiar with that case."

"Well, I remember it. My granddaughter, who lives in Chicago, was five, the same age as the little girl who went missing. It made me sick to think that something like that might happen to her."

"How long ago was this?" Rena asked.

"Well, my granddaughter is fifteen now, so I guess about ten years. I don't think they ever found that child. I hope that's not what we're dealing with here. As a parent, I'd want to know. Even if it was bad news."

A.L. stepped forward. "You don't happen to remember the child's name, do you?"

Mrs. Cannon shook her head. "I don't."

Looking up crimes in Dover would be enough for them to find it. "It was a pleasure to meet you in person, Mrs. Cannon," Rena said.

"You, too, Detectives. Don't touch the railing on your way out," she added.

A.L. was pushing buttons on his phone by the time Rena got into the passenger seat. To whoever answered, he said, "We need info on what is likely a cold case from about ten years ago. Dover, Wisconsin. Missing five-year-old. Similar circumstances to Emma Whitman. We'll be back in the office in ten minutes."

He hung up his phone. Neither of them said anything.

He drove and she tried to quiet her head, which was roiling with this new information. They parked in the lot and quickly walked inside. Then it was up the elevator. By the time they crossed the threshold of their office, they were practically running toward the manila folder that was on A.L.'s chair.

He opened it. Just one sheet of paper. He held it so that they could both read.

"Holy shit," he said after another minute.

Indeed. Corrine Antler, age five, had been dropped off at a day care and discovered missing approximately ten hours later. No ransom. She had never been found.

Rena gripped the back of the chair. "So similar," she said softly.

"Too fucking similar," A.L. said. "We're going to Dover."

Six

The lead detective on the Corrine Antler case had been Doug Franklin. He'd retired from the Dover Police Department two years earlier and most nice days could be found on the golf course. A.L. got this from Franklin's former supervisor, who was still riding a desk for the Dover PD.

"I wasn't here when the Antler case happened," Brent Smoke said. "I was hired three years later so it was technically a cold case. But I know that Doug Franklin thought about that child every day, that he never stopped trying to figure out what had happened to her. I'm sorry the two of you are mixed up in something similar. I'd be happy to let you look at our file."

A.L. wanted to talk to Doug Franklin first. "I'd appreciate any help that you can give us to connect with Mr. Franklin. Perhaps his cell phone number."

"We don't, as a rule, give out a former employee's personal cell number. Even to other officers. But I'll give him a call. See if he's available. Why don't the two of you have a cup of coffee in the waiting area?"

Neither Rena nor A.L. was likely to turn down coffee. It was hot and slightly bitter but no worse than what was brewed at the Baywood PD. And they barely had time to finish a cup before Brent Smoke came to find them.

"He'll meet you in the clubhouse," he said, passing an address to A.L.

"Thanks for your help," A.L. said. "We'll likely be back later to look at the file. If you could grease the wheels on that, it would be appreciated."

"Consider it done. Good luck."

A.L. and Rena walked back to his vehicle and plugged the address into the GPS. Thirteen miles. They were halfway there when Rena turned to him.

"This makes me think of Golf Course John."

Last spring, he and Rena had been investigating a serial murderer and had stumbled upon Golf Course John, a pleasant enough twenty-two-year-old man who worked behind the counter at the Baywood Golf Course, who A.L. had wanted to kill once he'd voluntarily disclosed that he was dating A.L.'s then sixteen-year-old daughter. "I try not to think of him," A.L. said.

"You're confident that's over?" Rena asked.

"Traci says it is. I am bothered by the fact that she's going to homecoming with the same boy she went to prom with."

"Why does that bother you?"

"Well, she says they're just friends."

"I'm still unclear. That should make you happy."

"You would think. But she went to prom with him because she couldn't go with Golf Course John since he was too old. I can't help but wonder if the same thing isn't still happening."

"So ask her?"

"I have to assume that she's telling me the truth until I have proof that she isn't."

Rena gave him a look. "Tess is coaching you, isn't she?"

He shrugged, keeping his eyes on the road. "She has a good relationship with her daughter. I could do worse than take her advice."

"Agree. But I always thought you had pretty good parenting instincts."

Now he glanced at her. "That sounds like a compliment, Morgan."

She smiled. "What do you think Doug Franklin is going to tell us?"

"More than the file would. That's why we're going to see him."

When they walked into the clubhouse, a man sitting at a corner table waved them over. He was sixty-something, wearing plaid shorts and a bright green shirt. He glanced at their badges and motioned for them to take a chair. "Tell me what's happened," he said, not bothering with any pleasantries.

Rena leaned forward. "Five-year-old female was dropped off by her grandmother at day care. At the end of the day, when her father came to pick her up, it was discovered that she hadn't been there the entire day. Grandmother swears she handed her off to her teacher at the front door. Teacher says it never happened. She's been missing for almost twenty-nine hours at this point."

He nodded. Rubbed his forehead with his index finger and thumb. "Corrine Antler was dropped off by her father. He walked her into the building. She ran ahead. He was fifteen to twenty feet behind. Once he saw her enter her classroom, he left. This was the same routine that they'd followed for months. Her mother came to pick her up that afternoon. She wasn't there and the teacher in her classroom said that she'd never seen the child."

"You never made an arrest," A.L. said.

Doug Franklin shook his head.

"Did you like anybody in particular?" A.L. asked.

"A few different people, at various times. There was a janitor who cleaned the building who had a short rap sheet and a belligerent attitude. But I turned over every stone in that man's life. I found some shit but never any sign of Corrine."

"You know where this guy is now?" A.L. asked.

"He's dead. Three years now," Doug Franklin said. "One of the last things I did before I retired was update the Antler file with his obituary."

"Anybody else?" A.L. asked.

"There was a neighbor who lived across the street. Single lady. Never married, never had any children. I had a witness who claimed they thought they saw a child watching television in her living room. But we couldn't find any physical evidence that tied Corrine to that house."

"She dead, too?" A.L. asked.

"Nope. Still lives in the same house."

"You think it makes any sense for us to pay her a visit?" Rena asked.

He raised one mangy eyebrow. "You got a missing kid. You got to do everything you can and then one more thing."

Rena nodded. "Her name?"

"Rosemary Bracken. Second house from the end of the block."

"The parents were never suspects?" A.L. asked.

"We looked at them, of course. But they were... well, I guess the best word would be *wrecked*. Just wrecked. They aged about ten years the first week. After a month, it hurt to look in their eyes. They're better now, you know. Had to go on. They had a seven- and a ten-year-old at the time. The seven-year-old just graduated from high school last spring. They invited me to the house for the party. We got to know each other pretty well over the years."

A.L. and Rena exchanged a glance. The idea of socializing with the Whitmans in ten years because they'd bonded over a missing child who was never found made him want to throw up. Rena appeared to concur. "Anything else that we should know?" he asked.

Doug shook his head. "Your case is remarkably similar," he said thoughtfully. "Is it even possible that it could be the same person responsible for both crimes?"

A.L. thought he heard the faintest bit of hope in the older man's voice. He understood. The case haunted Doug Franklin. If it was the same person and he and Rena managed to find the asshole, then there could be closure here in Dover. "I don't know. We can't ignore the possibility. We've got an eyewitness who places two strangers at a restaurant across the street from the day care the night before Emma disappeared. That sound remotely familiar? These guys were described at early to midthirties. Ten years ago they'd have been early to midtwenties. Both white. One is a redhead with a sleeve tattoo."

Doug Franklin tapped his index finger on the table. "The janitor had a kid. He was maybe nineteen or twenty. Red hair. I don't remember any tattoos."

Those could have been acquired in the last ten years. "You know where the kid is?"

Doug Franklin shook his head. "The janitor's name was Trapper Frogg. I don't remember what his kid's name was, which is weird because it was an odd one. Old age, I guess. It'll be in the file somewhere. I remember talking to him."

"Great," A.L. said. "We also want to talk to Corrine Antler's parents. Just to see if there is any possible connection between them and the Whitmans or anybody else intimately involved in this thing. Can you set that up for us?"

"Yeah, I think so. They're both teachers so they get off work by 3:30. Can the two of you hang around until then?"

He and Rena nodded. "We'll take a drive by Rosemary Bracken's house. And then spend the time reviewing the case file," A.L. said. "Brent Smoke already offered it to us."

"The new guy," Doug Franklin said, his tone not complimentary. "Always wanted to shake things up. Like what we'd been doing for the last thirty years was all wrong."

Doug Franklin had twenty years on A.L. He'd

earned his "Old Guy" stripes. But still, it made A.L. uneasy. Was he on his way to being him? Pissed off about the inevitable change that barreled toward them every day, like a goddamn speeding train.

A few months ago he'd have spent no time thinking about it. But that was before Tess. Who had triumphed over tragedy and likely wouldn't bother wasting too much time with somebody who couldn't realize that the good old days might have been great but they were fucking gone.

"Thank you for your time," A.L. said.

"You'll let me know, right?" Doug Franklin said, standing up. "If there's anything in your case that might mean something to me."

"Will do," A.L. promised.

They found Rosemary Bracken's house without any trouble. The yard was mostly dirt and the house was a square box, painted a dull gray, with one lone red petunia in a small pot next to the front door. "Nice landscaping," Rena said, nodding at the flower. "Doesn't make me hopeful."

"My uncle Joe lives in a similar place. Some people are just low-maintenance."

"Right. If a fifteen-year-old girl comes to the door who answers to Corrine, I'll remind you that you think this falls within the normal range." She turned her head to look at the day care across the street. It was a one-story brick-and-frame building. "This is so weird. I know the building doesn't look like Lakeside Learning Center but the location is similar. On a corner. Open field behind it. Houses. A few small businesses."

"No psychic," A.L. said.

"We haven't met Rosemary yet."

They got out of the car. Rena knocked on the door. She was just about to knock a second time when it opened. It wasn't a fifteen-year-old girl but rather a woman, maybe midfifties, wearing black-and-red pajama pants and a faded black T-shirt that appeared to have been washed about three hundred times. "Ms. Bracken?" Rena said.

"Yes."

"I'm Detective Morgan. This is my partner, Detective McKittridge." They both held their badges steady while the woman inspected them. "May we come in?"

"Why?" she asked, not moving.

"We're from the Baywood Police Department, about a hundred miles south of here. We are investigating the disappearance of a five-year-old from her day care. We understand that a similar crime occurred here in Dover about ten years ago and that you lived here at the time."

While she spoke, Rena closely watched the older woman's face. But there was no response. Not a blink, a twitch, a gasp, or anything that resembled a normal reaction to hearing that a child was missing. When she was done talking, there was an uncomfortable silence. Then finally, the woman stepped back and motioned for them to have a seat in the living room. There was a couch and one chair. A.L. and Rena both sat on the couch.

"I'm not sure how I can help you."

"Do you remember the missing child from the day care across the street?" A.L. asked.

"Of course. It was huge news in a town this size. Horrible news."

She said the last sentence without emotion, as if she might be talking about the price of milk going up. "Did you talk to police at the time?" Rena asked.

"I did. I suspect many of the neighbors did. I believe I got some extra scrutiny because some idiot reported that they saw a child on my couch, watching television."

"Did that make you angry?" A.L. asked.

The woman shrugged. "It was a waste of everyone's time. I didn't like that."

"I see. What is it that you do for a living, Ms. Bracken?" Rena asked.

"I transcribe medical records. From my home."

"You always work from home? Never go into an office?" Rena asked.

"Never. It's part of my deal. I don't like to go out but I'm a very good transcriptionist. With electronic medical records, many physicians input their own data but there are still some that refuse to do that. They want their transcription turned around quickly. I'm nocturnal. I work at night and sleep during the day, so that allows me to have whatever they've left in their queue by 10:00 at night back to them by 6:00 in the morning. They like that." She glanced at the clock. "These are my sleeping hours. I was just drifting off when you came to the door."

"Sorry about that," A.L. said easily in a tone that told Rena he didn't mean it. "Where were you this past Wednesday around 7:30 in the morning?"

Rena felt some satisfaction. She was now not the only one creeped out by the woman. A.L. was done tiptoeing around.

"I finished work early on Wednesday, probably by 6:00. So I guess I was getting ready for bed," she said.

"Could anyone verify that?" A.L.

The first hint of a smile crossed her lips. Just a hint. "No."

"Do you own a vehicle, Ms. Bracken?" Rena asked.

"I do. A 1982 Buick Regal. Green. License plate RB 5050."

A car that old wasn't going to have GPS.

A.L. stood. "Thank you for your time. Can we have your cell number in the event that we need to contact you?"

"No cell. Just a home number." She rattled it off and A.L. wrote it down in his notebook.

Rena had her hand on the doorknob when Rosemary Bracken spoke again. "I hope you find your little girl. I really do."

Rena managed a tight smile and walked out the door. She could hear A.L. on her heels. Then he stopped. She turned to see what was holding him up.

He'd taken three steps back toward Rosemary Bracken, who stood in her door, watching them. "Had you ever met Corrine Antler?"

"No."

"Did you know her parents? Had you ever met them?"

Rosemary shook her head. "I didn't and I still don't."

A.L. nodded. "Thank you for your time." He turned and easily caught up with Rena. Once they were back in his vehicle, she let out a loud breath. "That is one odd woman."

"*Odd* doesn't equate to kidnapper of young children," A.L. said.

"No GPS in vehicle or cell phone. Limits our ability to track her movements. 'I'm nocturnal.'" Rena said it in the same flat tone that Rosemary Bracken had used. "How about 'I'm a weirdo and it's better if I just hide in my little hole.'"

A.L. said nothing. Just sat behind the wheel and stared at the day care across the street.

"What?" Rena asked finally. "And why did you ask her if she knew Corrine Antler's parents?"

"I keep thinking about Traci at five. If we believe the grandmother and assume that Emma was at some point in the building, it's possible for me to see her getting distracted by something she saw outside the back door and going to investigate. Kids are very curious at that age. Now she's outside. I see three possibilities. Somebody set something up to deliberately lure a child outside. They scooped her up. Or, it wasn't deliberate but somebody just happened to be there, saw an unaccompanied child, and took her. Crime of opportunity. Or, nobody was there and she simply wandered away."

"Of those," Rena said, playing along, "I see the crime of opportunity as the least likely."

"Agree. And if she wandered away, why haven't we found her? Lots of people looking for her. I don't think she's out there."

"So that leaves number one," Rena said. "Somebody lured her outside and took her."

"Which brings me back to Traci. Earlier I was thinking this but now I'll just say it. At five, she understood stranger-danger. I don't think she would have willingly gone with anybody she didn't know or at least hadn't seen before."

"So the bad guy either was a known guy or…took Emma against her will."

"Both possible," A.L. said. "But if it's against her will, wouldn't there be some struggle? Some noise. Something that someone noticed?"

Rena shrugged. "Not hard to overpower a five-year-old child. To silence."

"I know. But my mind is hung up on the fact that I think she had some familiarity with whoever took her. That's why I asked Rosemary Bracken if she knew Corrine Antler or Corrine Antler's parents. To see if she had any familiarity."

"Don't you imagine that Doug Franklin asked her that?"

"I suspect so. It might well be in the file. Which we should go review." He put his SUV in Drive and pulled away from the curb.

"What if it was somebody Emma knew very well who lured her outside? Somebody she wouldn't have any qualms about going with? Somebody like…one of her parents?"

"Ugly goddamn theory," A.L. said, without emotion.

"I know. But you and I both noticed the strain between the Whitmans. It wouldn't be the first time that a parent harmed a child to hurt a spouse." They'd both seen that just two years earlier when a child had been beaten severely by his father to make the mother pay for her infidelity. It had been a gruesome, ugly case that had been horrible to investigate.

"I know," A.L. said. "We can't discount the parents."

"Or the grandmother. Our discussion five minutes ago was predicated on us believing the grandmother."

"We know she got to the day care. She told us her route and we were able to verify that with street cameras. And we see her at the end of the block and there's no child in the back seat. So I think we've got a good reason to believe the grandmother."

"But she's the only one with a criminal record. And one of the charges was child endangerment."

"I know. She's on the list," A.L. said. "We're going to ask her all about that. But right now, we need to go review the Antler file and then talk to the parents. We look for any connection between them and the Whitmans. I think I might like to talk to whoever was managing the day care at the time of Corrine's disappearance."

"I got a text from Ferguson. He has meetings set up with the remaining day care teacher and the cook today."

"Make sure he asks about their relationship with Kara Wiese. Do they like her, trust her, et cetera?"

Rena nodded and picked up her phone. Once she was done, she put her phone away. "If Emma knew who took her, maybe it wasn't her parents or her grandmother but a family friend. Or maybe the parents of one of her little friends, somebody she trusts."

"All possibilities." He didn't sound discouraged.

She understood. There was still hope. "I'm going to need to eat some lunch pretty soon." She picked up her phone. Punched a few keys. "There's a little diner two blocks from here."

"Good enough," A.L. said.

The BLT was better than he expected and the French fries were so hot he burned his tongue. Rena had ordered some kind of salad and a cup of soup. They were getting some interest from the locals who were sitting at the counter. Strangers in a small town got noticed. It was the nice thing about small towns. The bad part was you had to drive twenty miles to buy toilet paper and paper towels.

And schools in small towns had taken a hit. Many small districts had consolidated into larger, trying to stay afloat.

Thankfully, not in Baywood. They appeared to have a solid balance sheet and had maintained a reputation for excellence. And when Traci had taken her ACT, albeit for the second time, her score had shown that. She could go most anywhere her little heart desired. And he was determined to figure out a way to pay for it. But the last time he'd talked to her about it, she'd been indecisive. Maybe UW in Madison. Maybe Marquette in Milwaukee. Maybe University of San Diego. He'd shaken his head at that. He wanted her to spread her wings but she needed to do that in the Midwest. And since he'd be writing a big check, his vote counted.

"Don't screw around too long," he'd warned her.

Were the Whitmans ever going to get to have the same conversation with Emma? Were they going to get to see her roll her eyes and toss her hair but then be the lucky recipients of a kiss on the cheek before she flounced out of the room?

He pushed his half-eaten sandwich to the side, no longer hungry.

Or was the sunlight going to be ripped out of their lives forever?

Seven

He parked in a visitor spot to the left of the front door of the Dover Police Department. Once inside, it was just minutes before he and Rena were settled in a small room with a table and four chairs. Sometimes they split a file to get through it more quickly. This time, they sat side by side, looking at each piece of information together. Before they could flip the first page, A.L.'s cell phone pinged. He looked at the text, then at Rena.

"Doug Franklin got ahold of the Antlers. They can see us at four at their house." A.L. checked his watch. "We've got two hours to get through this."

"Do we have an address?" Rena asked.

"Yep," A.L. said, flipping the first page. For the next ninety-plus minutes, they relived the journey taken by Doug Franklin and others. It was sobering. Could easily see the increasing frustration by officers as the days wore on. Case notes were shorter, almost terse.

Cops were human. They got pissed off, too. Couldn't show it but sometimes it bled through on the pages.

"I'm getting the impression that Doug Franklin really didn't like Rosemary Bracken," Rena said thoughtfully. "Can't say that I blame him."

"He's got a missing kid and she can't even be bothered to answer the door when he knows that she's inside the damn house. He's more restrained than me," A.L. admitted.

"You'd have broken down the damn door."

"Maybe," A.L. admitted. "Multiple discussions with Trapper Frogg. He seems like a bit of an ass."

"Yeah. Smart answer for everything." Rena pointed to a line. "Here's where Doug asks him about his son. Oh my. Coyote. His son is named Coyote."

"Franklin did say it was odd. But Christ, with a last name of Frogg, don't you think the parents could have gone with Mike or Jim? The kid was going to have to endure enough."

"Appears that he was nineteen, living at home, working a part-time job at a burger joint. Not much else here."

They flipped through the remaining pages and finally he closed the file. "I got the day care director's name. Brenda Owen. We're going to need to see if she's still around."

Rena picked up her phone. In a couple clicks, she showed A.L. an address. "I'll bet this is her. We've got time to drive by her house. See if she's home."

"Let's do it." A.L. sighed. "I didn't see any obvious misses."

"Me, either," Rena said. She sat back in her chair and stretched her neck. Then leaned forward, her forearms on the table. "Do you think it's possible that someone was so successful in their first attempt to grab a child that ten years later, they come back and replicate the crime?"

"I don't know. But we're going to ask for some assistance from the state. I want to see every abduction or attempted abduction involving a day care center in the entire country for the last twenty years."

"Probably a good idea," Rena said. "Like Doug Franklin said. A missing kid. You do everything and then one more thing."

"In that vein, let's get going. We'll try Brenda Owen's house. That should be fairly fast. And then head over to the Antlers'. It would be good to get back to Baywood then, because I think we ought to talk to Elaine Broadstreet again tonight."

Brenda Owen lived less than ten minutes away from the police station. On the way, they passed through the heart of Dover, which wasn't much. The downtown was a three-block-long Main Street. A.L. counted five bars.

But Brenda's house, which was two blocks off Main, was on a sweet little tree-lined street with lots of story-and-a-half Cape Cods. They found her address and knocked. A woman, early sixties, answered the door.

"Afternoon, ma'am," Rena said. "Are you Brenda Owen?"

"Yes."

"The Brenda Owen who was a director of a child-care center here in Dover about ten years ago?"

"Yes. Who are you?"

"I'm Detective Morgan and this is Detective McKittridge." They held out badges. "Can we have a minute of your time?"

The woman looked over their shoulder, as if to verify that they'd arrived in a cop car. She was going to be disappointed. A.L.'s SUV didn't look special. Although Rena knew from personal experience that it ran pretty damn smoothly at over a hundred miles per hour.

"Perhaps out here," the woman said. She stepped onto the small porch. There was only one lawn chair. None of them sat.

"On Wednesday, in Baywood, Wisconsin, a five-year-old girl disappeared from her day care."

"I know," the woman said.

"And how did you know that, ma'am?" Rena asked, keeping her voice level.

"I saw it on the news. Then I looked online at the articles in the Baywood newspaper. Then I spoke to Alice Quest."

"Do you know Alice Quest?"

The woman shook her head. "No. But what I would have given ten years ago if somebody had reached out to me and said that they understood the terror. It's... hard for someone to understand, but part of what makes the situation so terrible is that you feel very alone. Even your friends, people you've known for years and imagined cared for you, turn against you. No one wants to support the person who let this happen."

"You were the director of the day care when Corrine Antler went missing in what seems to be a similar situation," Rena said.

"Yes. I'd been the director for over ten years. Nothing bad had ever happened. We'd never even had a broken arm on the playground. But everybody forgot that pretty quickly."

"I'm sorry that happened to you," Rena said.

The woman shrugged. "Of course, it's not about me. It's about Corrine Antler and her parents. Her siblings. But I called Alice because I'm probably the only one who understands what she's going through."

A.L. shifted, maybe to get the late afternoon sun out of his eyes. "I imagine you might have had your suspicions about what happened?"

"I was confident that Corrine had somehow gotten outside and wandered off. And at first, I guess I imagined that she'd be found pretty quickly. It wasn't until we were about two days into it that I realized that it wasn't going to turn out okay. That nothing would ever be right again."

"Did you ever adjust your thinking about the cause of her disappearance?"

Brenda stared at them. "I never thought it was anybody from the day care. My staff. Other parents. I just couldn't see that. But then again, I also couldn't imagine that a stranger had gotten inside our day care and that nobody had seen him or her. So, no. I guess I didn't. But now…now that it's happened again, maybe I was wrong."

Her words hung in the warm afternoon air. It was a beautiful fall day but Rena felt a chill cross her body. It had been ten years. Was it even possible that someone had taken both little girls?

"We're on our way to talk to the Antlers," A.L. said.

Something passed in Brenda's eyes but she said nothing.

"Do you still see them?" Rena asked.

"No."

Something wasn't right. "Dover is pretty small. That probably has to happen."

"The Antlers have never forgiven me. Once, when I was in the grocery store, I saw Mrs. Antler come in. Our eyes met. She…turned around and left the store. Left her cart right there in the aisle. Guess she couldn't stand to be in the same place I was."

"Did you continue to manage the day care?" A.L. asked.

"The day care only stayed open another six months. Then it closed. It was closed for more than six years before somebody else purchased the building and reopened it. I wasn't interested in trying out for my old job."

"Where did you work after the day care closed?" Rena asked.

"I didn't. This is a small community. Everybody knew the story and quite frankly, nobody wanted to hire the woman who lost Corrine Antler."

Not much to say to that. Rena looked at A.L.

"Have you ever been to Baywood?" A.L. asked.

"No."

"Know anybody in Baywood?" A.L. came back.

"No. Although I told Alice Quest that I could drive down sometime next week if things weren't better."

Was it odd that she was so quick to bond with Alice? Maybe not. She and Alice were an unfortunate minority. "I imagine Alice appreciated that," Rena said.

"I guess. She's still in the hopeful stage that the nightmare is going to end. For her sake, I want her to be right."

Patsy and Greg Antler lived in a two-story house at the edge of town. The paint was fresh, the leaves were raked, and while it was way too early, there were pumpkins flanking the front door. While they waited for their knock to be answered, A.L. thought about all the damn pumpkins he'd carved over the years with Traci. How excited she'd been when she'd finally been able to hold the knife and cut on her own.

Little steps toward independence.

Memories.

When the door swung open, he was surprised to see Doug Franklin. "Patsy and Greg asked me if I could stay," the man said.

"No problem," A.L. said.

Doug led them down the hall and into a family room filled with soft leather couches and matching recliners. Patsy and Greg sat on one couch. They were both midforties and maybe thirty pounds overweight. They stood as he and Rena entered. "Detectives McKittridge and Morgan," he said as he and Rena both showed badges. "Thank you for seeing us."

"Of course," Patsy said. "Can I get you something to drink? I have coffee made." Her tone was pleasant but he didn't get the impression that she was relaxed. Her jaw was tight and her eyes were wary.

He and Rena both shook their heads. "Thanks but no. We don't want to take up too much of your time," Rena said.

Greg motioned for them to take a seat. "Another little girl," he said. He obviously wanted to cut to the chase.

"Yes," A.L. said. "She's five and went missing from her day care. And while not exact, the circumstances are similar enough to yours that we wanted to have a conversation with the two of you."

"Do you think it's the same person?" Patsy asked. "Could it be?"

Again, there was the hope. That perhaps finally this would lead them back to Corrine.

"We don't have any reason to think so," Rena said, her voice gentle. "The parents are Leah and Troy Whitman. Do you know them?"

Both Patsy and Greg shook their heads.

"Troy owns his own automotive garage business and Leah is a paralegal at the Bailey Shepherd Law Firm," Rena said.

"I'm sorry," Greg said. "I don't think either of us has even ever been to Baywood."

"I was there once," Patsy said, correcting her husband. "Maybe seven or eight years ago. For a bridal shower for my younger sister. Her college roommate was hosting."

"What's your sister's name?" A.L. said, pulling out his notebook.

"Toni Krider. She lives in Denver now."

"And the person who hosted?" A.L. said.

"Uh…" Patsy stopped. "I guess I don't remember her name. She was a bridesmaid, dark hair, very pretty. I think they were roommates in college." She shook her head. "I'm sorry," she said. "So much of those first few years after are really a blur." She paused. "Like you're living but not really living."

Going through the fucking motions of life. "I understand," A.L. said.

"I could ask my sister," Patsy said.

Rena handed her a business card. It was a long shot but any information was better than no information.

"That would be great. Either my office or my cell is fine," she said.

"I wish we could be more helpful," Patsy said. Sincerity rang in her tone. "I hate to think of another family going through…well, going through what we went through."

Hell, A.L. thought. They'd been to hell and back. A.L. closed his small notebook and put it in his pocket.

Rena stood up. "We're just grateful for your time. We'll be going—"

"Do the Whitmans have other children?" Greg asked, interrupting Rena.

"No, sir. They don't," A.L. answered.

"I can't imagine," Patsy said, looking at her husband.

"It was the only thing that saved us," he said, blinking his eyes fast. "We had to keep going because we had two other children who needed us. We did the best we could but I suspect our sons would tell you that there were some rough years. The grief just…consumes a person. It's hard to imagine ever finding joy again."

"You do," his wife said, her hand on his arm. "Eventually. But…" Her voice trailed off. She stood up and started walking for the door. She evidently didn't intend to finish her sentence.

She didn't need to. A.L. knew. *Eventually. But not really*.

Rena let out a loud breath once they were in their vehicle. "That was excruciating. Even now, ten years later, their pain is palpable."

"It was pretty goddamn bad," A.L. agreed. His

throat felt closed up and he had a monster of a headache behind one eye. Corrine Antler would be fifteen, just a few years shy of Traci. If that had been him and Jacqui instead? Hell. He might have just put a bullet through his brain. "We keep asking questions," he said. "Until we figure out what happened."

The hundred-mile drive back to Baywood took ninety-eight minutes. A.L. and Rena took the elevator to their office. It was after six but all four of the other detectives on the Baywood Police Department were still working, most of them tapping on computer keyboards. Documentation was a part of the job.

A.L. pulled out a chair. Rena had detoured for a cup of coffee. By the time she got to the desk with a cup for both of them, he was flipping through his notebook. Looking for something. Anything that could lead them in the right direction. "Leah said that she left the house before 7:00. That Emma wasn't yet up."

"Yeah," Rena said, looking at her own notes. "She had a meeting in Madison."

"What meeting?" A.L. asked, thinking that he'd missed something in his own notes.

"I don't have it," Rena said.

"We didn't ask," A.L. said.

"Didn't seem like the most important question at the time. Is it now?"

A.L. picked up his keys. Tossed them from one hand to the other. "Gives us a reason to talk to her again."

"You think that's important?"

"I don't know," A.L. said.

Rena put down her coffee cup. "Everything and one more thing. Let's go."

But before they got to the door, Ferguson waved at them to hold up. "FYI, you two. Faster got some heat from James Adeva at the press conference this morning. I don't think he's happy."

Adeva was a crime reporter for the *Baywood Bulletin.* Pushy, detail-oriented, with the memory of an elephant, he was pretty good at his job. He caught inconsistencies and turned them into headlines. Chief Faster, who could sometimes play fast, no pun intended, and loose with the facts probably had nightmares about him. "Anything specific in his craw?"

"Nope. Just general astonishment that a child could be missing for more than a day and the police don't appear to have anything."

"Fine. What do we know from the remaining teacher and the cook?" A.L. asked.

"I spoke first to the teacher, Tanya Knight. She's thirty-four and has been at the day care for three years. Loves her job. The kids, her coworkers, her boss. Loves them all."

"I'll bet you're glad you didn't have to do that interview," Rena said, looking at A.L.

"I'm not philosophically opposed to happy people," he said.

"Yeah. But they make you nervous," Ferguson said, smiling at Rena.

"Did you ask her specifically about Kara Wiese?" A.L. asked.

"Yeah. Kara is a team player, always willing to help. Good with the kids."

"Okay. What else?"

"She knows Emma Whitman because Emma was

in her room last year. She's sick about the situation because she just—"

"Loves Emma Whitman," A.L. said, finishing the sentence.

"Yeah. Anyway, she was at work on Wednesday. She co-teaches with Olivia Blow but since she was ill, Alice Quest was in the room. Tanya said she starts at 7:30 but generally gets there by 7:00 because her husband drops her off on his way to work. On Wednesday, when she got there, that's when she found out that Olivia was absent because Alice was already in the room."

Rena flipped through her notebook. "That meshes with Alice's recollection. Alice said that she was in a classroom beginning at 6:30 that morning and only took a few short breaks out of the classroom the entire day."

"You search her house?"

"Yeah. I asked, she gave permission. She's a terrible housekeeper. Has cats. There was almost enough cat hair in the small bedroom to hide a five-year-old."

"I like her better now," A.L. said. His own cat could shed about three pounds of hair a week.

"Don't be sexist," Rena said, to both of the men. "Maybe her husband is the terrible housekeeper," Rena said. "Perhaps her job is to mow the yard."

"Yeah, well, that needed doing also. I did see a big motorcycle in the garage so maybe they spend their time riding that instead of taking care of the house."

"What did you walk away thinking?" Rena asked.

"That she's a nice lady. But just to make sure I had a good read, I went to her kids' school afterwards and chatted with the principal. Kids are well behaved.

There's never been any issues with either Tanya Knight or her husband. In fact, Tanya is a frequent volunteer and guess what, everybody loves working with her."

"What about Benita Garza?" Rena asked.

Ferguson flipped pages in his notebook. "She's late fifties. Used to—"

A.L. held up a hand. "Wait. Back to Tanya Knight. You said she's thirty-four. What does she look like?"

Ferguson shrugged. "White. Nice shape. Blond hair."

"Long or short?"

"Chin length. Straight."

"How tall is she?"

Ferguson rubbed his chin. "Five-five, maybe five-six. If it's important, I can call and ask her."

"No. That's good enough. Back to Benita."

"Benita worked at the button factory full-time but retired about a year ago. Stayed home for about three months before she started working at the day care. Her grandchild is enrolled there. Her shift is from 10:00 to 2:00 every day. Said it's the best job she's ever had. She did work on Wednesday but did not arrive until about 9:45. Said that she didn't know anything was wrong until Wednesday night when Alice Quest called and asked her if she'd seen Emma. She couldn't believe that the child was missing."

A.L.'s father and uncle worked at that same factory. They likely knew Benita. "Her house?"

"She lives with her daughter, son-in-law and their two children. Cute farmhouse at the edge of town. Much cleaner than the Knights' abode."

"So you've cleared them both?" Rena asked.

"Didn't see anything that makes me think we should look at them any harder," Ferguson agreed. "Anything else?"

"Nope. Not right now," A.L. said. "Thank you."

"No problem."

Rena waited until Ferguson got back to his desk across the room. "I feel like we're living Doug Franklin's life. He cleared all the people at the Dover day care."

"I know. This sucks. But did you think Ferguson was going to open a bedroom door somewhere and there would be Emma Whitman, playing with some dolls?"

"No. But I also can't stand the idea that it's been roughly a day and a half since Emma was dropped off and we don't appear to be close to an answer."

"We don't know how close we are. Right now it's hard to see how much incremental gain we've had but I have to believe with every conversation we know a little more. When we turn over the right stone, we're going to know it."

"Listen to you, Mr. Optimist. Maybe you should call Tanya Knight and ask her to go to lunch. You could have a bunch of glass-half-full conversations," Rena grumbled. "You were asking all those questions about her physical appearance just to make sure that Elaine couldn't have gotten her mixed up with Kara Wiese."

"Yeah. But Kara Wiese is barely five foot. With long brown hair versus short blonde. Come on, let's go."

They walked downstairs and got into A.L.'s SUV. He started it and pulled out of the lot. Got about three blocks before turning to Rena. "I know I said that I wanted to check in with Leah but I think I want to talk to Elaine Broadstreet again first. The questions we have for her are bigger than the questions we have for Leah."

"You think she's still at Leah's house?" Rena asked.

"If she is, we need to do it somewhere else. I don't think we'll get the truth otherwise."

"I'll call her," Rena said. Elaine answered her phone on the second ring.

"Hello."

"This is Detective Morgan. I'm with Detective McKittridge and we'd like an opportunity to meet with you. Are you at home?"

"Uh…no."

"Can you be there in fifteen minutes?" Rena asked.

"I don't…" the woman said, her tone irritated. There was a pause. "Of course," she said, her tone very different.

She either didn't want to appear argumentative to the police or maybe she didn't want her daughter to know who was calling. Hard to tell. Rena didn't much care. "Thank you. We'll see you then." She ended the call.

"What's her address?"

Rena gave it to him.

With a quick tap on the brakes, A.L. turned. The car behind him let loose a sharp blast of their horn.

Rena gave him a look.

"I know a shortcut," he said.

He likely does, she thought. He'd grown up in Baywood. Had left for a few years, walked a beat in Madison, and later did some years in SWAT. But, as he told it, he'd been lured back to Baywood in hopes of saving his marriage. It hadn't worked.

And he'd eaten dinner alone for a long time. But now was dating Tess.

That was the big news. The two of them had saved Tess from a serial killer just months earlier. "I never got a chance to ask," she said. "How was California? You and Tess still okay?"

He gave her an amused look. "Familiarity breeds contempt?" he said.

"*Contempt* is a harsh word. And, anyway, it would be difficult to ever dislike Tess."

He laughed. "Good one," he said. "Too much of me, that's another story."

Now it was her turn to smile. "So I can assume it went well."

"Yeah. It did."

She waited, hoping he'd let another morsel drop. But she knew it was unlikely. "I'll just have to use my imagination," she said, letting him know where her head was going.

"Make it good," he said. He pulled up in front of Elaine Broadstreet's house. "I think we beat her here," he said.

"Doug Franklin talked to Corrine Antler's grandparents," she said.

"Saw that in the file."

"So what we're doing makes all the sense in the world, especially given her criminal background and the fact that there's some time unaccounted for. But it just feels horrible. A grandparent, for God's sake."

"My dad is crazy about Traci," A.L. said. "Always

has been. Acts like an idiot when she's around, always teasing her, trying to make her laugh. I keep telling him that she's seventeen now, not a little kid anymore. But he can't seem to help himself."

"And Traci is such a good kid that she plays along."

"Most of the time. It is weird, though. He never did that with me or my sister, Liz. After Traci was born, it caught me off guard. Like I was the one with the baby but he was the one who changed."

Rena looked out her side window. "I wish my mom was going to be here. For my baby."

"Cancer is a fucking thief," he said.

Her mom had been dead for three years and it still hurt. "Gabe's mom will be over the moon." It wasn't the same but it would be nice. "His whole family will be."

Elaine Broadstreet's car turned into the driveway of her small ranch.

"My grandmother helped raise me," Rena said. "I trusted her as much as I did my mother."

"We don't know that Elaine has betrayed that same trust," he said.

"Maybe she had a mental lapse, you know, the same kind of thing that happens to a young parent who gets preoccupied on their way to work and leaves their baby in the back seat of a hot car for eight hours. Nobody can ever understand how that happens but it happens every year, to multiple kids. To good, caring parents."

"So you're back to she got Emma inside and then spaced out and left her there unattended? That still doesn't explain why her signature isn't on the sign-in sheet."

"I know. But I want to make it safe for her to tell us the truth," Rena said.

They gave her a couple minutes to get settled and then knocked on the door. Once inside, they saw that Elaine Broadstreet's home was nicely furnished with leather couches and solid wood end tables. The floors were hardwood and the rugs on them looked expensive.

Milo's Motors either paid better than he might have expected or she was luckier at the gaming tables than most. They'd get to that.

"You wanted to talk to me," Elaine said. She'd settled on one leather couch. He and Rena had taken ends on the other.

"How was today?" Rena asked, her tone caring. It reminded him of something she'd said once—that he had very little time or tolerance for small talk. Or something like that. It was true. And it was a fault. Because right now, Rena was spot-on. Elaine Broadstreet's culpability was yet to be determined. But what they did know was that her grandchild was missing. And for that reason alone, she deserved great consideration.

"Difficult," Elaine said. "We all jump every time Leah's cell phone rings." She paused. "People have been wonderful. So caring. One of Troy's friends started a fund-raising page and donations poured in today. Just poured in."

A fund-raising site. A.L. supposed it was to be expected. It was easy enough to do and it left people, those who started it and those who contributed, feeling good. It was a relatively easy way for a person to let the Whitmans know that they cared. "What do Troy and Leah think about that?" A.L. asked.

"I think Leah was a little embarrassed. I guess it seems a little bit like charity. But Steven told them that it only made sense, that they might have a need for it. Like to offer a reward," Elaine explained.

Or to pay for private searchers once the initial frenzy dies down, A.L. added silently. He hoped like hell it didn't come to that. "Who is Steven?"

"Steven Hanzel. He's Troy's best friend and he's the one who started the fund-raising site. He works at the bank. I think he's a loan officer."

A.L. wrote the name down in his notebook. It was time to get down to business. "We have a few more questions about the day you dropped Emma off."

Elaine nodded. "I suppose that teacher is still saying that she never saw me."

"Let's just say that the two of you have different recollections of the morning," A.L. said. "Have you had any second thoughts about what you told us?"

"No."

Rena leaned forward. "Is it possible that you walked Emma into the day care but didn't hand her off to anybody? I mean, Emma sounds like she was pretty mature. Maybe she knew where her room was? Maybe she said *I've got this* and you kissed her goodbye and left without actually seeing her go into a room?"

Elaine said nothing.

"I totally get how that could happen," Rena said.

"Do you have children, Detective?"

"No," Rena said, her tone level.

"Then I'm not sure you're qualified to *get* anything. But in any event, that's not what happened."

Elaine was no shrinking violet. She was pissed and she wanted Rena to know it. A.L. didn't worry that Rena would lose her cool. She was too seasoned for that and had been baited by those much more skilled. "So, Elaine, we're to understand that your previous statement stands without correction," A.L. said, his tone friendly. "You handed her off to Kara Wiese and you signed the sheet on the clipboard by the office before you left."

"All of that is still correct. I know that I didn't mention signing the sheet initially but I've been over it a thousand times in my head. I did that. I'm sure of it."

"Okay," A.L. said. "Do you happen to know Tanya Knight?"

"Of course. Emma was previously in her room." She paused. "I know the difference between Kara Wiese and Tanya Knight if that's what you're getting at." She was back to being pissed.

She reached for a candle that was on an end table. Turned it. Just so. Took a nice long look out her front window.

They waited.

"I do actually have a correction to my statement," Elaine said finally, looking at Rena. "But I'm guessing you maybe already know that."

Eight

"We're listening," A.L. said.

Elaine sighed. Settled back on the couch, as if this was going to be lengthy explanation and she wanted something solid behind her. "After I left Emma at the day care, I drove to the Wildwind's Casino."

A.L. knew the place. It was twenty-five miles west of Baywood. His dad and his uncle Joe went there at least once a month. Said it was for the buffet, but A.L. didn't think so.

"I got there shortly after 8:00. I left by 9:30 so that I could get to work by 10:00," Elaine added.

"That's a pretty exact recollection," Rena said.

"It's what I do three or four days a week. Not that hard to remember."

A.L. considered the information. It added up. Milo had said that she was a gambler. Said that she generally arrived at work about ten. "Why did you lie the first time?" he asked.

Elaine looked at Rena. "You asked the question in front of my daughter. She…hates that I gamble. We've had words about it. So I hide it from her. I didn't think it would be a big deal."

A.L. looked around. "This is a real nice house in a real nice neighborhood. You must do pretty well at the casino."

"The casino always ultimately wins," she said. "Everybody knows that. But there have been times that I've done okay. I just enjoy it. Maybe that's what makes Leah angry. But, quite frankly, it's not really Leah's or anybody else's business how I choose to spend my time or my money. I choose what makes me happy and I don't need anybody's approval."

Elaine was now even more pissed off. They must have been *some* words.

Rena leaned forward, put her notebook and pen on the table. "You were arrested for child endangerment and illegal narcotics," she said.

Elaine didn't flinch. "Yes. I had a bad habit and I paid a price for my stupidity. Marijuana. Cocaine. Pills. I was a regular user. I was collateral damage, got caught up in a sweep that was focused on somebody else. But there were witnesses who testified that I'd done the drugs in my home, in front of my child. It was true. I never let her touch them but…that hardly matters, right?"

"No," Rena said, her voice hard.

"I did my time," Elaine said. "And it was the best thing that could have happened to me. I kicked the habit."

"Leah knows?" A.L. asked.

"Of course. During my jail time, she was in the foster care system. Had to change schools. It was hard on her. Hard on both of us. But we made it through. Got past it. It was just Leah and me for a lot of years. She was in high school when I married Bert Broadstreet. He was a good man. Unfortunately, he died eight years later. Heart attack. This," she said, waving her hand around her house, "is because of Bert. He had always been a good saver and quite frankly, I'm benefiting from that today."

"Would you say that there's lots of friction between you and your daughter?" A.L. asked.

Elaine shrugged. "I don't know if it's friction. It's just lately she seems determined to find fault with me, to find fault with the things I do. To have others find fault with me." She stopped. "Never mind. Now is certainly not the time to be dwelling on that."

"Is your daughter's marriage in good shape?" A.L. asked.

"Why would you ask me that?" Elaine responded, her tone sharp.

"Because I thought I detected a hint of…something," A.L. said. "Something that told me that everything wasn't exactly right."

Elaine scratched her ear with her right index finger. "I've noticed that lately, too," she said. "I haven't asked. And Leah hasn't volunteered any information."

"You don't have any reason to believe that either one of them is in any way responsible for Emma's disappearance?" A.L. asked.

"Absolutely not," she said. "They both love that little girl. With all their hearts."

A.L. glanced at Rena. When she folded up her notebook, he stood. "I think we're done," he said.

Elaine stood, too. "For what it's worth, I'm sorry I wasn't completely forthcoming earlier. It's just complicated. I try not to disappoint my daughter if I don't have to."

It was dumb to lie to the cops but A.L. somewhat understood the circumstances. She'd been attempting to avoid a confrontation with her daughter. He wasn't always absolutely forthcoming with Traci. For example, she knew that he'd recently been to California on vacation but didn't know that he'd gone with Tess.

"Did you tell Milo about the conviction?" Elaine asked.

A.L. shook his head. "Nope. Didn't see the need. If he'd done a background check on you, he'd have found the information himself."

"If I can keep it from my son-in-law, too, that would be best."

"You don't think Leah has told him?" Rena asked.

"We haven't talked about it for years but the last time we did, she said that she hadn't. She didn't do that for me. Like I said, it was a hard time for her. She told me that she'd put it behind her. She told me that there was nothing to be gained from dusting off the drama and giving it air."

"We'll attempt to keep your confidences as much as we're able," A.L. promised, knowing better than to ever promise absolute confidentiality. Sometimes shit happened and every scab got scratched and ripped open.

"I appreciate that. But know this, Detectives. If it

helps you find my granddaughter, I don't care if it's the lead story in the *Bulletin*."

"Right. Good evening." He and Rena walked back to their car.

When they got inside, Rena turned to him. "Well, I definitely didn't see any cognitive failure. As my grandmother might have said, Elaine Broadstreet is full of piss and vinegar."

"Agree."

"I have to admit, I was a little surprised when you asked Elaine her opinion on the Whitmans' marriage."

"Yeah, I know. But there's something about her that I like."

"She's a felon and she lied to us."

"There is that." A.L. flipped through his notes. "What do you think about this Steven Hanzel and the fund-raising site?"

"Not surprised," she said. "They might need it."

"Yeah."

"Do you really think that Leah hasn't told Troy about her mother's *small* transgressions and subsequent time in jail?" Rena asked.

"I don't know. And I'm not sure of a way to ask him without tipping our hand. I guess we could ask Leah if it comes to that," A.L. said.

"Tough on a kid to suddenly get dumped into the foster system and have to change schools," Rena said.

Rena's phone dinged. She picked it up. Studied it. Made that weird face she always did when something wasn't quite right.

"What?" A.L. asked.

"We got Kara Wiese's phone records."

"And?"

"There's something odd. Well, maybe odd," Rena qualified. "I had asked them to specifically look for outreach to banks or financial institutions, based on the fact that Claire Potter thought she might be trying to buy a house."

"Good call. Follow the money."

"Well, there were seven calls to Baywood Bank in a two-week period about two months ago. And then nothing after that."

"Maybe the deal fell through," A.L. said.

"Yeah. Maybe."

"But when Claire was talking about Kara stepping out to take a telephone call, it seemed as if that was recent. Not months ago."

"It's time to talk to Kara Wiese again," Rena said.

"She's the other major player here. If we believe Elaine Broadstreet, then we can't believe her."

"You believe Elaine? Even after we know she lied to us once."

"I understood her motivation to lie about where she went before work," A.L. said. "We should be able to easily verify her arrival at the casino. Nobody walks in those doors without being on camera. Same for leaving. We know she spent the rest of the day at work. So if we can account for her time, it seems unlikely to me that she's a bad guy here."

"Kara Wiese was at work all day yesterday. How can she be the bad guy?" Rena asked.

"I don't know. Maybe there are no bad guys. Maybe Emma just took off."

"Not if Elaine is right about signing her in on the clipboard," Rena said.

"Devil is always in the details," A.L. said.

"It's been almost thirty-four hours," Rena said. "A long time for a five-year-old to be wandering about undetected. She'd be hungry, cold, missing her mom and dad."

A.L. didn't answer. There were no answers. "I'll ask Ferguson to help with verifying Elaine's time at the casino. Now, let's go see Kara Wiese."

"Want me to call first?" Rena asked.

"Nope. We'll take our chances that she's home."

She put her hand on the door handle. "You know, if we believe Elaine and we also believe Kara, and we don't think Emma simply wandered off, somebody who was inside the day care took Emma."

"A stranger? Are we back to crime of opportunity? Stranger walks into a day care, the office is unmanned because Alice is covering a classroom, and sees an opportunity to abscond with a child?"

"Would a stranger be detected?" Rena asked.

"Not necessarily. The teachers are all in classrooms. The cook has yet to arrive. Parents are coming and going but not everybody knows everybody else."

"Or was it a parent, somebody who had a good reason to be there, a reason nobody would question. They drop off their own kid and then wait for the opportunity to take Emma. Or maybe any child would have done?"

"That scenario makes me want to lose my lunch,"

A.L. admitted. "But it doesn't seem too likely given that Elaine is so confident that she handed Emma off to Kara. If not Kara, it had to be somebody who looked an awful lot like Kara." He paused. "You know my uncle Joe and my dad look an awful lot like one another. People still get them mixed up."

"You think Kara Wiese's sister was there?"

"Her sister, her mother. An aunt possibly. I think we need to figure out if any of those people exist and are in the area," A.L. said.

"We could simply ask Kara," Rena said.

"I don't think so. Let's do this on the QT. Alice included her Social Security number in the information she provided to us on each staff member. That should be enough."

"I'll get it in play," Rena said.

On the way to talk to Kara, Rena's phone rang. "Detective Morgan," she answered.

"This is Michael Purifoy, returning your message."

"Thank you for calling, Mr. Purifoy." Rena dug into her bag and pulled out her copy of the sign-in sheet for Kara Wiese's room. Then put the phone on Speaker so that A.L. could hear. "Mr. Purifoy, I want to talk to you about yesterday morning at Lakeside Learning Center. I've reviewed the sign-in sheet and you signed your son Jake in at 7:18. Is that correct?"

"That sounds right."

"Do you recall, Mr. Purifoy, if there was a teacher in the room?"

"Kara was there."

"You're absolutely confident of that?" Rena asked.

"She's a baseball fan and we talked about the Brewers' chances to make the playoffs. Yeah, she was there."

"Thank you, Mr. Purifoy. I appreciate you calling me back."

"No problem, Detective. Goodbye."

"Well, that's that," Rena said, putting her phone down on the console.

"Good to know before we got to Kara's," A.L. said.

"Again, you sound almost positive. It's starting to scare me," Rena said. "Like you've made a pledge to look for the silver lining."

"I don't make pledges."

"We're almost going past the learning center. Even though they are closed, I have a feeling that Alice is probably there. I'd like to talk to her about the phone call from Brenda Owen. That would have been a pretty startling call to get."

"Okay." Five minutes later, they pulled up in front of the day care. The police tape from the previous evening was gone. Earlier that day, he and Rena had gotten a text that they were moving the command center for the search team to the city park that was three blocks away. That would allow this neighborhood to get back to some semblance of normalcy.

They found the woman in her office. "How's it going?" Rena asked.

"Any news?" Alice asked immediately.

Rena shook her head. "Nobody is giving up."

"I heard there were still many, many people searching," Alice said.

"Yeah." Rena had heard hundreds. There were feet on the street, both human and canine, and there were drones in the sky. A hotline had been established and publicized. So far, there had been six calls about possible sightings. Each had been meticulously followed up on by other officers. Each had been disappointing. "We thought you might be here."

"Yeah. Just felt right. Plus I'm fielding lots of calls from parents. I did send everyone a message that we would reopen tomorrow. I think that was good news. I... I guess I hope it was good news. Parents are scared."

Rena wasn't sure what to say. Of course the focus had to be on Emma and the whole Whitman family but there was no doubt that this put Alice and the Lakeside Learning Center in a bad spot. Bad enough that they might not recover if one considered Brenda Owen's experience. Maybe parents were right now trying to find other childcare arrangements and enrollment would rapidly decline over the next couple weeks until the center ultimately closed.

It was a minute concern in comparison to a missing child but still, she understood Alice's concern. But Alice wasn't without blame. They'd be in a significantly better position if she'd had cameras around the place.

"We spoke to Brenda Owen today," Rena said.

Alice's head jerked. "You were in Dover?"

"Yes."

"It was good of her to call," Alice said.

"Did you know about Corrine Antler before Brenda called?" A.L. asked.

"Why would I have?" Alice said.

"Not familiar with Dover?" Rena asked.

Alice shook her head. "No," she said. Her phone rang. She glanced at the number. "I'm sorry but I really should take this."

"No problem," A.L. said. "We were on our way somewhere else and just thought we'd stop by."

Tess Lyons wandered around the mall food court, unable to make up her mind. Pizza? Thai? Steak sandwich? Tacos?

Finally, after two trips around the half circle of options, shredded chicken tacos and chips and guacamole were crowned the winners. She carried her tray in her right hand. With each step, her shopping bag that hung off the same arm, awkwardly bumped into her leg.

It really had been easier with two arms and two hands.

Soon, she thought as she slid her tray down onto a table and took a seat. She'd had her third appointment and her prosthetic arm was in development, as the lab liked to say. Her daughter, Marnee, had teased her about the process, saying that this was the first thing she'd come across that couldn't be ordered on Amazon and delivered the next day. A.L. had volunteered to come to every appointment but she'd declined. It was just something she had to do. On her own.

It would be unique to her needs, her hopes for functionality, her desire for aesthetics. "It's okay to want it to look good," her prosthetist had said.

Looking good was relative, Tess knew.

She likely wasn't as concerned about that now as she had been. Time had a way of helping one deal with things. It offered a chance to develop perspective. She could have died on the beach that day. But, instead, had been offered a chance to have a life.

Different.

But no worse.

A.L. had said it didn't matter to him if she pursued a prosthetic. She believed him. Which mattered a great deal more than she would have admitted to anyone. He wasn't a guy to wax poetic about a relationship but she knew, one look into his eyes told her, that he really did believe she was beautiful.

They'd had fun in California. Had slept late and eaten long lunches and had cocktails on the deck at sunset. He'd stood shoulder to shoulder with her as she stared out into the ocean and later had held her one hand tightly in his own as they'd strolled at the water's edge, the surf gently lapping at their bare feet.

He'd looked really good with a tan. And the rest had seemed to do him good. Had smoothed out the lines around his eyes, lightened the dark circles that settled in when he worked too hard. He hadn't shaved for a week and she'd teased him about the gray that showed in the short whiskers.

He'd seemed unconcerned. She liked that.

She bit into her first taco and chewed. Was halfway done with it when, at first, she thought that thinking about A.L. was making her see things. But then she took a second look and was confident that she was right. It was A.L.'s teenage daughter across the way. Even though she had only met Traci once, she was confident it was her. The girl's hair was dark like A.L.'s and she wore it long, well past her shoulders. She had A.L.'s eyes and what Tess assumed was her mother's nose.

Traci had just picked up a plate of Thai food and was scanning the food court, looking for a spot. Tess put down her taco and waved. Traci hesitated, then waved back. Tess figured that would be it. She was surprised when the young girl headed her way.

"Hi, Traci," she said, when the girl was still five feet away.

"How's it going, Tess?"

"Good. I need new shoes and I'm a sucker for a food court," she said. She glanced at Traci's plate. "That was a runner-up."

"I'm going to get a piece of pizza if I'm still hungry after this," Traci said.

Tess smiled. "My daughter, Marnee, is just four years older than you and her appetite pretty much rules her daily life. Are you here with friends?" she asked.

"Nope. Just me. Mom had a meeting tonight so she said I should grab something when I was out." Traci continued to stand by the table, tray in hand.

"Would you…like to join me?" Tess asked.

"Sure," she said, without hesitation. Traci pulled out her chair and sat. She unwrapped her plastic silverware and started eating.

"Senior year, right?" Tess asked. The one and only time she'd met Traci had been at A.L.'s apartment this summer. The two of them had cooked out burgers and he'd invited Traci to join them for dinner. He'd done a good job of prepping his daughter in advance as there had been no awkward questions that night about her amputated arm. No odd looks. Just some simple conversation about Traci's waitressing job at Pancake Magic and the rock concert that she'd been to in Madison.

"You look really tan," Traci said.

Tess smiled. "I got some good sun in California."

Traci put down her fork. "When were you in California?"

Tess got a bad feeling. But she was in it with both feet now. "Just a few days ago."

"You were with my dad?"

"Yes." Tess pushed her tray aside, leaving half of her guacamole dip.

"I didn't know that," Traci said.

Which was weird, in that Tess knew A.L. and Traci had had dinner the night before the two of them had left for their trip. Why the hell hadn't A.L. simply told her the truth?

Dark thoughts, which she perhaps might not have immediately jumped to before the loss of her lower left arm, popped into her head. Was A.L. ashamed of her? Did he not want others to know that he was attracted to her?

Was he simply an asshole?

No. She immediately dismissed that one. A.L. was

sometimes short, borderline rude, many times preoccupied with work, but he was not put off by her arm or lack thereof. And he was not the kind of guy who frankly cared what anybody else thought.

Except perhaps his daughter.

"Does that bother you, Traci? That I was in California with your dad?" She wasn't going to dance around it.

Traci shook her head. "No. But I was worried about him being out there by himself. That he'd slip on a rock and go over a cliff or something. I guess it pisses me off that he didn't tell me the truth."

"I think your dad would rather cut off *his* arm before upsetting you. I'm sure he had his reasons."

Traci picked up her fork. Took two bites. "Do you like him?"

Maybe she should stick to a one word answer. *YES.* But that seemed inadequate. "You know your dad and I met in unusual circumstances." She'd been the target of a serial killer who had come really close to successfully snuffing out her lights for good.

"And I've had some things to deal with," Tess added, glancing at her arm that ended two inches below her elbow.

"Uh-huh," Traci said.

Tess heard, *Yeah, great. But you didn't answer my question.*

"It's good," Tess said. "Right now, it's very good."

"Right now?" Traci repeated. "You're thinking this is short-term?"

"You really are your father's daughter," Tess said.

She hoped it wasn't a summer fling but those were conversations that hadn't yet taken place. "It's just early in the relationship," she hedged.

"He hasn't really dated much since he and Mom got divorced. When he did, I certainly never met any of them. I guess I was surprised this summer when he had the barbecue. He told me about your accident. I think he wanted to make sure that I didn't stare. I guess that's when I first thought that this might be something different."

"I was nervous to have your dad meet my daughter," Tess confessed. "I didn't want her to get too hopeful," Tess added, wanting to be as honest as she could.

Traci stared at her. "I don't know what I hope for. For so long after the divorce, I hoped that Mom and Dad would get back together. But now, I really don't think that's going to happen."

Tess said nothing.

"I don't want him to be alone," Traci said, proving that she was pretty mature. "I mean, I'm off to college next year."

"Right," Tess said.

Traci stared at her. "I should probably be going." She gathered up her tray. "It was good to see you again, Tess. And my dad, well, he said he had a really good time in California."

Tess watched her walk away. Then picked up her phone and sent a quick text to A.L. Met Traci by chance at the mall. We ate together. She knows that I was in California with you.

She pushed Send before she could rethink it. A.L.

needed to know so that he didn't get caught in a lie with his daughter. They could deal with why he'd kept it a secret at a later time. Definitely after the police had found the missing five-year-old.

A.L. got the text from Tess just when he and Rena were about to park in front of Kara's house. "Fuck," he said.

Rena looked around quickly, as if expecting trouble. "What?" she asked.

A.L. waved a hand. "Nothing."

"Tell me," she said. "I need something to take my mind off the fact that we're more than twelve hours into this day and not much closer to a happy ending."

"Tess ran into Traci at the mall," he said.

Rena waited. Finally she said, "And Traci told her that her butt looked fat in the dress she was trying on?"

A.L. frowned at her. "Of course not."

"Then what is making you suddenly act as if your cat prefers me over you?"

"That will never happen," he said. Then he sighed. "I didn't tell Traci that Tess was going to California with me. And now Tess knows that."

"And she's going to wonder why?"

"I imagine," A.L. muttered.

"So tell her why."

"Nothing to tell."

"Not sure I understand," Rena said.

"Nothing to tell because I'm not sure why I didn't tell Traci or Jacqui or anyone but you. I just didn't."

"Because you don't like people knowing your business," Rena said.

He hated that. "Maybe."

"But maybe not?" Rena said. She could always get to the heart of the issue. "Maybe there was another reason?"

"I just said, I don't know."

Rena reached for the door handle. "You should really try not to screw this up with Tess. I like her."

"Thank you for your counsel. Very helpful." Tess wasn't going to buy that he'd simply forgotten to mention it to Traci the night before they were leaving town.

He took the moment to send a quick text back to Tess. Thanks. We'll talk later.

He pushed Send. There was no immediate response. He tried not to read too much into that.

Nine

Rena knocked on Kara's door. When she opened it, Rena thought the woman looked tired, and her nose was sunburned. "Can we come in?" she asked.

"Of course," Kara said. She stepped back.

Her house was a midsize ranch with a great room off the kitchen. Kara led them there. It smelled of lavender. Rena saw the lit candle on the fireplace mantel and figured that was the reason. "Is your husband home?" she asked.

"Working," Kara said. She looked at the clock. "Well, by now, close to done with work. But like I said before, he'll stop for beers with his friends."

Kara Wiese was perhaps more understanding than Rena. If that was Gabe, she wouldn't care if he had drinks with his friends occasionally, but every night after work? That seemed excessive. "Are we interrupting your dinner?"

"Difficult to think about things like food. I just got home about an hour ago. We searched all day."

"I've shared the notes of our initial discussion with

Detective Morgan, so she's up to speed," A.L. said. "Since that time, is there anything that you've thought of to add to that or perhaps modify in any way?"

"No."

"I wanted to show you the sign-in sheet from near the office," he said.

Rena reached for her bag and pulled it out.

"Is that your writing?" A.L. asked, pointing to the date.

"Yes."

"And when did you write that?"

"On Wednesday morning. When I got to work."

"When we talked earlier, you said that the first thing you did was make coffee," A.L. reminded her.

"I guess I did. I'm sorry. I forgot about this. It's just something I do."

"Okay, thank you. Now I want to focus a bit more on reasons why you might leave your classroom," A.L. said. "Can you walk me through those again?"

"I leave the classroom to use the restroom."

"What about for lunch? Or to get lunch for the kids?"

She shook her head. "We eat in the classroom. If we've brought something from home, we eat that. Otherwise, the cook delivers our lunch and the kids' lunches at the same time."

They were working through lunch. Rena thought that was probably illegal, but that wasn't her issue right now. "Any other reason that you'd leave your classroom during the day?"

"I guess I'd also leave it if I got a text from the office indicating that I was needed there."

"A text?" Rena asked.

"Yes, that's how Alice communicates with us. She knows that we all keep our phones handy. I mean, really. Who doesn't anymore?"

It was the perfect segue to ask her about her phone usage. "Alice never calls your phone?" Rena asked.

"No."

"But you must get other phone calls, right?" Rena asked. "Or need to make some. What happens then?"

Kara shrugged. "I can't speak for others but I guess I would look at the number of who was calling. If I knew it, then I might answer. If not, I'd let it roll over to voice mail."

That was reasonable. She did the same thing. But Kara had only answered half the question. "But what about outgoing calls?"

"I… I don't make that many outgoing calls. But if I did, like to my dentist or my doctor, I'd probably step out into the hallway quickly."

"Are you or have you recently been attempting to secure financing to buy a house?" A.L. asked.

"What?"

A.L. repeated the question.

"Um…no. Why would you think that?"

"One of your coworkers thought you might be working on securing financing."

She shrugged. When it didn't appear that she was going to offer anything more, Rena said, "I've reviewed your phone records. A few months ago, there were numerous calls to the Baywood Bank. Can you explain who those calls were to and what the purpose was?"

Kara smiled. "Oh, a few months ago. I'm sorry, I spaced out for a minute. I guess I'm more tired than

I thought. We were considering *refinancing* a few months ago but got busy and dropped it."

Again, it made sense, thought Rena. She and Gabe had gotten a mortgage just two years ago. If refinancing was anything like financing, it could be a pain in the butt. You had to get tax returns and bank statements and your employer had to verify your employment.

"Did you work with anyone in particular at the bank?" Rena asked.

"I'm sorry, I don't recall. I think I might have talked to a couple different people," Kara added. "You know, I don't think banks actually want you to refinance. Otherwise they would make it easier."

"You are aware that Elaine Broadstreet has said that she handed Emma off to you," A.L. said.

"Yes."

"You've indicated that this could not have happened, that you were in your classroom until after 7:30, when Claire Potter arrived," he continued.

"Yes."

"Is there anyone at the day care, another teacher, a parent, a vendor, anybody that you can think of that she might have thought was you?"

Kara appeared to be considering the information. "I've been teaching in the same room since I started. So there are parents of three- and four-year-olds that I don't know. So, I'm sorry, I don't think I can answer that question very well."

"No problem," A.L. said easily.

Kara glanced at her watch. "If there's nothing else, I think I'd better try to catch some sleep. I'm afraid I got very little last night and with being out in the sun all day, I'm pretty much tapped out."

"That will do it," A.L. said. "Thank you for your time."

"Of course."

"Do you think it's too late to go see Leah?" Rena asked once they were back in their vehicle. "It's a little past 8:30."

"I doubt she's sleeping. And we told her that we'd check in every day."

"You're right," Rena said. "Let's go."

When they knocked fifteen minutes later, Special Agent Monty Connell answered the door. "Detectives," he said.

"We need to talk to Leah," A.L. said.

"Anything we should know?" the agent asked.

"Nope. Just following up on some missing info," A.L. said.

"Okay. Have a seat," Monty said, motioning them towards the living room. "I'll get her."

When Leah walked in alone three minutes later, he and Rena still stood in the middle of the living room. She did not greet them. Her light blue sweatpants dragged on the ground and her gray sweatshirt had a stain on the shoulder. She had her hair pulled back in a ponytail and was wearing no makeup with the exception of some smeared mascara under both eyes.

A.L. figured it had probably taken just about everything she had to be clothed and upright. If he had to guess, she'd probably not eaten, either.

"Is Troy home?" Rena asked once they were seated,

him in the chair, Leah and Rena on opposite ends of the couch.

Leah shook her head. "Searching. I wanted to go, to switch places with him. But he wouldn't do it."

"Maybe he feels as if he needs to physically be doing something," A.L. said.

"He said..." She stopped. "He said if they find something, he doesn't want me to have to see...it."

That had to have been a damn ugly conversation for them to have.

"Hard to know, of course, whether that was the truth or not," Leah added.

And like before, A.L. was struck by the fact that the Whitmans did not seem to be drawing strength from one another. Hard time to be alone. "Have Troy's parents arrived?"

Leah shook her head. "They've called. Several times. Said they would come but that they didn't want to be a bother."

If this had happened to him and Jacqui when Traci was five, nothing would have kept his dad or Jacqui's parents from being there. But everybody coped differently. Neither he nor Rena said anything.

"If you need to talk to Troy, my guess is that he'll be home soon," Leah said. "They won't search too long after dark."

"Actually, we had a question for you. We were reviewing our notes from our initial conversation," A.L. said. "You left the house early on Wednesday because you had a meeting in Madison. Who were you meeting?"

Leah stared at him. "Why does that matter?"

"Just making sure that we've got full information." He was getting a bad feeling.

"It's very difficult for me to think about anything but Emma," she said. "My head is swimming."

A.L. said nothing.

After an awkward pause, Leah said, "I met a prospective client."

"What was his or her name?" Rena asked, pen in hand. "And contact number?"

"I… I don't have it," Leah said.

"But there would be someplace you could check," Rena said, her tone still gentle. "An email setting up the meeting? With an assistant?"

Leah turned her head and stared out the living room window. A.L. followed her gaze. The outside lights were on, making it easy to see the mums in nice-looking concrete planters. Reds. Yellows.

A.L. and Rena exchanged a quick glance but neither spoke. Finally, Leah turned back to them. "There wasn't any client or any meeting."

A.L. thought about the Whitmans' relationship and figured Leah's next sentence was going to be that she'd met a man. That she was having an affair.

"What were you doing, Leah, that you needed to leave the house early?" Rena asked. Her tone was still polite but less gentle than before. It was time to cut the bullshit.

"I drove to the Wildwind's Casino. I…expected my mother to be there. She's a gambler. She has a problem."

Neither A.L. nor Rena acknowledged that this was old news.

"You were meeting your mother?" A.L. said. Elaine had said nothing about this.

Leah pursed her lips. "No. I wanted to be there, in place, before my mother arrived."

In place. What the hell? "For what purpose?" A.L. asked, careful to keep his tone neutral.

"Well, if you must know, I was videoing her. She has a favorite spot and I wanted…a good angle."

A.L. considered his next question. "What were you going to do with the video?"

"I don't know," she said.

She was lying. A.L. was pretty confident. "So you got up early to video your mother, without having any express purpose for the video?"

"I don't like how my mother spends her time and money," Leah said. "I don't expect you to understand. It's hard for other people to…get it."

"Maybe not as hard for us as for others. We know about your mom's criminal conviction," Rena said. "We know that you spent some time in a foster home."

"I don't like to talk about that. It was a long time ago," Leah said.

But not forgotten. Or forgiven? A.L. leaned forward. "So you left your house before 6:30. And you drove directly to the casino?"

"Well, I stopped for coffee on the way. But, essentially, yes," Leah said.

They'd be able to verify her time of arrival. "Did you talk to your mother at the casino?" A.L. asked.

"No. After she left, I waited another five minutes and I left. I drove straight to work. You can ask my boss about that."

We will, A.L. thought. But he was pretty confident that they were getting the truth this time. "Have you shared the video with anyone?" he asked.

Again, Leah took her time in answering. "With my attorney. That same morning."

"I thought you said that you didn't know what you were going to do with the video?" Rena asked.

"I don't. But I know that I went to a lot of trouble to get it and I wanted to make sure that there was a safe copy."

"You work at a law firm," A.L. said. "Are you using an attorney from your own firm?"

"No. I certainly don't need anyone there knowing my business." Leah stood up, her hands on her hips. "All of this happened before Emma. And if you don't mind, I really don't think it's a good use of my time right now talking about it. My child is missing. Could we keep our focus on what's really important?"

Leah and Elaine were playing some kind of weird cat-and-mouse mother-daughter game. God knew that Traci could go round and round with Jacqui sometimes. He tried never to get in the middle of their deal and he wasn't too interested in getting sideways between Leah and Elaine, either. But there was one thing that needed to be hashed out. "You were in the room when your mom told us that she'd gone to work immediately after dropping off Emma. You knew that was a lie but you never said anything."

"My mother is a lot of things but one thing I know is that she loves Emma. She would never do anything to hurt her."

It was probably time to be blunt. "Your mom said

that she handed Emma off to Kara Wiese. And then she signed in on the clipboard hanging by the office. Her signature isn't on that paper," he said. "So it looks as if she's mistaken. Is it possible that she's also mistaken about handing off Emma to Kara?"

"No. She would never, never, not make sure that Emma was safe before leaving. I can't explain the sign-in sheet. Maybe she didn't do that. It doesn't matter."

"I know it seems like a little detail but it's actually a pretty big thing. If she didn't sign it, then it's possible that Emma wandered off. If she did, then that's pretty much off the table because it means that somebody switched out that sheet before the next person signed in at almost nine o'clock."

"If she says that she did it, I believe her," Leah said.

Was that true or did Leah have another reason to know that Elaine wasn't responsible for Emma's disappearance? Because Leah was? Or maybe Troy? Maybe that was the cause of the permafrost between the two of them? It wouldn't be the first time that one parent covered for another parent after something unfortunate had occurred. They did it because they felt as if they had to—but yet they hated the other person for putting them in that situation.

"Leah, we've talked to her boss. He tells us that your mom is making mistakes that she's never made before. Potentially costly mistakes. And you mentioned that she repeats herself. All this makes us less sure than you that everything happened the way she says it did."

Leah's face was so rigid she almost looked frightening. Rena wasn't sure she was breathing. "My mother is sharp as a tack," Leah said. "She's not making mistakes at work."

"We talked to Milo," A.L. said. "He would know."

"He doesn't know shit. I know. I know because I'm the one who changed the spreadsheets. I did it."

It was a *what the fuck* moment if there ever was one. A.L. looked at Rena. She was staring at Leah, like the woman might have two heads.

"You wanted Milo and others at work to think poorly of your mom?" he asked.

"That and I wanted to drive her a little bit crazy," Leah said. "It felt good to know that she might be losing some sleep over it. God knows there were plenty of nights I couldn't sleep when I was in foster care. But nobody cared then and nobody cares now."

"Does Troy know what you've been doing?" Rena asked.

"No. Listen, I'm tired. I need to rest," Leah said.

"That's probably a good idea," A.L. said.

They were at the door when Leah spoke again. "You think I'm a horrible daughter, don't you?"

"We have absolutely no opinion about that," A.L. said.

Rena waited until they'd pulled away from the curb. "I do sort of think she's horrible. A video of her mother gambling at her lawyer's office already is one thing. But tampering with her computer, altering work, that's another whole level of maliciousness. She needs therapy."

"I think there's a lot of suppressed rage there. But at least now we know that Elaine isn't slipping. Maybe she did sign the sheet."

"And whoever took Emma also took the sheet," Rena said. "It makes it harder to see this as a crime of opportunity. I think somebody planned to take Emma Whitman. The questions is, why her?"

Ten

Why Emma Whitman?

The question bounced around in his brain as he drove away from the Whitman house. "I don't know," he said finally. "I just don't know."

"All we can do is get back to basics. While I can't see Leah making up any of that story since she looks bad, we should at least talk to Leah's employer. Verify her work hours on Wednesday," Rena said. "Also verify her presence at the casino."

"Too late to do that tonight. I suppose we're going to have to call it a day." They'd been at it since early morning, after just a few hours of sleep. The two-hundred-mile drive there and back from Dover in the warm September sun hadn't helped.

"You're probably right. We'll hit it hard tomorrow," Rena said. "By then, Emma will have been missing forty-eight hours."

He understood what she wasn't saying. If the searchers hadn't managed to find her in that amount of time, it wasn't looking good. "You think it's weird that Perry and LuAnn Whitman aren't camped out at Leah and Troy's house?"

"You don't buy Leah's explanation that they didn't want to be a bother?"

"Family unites at a time like this. I think we need to talk to them."

"Equal opportunity police interrogations for all grandparents," Rena said.

"You and I both know—"

"Yeah, yeah. Family gets looked at hard for a reason. It's just so damn hideous."

"It is what it is," A.L. said.

They were both quiet as he drove Rena back to get her car. Once in the parking lot, he turned to her. "See you tomorrow."

She opened her door, stood and slung her purse over her shoulder. "Are you going to see Tess?"

"I don't know," he said honestly. "I might call her."

"I don't think you do your best work on the phone," Rena said. "You should go see her."

"You should go home," he said.

Before she shut her door, she said, "I know what I'm talking about. You should listen to me."

He watched her walk to her car, get in and then pull out of the lot. He took his foot off the brake and was right behind her.

His first instinct was to let things settle a little bit.

But Rena probably was smarter about these things than he was.

He picked up the phone and called Tess.

"Hi," she said.

"Did I wake you?"

"No. But I did read in one of my magazines that a man doesn't necessarily respect a woman who responds to late-night booty calls."

She was teasing. The tension in his chest eased. "How do you know this is a booty call?"

"Hmmm. I guess maybe it's just wishful thinking."

His heart sped up in his chest. "We can talk about Traci," he said. "And California."

She giggled. "Oh don't worry. We will. Probably afterward but definitely before I tell you where I hid your pants."

Ten minutes later, he knocked on her door. She opened it, gave him a look of mock confusion, and said, "I'm sorry. I thought you were my Uber driver."

"Where you going?" he asked.

"Some place very fancy. Very expensive. Fourteen-dollar glasses of wine."

He stepped inside and shut the door behind him. She looked good. She was wearing blue-and-white-striped pajama pants and a small, strappy blue shirt. No bra. "Those kind of places have a dress code," he said.

"No worries. I've got a little black dress laid out on my bed." She leaned in and kissed him. "I missed you," she said. "How's the case?"

"Frustrating." She wouldn't expect any details.

"I keep thinking of Marnee at five. How frightened she'd be." With the palm of her hand, she gently stroked his face. "There's no way for Emma Whitman to know this, but she's lucky to have you working on this."

"You think so?" he said.

"Oh, yeah. I know you won't give up. I've had

some personal experience with your tenaciousness. You found me even when I didn't want to be found."

"And you cooked Rena and me dinner. Shrimp and pasta as I recall. It was good."

"No dinner tonight but a little snack." She led him into her living room. There was a plate of cheese and crackers and some red grapes. Also a bottle of wine and two glasses.

"Is this the fourteen-dollars-a-glass wine?" he asked.

She smiled. "It may end up costing you a great deal more than that," she said suggestively.

He smiled. "I've always been a fool with my money."

He took off his suit jacket, loosened his tie and sat down. Patted the spot on the couch next to him. She sat and snuggled close. Her skin was soft and she smelled good.

"This was a crappy thing to come home to after a really good week in California," she said.

"I'm sorry that I didn't tell Traci that you were going, too."

"I'm not asking for an apology, A.L. It's your decision who you tell what. I only sent the text because I didn't want you to be blindsided by your daughter."

"But you were probably curious as to why I failed to mention it."

She had her head in the crook of his arm. She looked up with a smile. "Didn't curiosity kill the cat?"

"You have a right to ask," he said. "I should have told her. But... I couldn't."

"Couldn't," she repeated.

"This," he said, waving his hand at the two of them, "is new to me. I haven't had this for a... Hell, maybe

I've never had this. I think I'm not ready for questions about the relationship. I want to keep everybody outside the fence right now. It's so new, so good, that it feels weird to talk about it. Like I'm not protecting it enough."

She sat up. "Who needs a fourteen-dollar glass of wine when you say things like that?" Then she leaned in and kissed him. Hard. And he felt the response roar through him.

"I want you," he said.

"Take me," she answered.

He slipped his hands under her shirt and pulled it over her head. Then her pajama pants and panties came off. She was gloriously naked in his arms.

"You have too many clothes on," she said. "And I'm not able to help much."

Yeah, things like buttons and zippers were a challenge with one hand. "No worries," he said. "Just keep kissing me."

And she did. And somehow, they made it down the hallway to her bedroom, dropping his clothes in a path along the way. They fell into her bed and when he was finally inside her, he knew he was exactly where he needed to be.

Where he wanted to be.

It was the first peace he'd had in days.

Rena was eating a doughnut when he approached her desk the next morning. "Chop," he said. "Let's go. We got a psychic to talk to."

She licked her bottom lip. "Words I never thought I'd hear A.L. McKittridge say." She deliberately looked at her watch. "It's seven o'clock. No self-respecting psychic is at work yet."

"She will be," he said. "I sent an email to her very late last night, asking if we could meet this morning. I got a response right away. She said okay but that it would need to be early. She's doing a group reading and won't be available for most of the day."

"What's a group reading?"

"Not something I want to be part of. That's why we're going now."

"So you were working last night. You didn't go to see Tess."

"I only did a little work last night and for your information, Ms. Nosy, I did go see Tess."

He'd stayed the night. After they'd had sex, they'd finally had a little wine and enjoyed some cheese and crackers. It was only after she'd fallen asleep that he'd gotten around to sending the email to the psychic.

"She's not pissed at you, then?"

"I'm pretty sure she's not."

Rena narrowed her eyes. "Okay, then. Meanwhile, back at the ranch, since Ferguson was already working on verifying Elaine's time at the casino, I asked him to also make sure that Leah was there when she said she was."

"Very good," A.L. said.

Rena swallowed the last of her doughnut and took a big drink of her coffee. "And Kara Wiese has no siblings. Her parents died four years ago. Car accident. And her mother's only siblings were two brothers. Her father had a sister. She's alive and lives in Utah. I saw the photo from her driver's license—looks nothing like Kara."

"It was worth a shot."

"Absolutely." She balled up the napkin her doughnut had rested on and threw it in the trash. "I'm ready for the psychic. Maybe I'll get my fortune read while I'm there."

While the day care and the house next door to it had probably been built in the 1950s, the house that the psychic saw the future from was probably thirty or forty years older. It was a tall and narrow two-story, all brick, with leaded glass windows, and a big, heavy wood door that had an actual knocker. A.L. used it to announce their arrival.

It took about a minute for a woman, maybe midforties, wearing jeans and a gray T-shirt to open it. She had long brown hair pulled back in a low ponytail and a nice face.

"Genevieve Louis?" he asked.

"Yes. Sorry it took me a minute, I was upstairs."

She didn't much look like a psychic. Although to be honest, she was the first one he'd actually met. "Detectives McKittridge and Morgan," he said. They both held out badges but she barely glanced at them.

"Please come in. Would you like a chair?" she asked.

That would leave her standing, since there were only two. The group readings must occur elsewhere.

"We're fine," he said.

"We want to talk to you about Emma Whitman," Rena said. "She's the missing five-year-old."

"From the day care."

"Yes," Rena said.

"I've been thinking about her 24/7," Genevieve said.

"Why's that?" Rena asked.

"I'm not sure," Genevieve admitted. "I mean, it's a horrible story. But it seems to have consumed me. Maybe because it happened so close to here."

"Were you here on Wednesday morning? Around 7:15, 7:30?" A.L. asked.

"Not here," she said, motioning to the space around them. "I don't open until 10:00. But I would have been upstairs. In my apartment."

"Convenient," Rena said.

"The reason I rented this location," Genevieve explained. "I like to have all my energy centered, not spread too thin."

"Right," A.L. said. "You didn't happen to see Emma Whitman walk away from the day care?" he asked, knowing it was all but impossible. If she had, she'd no doubt have come forward right away.

"No. I slept until almost 9:00 that morning."

"No unusual noises? No dogs barking?" Rena asked.

"Sometimes people hear things but they don't realize the importance at the moment," A.L. added.

Genevieve smiled. "I'm pretty attuned to any stimuli."

"And you didn't see or hear anything unusual?" Rena said.

Genevieve shook her head. "But I don't think she walked away."

A.L. stared at the woman. "Why do you say that?"

"I told you, it's been consuming me. I see her in a car."

"See?"

Her glasses had slipped down her nose and she deliberately pushed them up. "Yes. See."

"Do you see anything else?" Rena asked quickly, probably afraid to let him speak.

"She's not unhappy."

No one said anything. For a very long minute.

"Uh…can you describe the car?" Rena asked.

Genevieve shook her head. "I'm not sure it's even a car. But I think it's a vehicle of some kind."

"The driver?" Rena asked. "Male? Female?"

"I'm sorry. It's always just her. Little Emma."

"What was she wearing?" A.L. asked.

"I've read the description in the newspaper. I could recite that and maybe you'd believe me more or less. I don't know. But I'm not seeing clothes. Just her sweet face with her brown hair blowing in the wind."

"When did you first have this…uh…vision?" Rena asked.

"When I first woke up. It was at least an hour later that I heard what had happened at the day care."

She looked directly at A.L. as she spoke the last sentence.

"And have you had any other visions?" A.L. asked, as if finally finding his voice.

Genevieve shook her head. "I'm sorry, no."

"If anything comes up that might be helpful to us, we'd appreciate a call," Rena said, handing the woman her card.

"I'll do that. I hope you find her. I really do."

"Have you ever met Leah or Troy Whitman, the child's parents?" A.L. asked.

"Not that I'm aware. I suppose it's possible. The day

care will have a bake sale every couple of months to raise money for activities and I try to support them."

"So you know Alice Quest and perhaps some of the staff?" A.L. asked.

Genevieve nodded.

"Got any feelings one way or another about them right now?" A.L. asked.

"As if whether or not they're involved in Emma's disappearance?" Genevieve clarified.

"Any feelings?" A.L. said, keeping it broad.

"I'm sorry. I don't. All I can tell you is that I'm confident that it was Emma that I saw, her hair was blowing in the wind, and she didn't seem scared or unhappy."

"Thank you," Rena said. She opened the door and motioned for A.L. to precede her out. When they were far enough from the door not to be heard, she turned to him. "I thought for a minute you were going to ask her to help with the investigation."

It wasn't unheard of. But definitely not generally his thing. But they were into the third day. This was excruciating. "If I'd thought she had more to offer, I would have," he said.

"Not unhappy," she repeated. "If we believe in this *vision*, that supports our theory that it wasn't a stranger."

"Agree," A.L. said. "For what that gets us."

"I really didn't get the feeling that she's a crack-pot," Rena said.

"You believe in psychics?" A.L. asked.

"I believe that there are people who are better connected to what's going on around them than others.

And that maybe they have the ability to feel things, hell, maybe even see things, that the rest of us can't."

"If, and this is a big if, she's right, then Emma was in some kind of vehicle but not unhappy about it. Hair blowing in the wind," A.L. said.

"Multiple people have looked at street camera video. Nobody has picked up a little girl being driven in a vehicle."

"I know. We're back to crackpot."

Rena started heading back to their vehicle but he stopped her. "There's one more thing we need to do now that we're in this neighborhood."

"What?"

"Remember Coyote Frogg? I asked Ferguson to try to find him. He would be twenty-nine years old. There's no record of him being employed since 2017. Yet he never collected any federal or state assistance after that. And there's been no electric bills, gas bills or telephone bills in his name since around the same time."

"So he dropped off the grid."

"We all know that's almost impossible to really do. But he's been pretty much a shadow. He did seek some medical treatment about six months ago in Milwaukee for a chemical burn. Told the doctor that he was a student and he'd been doing an experiment in his basement."

"Cooking meth?" Rena asked knowingly.

"Good a guess as any. But we were able to get a recent photo out of his medical record and I had Ferguson scan it and send it to me. I want to show it to Mr.

Gibacki at the Panini Playground." He held out his phone and let Rena see the photo.

"Definitely meth," she said.

Heroin was the drug of choice for many but that didn't mean the meth industry had died out. Far from it. While most of the meth circulating came in via Mexico, cheaper and stronger than ever, there were still some local cooks. They had to work harder to get the ingredients and ultimately produced in limited quantities, but there was enough money in it to keep them doing it.

A.L. glanced at the photo again. The years had not been kind to Coyote Frogg. He skin was pasty white and another twenty pounds would have kept him from looking emaciated. But he did have a hell of a head of red hair. It wasn't terribly long in the photo, just falling below his chin. It was a head shot so there was no way to see whether he had a sleeve tattoo. The detail in the medical record likely would have included it but they'd only been able to obtain the photo. A warrant would be necessary to get more.

Mr. Gibacki had described shoulder-length coarse red hair.

Hair could grow. That's why they were going to let him take a look.

The Panini Playground wouldn't open for hours but there was a car parked behind the restaurant. A.L. knocked on the back door. It opened a few inches and A.L. shifted so that the man could see him. "A minute, sir?" A.L. said. "We have something we'd like to show you."

The door opened and Mr. Gibacki came out. "Detectives?" he said.

"We have a photo we'd like you to look at, sir. To see if you recognize it as one of the men that you kicked out of here on Tuesday night." A.L. pulled his phone. Thumbed through his messages. Held the phone out for the older man to see.

Mr. Gibacki stared at it. For a whole minute. Finally, he looked up. "His hair was much longer, more wild-looking. But I think it's him."

As A.L. and Rena brought Chief Faster up to speed on Coyote Frogg, his eyes started to dance. It took just seconds, really, for the man to make several leaps in logic. One, that Coyote Frogg's father had been a person of intense interest in the Corrine Antler disappearance. Two, that perhaps the Dover police had been too focused on the father and had not spent enough energy on the son. And three, if Coyote Frogg could be found, there was a chance to solve not one but two kidnappings.

What didn't get said was that it just *felt* better that it was a stranger than a family member.

Faster rubbed his hands together. "I've already had a call from the mayor this morning. His office is getting lots of pressure to solve this case. When people don't feel as if their children are safe, they don't have much tolerance for anything else that isn't quite right in the community. He's going to be happy to hear this news."

A.L. said nothing. His own heart had beat fast when Mr. Gibacki had identified Coyote Frogg's photo as the same man he'd booted from his restaurant on Tuesday night. He understood the interest in finding Coyote Frogg. But he also knew that eyewitness testimony was more unreliable than most people realized. Mistakes were made all the time.

"I want the two of you back in Dover. The Frogg family lived there for more than twenty-five years. There have to be distant relatives or former friends, somebody who can lead us to Coyote Frogg."

"We're going to need a warrant to get more information out of the medical record," A.L. said. That would include information on the patient's tattoos."

"I'll get it for you," Faster said. "And I'll fill in the FBI and others."

The man had a head of steam going and there was no sense in trying to convince him not to get too focused on one person. He'd never been a great cop and he never would be. And right now, he was in charge. So that meant A.L. and Rena were going to Dover.

And he could be right. A.L. didn't want his own issues with Faster to cloud the possibility that this really could be the break they were looking for. "Ready," he said, looking at Rena.

She stood. And ten minutes later, they were on the road. A.L. was driving.

"Let's try Perry and LuAnn Whitman now," he said. "Do you have their numbers?"

"Yeah," Rena said, flipping pages in her notebook. "Which cell do you think I should try first?"

"Try LuAnn. I think women are better about answering their phones."

"Are you slamming women?"

He lowered his chin and gave her a stare. "I was complimenting women, the whole damn group of you.

For your information, there are many things that I think women do much better than men."

"Damn straight," she muttered. She dialed and pushed Send. It was answered on the second ring.

"Hello."

"Is this LuAnn Whitman?"

"Yes."

"This is Detective Morgan of the Baywood Police Department."

The quick intake of breath was audible. LuAnn was steeling herself for bad news.

"I am not calling with news about Emma. But rather, I have just a few questions for you and your husband, if he's available, that might help us as we continue to investigate."

"For a minute I was sure…" Her voice trailed off.

Rena understood. The woman didn't want to put what she'd been sure of into words. Too ugly. Too harsh. "My partner, Detective McKittridge, is also on the line. I'm going to put you on speaker phone."

"My husband is right here. I'll do the same," she said.

There was a slight pause and then a man said, "Hello, this is Perry Whitman."

"Detectives Morgan and McKittridge here, Mr. Whitman," Rena said. "Thank you both for being available to talk to us. May we call you LuAnn and Perry?"

"Of course," LuAnn said.

"First of all, let me say that we're both terribly sorry that this has happened to your family and we're doing everything we can to find Emma," Rena said.

There was no response. Hard to know if Troy and

or Leah had said anything about them to LuAnn and Perry.

"We understand that you live in Milwaukee. Have you lived there for some time?" Rena asked.

"Eighteen years. Troy was just starting high school when we moved in," LuAnn said. "He turns thirty-two next month."

A.L. and Rena looked at each other. It was going to be a really bad birthday party if Emma's chair was empty.

"Do you work in Milwaukee?" A.L. asked.

"I retired about three years ago," Perry said. "I worked in logistics for a manufacturing company here in Milwaukee."

"I'm working part-time at Brookfield Square mall. At Pagany Chocolates. Gets me out of the house," LuAnn said.

"Can you tell us about your day on Wednesday?" Rena asked.

"Well, we got a call from Troy sometime after 6:00 that evening," Perry said.

"Let's start from the beginning of the day," Rena said, trying to redirect them.

"Well, I have dialysis three mornings a week," Perry said. "Monday, Wednesday and Friday. That starts at 9:00 but I'm always there by 8:30. Takes about four hours. So I'm there until about 1:00."

"Where does this occur?" Rena asked.

"There's a dialysis center about four blocks from our house. Broadhurst Pavilion."

Pavilion. What a nice word for a place where they stuck needles into you and cleaned out your kidneys.

"Thank you, Perry," Rena said. "After 1:00, what did you do?"

"I always come home and take a nap. Then I watch a little television. That's what I was doing when Troy called."

"And your day, LuAnn?" Rena asked.

"I got up about 7:00 and walked the dog. Then I showered and drove to work. Our store opens at 9:00. I was there until 2:00. Then I drove home. Oh, wait. I think I stopped at the store on my way home. Yes, that's right. I needed ketchup for the meat loaf I was making." She paused. "I guess that was a waste. Neither one of us ate a bite of dinner that night. I threw the meat loaf away."

"So you were at home when Troy called?" A.L. asked.

"Yes. Watching television with Perry. It was just so unbelievable. It still is. And we feel so helpless here," LuAnn said. "We just sit here and wait for the phone to ring."

"I'm sure that's difficult," Rena said.

"We've been told that's about all we can do," Perry said. There was a hint of hurt in Perry's tone.

"I'm sure that Leah and Troy are comforted by your support," Rena said.

"We love that little Emma. She's the sweetest thing. And the idea that she may be lost or hurt or…" Her voice caught in a sob.

"It's okay, honey," Perry said softly, clearly speaking to his wife. "I'll do this."

It hit Rena that Perry and LuAnn were supporting each other the way she and A.L. had expected that Troy and Leah would.

"Truth is, Detectives, we're not as close to our son and daughter-in-law as others are to their children," Perry said.

Leah had said that they were lovely people. "Why is that?" Rena asked.

"It would be convenient if we could blame our daughter-in-law. But that wouldn't be true," Perry said, finishing the thought. "We maybe said some things that we shouldn't have said to Troy when he was considering buying Garage on Division."

"We just weren't confident that it was a good decision," LuAnn said, evidently having composed herself enough to speak. "But there was no talking him out of it."

"Why didn't you think it was a good decision?" A.L. asked.

"I thought he was paying too much for the business. I wanted to see the financial statements but he told me that he'd looked at them and was satisfied," Perry said. "I didn't want to see him take on that much debt."

"Did he ask you to help him with the purchase?" A.L. asked.

"No. I think he knew that we'd be uncomfortable with that. He worked all that out with Steven," Perry said.

"Steven?" Rena asked.

"Steven Hanzel. He's a banker in Baywood. But we've known him since we moved into this house. He lived across the street. Troy and Steven were best friends. Actually, both our boys were friendly with Steven," Perry added.

"We always thought that's why Troy moved to Baywood, because Steven was already there," LuAnn said.

Rena looked at A.L. "What do you think of Steven?"

Neither one of the Whitmans responded. Finally, LuAnn said, "Well, Steven has never suffered from a lack of self-confidence."

"He was a cocky shit," Perry said. "But he got better with age. Got a college degree. We didn't know his wife but we've met his little girl at one of Emma's birthday parties. I think he's got a little boy, too. Hard on kids when the marriage doesn't work out."

Hard on parents when their adult children pushed them away. "You mentioned your other son?"

"Yes, Travis. He's two years older than Troy. He doesn't live too far from us here in Milwaukee. We called him on Wednesday night, once we'd talked to Troy. He came over right away. That helped."

Neither A.L. nor Rena volunteered that Travis had known first. "Are Troy and Travis close?" A.L. asked.

"Well, they fought like caged tigers when they were kids," Perry said. "But I think that they get along pretty well now."

"This is a difficult question for me to ask," Rena said. "But do either of you have any reason to believe that either Troy or Leah could have something to do with Emma's disappearance?"

The question hung in the air.

"Both Leah and Troy love that little girl with all their hearts," Perry said. He didn't sound angry that the question had been asked.

"But we also don't think that she wandered away from the learning center. We talk to Emma on the phone at least once a week. She loves going there. Talks about her teachers all the time," LuAnn said. "She's a very responsible little girl. Knows right from wrong."

"Somebody took her," Perry said. "Somebody took our sweet baby away from us."

"They're hurting on so many levels," Rena said, once she'd ended the call.

"Yeah, that was bad. I'm going to pull off here," he said, nodding his head in the direction of a highway rest stop. "I want to check my notes."

"I might use the little girls' room while we're here," Rena said. She held up her sixteen-ounce coffee cup in further explanation.

"You rent coffee, you don't own it," A.L. said, sounding preoccupied.

When she got back into the vehicle, he was drumming his fingers on the steering wheel. "During that first conversation with Troy and Leah, Troy called his parents before the Amber Alert was sent. I asked him about his relationship with his parents. I have in my notes that he verified it was a good relationship."

"Maybe he just didn't want to get into the weeds. Not what was important to him at the time," Rena said.

"Possibly."

"Or he's in denial about relationships he has with others. Maybe if we asked him, he'd say that he and Leah have a good relationship."

"Okay."

"You don't sound convinced," Rena said.

"Maybe he didn't want us to have any reason to follow up with his parents," A.L. said.

"They didn't tell us anything of great importance," Rena said.

"They told us that they didn't think Garage on Division was a good buy. That they wanted to look at the financial records but Troy didn't let them. Remember the story you shared about the conversation at the Morgans' dinner table? Maybe it wasn't just an ugly rumor that Danny heard. Maybe the business is in trouble."

"Are we going to ask Troy for his financial records?" Rena asked.

"I don't know," A.L. said. "I want to talk to Troy again before we make that decision."

"During that same conversation, Leah said that LuAnn and Perry were lovely people," Rena said. "I remember her using the word *lovely* just because not that many people use that word regularly. Now, in retrospect, she didn't really answer the question of whether there was a good relationship."

"Maybe she doesn't understand the relationship. Perry made it sound as if the concerns about buying the business were voiced to Troy. Maybe Troy never told Leah. So all Leah knows is that the relationship soured for some reason but can't put her finger on why."

"Complicated," Rena said. "Sounds as if their relationship with Travis might be better. For their sakes, I hope it is. Do you think we should follow up with Travis?"

"Everything and one more thing. Let's call him now," A.L. said.

Rena entered his number in her phone and pushed Send. It rang four times before flipping over to voice mail. "This is Detective Morgan from the Baywood

Police Department. Please return my call at your earliest opportunity." She closed by reciting her number twice, even though it should pop up on his caller ID.

"Switching gears," A.L. said. "What do you remember about Trapper Frogg and his son, Coyote, from when we looked through Doug Franklin's file?" he asked.

"Coyote Frogg was the only child of Trapper Frogg and his wife, who were married late 1980s and divorced in the late 1990s when he was ten. Trapper Frogg died three years ago. Coyote was mentioned in the obituary but there was no other family. Although I think I did see a note that the ex-wife was living in Las Vegas. I don't think Doug talked to her. Can't remember her name."

"Dusty," A.L. said. "That was his wife's name. You're right, Franklin didn't talk to her. I think because Trapper told him that there'd been no contact between her and either Trapper or Coyote for many years."

"Why do you ask me when you already have all this in your head?"

"Testing you," he said.

She raised her middle finger in a friendly salute. "Test this."

He smiled. "Faster wants us to wrap this up with a bow."

"Did you see the front page of this morning's paper?"

He had. The headline had been Fund-raising Site Established for Missing Child. He'd skimmed the article. It had given a basic update on continuing search activities and then devoted three paragraphs to how people could donate to the Whitman family. "I imagine the money will flow in," he said. "By Monday, the headline is going to be Baywood Cops Can't Find Their Own Asses."

"Which explains Faster's motivation. The press is still playing nice but it won't last. The mayor is already calling him."

"Can you text Brent Smoke and ask him to pull Trapper Frogg's last address?" A.L. asked.

"Why? I thought you said that Coyote hadn't been seen or heard from since 2017. You don't think he's hiding out at his dad's old house, do you?"

"No. But prior to dropping off the grid, he had a checking account. Ferguson was able to find a deposit for forty-seven thousand dollars."

"Chump change in the drug world," she said.

"Right. But this was a wire transfer, from one bank to another. I'm betting it was legitimate money from the sale of his dad's house. We're going to go talk to the buyer. See what he or she knows."

She picked up her phone. Touched some numbers. "I'm sort of disappointed in you that you can't remember the address. It was probably mentioned at least once in those hundred pages or so that we reviewed. Perhaps your memory isn't that good."

"I'll remember forever that you're a pain in the ass. I know that it was Cleveland Avenue but I don't want to waste time circling the block."

Fifteen minutes later, she had confirmation from Brent Smoke's assistant that it was 470 Cleveland Avenue. They would start there and then widen the circle. Maybe there would be a helpful neighbor who had known Coyote Frogg, who might be able to point them in the right direction.

They were fifteen minutes away when A.L.'s cell buzzed. He looked at the message. "Ferguson has verified that both Elaine and Leah were at the casino on Wednesday morning. Leah arrived first, coffee in hand. Then Elaine. Elaine left, Leah followed. Times match what both the women said."

"Well, that's that, I guess," Rena said. She was quiet for a minute. "I didn't want it to be Leah. She's doing some sad shit with her mother but still, it's her child."

"Yeah. That would be bad."

The Froggs had lived at the very edge of Dover, near a set of railroad tracks. It was a small house, maybe a two-bedroom. There was a man on a ladder painting the exterior of the house. "That's some paint," A.L. said. It was a cross between red and burgundy and was starkly different than the white he was trying to cover.

He parked his vehicle and he and Rena got out. They approached from an angle where the man would see them coming. They didn't want anybody falling off and cracking his head open.

"Morning, sir," A.L. said.

"Morning," he replied, his tone cautious.

Maybe he thought they were from the city. That one of the neighbors had complained about the new paint. "I'm Detective McKittridge and this is Detective Morgan. We're from the Baywood, Wisconsin, police department. Can we have a minute of your time?"

The man didn't answer but he did climb down. He was young, maybe twenty-five.

"What's your name, sir?" Rena asked.

"Dawson Ladle," he said.

"Is this your house, Mr. Ladle?" she asked.

"Yeah."

"How long have you lived here?" Rena followed up.

"Almost three years."

"Did you purchase it from Trapper Frogg?" A.L. asked.

"Well, sort of. It was Trapper's house but I actually bought it from his son, Coyote, after Trapper passed away."

"Do you know Coyote Frogg?" A.L. asked.

Dawson Ladle shrugged. "Dover is pretty small. Most everybody knows everybody else. So, I guess you could say that I knew Coyote. He was a senior in his school when I was a freshman. He didn't pay any attention to me but he ran track his senior year and made State so I knew him. I saw the sign in the front yard when he put the house up for sale and it was in my price range. I was surprised that he wasn't keeping the house but he didn't seem to want anything to do with it."

"Where was Coyote living at the time?" Rena asked.

"I'm not sure," Dawson said. "I don't think it was anywhere in Dover. He made it seem as if it was a hassle to come back, even for the closing."

"When's the last time you saw Coyote?" A.L. asked.

"At that closing," Dawson said. "Once the paperwork was signed and I'd written a check, he couldn't wait to get out of here."

"What title company handled the sale?" A.L. asked.

Dawson closed his eyes. "Mc... Mc... McPherson Title," he said, opening them.

It might give them a place to start. The title company might have an address for Coyote at the time of the sale. "Do you recall any of Coyote's friends?"

"I don't know much about him after he got out of high school. But in school, he and Chuck Hayes were buddies. I can still see them in Chuck's car. He had an old Mustang convertible. Black. I think it was a '67 or a '68. And the two of them rode around in that car, looking for trouble. I thought they were so cool."

"Did Coyote and Chuck find lots of trouble?" Rena asked.

Dawson smiled. "I don't know. But it was fun thinking that they did." He paused. "Is Coyote in trouble now? Is that why you're asking all these questions about him?"

"Just trying to locate him," A.L. said easily. "Appreciate the tip on Chuck Hayes. Where does he live?"

"Behind the high school. Biggest house on the street. Red brick."

They'd seen the high school on the first visit. "Anything else you can think of that might lead us to Coyote?"

"No. But if you find him, can you tell him it would have been nice to know that the backyard floods every spring. But I guess that's just buyer beware," Dawson added, his tone good-natured.

"Good luck painting the house," Rena said. "Nice color."

"My girlfriend picked it out," Dawson said. "I'm not so sure about it. But if she moves in, it will be worth it."

"That's so nice," Rena said, when they were back in the car. Then she glanced at A.L. "What? No smart remark that I'm a romantic fool."

"Nope."

"Are you feeling okay? Need more sleep? An iron pill? Testosterone cream?"

A.L. ignored her and checked something on his phone. He turned the corner.

"Where are you going?" Rena asked. "The high school is the other direction."

"I know. We're going to do a quick swing by McPherson Title."

"Tess still working at Hampton Title Company?"

"Yeah. The stories she tells about Clark Hampton make me think he's kind of a goof but she likes her co-workers and likes the work. No reason to be looking for anything else. I think she really appreciates how flexible they were when she needed time off last spring."

"She'd had part of her arm bitten off by a shark. I think most people might have needed a moment."

He saw the sign for McPherson Title and pulled into a parking spot. The door was unlocked and they walked in. There were two women working at desks and what appeared to be two offices and a restroom toward the back.

"May I help you?" one of the women asked. She did not get up from her desk.

A.L. approached and offered his card. "Can I speak with whoever is in charge?"

That got her up. "Of course." She walked quickly to the back office. Knocked on a door. Then opened it and stuck her head inside. In less than a minute, she was back with a middle-aged white guy trailing behind.

"I'm Marcus Page," the man said. "We can talk in my office."

Marcus led them back the direction he'd come from. Once inside the midsize office, he motioned for them to have a seat at the small corner table with four chairs. Once he was seated, he said, "What can I assist you with?"

"Mr. Page, we're working on an ongoing investigation and want to have a conversation with someone who we believe you might have some information on. McPherson Title was the title company that assisted with the sale of his property a couple years ago. We're hoping that you'd have an address?"

"Who is the individual?"

"Coyote Frogg."

Marcus Page's facial expression didn't change. But suddenly he was tapping the end of A.L.'s business card on the table in a staccato beat. "You're from the Baywood Police Department."

"Yes, sir," A.L. answered, even though it hadn't sounded like a question.

"The only thing that the police in Baywood are working on right now is the disappearance of Emma Whitman."

Rena leaned forward. "Mr. Page, how is it that you know Emma Whitman's name?"

"I imagine most people in this town know it. Or at least most people of a certain age. Because when we heard the news, it took us back ten years, just like that." He stopped tapping and very carefully laid A.L.'s card on the table. "My daughter was Corrine Antler's best friend. They went to the same day care. She was there the day Corrine disappeared."

"That must have been a horrible time," Rena said. "For your child. For you."

"Coyote's father worked at the day care. And now you want to talk to Coyote about another missing child." He sounded very angry. "Did the police miss something here ten years ago? Did they?"

"Mr. Page, I would encourage you not to connect too many dots that are really just specks of dirt on the paper," A.L. said. Christ, he had not expected this. It was as if they'd scratched a scab and ended up rupturing the femoral artery.

"Do you have any idea what it's like to explain to your five-year-old why her best friend is never coming back to day care? Why they're never going to play together again?" He pressed his lips together. "I'm sorry," he said. "You know, my wife and I didn't let our daughter play outside for almost a year. We…we were afraid that the person who'd taken Corrine would see her and come back for her."

Suddenly, he pushed back his chair and walked to his desk. He sat down and started punching keys on his desktop computer. "We scan every piece of paper in every file."

They let him work. And four minutes later, he looked up. "The only address we had on Coyote Frogg was the address of the property that was being sold."

"We appreciate your time," A.L. said.

"Just find the bastard this time, will you?"

Neither of them said anything as they left the title company and drove to the high school. Rena felt mentally bruised. And exhausted. Corrine Antler's disappearance had changed people. Was this the journey that so many in Baywood were just beginning? Naive still to the trauma that would set in, unaware of the bitterness they would shoulder going forward. It was a depressing thought.

When A.L. pulled up in front of a two-story redbrick house, she studied it. It was big, certainly bigger than any of the neighbors'. And it had an attached four-car garage. Perhaps there was still a vintage mustang behind one of the doors.

They knocked and a teenage boy answered. He was wearing a faded University of Wisconsin T-shirt and pajama pants and had a cell phone in his hand. "Is your dad Chuck Hayes?" A.L. asked.

"Stepdad."

"Is he at home?"

"No."

Rena gave the kid credit. He wasn't giving anything away. "I'm Detective Morgan and this is my partner, Detective McKittridge. Your stepdad is not in trouble and there's nothing wrong but we do need to talk to him."

"He's playing tennis. At the community courts."

Rena pulled her phone and used the map function. "Right here?" she asked, pointing at the screen.

"That's the one," he said.

"Thank you," Rena said. By the time they got back to the car, the kid was already talking on the phone. Maybe to call his stepdad to warn him that the police were looking for him. Maybe his best friend to laugh about the same.

They found Chuck Hayes sitting on a bench, on the

side of an empty tennis court, no partner in sight. Both Rena and A.L. flashed badges. "I assume your stepson told you we were coming, Mr. Hayes," Rena said.

"Please, Chuck is fine. And, yes. You made his day," Chuck added dryly. "He said that if I end up being handcuffed, that somebody needs to get a photo. That's why I sent my tennis partner on his way."

"Restraints are not generally required," Rena said. "We just have a few questions about someone we believe you were acquainted with in the past. Coyote Frogg."

Chuck Hayes's eyes grew serious. "Is he dead?" he asked.

"Not that we know of," A.L. said. "Interesting first question, though."

Chuck ran a hand through his short brown hair. "Coyote was my best friend in grade school all the way through high school. I went to college, he didn't. It was a divide we couldn't breach. We saw each other socially a few times after I got out of college and moved back to Dover but...our lives were pretty different. I was busy with a wife and kids and, well, he wasn't."

"What was he busy with?" A.L. asked.

"Alcohol. Drugs. I don't want to talk poorly about him but I did hear that he was dealing and sampling some of the product."

No surprise there. "Can you think of somebody who might have kept in contact with Coyote after high school?"

"He was hanging with people who I would have crossed the street to avoid. I wasn't interested in learning their names."

"Did you know Coyote's mom?"

"Yeah, sure. Dusty. Coyote used to call her by her first name. If I'd have called my mom by her first name, I wouldn't have sat down for two weeks."

"Understand," A.L. said. "Do you remember when she left?"

"I don't know. Maybe we were in fifth or sixth grade."

"Did Coyote talk about her after that?"

"Not if his dad was around."

"Do you know if he ever saw her?"

"I remember him talking about her one time. I was a freshman or sophomore in college, and I was home on break. Coyote and I were still trying to hold the friendship together. He came over to my house. Said that he was getting out of Dover, that he was going to go live with his mom."

"Did that happen?"

"I don't know. Maybe. I'm not sure I saw him after that."

"Okay. Do you recall, Mr. Hayes, when Corrine Antler disappeared?" Rena asked.

"That was the little girl from the day care, right?" he verified. "That was a while ago."

"Ten years ago," Rena said. "Did you know her or her family?"

"No."

"Did Coyote ever talk about her or her family, either before or after Corrine's disappearance?" Rena asked.

"We might have talked about it afterwards."

"Do you recall anything specific that Coyote might have said about Corrine Antler?"

"Just that the police were crawling up his dad's ass... sorry," he said, looking at Rena. "They talked to his dad a bunch of times because his dad worked at the day care that she disappeared from. Now that I think about it, I do remember one thing he said. That the police dug up his dad's garden."

"Did he think his father had anything to do with the disappearance?" A.L. asked.

"I don't know. Christ. That's not the kind of thing you ask your friend."

"Did *you* ever think that either Coyote or his dad had anything to do with the disappearance?" Rena asked.

Now Chuck narrowed his eyes. "Detectives, you've got a lot of questions about something that happened ten years ago."

A.L. closed the distance between him and Chuck. "Another five-year-old girl disappeared in very similar circumstances in Baywood this past Wednesday. We have an eyewitness who put Coyote Frogg in the vicinity the previous night."

"Well, fuck me," Chuck said. "Sorry," he added, again in Rena's direction. "I've been out of the country on business this past week, just got home late last night. I'm behind in my news. But now something makes sense. I got an email yesterday asking for a contribution. I only glanced at it but I did see that it came from a guy I know in Baywood. His bank and my investment company are owned by the same holding company. We cross-sell a few products."

"What's his name?" Rena asked.

"Steven Hanzel."

"Are the two of you friends?" Rena asked.

"No. We have common friends. He's…let's just say, I'm a happily married guy and when I travel, I'm in my hotel room by 8:00, alone."

"And he's not."

"That's what people say. But I guess this shows that he's an okay guy. I mean, he's reaching out pretty broadly to raise money for a good cause." He paused. "I just can't get my head around the fact that the Coyote Frogg that I knew could have anything to do with a missing child. But believe me, if I had any information about him, I'd tell you. I got three kids. Anybody who hurts a child isn't even human and I'd be the first person to step on them in the street."

A.L. and Rena both handed Chuck a card. "Please call us if you remember anything else that might be helpful," A.L. said.

Ten minutes later, Rena spread butter on her strawberry French toast. She loved places that served breakfast all day. A.L. had gone for the more traditional burger and fries for lunch.

A.L. drank his coffee.

"Ten years ago, Doug Franklin documented that Coyote Frogg was not in contact with his mother."

"He was nineteen at the time. Maybe this conversation between Coyote and Chuck occurred after that. If Chuck was a sophomore, the two young men might have been twenty."

"Do we contact Dusty?"

"I don't know if it's worth it."

"Faster isn't going to be happy with what we've got," Rena said.

"We can't manufacture facts," A.L. said. "But you're

right, if there is one stone left unturned, Faster will use it to bash us over the head. I'll reach out to Dusty."

"Okay. I think we need to get back to Baywood."

"Maybe swing by Troy and Leah's house. Check in," he said. "Still have to talk to Leah's employer, too."

"Maybe you could do that and I'm going to start calling the parents who dropped their kids off around the same time. We already have talked to those in Emma's class who fall into that group but we need to look broader, at the other classroom. Those parents would have been going in and coming out of the main lobby area around the same time as Elaine Broadstreet. Maybe they saw something."

"That's fine. Although the times don't always make sense on the sheets." A.L. opened the file folder near his right hand. "For example. Here's the sign-in sheet from the other room. First parent signs that they dropped their kid in at 7:07. Next one at 7:12. Next one at 7:10."

Rena shrugged. "Slow watch. In a hurry. Bad with details. A thousand reasons."

"Sloppy system, that's all I'm saying," A.L. said.

"I suspect Alice Quest will be instituting a whole host of new and improved systems in the coming weeks. Maybe she was sloppy. Maybe just casual. Because she thought that would be enough." But now a kid was missing and every detail of her operation was under scrutiny.

"There were holes in her processes but I think she genuinely cares about the kids and their parents," A.L. said.

"Yeah. And if we don't find Emma, her life is never going to be the same."

"Fuck that," A.L. said. "You were part of the conversation with Marcus Page. If we don't find her, none of our lives are ever going to be the same."

Eleven

Ten minutes after A.L. and Rena had arrived back in Baywood and gone their separate ways, A.L. had his hands full. With a crying woman.

Not any of the women regularly in his life. A woman that he'd never met until three minutes ago. But she was clearly having a bad day and he was maybe the worst person in the world to offer assistance.

"I'm sorry. I can't stop crying. I have a five-year-old daughter and I just can't imagine what the Whitmans are going through. Leah is such an important part of our family."

In this case, the *family* was the Bailey Shepherd Law Firm. A.L. nodded at the receptionist. "I can come back."

"No, no. If I can help in anyway, I want to. I do. Let me page her."

Her was the human resources manager, who was apparently not in her office.

"Oh, God." Julia Spear reached for more tissues. He knew her name because she had a big gold nameplate. "No, just wait," she said.

She punched some keys on her desk phone and seconds later, it rang. "There's a detective here to see you. It's about Leah," she whispered. Not quite softly enough that he didn't hear it. She hung up. "Greta will be right here."

"What's Greta's last name?"

"Greta Pistolle. I thinks that's French."

As long as she spoke English, he was going to be happy. He wandered a few feet away from the reception desk, afraid that if he stayed too close, his proximity might prompt more tears.

Greta Pistolle was midforties. She wore a dark business suit and a white blouse. He sensed a rather nononsense attitude as she approached, so he was a little surprised when she took a minute to stop at the desk and check on Julia. "Take a few minutes," she told the woman gently.

Then she approached. "Detective McKittridge, I'm Greta Pistolle, the human resources manager here at Bailey Shepherd. Let's go to my office."

Once there, with her behind the desk and him sitting in front of it, she offered up a smile. "Julia is an excellent receptionist with a very kind heart. The type who sends cards to the rest of us when our pets are ill or hurt."

Before Felix, he'd have laughed at that. Now, he realized it would be hard if the cat was in a bad way.

"Obviously, this issue with Leah and her family is far more serious so she's having a little trouble coping," Greta said. "Now, what can I help you with?"

"Can you verify how long Leah has been employed with Bailey Shepherd?" A.L. asked.

Greta turned her chair so that she faced her computer. A few clicks later, she said, "Two years this December."

"I understand she's a paralegal."

"Senior paralegal. She was hired as a paralegal but got promoted about six months ago."

Leah had not made the distinction. Maybe it wasn't that big of a deal. "What can you tell me about her work?"

Greta shrugged. "Of course I don't see it every day but given the recent promotion, I think you can safely assume she's doing just fine. It's unusual for a paralegal to get to be a senior paralegal so quickly. Normally, it's at least three years. But I recall her supervising attorney saying he thought Leah was something special."

"His name?" A.L. asked.

"Devin. Devin Raine. He's not here today. He volunteered to search. We'd probably all be doing that but the business has to keep running."

"Can you tell me about Leah's work hours?" A.L. asked.

She shook her head. "You'd have to ask Devin. Our paralegals are salaried and their timekeeping is done on an exception basis. If we don't see an exception noted in the time records, such as vacation or sick, we assume they were here."

Probably an okay assumption except for when Leah was at the casino, secretly videotaping her mother.

"Can you give me Devin's direct line?"

Again, she turned to her computer. "This is his cell. I suspect that's where you'll have the best chance of reaching him. How is Leah doing? I keep wanting to call but I don't want to bother her."

"That's probably a good decision," he said. "Thank you, Ms. Pistolle." On the way out of the building, he spent a minute in the lobby, where they had photos of all the lawyers. Devin Raine was a good-looking guy. Dark blond hair. Blue eyes. Maybe early fifties with a tan fit for the most selective of golf courses.

As he walked out of the law firm, he was dialing the man. It rang four times and went to voice mail. Guy probably didn't answer any numbers he didn't recognize. A.L. left a message asking for a call back.

Then he drove to the Whitmans' house. There was a news van parked on the street, across from the house. He did a slow drive-by. Didn't look like there was anybody in it. He did a U-turn in the street and parked across from it. He found Leah in her kitchen. Sitting at the table. Staring at her hands. The agents still at the house were in the living room. "Just checking in, Leah, like I said I would." There was no need to tell her that minutes ago he'd been having a conversation about her. Or that they had questions about the financial solvency of her husband's business.

"How are you doing?" he asked.

She shrugged. "Last night I dreamed that I could hear Emma in her room. I woke up and ran down the hall. I...think I might be losing my mind."

"You're not. You're under a huge amount of stress."

"I stayed in her room. All night. Her sheets smell like her." Leah's voice cracked.

He could feel his own throat closing up. "Is Troy out searching?" A.L. asked.

"He was. They sent him home to sleep. But he's not sleeping. He's in the garage," Leah said. "With Steven Hanzel," she added. "I don't like it when they smoke in the house."

"I think I'll take a walk out," he said.

The Whitmans had a two-car garage, detached. It sat more than fifty feet back from the house, making it a long trek in the pouring rain with groceries. But today it was sunny, the temps hovering in the midseventies. A.L. made his way past a late-model four-door blue truck and found Troy and another man sitting on lawn chairs in the empty side of a two-car garage.

The truck blocked their view of the street and blocked reporters and curious others from having a look at them. Troy wasn't smoking but the other man was. A pack of cigarettes lay on the cement floor, almost squarely between the two chairs.

Maybe Troy had needed a cigarette? Maybe that had driven him from the house? Or maybe he'd simply needed to get away from the horrible silent waiting. The hovering agents. The pain in his wife's eyes. Maybe he'd wanted to sit with his friend for a minute and pretend that it was any other lazy afternoon?

Or maybe he was an asshole who didn't understand that part of his job as husband and father was to step up in the tough times.

"Troy," A.L. said in greeting.

He waved but he didn't get up. He looked very tired.

"I'm Steven Hanzel," the other man said, his voice too loud. He bounced up and extended his hand.

"Detective McKittridge," A.L. said.

"I'm assuming there's no news," Troy said. "Otherwise, Leah would have beat you out here."

"No news, sir."

"It's crazy," Steven said. "Just crazy." His cell phone buzzed and he picked it up. Looked at the screen for a couple seconds. Then the phone went back into his shirt pocket. "Good news is that we've picked up another twenty grand."

Troy nodded. "Fund-raising site. Steven got it going," he said, apparently for A.L.'s benefit.

"I heard something about it," A.L. said.

"Least I could do," Steven said. "People want to help. Donations are coming in from all over the country. It's amazing. Just...crazy."

Crazy was evidently Steven Hanzel's go-to word. And while A.L. wasn't a guy normally hung up on political correctness, it seemed rather gauche to be talking about the money pouring in. But then again, Hanzel was a banker. His world was money. His repeated use of the word *crazy* made A.L. think of those first few minutes after he'd met Leah and Troy on Wednesday afternoon. Leah had said it was terrifying and Troy had seemed to correct her by saying it was crazy. Were Troy and his friend together so much that Troy was picking up his vocabulary?

"I was hoping to have a minute," A.L. said, looking at Troy.

"Of course," Troy said. He glanced at his friend. "I'll see you later."

"Oh yeah, yeah. That's fine. You call me. Whenever, you know." Hanzel talked as he walked backwards out of the garage.

A.L. waited until he had turned and gotten halfway back to the street before speaking. "I wanted to ask you about your business."

"Why? What's that got to do with anything?"

He sounded almost panicked.

"We can't ignore the possibility that Emma's disappearance is somehow related to an issue that somebody might have with you. Perhaps a disgruntled customer. An angry former employee."

"I got three guys working in my shop. The same three guys who have been working there since I bought it. Hell, even before that."

"Names?" A.L. pulled out his notebook.

"Davy Grace, Pete Seoul, Cory Prider. Listen, I've known these guys since I was in high school. Davy was in my same class. Pete and Cory are older but that doesn't mean anything. I'm their boss but we're also friends."

"Never any issues?"

Troy threw up his right hand. "Hell, yes, there are issues. Sometimes they screw up. Sometimes they even do shitty work, which really pisses me off because they're better than that and with so much competition, that will kill you."

"How's business?" A.L. asked.

"Fine. Yeah, it's fine."

"Not sorry you bought it?"

"No. Why would I be?"

"Just asking," A.L. said. "Owning your own business is tough. If there's nothing left at the end of the month, you don't get paid, right?"

"We're doing just fine," he said.

A.L. decided to let it go for the time. "You been in touch with any of your employees?"

"Not today. They knew I wasn't going to be in."

A.L. would swing by the garage next. "Let's talk about your customers. Any problems with anybody lately?"

"No. I mean, maybe."

"Which is it?" A.L. asked.

"Davy did some work on a vehicle earlier this week and he forgot to clamp a hose or if he did clamp it, it popped off. Anyway, long story short, customer drove the vehicle out of our shop, got halfway home with her seven-year-old and five-year-old and the engine overheated. She had a cell phone and called her husband. But before he could get there, another vehicle stopped. A couple redneck assholes. Didn't touch her but I guess they scared her pretty bad. Anyway, husband arrives, assholes leave, and wife calls us to tell us we'll be hearing from their attorney."

"Did you?"

"Not yet. I offered six free oil changes. Wife told me where I could shove them."

"Did you fix her car a second time?"

"Nope. They had it towed to Morton's Garage."

"What's the customer's name?"

"I do not want you going to see her. Maybe she's over being pissed. This could just stoke the fire and she decides to call the fucking lawyer. I can't be sued. I can't…" He ran his hands over his short hair. "Listen, she's got kids of her own. She isn't going to do something to one of mine."

"Unfortunately," A.L. said, "we don't know if that's

true. Maybe she feels that you endangered her kids and now she wants to return the favor. What's her name?"

"Gi-Gi. Gi-Gi Thompson. Her husband's name is Barrett."

A.L. wrote it down. "Anybody else that might have a beef with you?"

Troy pressed his lips together. Looked at the back of his house. Then shook his head. "I can't think of anybody."

"Get along with your neighbors?" A.L. asked.

"I had words this summer with a guy whose dog was shitting in my yard but other than that, it's good."

"What was his name?" A.L. asked.

"There's no need to go talk to him. I dealt with it. It's over."

"It's better if we decide who we need to talk to," A.L. said. "What was his name?"

"I don't even know his name. But he lives across the street, a couple doors that way. His house has the ugly blue siding."

"Thank you. If you think of anything else, please let us know."

"Yeah, sure." He started to reach for the pack of cigarettes but pulled his hands back and stuffed each hand under a thigh.

He'd been fast but not fast enough. His hands were trembling.

Troy Whitman seemed about to break.

A.L. found the neighbor with the blue siding sitting in a lawn chair in his garage. Figured it was a thing in the neighborhood. He was not smoking but he did have two empty bottles of cheap beer next to his chair. He was retirement age with thinning gray hair and wore an old Rolling Stones T-shirt and blue jeans.

"Hello," A.L. said. "I'm Detective McKittridge with the Baywood Police Department." He held out his badge, gave the guy plenty of time to look at it. "What's your name?"

"Why? Am I under arrest?" the man asked, his tone serious. Then he smiled. "Just screwing with you. Roger Martin."

"Thank you, Mr. Martin. I wanted to ask you about your relationship with Troy Whitman."

"We don't have a relationship. He lives down the street. That's it."

"He said that the two of you recently had words after he complained about your dog taking a dump in his yard."

The man smiled again. "I've been walking my dog past his house for two years, ever since we moved in here. Didn't realize who he was until my wife took her car to his garage about two months ago. Thank God I got a quote before I had him do the work. A thousand bucks. Double, literally double, what the guy six blocks down the street charged me. I told Lois that Troy Whitman was a crook. That's when I decided to let my dog shit in his yard. After all, he's shitting on his customers."

Troy hadn't said anything about a disagreement over a quote. "Did you and Troy discuss the quote?"

"No. Maybe Lois called them up and told them we were taking it somewhere else. I don't know and

I didn't care. I hate it when people think they can rip senior citizens off."

A.L. did not think this man had a five-year-old hidden in his house. "Are you aware that Mr. Whitman's daughter is missing?"

"You couldn't be alive in Baywood and not know that. Goddamn shame. Nobody deserves for that to happen. I may not like his business practices but I wouldn't wish that on anybody."

"Where were you, Mr. Martin, on Wednesday morning?"

The man gave A.L. a look that told A.L. that he was now the equivalent of dog shit. "Lois and I volunteer at the homeless shelter on Portuana Street every Wednesday. We were there by 8:00 and didn't leave for several hours."

"Okay. Thank you," A.L. said. "I won't take up any more of your time."

"I got a lot of time," Roger Martin said. "I sit here a good portion of the day. And sometimes, at night, when my back is bothering me, I come out here, too." He paused. "You know, I can see the Whitmans' driveway from right here."

A.L. moved to a spot behind Roger Martin's chair. He did have a good view of the house and the start of the driveway. Couldn't see as far back as the garage, however. There was a reason the man was making a point of the view. "Ever see anything interesting?" A.L. asked.

The man shrugged. "Lots of coming and going from the Whitman house. Real late at night sometimes.

Maybe he's fixing cars 24/7. I just don't know. Guess I don't have anything more to say about that."

Roger Martin really didn't seem to care for Troy Whitman.

"Goodbye, sir," A.L. said.

"Back at ya. Hope you find that little girl. I really do."

Rena focused on the kids who had been signed in between 7:10 and 7:25. There were five. She cross-referenced the kids with the parent list and called the first number.

"Hello," a woman said.

"Is this Angie Tate?"

"Yes."

"This is Detective Morgan from the Baywood Police Department. Would you have a few minutes that I could ask you a couple questions in relation to the Lakeside Learning Center?"

"Yes, of course."

"You have a daughter in the three- and early four-year-old room, right?"

"Right. Jenna."

"On Wednesday, you signed her into her room at 7:14. Does that ring a bell?"

"Yes."

"Great. When you arrived, do you recall seeing anyone in the lobby area, either near the office area or even in the larger play space?"

"There were people coming and going, about the same as usual. It's sort of a common drop-off time. People trying to get to work by 8:00, I guess."

"Did you see anybody who looked out of place or odd, like they didn't belong there?"

"If I'd have seen anything like that, I'd have already said something to somebody."

"Of course," Rena said. "But I just have to ask the question. How about teachers or staff employed by the center? Were any of them in the lobby?"

"No. I'm confident of that."

"Okay. One last question, do you know Elaine Broadstreet?"

"That's Emma's grandma, isn't it?"

"Yes. Do you know her?"

"I don't *know* her but I'd recognize her. She's always very friendly."

"Do you recall seeing her on Wednesday morning?"

"I never saw her or Emma."

Rena thanked the woman and hung up the phone. She tried to hang on to what A.L. had said, that they perhaps couldn't see incremental gain but with every conversation they had to be getting closer. But it was hard. It seemed as if Emma Whitman was truly just gone.

She drew in a breath and looked up the next number.

A.L. called Rena from his vehicle. "How's it going?"

"I've managed to get ahold of four of the five parents who dropped kids off around the same time as Emma," she said. "I didn't get anything from anybody."

"There's always one more."

"Actually two. There is one parent who didn't indicate a drop-off time who we should probably contact."

"Okay. I can work on those. But for now, I want to

swing by and pick you up. We need to visit Garage on Division."

"I was hoping I could go home smelling like oil tonight. People really don't realize how glamorous police work is," Rena said.

"And they don't give a shit," A.L. said. "See you in fifteen."

Rena was standing outside holding two cups of coffee when A.L. pulled up. She got in and handed A.L. one.

"Thank you," he said.

"How were the Whitmans? Leah videotaping or sabotaging anybody new?"

"She thought she heard Emma crying in her room last night."

"Christ. Sorry, it was a bad joke. I hate this."

"I know. I'm not sure Troy is in much better shape. He's literally shaking. But I think he has more support than Leah seems to. At least his friend was over at the house."

"Who's that?"

"Steven Hanzel. He started the fund-raising site. I guess it's going well."

"One good thing about the internet and social media. Somebody in Utah who has never met you can push a button and money comes from their account into yours. Magic."

"Makes the old days when we circulated printed flyers when somebody was missing seem pretty archaic," A.L. said.

"Not so archaic. I saw volunteers out this morning, tacking up posters of Emma onto telephone poles."

"Do everything you can and then one more thing," A.L. said. "Speaking of which, I didn't get a chance to call Dusty Frogg yet."

"She's probably not our highest priority."

"I did, however, speak to Roger Martin. He's a neighbor who appears to encourage his dog to shit in the Whitmans' yard."

"Nice."

"Yeah. He thinks Troy tried to gouge his wife, Lois, on some repair work."

"You think he has anything to do with Emma's disappearance?" Rena asked.

"Nope. But he made sure I knew that Troy Whitman leaves his house late at night sometimes."

Rena shrugged. "Gabe and I sometimes go out for breakfast at midnight at the diner on Forest View. It's not a criminal activity."

A.L. nodded. "Especially if you're getting the biscuits and gravy. That place knows what they're doing."

He turned and pulled into a space to the side of Garage on Division. There were two other cars parked nearby, both empty. The building had three bays and all the doors were up, probably to let some fresh air in. He could only see one car about four feet in the air, supported by a hoist. The other two bays were empty. He didn't see any people working. "Speaking of knowing what they're doing, this place doesn't seem to be doing much."

"That looks like the office," Rena said, pointing to a door at the far end of the building.

"Yeah." It was difficult to see through the mostly

closed blinds but he caught a shadow of something or somebody. "Let's go," he said.

A bell rang when he opened the door. There was a chest-high counter with a computer and a printer on it. Also a landline phone and a potted plant that looked as if it hadn't been watered for a while. Behind the counter were two old-looking office chairs. In front of the counter and to the left was a small waiting area with three equally old guest chairs, the folding variety type, and a water cooler with a sleeve of paper cups on the table next to it.

"Hello," A.L. called out.

"Hey, there," came the response from somewhere in the back. It was a man, his voice a little gravelly. "Be out in a minute."

It was probably less than that when a man hurried through the back door. "Afternoon. What can I do for you, folks?"

"I'm Detective Morgan and this is my partner, Detective McKittridge." They both held out badges. "And you are?"

"Davy Grace, ma'am."

She really hated being called ma'am. Made her feel about eighty.

The man was late twenties with a wiry build. The thumb on his right hand was badly bruised. Rena noticed that as he wiped his hand on a dirty rag before offering it to her and then A.L. "Thanks for making some time for us," Rena said.

"Never had the police come see me at work before," he said.

"Just a few questions," Rena assured him.

"Can we do this outside?"

"We can," she said.

He led them out to the side of the building, where he promptly lit up a cigarette. They were facing west and the late afternoon sun beat down on them.

"I think I know why you're here," Davy said. "We all feel horrible about what's happened. Emma is one of the sweetest little girls I've ever met."

"How long have you worked here, Mr. Grace?" A.L. asked.

"I been here going on seven years."

"So you were here when Troy Whitman bought the business?" Rena asked.

"Yes, ma'am. And I was damn glad that he did. I live less than a mile from here and I like my commute, if you know what I mean."

There wasn't much bad traffic in Baywood but Rena did understand. Gabe had said something very similar recently now that he had quit his job as a financial consultant where he might put on hundreds of miles a week and become a full-time student again. He only had to be on campus two days a week. Everything else was done online.

"How would you characterize your relationship with Troy Whitman?" Rena asked.

"He's the boss. I respect that."

"Respect him?" A.L. asked.

"Uh…sure. Of course. I mean, he's made some mistakes. We all have. But I've known Troy my whole life. We were in school together. Hell, I was the one who told him the garage was for sale."

"Troy told us that there'd recently been a situation where a couple was very upset because the wife brought her car in, you worked on it, and then later that afternoon, it stalled out on the highway."

Davy's eyes darkened. "He told you about that, huh?"

"Only because we asked him if there might be any customers who were upset with him or the garage."

"Well, okay then."

Davy was a little touchy. "Do you think Mr. or Mrs. Thompson might have been angry enough to do something to hurt Troy Whitman or his family?"

"They said they were going to sue. I don't think that's happened. Least I haven't heard anything. But if you're asking if I think they would have hurt Emma, well, that just doesn't make sense. Only an asshole would do that and while they were both upset, I didn't get the impression that they were that kind of people."

"We'd like their home address," Rena said. "That would be on their paperwork, right?"

"Yeah." Davy took one last puff off his half-smoked cigarette and threw it to the ground. He put it out with the heel of his work shoe. "We can get it inside."

When Rena saw the address, she didn't recognize it. "Where is this?" she asked, as she copied it down.

"It's way out there, in the county, in one of them new houses that they're building around Lemming's Lake. I hear some of the houses are going for a million dollars," Davy said.

It would be more than a forty-five-minute drive. Long way to come to get a vehicle serviced. Although to be fair, there probably weren't that many other full-service garages that would have been closer for them.

"Thank you," she said. "Were you here at the garage this past Wednesday?"

"Uh…no. I was out of town, at a funeral."

"Where was the funeral?" A.L. asked.

"Dover. It's north of here."

About ninety-seven miles, to be exact. She'd never been to Dover, never heard much about it. Until Emma Whitman had gone missing. Now it seemed to be popping up everywhere. "Whose funeral?" she asked.

"My uncle's."

"His name?" A.L. asked.

Now Davy frowned at them. "I don't see…"

"Just making sure we've got full information," Rena said pleasantly.

"Burt Chrysler."

"Like the car?" A.L. asked.

"Just like it," Davy said. "People always ask that. He used to kid around, tell people that his other house was in Detroit. I used to love to see their faces. Spent almost every summer with Uncle Burt when I was a kid."

"In Dover?" A.L. asked.

"Of course. He didn't really have a house in Detroit."

A.L. pressed his lips together.

"You were in Dover all day?" Rena asked.

"Couple hours. There was a nice lunch after the funeral."

"What did you do the rest of the day?" A.L. asked.

"Drove around. I like to do that."

"Was anyone with you?" A.L. asked.

"No. I asked my cousin to go but I guess she didn't feel quite the same about Uncle Burt."

Maybe hadn't wanted to be in a car with Davy for

any length of time. "Mr. Grace, do you know a Coyote Frogg from when you visited the Dover area?"

Davy shook his head.

"He has memorable red hair," Rena said.

"I like redheads," Davy said, looking at Rena's hair. Gross. "Mr. Grace, are you the only one working today?"

Davy shrugged. "Yes. Both Pete and Cory got some kind of flu. Or so they say." He smiled.

"You think that might not be true?" A.L. asked.

"They're probably fishing. They know that Troy has his head somewhere else so there's little danger of it catching up to them."

A.L. had said that Troy had known Pete Seoul and Cory Prider for a long time. But now they were potentially goofing off while Troy was dealing with something horrific. With friends like that, who needed enemies? "You happen to have phone numbers for Pete and Cory?" Rena asked.

"Cell numbers," Davy said.

"Good enough," she said. They would call and ask the two to come to the station to answer some questions. That should get their attention.

Pete Seoul and Cory Prider had indeed been fishing. Pete's nose was sunburned and Cory's pants looked as if he'd fallen in. They both looked to be in their early forties. They took Cory first.

"You got a Coke or something?" Cory asked as he leaned back in his chair.

Rena started to get up but settled down as A.L. said, "No."

"Water?" Cory asked.

Rena didn't budge. She knew what was coming. A.L. had made up his mind. These guys were pieces of shit.

"No," A.L. said. "You were absent from work today?"

"Yeah."

"Sick?" A.L. asked.

Cory shrugged, maybe a little sheepishly. "Mental health day."

If he'd needed fresh air, he could have joined the volunteers searching for Emma. "I imagine Troy Whitman's mental health isn't all that great right now," she said. "Probably doesn't need to be worrying about his business."

"We did him a fucking favor. If we don't work, we don't get paid. And quite frankly, there is barely enough to keep Dutiful Davy busy."

"You don't like your coworker?" Rena asked.

Cory shrugged. "He's…let's just say that he's a simple guy. And sometimes that can get on a person's nerves."

"Not enough work. Not crazy about your coworker. Doesn't sound as if there are great benefits. I guess I'm curious why you stay," A.L. asked.

"Some work is better than no work. And I like Troy Whitman well enough. I feel damn sorry for him. A missing kid is bad."

"You have children, Mr. Prider?" Rena asked.

"No wife, no kids. That I know about, anyway." He smiled without showing any teeth.

Neither A.L. nor Rena smiled back. "Walk me through your day on this past Wednesday."

Prider let out a loud sigh. "I left my apartment around 6:30. Stopped at Pancake Magic for breakfast like I usually do, and got to work about 7:15. I was the first one there. I unlocked the doors, made the coffee and finished a brake job on a car that had been left overnight."

"Who got to work next?" Rena asked.

"Shit, I don't know. Davy or Pete. One of them. I was busy, you know, and it ain't my job to babysit them."

"You're sure they were both at work that day?"

Prider leaned back and looked at the ceiling as if the answer was written there. "Now that I think about it, Davy wasn't at work that day. So it was Pete. But don't ask me what time he got there. I don't fucking know."

"Do you *recall* what time Troy came to work that morning?" A.L. asked, his voice hard.

Cory scrunched up his forehead. "I think he was there by 9:00."

"Is that earlier or later than usual?" Rena asked.

"Later," Cory said. "Lots of mornings, he's there when I arrive. Already has the coffee made."

"Did the two of you happen to talk about why he was later than usual?" A.L. asked.

"No," Cory said. "He's the boss. He can come in whenever he wants. None of my business."

"Have you talked to Troy in the last couple of days? Since Wednesday?" A.L. asked.

"No. I sent him a text when I heard the news about his daughter. Just told him we were all pulling for him."

"Did he respond?" Rena asked.

"I think so. He said thanks or something like that."

"When you're absent, do you call in before your shift?" Rena asked.

"Sometimes. But I didn't want to bug him today. We do time sheets. That's how he knows what days to pay us for."

"Do you know Leah Whitman?" Rena asked.

"Of course. She comes by sometimes. Calls the business phone when Troy isn't answering his cell."

"Does he not answer his cell often?" A.L. asked.

"Only when he doesn't want to talk to his wife," Cory said, once again doing the weird smile with no teeth.

They needed to end this. Before she got sick. It was way worse than Davy saying he liked redheads. Rena stood up. "Thank you for your time, Mr. Prider. If you should think of anything that might help us find Emma Whitman, we'd appreciate a call." Both she and A.L. passed over cards.

"Sure," he said.

Rena escorted the man out of the building, using a door that didn't require her to pass by Pete Seoul, who was still waiting. While Cory Prider had given them nothing that was especially helpful, she still didn't want the two of them comparing stories.

Once she deposited Prider on the sidewalk, she returned to the conference room where A.L. sat. He was reviewing his notes.

"If he's a regular at Pancake Magic, Traci probably knows him," Rena said.

"I'm going to pretend that I have no knowledge that the likes of him has any intersect with my daughter. Do you feel as if you need a shower?" A.L. asked.

"Sort of. What do you think Troy Whitman was doing between 7:15 and 9:00? His house is only a fifteen-minute drive to Garage on Division."

"I know. That's what I was checking in my notes. He said that he was anxious because he doesn't generally do mornings, that Leah did them. That meshes with Prider saying that Troy is usually the first one in."

"But not on Wednesday," Rena said. "We're going to need to ask him."

"Yeah. Let's finish up with Pete Seoul first."

Rena fetched the man from the waiting room. He was probably about the same age as Cory Prider but he carried some extra weight in his belly and his right knee looked a little stiff when he walked.

"Mr. Seoul, we'd like to talk to you about your job at Garage on Division," Rena said.

"Okay."

"How long have you worked there?" she asked.

"Twenty years."

"You've seen some changes I suspect," she said.

"More than some."

"Help me understand that better," she said.

"Simple. Used to be I could tell you what was wrong with a car by listening to it. Now I got to hook it up to a machine that tells me."

He didn't sound angry. Just matter-of-fact. "So you were employed at the garage when Troy Whitman purchased it."

"Yeah."

"How did you feel about that?"

"Okay."

Rena smiled at the man, trying to remember that

honey could be better than vinegar. "What's your re-lationship with Troy Whitman?"

"He's my boss."

"I understand that," she said. "Are you friends out-side of work?"

"No."

"Do you know his wife?"

"Not really."

She was not a dentist but she was pulling teeth. "Mr. Seoul, can you walk us through your day last Wednesday?"

"I worked."

A.L. leaned forward. "What time did you arrive at work?"

"Seven thirty. That's when I always arrive. I leave my house at 7:21 and it takes me nine minutes to get there."

"Was anybody else at the garage when you arrived?" A.L. asked.

"Cory Prider."

"What time did Davy Grace or Troy Whitman ar-rive?"

"I don't think Davy worked that day. Least I never saw him. Troy rolled in when I was taking my break. I take that from 9:00 to 9:15 every day."

She just bet he did. "Mr. Seoul, are you aware of any customers or other employees who might be angry with Troy Whitman?"

He shook his head.

"We're aware of a complaint that came in from a Mr. and Mrs. Thompson after their car was worked on at the garage and subsequently had trouble."

"I didn't work on that car."

"Right."

"Have you spoken to Troy Whitman since the disappearance of his daughter?"

Pete Seoul shook his head.

She was going to give it one more shot. "Anything else that you can tell us that might be helpful?"

"Nope. But I guess I have been thinking about Troy's storage shed."

A.L. put his pen down. "I've been to Troy Whitman's house. There's no storage shed."

"Not there. At Alcamay Corners. He rents a unit there." The man stood up. "Just saying, it might be a good idea if somebody checked that."

Twelve

Alcamay Corners. Everybody in Baywood knew the intersection of Alcamay Road and Main Street. On one corner was the Alcamay Funeral Home, the biggest and busiest funeral home in Baywood. On the second corner was a cemetery, making it a quick and convenient trip for the dead. On the third, a restaurant. They had a nice room for the funeral lunches. On the fourth and final, rows and rows of storage sheds. Maybe the dead people's furniture got stored there.

"Fuck," A.L. said when Rena got back to the room after escorting Pete Seoul out. They'd hardly been able to get him out fast enough.

"You don't really think…"

"I don't know what I think. But we need to take a look. Right now," A.L. said. "Not only do we have a storage shed that we haven't looked at, we've got an unexplained absence if both Pete and Cory are right that Troy didn't show up for work until 9:00."

"Are you going to call Troy? Leah?"

"Nope," A.L. said. They'd done a property search

on their names. Standard procedure. Nothing had come up. A rental unit wouldn't.

"We'll need a warrant," Rena said. "I'll figure out who owns those storage sheds and which unit belongs to Troy."

"Make it quick, Morgan. I'm going to give Faster's office a heads-up."

Forty minutes later, they were on their way. The owner had agreed to meet them at Unit 49, which Troy had rented for the prior seven months.

"I want to know but I don't want to know," Rena said. "Does that make sense?"

It did. The possibilities of what they might find in the shed were enough to make the most experienced cop shaky. A.L. could feel his own stomach churning. Bad things happening to a child were horrific enough, but the idea that the parent could be responsible was so goddamn dark that A.L.'s chest felt heavy and it was work to breathe. "He'd have fooled me," A.L. said. "I know the parents are the first place we look but I have to admit, I didn't like either Troy or Leah for this."

"Same," Rena said. "I hope our guts were right."

"We'll know in five minutes."

Right on the edge of 7:00 p.m., they made a right-hand turn onto the property. There were rows and rows of big storage sheds, the kind that had garage door openings. Rena pointed toward the left. "Try that row," she said, pointing at the second to last.

It was the third from the end. There was already a white pickup truck parked by it. A man, maybe fifty, wearing jeans and a short-sleeved shirt, got out. He waved at them.

A.L. beached it and he and Rena got out fast. Both carried flashlights. Now that they were here, A.L. couldn't get the goddamn shed open fast enough. "Detectives McKittridge and Morgan," he said. "Can you open that?"

"I can." The man looked down at his feet. "If you're looking here for the reason I think you're looking here, I hope like hell that you're wrong."

A.L. didn't answer.

The man handed A.L. a garage door opener. Then he went back to his truck. Likely afraid of what he might see.

A.L. pushed the button. The door inched up.

A.L. looked at Rena. He was pretty sure she wasn't breathing.

Then the door was halfway up. Dark inside. They flipped on their flashlights.

Five more inches.

"Jesus," Rena whispered.

Indeed.

"What the fuck is this?" A.L. asked.

Rena had no words.

A.L. took two steps into the garage. Had to stop there. Because there was a zebra in his way. A stuffed one, that is.

And the zebra had friends. Lions and tigers and bears. Oh my. And on the shelves that lined two walls, there were possums and squirrels and, yep, that was a hawk. She looked at A.L.

"Close your mouth," she said softly. She found a light switch and flipped it.

He turned to look at her. "Take a good look around."

"That's all you're going to say?" she asked incredulously. "Take a good look around," she repeated.

"I don't know what else to say," he said.

"You think Troy did these himself?" Rena asked. She was moving carefully among the animals, making sure that there was no five-year-old child hidden somewhere. "That he's a taxidermist?"

"I don't know. Some of these seem pretty old," he said. "Like this one," he said, pointing at a stuffed monkey that looked as if it had seen better days. Better dead days, that is.

"Right," she said. "You think he forgot about this place or is this a secret he's trying to hide?"

"Leah never said anything about it, either."

"Maybe she's embarrassed. Or maybe she doesn't know." Rena paused. "I'm not going to be the one to tell her," she added.

"Pete Seoul deliberately led us here," A.L. said.

"Yeah, that's interesting," Rena said. "I guess it's possible that he knew about the storage shed but never had the opportunity to get a glimpse inside. Or he had and he wanted us to know that Troy Whitman had an unusual...habit, collection, fetish... Hell, I don't know the right word."

"When I talked to Troy, he made it sound like he and Davy, Cory and Pete didn't just work together but they were good friends. I sort of got that feeling from Davy, although I think he's just a friendly type. I definitely didn't get that feeling from Cory or Pete."

"Agree. Is this more of what we saw between Troy and his parents? He either can't help but paint a rosy picture or he's obtuse to the way things really are."

"Whatever, we're done here."

They flipped the light off, stepped outside the garage and A.L. closed the door. They walked back to the truck, where the owner still sat.

"Everything okay?" the man asked.

"Yeah. Fine," A.L. said.

"Whew. That's a relief. I like Troy Whitman and I've been feeling real bad for that family. My wife and I made a donation to the fund. We were happy to do it. We got three kids of our own. Just wanted to do something to help, you know."

"Thanks for meeting us here," Rena said. They got into A.L.'s vehicle and drove off. "You know, in the movies, after the bad guy kills somebody, they do a flashback to when he was a kid and he killed the neighbor's cats. That isn't this, is it?"

A.L. didn't answer.

"I saw a story once about a guy who collected toenail clippings. That would be even odder, right?" Rena said.

Now A.L. gave her a sideways glance.

"I'm rambling, I know," she said. "That was just so…odd. I'll be quiet now." She sat for a minute. "I don't like it that Davy Grace has a connection to Dover. That he was, in fact, in Dover the day that Emma went missing. And that he spent substantial time in Dover."

"Agree," A.L. said.

"I'm going to follow up on the uncle's obituary."

"I'm going to go talk to Troy and get an explanation of where he was between 7:08, when Elaine pulled away, and roughly 9:00 when he arrived at work."

"Maybe he was at the casino, filming Leah who was filming Elaine," Rena said.

"That would be fucked up, wouldn't it?" A.L. said, shaking his head. "After that, I think I'd better go see Barrett and Gi-Gi Thompson."

"I wonder if Gi-Gi is short for something."

"I'll make sure to ask her," A.L. said.

Troy was no longer in the garage. He was in the basement. Leah was in bed. A.L. got all this from a young FBI agent who was playing solitaire on his computer at the dining table.

Everybody filling in hours in their own way.

A.L. opened the basement door and walked downstairs. He saw Troy stretched out on an old leather recliner, a TV remote in one hand and what looked to be a cocktail in the other. He was flipping through channels.

A.L. knocked on the wall. Troy looked over his shoulder. "News?" he asked, putting his footrest down.

A.L. shook his head. "Sorry, no." Without invitation, he sat on the couch. "Have a minute?"

"Yeah," Troy said, shutting off the television. "I wasn't watching anything. Can't concentrate."

A.L. was reminded of something that Doug Franklin had said about Corrine Antler's parents. That in a week they'd aged about ten years. It had been about half that for Troy Whitman but he looked well on his way.

His eyes were dark, his hair was unkempt, and it looked as if he was sleeping in his clothes. "Did you hear," he asked, "that one of the drones thought they had something today?"

A.L. had. One of the heat-seeking drones had identified an object in a barn. It had been promptly investigated. It had been a child, just two years older than Emma, watching over her dog that was having puppies.

"Guess the good news is that they found something that was there," Troy said.

"Right," A.L. said. "Nobody has given up hope."

Troy shook his head. "I think Leah has. She took some pills to go to sleep. Said she just can't stand this anymore. That's why I'm here and not out searching. I figured somebody needed to be here for the phone."

A.L. glanced at the empty glass. "Got to stay sober for that," he said.

"Stopped at two," Troy said. "When I really wanted the whole fucking bottle." He stared at A.L. "You got kids?"

"A daughter. Senior in high school."

"So you got your own worries."

"Not like this," A.L. said. "This is about as bad as it gets. We know that."

Troy said nothing.

They sat in silence for a few minutes. Finally, A.L. shifted. "I need to ask you about your day on Wednesday."

"Okay."

"What time did you leave for work?"

"After Elaine picked up Emma?"

"Right after? Ten minutes later? An hour later?"

"Pretty soon after," Troy said.

"And how far a drive is it to your work?"

"Fifteen minutes."

"So you estimate that you probably arrived at Garage on Division by 7:45 at the latest?"

"That sounds right."

"And what if I told you that your employees who were working that day estimate that you arrived around 9:00?"

Troy shrugged. "They're wrong."

"They seemed pretty confident."

"Maybe they didn't see me. I remember I was doing some paperwork up in the office. They're back in the bays, thinking about other things. Cars these days are complicated. You got to really be thinking about what you're doing."

It seemed reasonable. The office was separate from the rest of the garage. But both Cory and Pete had seemed sure. But could either man be trusted? "You recall any customers who came in on Wednesday morning who could verify that you were there?"

Troy shook his head. "Sorry. Nobody that I can think of."

"You've got a scheduling system of some type, right?" A.L. said. "Something that allows you to keep track of what vehicles are coming in for what type of service?"

"Yeah."

"On a computer?"

"Yeah."

"I'd like to see that for Wednesday. In fact, for all this week."

"I can't access it from home," Troy said quickly. "And I shouldn't leave right now."

He could be a hard-ass and demand that they go right now. Or, he could get a warrant and they could confiscate the computer. He decided to take a more measured approach. After all, he could not forget that Troy Whitman had lost a daughter and there was still no real reason to suspect that he was anything but a grieving father here. However, if he found out that there was an unexplained absence of more than ninety minutes, all bets were off. "Then, tomorrow," A.L. said. "Early tomorrow morning."

"I'll print you off a copy," Troy said.

A.L. shook his head. "I'll meet you there at 8:00 with a technician. We'll have him or her get it off the computer." A.L. paused. "Don't go inside until we get there. Don't access your computer before we get there. Trust me on this, my person will know if you did and be able to find anything that's been modified, added or deleted." He was willing to cut the man a little slack but he wanted to make sure there was no question that Troy understood that this wasn't a suggestion but rather a demand.

Troy stared at him. "Anything else?" His voice was just short of hostile.

"Yeah. You should know that we executed a search warrant for your storage shed at Alcamay Corners. The landlord opened the door for us."

Troy said nothing.

"It would have been helpful if you'd mentioned that you had a storage shed."

"There was no reason to," Troy said.

"In the spirit of good faith and all," A.L. said. "Does Leah know about it?"

"She knows that I have an interest in taxidermy. She does not know about the extent of my collection or the rental unit. I used to keep a few of the pieces here, in the basement, but she didn't like looking at them when she came down to do laundry. She wanted me to sell them. I told her that I did."

But he hadn't. In fact, it sounded as if he'd obtained more since that conversation.

"You look as if you disapprove, Detective," Troy said, a challenge in his tone.

"Just don't think lies are the best foundation for a strong marriage. But that falls outside the scope of this investigation. Have a good night, sir," A.L. said. Then he walked out of the house and across the small yard. Sunset had faded into full-blown darkness. The end of another day.

But not for him. Even though his conversation with Troy had left him with a bad taste in his mouth, there were more people to talk to.

Gi-Gi was short for Georgiana. "My father had been George and was attached to the name," Gi-Gi Thompson explained. She, Barrett and A.L. were sitting at her kitchen table.

After learning that he was a police officer who wanted to talk about an incident that had happened at Garage on Division, the Thompsons had sent their two grade-school children upstairs to finish homework. Even though he'd arrived well after dinner, dirty dishes were still on the counter and the smell of tuna and noodle casserole lingered, at odds with the gleaming stainless steel appliances, the quartz countertops and the four thousand feet of living space.

"Tell me about your recent interactions with Garage on Division."

"We're pretty unhappy with the work that got done on our vehicle," Barrett said. "It put my wife and my children in a bad spot. A dangerous spot. Are you here about the report that we filed?"

"In a way," A.L. said. "I recently had a conversation with a few people who mentioned the incident."

Barrett looked at Gi-Gi. "I told you it was a mistake to post something about it." He looked at A.L. "She *loves* social media."

"That's not where I got it," A.L. said. "But if you could walk me through your experience, I'd appreciate it."

"My wife's car had been running rough for a couple weeks. We had used Garage on Division before and had been happy with the work. On September 9, we dropped it off and they had it for hours. Five hundred and sixty-two dollars later, I was promised that the vehicle was ready for pickup," Barrett said.

Gi-Gi leaned forward. "Barrett dropped me off at the garage and went back to work. I drove it to pick up our young children from school. I did that and was halfway home to our house when it died. Just died. Left us stranded. Well, the first thing I did was call Barrett."

"I was at work. Left as quickly as I could but it wasn't soon enough. A couple of redneck local boys stopped, supposedly to help."

"They had horrible teeth. You know, the kind that meth users have."

A.L. allowed himself to wonder how many meth users Gi-Gi Thompson encountered on a regular basis.

"I saw *Breaking Bad*," she added. "Every season."

There it was.

"If Barrett hadn't come when he did, there's no telling what might have happened. I mean, they were looking at my kids and it was giving me the chills." Gi-Gi stopped. Put her red-painted index finger into the air. "I just thought of something. What if… Oh, I can't even say it."

"Just say it, honey," Barrett said.

"What if those two men are behind Emma Whitman's disappearance? What if they took her? Oh, Barrett. Doesn't that just make you sick?"

Barrett Thompson looked at A.L. "My wife isn't accusing anybody but I've learned over the years not to dismiss her ideas. She's generally spot-on."

"Can you describe the men in greater detail?" he asked, looking at both Gi-Gi and Barrett.

"White," Gi-Gi said.

"Hair and eye color?"

"One had brown hair and the other had red hair. I don't remember their eyes. Creepy, if that's a color."

"Height, weight?"

Gi-Gi looked at Barrett. He was evidently the height and weight expert.

"They were both kind of wiry. The redhead, I'd guess five-ten, maybe one fifty," Barrett said. "The other was taller, could have been six feet. But not more than a hundred and seventy pounds."

"Any distinguishing marks or tattoos?" A.L. asked.

"Not that I saw," Gi-Gi said.

Coyote Frogg had a sleeve tattoo. Hard to miss unless he was wearing long sleeves. "Do you recall what they were wearing?"

"Dirty jeans. Shirts. Nothing memorable," Gi-Gi said.

"Long sleeves?" A.L. asked.

"Yeah, I think so." She smiled. "I guess that's sort of weird. It's been hot."

"What were they driving?" A.L. asked.

"An old Jeep. The kind where the sides come off," Barrett said.

"Color?"

"White. It was filthy, though," Gi-Gi said. "Looked as if it hadn't seen a car wash in several years."

"Noticeable dents or marks?" A.L. asked.

"Not that I noticed," Barrett said.

"Did you get a license plate?" A.L. asked.

Gi-Gi snorted, a most unladylike noise. Even Barrett looked surprised. "We were a little busy, Detective," she said.

He'd had enough of these people. But he had one more question. "When they drove off, what direction did they go?"

"North," Barrett said. "Away from town."

North. In the direction of Dover. A.L. stood up. "Thank you for your time."

It was almost 9:00 p.m. by the time A.L. drove back to the police station, the conversation with the Thompsons running through his head. The physical description was close enough to what Mr. Gibacki from Panini Playground had given them to call it the same.

When he got back to his desk, Rena was at hers. He quickly brought her up to speed on his conversation with the Thompsons. "Now, what did you find out about the funeral in Dover?"

"There was one. Burt Chrysler at the Smithe Funeral Home. No church service, everything at the funeral home. I reviewed the obituary and there was no specific mention of Davy Grace, although the obituary did say numerous nieces and nephews."

"Cameras at the funeral home?" A.L. asked.

"Yes. I'm going to go look at the relevant footage once they email it."

"You think it's worth it?" A.L. asked.

"I do. I can't explain it but I think Dover is important."

"You think we've got a serial kidnapper?"

"I'm not saying that," Rena said. "But I'm not going to ignore any Dover connection."

"You've got a good gut," A.L. said. "I think—" His desk phone rang. He picked it up. "McKittridge," he said. He listened. "I'll be right out." He carefully put the phone back in its cradle.

"What?" Rena asked.

Her damn gut. He held his cards close but still, she knew that shit was blowing in the wind. "Nothing," he said, his tone dismissive. Then realized that since he sucked at things like this, he might want to make good use of her gut and general knowledge of all things female. "Tess is in the lobby. Wants to see me."

"About?"

He didn't know but he didn't think it was good. They'd been seeing one another for months and she'd never felt the need to visit him at work. Now it was late on a Friday evening. "I'm not a fucking mind reader," he said.

"Well, then, I guess you're going to have to go talk to her," Rena said. She picked up her coffee and took a sip. She was enjoying this.

"I will." He pushed his chair back. The walk to the visitor lobby was short. And there she was, perched on the edge of the cheap vinyl-and-aluminum chair.

She stood up. Didn't smile. "I'm sorry to bother you at work," she said.

Something was definitely not right. "Not a problem. There's a conference room back here that we can use." He held open the door. She passed in front of him. She smelled good. He wanted to reach out, give her a hug, bring her body in close to his, but he kept his hands to himself.

"What's up?" he said, once the door was closed.

She licked her lips. "I got a call from Marnee. Guess who she ran into at her *school* dining hall?"

He had no fucking idea and wasn't sure he cared. But that clearly wasn't the right answer. "You tell me," he said.

"Your ex-wife."

"Jacqui?"

"You have more than one ex-wife?" she asked.

Of course not. "That's odd," he said. It was the best he could come up with. And it only came to him because Rena had said it earlier about the storage shed.

"Odd," she repeated. "It's not odd, it's damn ridiculous. And I won't have it, A.L. I won't have Marnee pulled into your ex-wife's drama."

Jacqui could be a pain in the ass but she wasn't the devil. "I don't think she's dangerous."

She stared at him. Her pretty blue eyes were fierce. "Are you deliberately missing the point?" she asked. "Your ex-wife was on my daughter's campus, in her dining room. Do you really think that was coincidence?"

"No," he said. "What happened?"

"Jacqui made up some bullshit story about having a friend whose daughter was interested in UW-Eau Claire and they were touring the campus together."

That probably was bullshit.

"Your ex-wife is stalking my daughter," Tess said. "I'll say it again. I won't have it. She is too important to me."

"I get that. My daughter is important to me, too."

"You can't understand. It's just been the two of us for a long time," Tess said.

"We're not really going to argue over whose daughter is more important to them, are we?" A.L. asked.

Tess closed her eyes. Took a breath. "No. I'm sorry."

"You've got nothing to be sorry for, Tess. Jacqui pulled a fast one. Traci no doubt told her about meeting you at the mall and she decided turnaround was fair play. I don't know what she's trying to prove but I'll tell her it needs to stop. Now. I'll let her know—"

He paused at the knock on the door. Took two steps and opened the door. It was Rena.

"I'm sorry to interrupt, A.L." Rena looked past him. "Hi, Tess."

"Rena," Tess said.

"What?" A.L. asked.

"We've got something."

Thirteen

Rena felt like shit interrupting A.L. and Tess. The tension in the room was palpable.

"Tess, I'm…"

His voice trailed off as Tess held up her hand. "I've said my peace. Just take care of it, Able."

Able. Rena stepped back to let Tess walk past her. She barely waited until Tess was through the double doors before turning back to A.L. "Your first name is Able?"

He shook his head. "No."

"Then why did she call you that?"

"Is that the important question now, Morgan? I'm hoping you knocked on the door for something else."

"Yeah. We have to go. The dogs picked up Emma's scent in the backyard of a house, about two miles out of town."

A.L. pulled his keys from his pocket. "I'll drive. Who owns the house?"

"Alice Quest."

His head snapped up. "You have got to be fucking kidding me."

Rena shook her head. Then started running to keep up with A.L., who was sprinting toward the door.

"That house has already been searched once," A.L. said. They were in his SUV and he'd taken the turn out of the parking lot fast. "As was her vehicle. And she was in a classroom. All damn day. She's the one who called the police."

Rena didn't answer. She had a feeling that A.L. was talking to himself.

It took less than five minutes to reach the address. There were already four other cop cars around the house. Two of them had their lights going. She also saw Chief Faster's SUV.

The man must have seen them arrive because he came out of the house just as they were going in. "We've searched the property," Faster said. "Emma isn't here."

"Was here, though?" A.L. asked.

Faster shrugged. "Dogs picked up her scent outside. Not inside."

Alice Quest lived in a small ranch with a one-car attached garage. Her lot was maybe a half acre, nicely divided between a front and a backyard. There were no outbuildings, no place to hide a child.

"What's the chance it's a fluke?" A.L. asked.

"FBI said that they were *very confident*. That's good enough for me," Faster said.

There was a play set in the back. One of those nice wooden ones, with two swings, a good-sized slide and a climbing wall. The ground beneath it was a fine mulch. Rena remembered that Alice had told her she had two granddaughters.

"Where's Alice Quest?" Rena asked.

Faster looked at his watch. "About right now, I'd say she's walking into the Baywood PD. We pinged her phone, found her having dinner downtown, and Blithe picked her up."

Rena felt ill. She really hadn't wanted anyone at the day care to be responsible for harming Emma. It was such a betrayal. Alice and the others were supposed to be the trusted ones, the ones who maybe didn't love the children as a parent would but goddamn it, would still step in front of the speeding train for them if it came to that.

What the hell would she do once her and Gabe's baby was born? Quit work? Was that the only real option because day care wasn't safe?

"The two of you should head back," Faster said. "I want you to question her."

"Okay," Rena said. A.L. didn't say anything, just started walking to his vehicle. They were headed back to town when he finally spoke.

"This doesn't make sense," he said.

"I know. Emma was outside but not inside? What kind of risk was that? There are neighbors."

"Not super close," he said. "And there's some trees that impair visibility into the backyard."

"Still. Are you going to abduct a child and let her play outside at your house?" Rena asked.

He shook his head. "She had to have had help. We have multiple witnesses who support the fact she was at the day care."

Once A.L. had parked, they walked inside and went to find Blithe. "Where is she?" A.L. asked.

"Room 2," Blithe said.

"She say anything?" Rena asked.

"Nope. She seems like a nice lady," Blithe said. "It's going to be a kick in the balls if she's the one."

How true, thought Rena. She had no balls but she clearly understood what Blithe meant. She turned and led A.L. back to the middle of their three interrogation rooms. When she walked inside, Alice Quest was sitting at the oblong table, a half-full plastic cup of water in front of her. She looked up when they entered.

"Detectives," she said. "I'm assuming there's news."

"Alice," Rena said, taking a chair. "Thank you for coming in."

"It doesn't seem as if I had much choice. It made for a rather awkward parting with my friend that I was having dinner with. I imagine she'll have a few questions."

"We picked up Emma Whitman's trail," Rena said.

Alice didn't flinch. Just kept her eyes on Rena.

"On your property."

"That's impossible," Alice said.

"We're sure she was there," A.L. said.

"Alice, tell us how she got there," Rena said.

"I have no idea," Alice said. "It makes no sense."

That was exactly what A.L. had said.

"She doesn't know where I live. I mean, maybe her parents have driven by and said Ms. Quest lives there but there's no way she could get herself from the learning center to my house. It's more than five miles."

"She was there, Alice," Rena said, keeping her voice gentle yet firm. Alice was talking and that was always better than having a suspect clam up.

Alice took a drink of water. Set her cup down. "I think I'm getting this. You didn't bring me in here to tell me news. You brought me here because you think I had something to do with Emma's disappearance."

"We believe Emma was recently in your backyard and we need you to tell us about that," Rena said.

"I don't have a clue. Emma Whitman has never been in my backyard. None of the children from the day care have ever been at my home. I don't mix business and pleasure. I give a lot of my life to the Lakeside Learning Center and generally, I'm pretty damn content to do that. But when I go home, I want to leave it behind."

"So you're saying that Emma has never been in your backyard or your home?" Rena asked.

"That's what I'm saying. And quite frankly, Detective, if this is going to go much longer, I want to call my attorney."

A.L. pushed his chair back and tapped Rena on the shoulder. "Excuse us for a minute," A.L. said, looking at Alice.

The woman nodded.

Once they were in the hallway, A.L. leaned close. "What's your gut saying, Morgan?"

"It's not very talkative right now. But we don't have enough to take this much further."

"Agree. But we start digging," A.L. said.

Rena nodded. There would be little they didn't know about Alice Quest. "I'll shake her loose," Rena said.

A.L. turned to walk back to his desk. Rena reentered Room 2. "Alice, we appreciate you coming in. That will be all for today."

"Do you believe me?" Alice asked. "Do you believe that I had nothing to do with Emma Whitman's disappearance?"

Rena said nothing.

"Listen to me, Detective," Alice said, her voice hard. "If even a whiff gets out that I might be a suspect, my business will be ruined. I'm not going to let the Baywood Police Department do that to me. Do you understand?"

Again, Rena was silent.

Alice reached for her purse, which had been sitting on the floor by her feet. She opened it, tore a piece of paper from a small lined notebook and wrote a name on it. She shoved it across the table at Rena. "That's my attorney's name. If you need anything else from me, you call her."

Sandra Whitley. Alice hadn't included a number.

"We'll do that," Rena said.

Alice picked up her purse and walked out of the room.

Rena went back to her desk. Pulled out her chair. Sank into it. "I don't know, I just don't know," she said.

A.L. was scrolling through his cell phone. He looked up. "We keep working the case. All we can do."

Rena leaned her head back, far enough that she could study the ceiling tiles. Finally looked at him again. "Tell me why Tess called you Able."

A.L. sighed. "When we were in California, I evidently spent a little too much time sleeping in a hammock. She was convinced that A.L. is short for Able Loafer."

Rena laughed so hard that she almost fell out of her

chair. "Thank you, A.L.," she said, when she could finally talk. "I needed that. I really needed that."

"Happy to help. Now I am going to take five minutes of personal time and go see my ex-wife and tell her to quit stalking Tess's daughter."

A.L. knocked on the front door of the house he used to live in. The house he'd liked. The house he'd painted and wallpapered, and where he'd cut the grass. The house that now felt very foreign to him.

The door swung open and Traci beamed at him. "Hey, Dad. It's late. I didn't know you were coming over."

"Spur of the moment," he said. "Did you check the peephole before you opened the door?"

"I'm the daughter of a cop. Of course I did. Checked it twice, to see if my visitor was naughty or nice."

"Smart mouth," he said, rolling his eyes. "Is your mom still up?"

"Yeah. In the kitchen."

"Is she still dating Craig?"

"Why? You want to get back together?"

"Just answer the question."

"Yes. I think she's happy."

"Good. Can you get her?" He stayed by the door, standing on ceramic tile flooring that he'd busted his ass to lay one summer weekend.

Traci narrowed her eyes. "Is this about me?"

"No," he said honestly. "No more questions."

"Okay. May the best man-slash-woman win." She bounced down the hallway, her ponytail swinging. Damn, he loved that kid.

In a minute, Jacqui walked down the hallway. She was wearing shorts and a T-shirt. She'd put on a few pounds over the last ten years and it was starting to gather around her hips. But she was still an attractive woman, he supposed. "Do you have a minute?"

She nodded, her eyes guarded.

Jacqui wasn't a dumbshit. She had to know that she'd crossed the line by going to see Tess's daughter. But she had never liked to admit that she was wrong and he suspected that wasn't going to be different today.

"I am aware," he said, "that Tess Lyons ran into Traci at the mall the other night. And I am also aware that you just happened to be on the campus of UW-Eau Claire in the dining hall where Tess's daughter eats."

"Is this an interrogation, A.L.?" she asked, sounding deliberately bored.

"No," he said.

"Then what's your point?" Jacqui asked.

"My point is, don't do that again. Don't go looking for Tess's daughter."

"But it's okay if she looks for *my* daughter. Is that how this goes?" Now Jacqui's voice was loud. He was sure if Traci had her door open, she was hearing every word.

"Shush," he said.

"Don't shush me."

He held up a hand. "Fine. Can you please keep your voice down so that Traci isn't a part of this conversation?"

Jacqui pressed her lips together. "Fine," she said.

"I… I don't ask you for a lot, Jacqui. I pretty much let you set the rules about when and where I get to see Traci. And you've been fair and we've managed to work through things. All I'm asking is that you not purposely screw up what I've got going with Tess."

She stared at him.

He stared back.

"Is that all?" she asked finally.

"Yeah. That's all."

She turned. "You can let yourself out, A.L."

He did just that. He was pretty sure he'd gotten his message across but whether Jacqui chose to heed the request was anyone's guess.

Fourteen

The next morning, Rena was drumming her fingers on her desk when A.L. arrived at 6:30. She looked as if she had something to tell him. "What?" he asked.

"We checked for the wrong sister," she announced.

"I've only had one cup of coffee. You're going to have to give me more than that."

"We checked to make sure that Kara Wiese didn't have a sister."

"And that her mother was dead," he added.

She waved a hand. "This is about sisters."

"Okay," he said. He pulled out his chair.

"Alice Quest has a sister," Rena said. "We never checked for that. There was no reason to."

"And this is important because?"

"Because she lives in Dover."

A.L. picked up his empty coffee cup and set it back down. "Very little in life is a coincidence."

"You always say that."

"Because it's true," A.L. said. "What's her name?"

"Melissa Wayne."

"Older? Younger?"

"Older by two years. Alice is fifty-two. Melissa just turned fifty-four. Alice lied to us. Looked us right in the eye and lied. We were talking about Brenda Owen calling her and we asked her if she knew Dover and she said no. Her sister *lives* there."

"She also said that she'd never heard about Corrine Antler. Guess we don't know if that's true or not," he said.

"I'm going to find out," Rena said. "I'm pissed at her and…I guess disappointed."

"Yeah, doesn't look good for Alice," A.L. said. "Do you think it's even possible that there is any intersect between Alice and Rosemary Bracken?"

"I thought of that. Nothing that I've been able to find thus far. But I think I'm going back to Dover."

"Your gut is talking to you again?" A.L. asked.

"I think its heartburn," she said. "Maybe you should go back to the psychic and ask her about Dover."

"I think I'm going to talk to a few more parents, ask some more specific questions about Alice."

"Are we in danger of missing the trees for the forest?"

"We're not going to ignore everybody else. But the dogs haven't picked up Emma's scent anywhere else."

"As irritated as I am that she lied to us, I can't get past the fact that if she really was responsible for Emma's disappearance and Emma was in her backyard, why didn't she simply just tell us that Emma had been there once? I don't know, make up something like she took the kids for a field trip and had to stop at home to check something and Emma got off the bus and wandered around the yard."

A.L. shrugged. "I don't know. Who knows why people say what they do?"

"Maybe she was just telling us the truth," Rena said.

"But still, you're going to Dover."

"I have to. Too many ties to that area to ignore it. Maybe I'll get lucky and run into Coyote Frogg."

"Any day you can stumble over a meth addict is a good day," A.L. said. "Keep in touch."

"Before I go, I just have to ask. How did your conversation with Jacqui go?"

"How do you think it went?"

"I don't know. I had this wild daydream that she threw herself at your feet and tearfully told you that ever since Tess came into the picture, she's realized how much she loves you and that she must have you back."

"That didn't happen."

"That's it. That's all I'm going to get. *That didn't happen.*"

A.L. sighed. "I talked. She listened or pretended to listen. I'm never sure which."

"What are you going to tell Tess?"

"Nothing. She asked me to handle it and I've done the best I can. What happens next is anybody's guess."

"I think you're pretending that you're not concerned but that is totally not true."

"You have somewhere to go, right?" he asked.

"Send Tess some flowers. Everybody loves flowers."

"Goodbye," he said. Then he turned his attention to his computer.

* * *

Flowers, huh? Once he knew that Rena was out the door, he tapped a few keys, brought up the website of the Petal Poof, the little store on the main street. It was a step back in time looking at their information. Months ago, one of their employees, Jane Picus, had been a victim of the serial killer who had almost killed Tess.

He'd liked the people at Petal Poof. Thought they had nice flowers.

It was Saturday so they'd be open, just not yet. Probably at nine.

He walked back to the break room and filled his cup with what looked like industrial-strength coffee. He didn't mind. The more caffeine, the better. When he got back to his desk, he reached for the list that Rena had been working on. He saw the two names of parents that she'd yet to reach.

He thought about calling but since Alice Quest had so nicely provided the names of the parents' employers and their telephone numbers if she had them, he saw the Shana Federer was employed by Baywood Bank. That made him think of Steven Hanzel. And made him think that it might be worth his time to visit in person. He knew the bank was open from eight to noon on Saturday mornings.

At eight thirty, A.L. arrived at the Baywood Bank. He asked the security guard at the door if he knew Shana Federer and the man pointed at the fourth teller window. A.L. waited in line, grateful that nobody came up behind him. Five minutes later, after some high school kid with a jar of change was helped, he put his badge on the counter and slid it so she could easily see it. "I'd like to talk to you for a few minutes."

She didn't ask why. Everybody knew what the police were working on. "I'll need to ask my supervisor," she said.

Four minutes later, she led him down a hallway to an empty break room. There were vending machines on one side, a microwave, refrigerator and sink on the other side of the room. A round table with six chairs in the middle. She pulled one back and he did the same. Before she sat, she removed her cell phone from her back pocket and put it on the table.

He showed her the sign-in sheet. "Can you describe your general drop-off process at the day care?"

"I guess," she said. "We've got a routine. Mia has been going there for over a year."

"I understand," he said. "Just walk me through it."

"We live just down the street from the day care. On the days that I start work later, Mia and I walk. On earlier days, I drive. That's what it was on Wednesday. I drove, parked and we walked inside. I usually glance in the office to say good morning to Alice. I started to do that but the office was empty. I assumed she was in one of the classrooms."

"Was there anybody else in the lobby?"

"There was a dad leaving as we walked in. I don't know his name but his son is in Mia's class. His name is Wyatt. They're pretty new at the day care."

"Okay. Then what?"

"I..." She closed her eyes. "I walked Mia to her classroom. Went inside as far as the cubbies and hung up her backpack. That's when I saw Alice Quest and I realized she was covering for Olivia Blow. Anyway, I waved to Alice, then I hugged Mia and I left."

"You signed the sheet?" he clarified.

"Yes," she said. "I did. That's just habit. I always do that immediately after I hang up Mia's backpack."

"And how did you know what time it was?"

"My phone. I always have it in my back pocket. Never wear any pants that don't have a back pocket. I know it's stupid, because I'm not so important that I couldn't miss a call, but I just feel better when I have my phone on me."

"Okay."

"Then I left."

"The building?" he clarified.

"I…" She hesitated, then scratched behind her left ear. "Actually I had to stop in the bathroom. I have IBS. Irritable bowel syndrome," she added. "Sometimes I need a bathroom rather quickly and that was one of those mornings where I didn't think I could wait until I got to work."

He'd already had one conversation about diarrhea with Olivia Blow and he didn't want to have another one now. But he wanted to make sure he had her full statement. "After you used the bathroom, what happened?"

"I left."

"Did you see anyone as you left?"

"No. I mean, I saw Kara in the bathroom but that was it."

"Kara?"

"Yeah. Kara Wiese. She's a teacher there."

Fifteen

Shana Federer had signed her daughter in at 7:08.

"If you went to the bathroom directly after you left Mia's classroom, what time do you think it was that you saw Kara Wiese?"

"This is embarrassing," she said.

"I'm sorry."

"I guess it would have been about four or five minutes later. I have to go urgently so it's generally pretty quick, you know. I had to get to work, too."

"Right." So that meant it was 7:12 or 7:13. Kara Wiese had been adamant that she hadn't left her classroom prior to 7:30 because Claire Potter didn't arrive until then and she couldn't leave the children alone in the room. "Which bathroom did you use? The one in Mia's classroom or the one in the hallway?"

"In the hallway."

"And you're confident that you saw Kara Wiese in the bathroom?"

"Well…yes. I mean, I thought it was her. We're not friends but I've seen her a bunch of times at the day care."

"Do you remember the conversation?"

"I don't know. She was standing at the sink when I came out of the stall. It was sort of embarrassing because…well, you know, it's always better if the bathroom is empty and I didn't know how long she'd been standing there. Anyway, I think I said good morning and she said good morning and I washed my hands and left."

"She was still in the bathroom when you left, still by the sink."

"I think so."

"What was she doing?"

"I don't know. I didn't really look at her that closely. Maybe she was doing her makeup. Sometimes that happens to me when I'm running late. I put my makeup on at work."

"Can I see the time on your phone?" he asked.

She looked surprised but she picked up her phone. He checked the time on it against his own phone. Same thing on both. So he was pretty confident that his data points were good.

"Was there anybody else in the bathroom with you and Ms. Wiese?"

Shana shook her head. "I should probably get back to my window."

"I understand." She probably expected that he was going to ask about the color of her poop next. "Thank you for your time."

"You're welcome. I'll walk you back to the lobby."

When they got there, Shana extended her hand. "Good luck, Detective McKittridge."

"Thank you." Over her shoulder, at one of the desks

in the far right corner of the bank, he saw Steven Hanzel. The man was sitting at a desk, turned so that his right side was to A.L. He was talking to a young couple who sat in chairs in front of his desk. A.L. was confident the man was unaware of his scrutiny. "You work with Steven Hanzel?" he asked.

She glanced over her shoulder. "I guess. I mean, yes. He's a loan officer so we don't interact very much."

Exuberant Steven Hanzel, who had set A.L.'s teeth on edge. Maybe A.L. had *sensed* that the man ran around on his wife. He should call the psychic up and tell her he might be some competition. "Is he…well-liked at the bank?" A.L. asked.

She shrugged. "I think so. We both went to Baywood High. Actually dated for a month or two when I was a junior and he was a senior."

"Small world," A.L. said.

"I think he did a good thing setting up the fund-raising site."

He heard something in her tone. "But…?"

She shrugged. "My sister-in-law is his manager. She's shared some things."

"Like what things?" A.L. asked.

Shana chewed on the corner of her upper lip, looking as if she realized that she might have said too much. No doubt what her sister had told her had been done in confidence. "I don't want to get my sister-in-law in trouble. I think she only told me because she knew that we'd dated at one time and that he'd dumped me for another girl."

Bingo. He was going to let Shana off the hook. It

would be better to get the info firsthand versus second. "What's your sister-in-law's name?"

She said nothing.

"I'm pretty sure I can work this so that she doesn't know that it was you who sent me her direction," A.L. said.

"Tamara Federer. I married her younger brother. She's divorced and went back to her maiden name."

"Does she work out of this location?"

"Yes. The VPs have offices on the third floor."

A vice president probably wasn't working on a Saturday morning. He said as much to Shana.

"Yeah, most don't. But my sister-in-law is a total type A and believes in leading by example. She's working."

"Okay. Don't call her to warn her. That will spoil the plan."

"I won't. Thank you."

A.L. walked directly to the bank of elevators on the far right side. He got in and pushed 3. When the doors opened, there was a reception desk immediately in front of the elevators. Nobody could miss it. And nobody could get by it without being seen.

The VPs evidently didn't want to have unexpected visitors.

He smiled at the middle-aged woman behind the desk. "Tamara Federer, please."

"Do you have an appointment?"

He pulled a business card. "No. But I am going to need to see her."

The woman picked up his card. Studied the info.

"Just one minute, Detective. You can have a seat in the waiting area."

The chairs on the third floor were a soft brown leather, nicer than the green fabric chairs that he'd seen in the downstairs lobby. He took a seat.

Tamara didn't make him wait long. He heard her heels before he saw her. She rounded the corner, wearing a black pantsuit that looked good on her. She seemed young for a VP, maybe just midthirties. Her hair was platinum blond, cut short, and she wore way more makeup than he preferred. But altogether, she was a professional package.

She extended a hand. "Detective McKittridge, I'm Tamara Federer."

"Thanks for seeing me."

"Of course."

"Do you have someplace where we might talk in private?" he asked.

"Follow me," she said. She led him down a long hallway, in the opposite direction of where she'd come from. She opened the door to a small conference room. He took a seat in another really good-looking leather chair. This one swiveled.

She sat, too, at the head of the table. "What can I help you with?" she asked.

"I want to talk with you about Steven Hanzel."

"Steven Hanzel who works here at Baywood Bank?" she asked, sounding surprised.

"Yes. I understand that you're his supervisor."

"I am. I… I guess you've caught me a little off-guard. In the past, I've had the opportunity to talk to the police just twice, and both times they had questions about customers. This is the first time I've had someone ask questions about an associate and I have to admit, it doesn't feel good."

"Please don't read too much into my questions," he said. "I am investigating the disappearance of Emma Whitman. I imagine you've heard about it."

"It's all anyone is talking about. I have a niece, she's just a year younger, who goes to that same day care."

A.L. kept his face blank.

"I told my sister-in-law that she should think about changing providers. I mean, really, what kind of place just lets a five-year-old walk out?"

"It's my understanding that Steven Hanzel is friends with Troy Whitman, father of Emma. And that he is responsible for setting up the fund-raising site. That put him on my radar."

"I'm keenly aware of his involvement in that."

It was an odd choice of words. "Keenly aware?" he repeated.

"When it first started, about three other VPs brought it to my attention. It made all of us a little uncomfortable that he was spearheading the effort. We didn't want it to appear that it was a banking-led thing." She held up a hand. "That sounded bad. It's a good idea, right. But just not something that we'd generally take a lead on because there's been a few situations with these efforts where the primary fund-raiser was working for his own gain. It would be problematic for Baywood Bank if that was the situation. So I immediately talked to him about it. And let me tell you, I read the fine print of how he's got everything set up. I felt good when I could assure my peer group that it was all aboveboard,

that the money would and could only go to the Whitmans. Steven evidently just felt moved to do something
to help. He was being a good friend."

"I guess I'm surprised that the bank felt so strongly
about it."

"Well, in truth, it probably had much to do with the
fact that it was Steven Hanzel. He's got a reputation
in the bank."

"For?"

"This will stay confidential between us, right, Detective?"

"As much as I can keep it," he said.

She sighed. "That's the same answer that I give. Steven Hanzel is an underperformer. He's a loan officer
who doesn't get very many loans closed. Loan officers
are basically sales representatives. And you'd think that
his personality would be a good fit for that. But for some
reason, he cannot seem to pull together the numbers that
we expect or certainly what his own peer group pro-
duces. And some of his decisions about loans have also
seemed questionable. So questionable that I'm reviewing every one that he authorizes above a certain limit."

"So why does he still have a job?" A.L. asked.

"Excellent question. I inherited Steven from another
VP who, quite frankly, isn't willing to address performance issues. Over the last six months, I watched him
closely and took every opportunity presented to me to
coach him on his work. And when that didn't have the
desired effect, I started with the bank's formal correc-
tive action process. Steven Hanzel has received several
written notices that his performance is lacking. Quite
frankly, he's on his last leg here."

"Seems like a lot of work for somebody who isn't doing the job."

"Steven suffered a pretty severe hearing loss when he got sick in college. Mono? Meningitis? I can't remember the reason. All I know is that it meets the definition of disability. Which complicates the issue for us. The bank doesn't like to get sued by former disgruntled employees. When we do, we want to make sure that we win the case easily. Good documentation is our friend. But just as importantly, from my perspective, is that I've earned a reputation here as somebody who gives people a chance. I've turned around poor performers. I really wanted him to succeed. But he just gets in his own way."

"How's he do that?"

"I'd be speculating and I don't want to do that."

A.L. shrugged. "I won't think less of you. In fact, right now, I'm thinking that you're pretty smart and talented and that you're a high performer, which is how you got to a VP position at what seems to be a fairly young age."

She smiled. "I have worked hard." She drummed a perfectly polished index finger on the table. "The bank does preemployment drug testing and four years ago, Steven Hanzel passed his. We only conduct ongoing testing when the work performance is such that we suspect that alcohol or drugs are affecting performance. I want to test him, but thus far my human resources department has put the brakes on that."

"You think he's a drug user."

"I wouldn't be surprised. My ex-husband was an addict and I see some of the same behaviors."

"Like?"

"Steven is a smoker so he makes a beeline outside every break and lunch hour. He stands near the south entrance, smoking and talking on his phone. Twice now, when I've walked by on my way to a midday meeting off-site, he's stopped talking. Not stopped as in listening. He was midsentence both times that he saw me and *boom*, he goes silent. I think he's making drug deals. But I've been told to manage him out of the bank based on his performance. So I'm biding my time."

Steven Hanzel was on thin ice and he knew it. It made A.L. wonder if he'd shared that information with his best friend, Troy Whitman. And while it could not be disputed that it was a good thing to get the fund-raising going, perhaps Steven would have been better served to focus on his job.

"Do you happen to know the balance of the fund-raising account?" A.L. asked.

"I saw Steven in the employee break room yesterday. He couldn't wait to tell me it was close to $160,000. I wish he watched his own numbers so closely."

That was real money. People were very generous. "I appreciate your time, Ms. Federer."

"I hope you find Emma and the person who is responsible for this."

"Me, too."

He left the bank and called Rena from the car. Filled her in. First on the fact that Shana Federer thought she'd seen Kara Wiese in the bathroom prior to 7:30. "Are you going to ask Kara about it?"

"Not just yet," he said.

She didn't ask why, probably figured he had a reason. After all, by Shana's own admission she *thought* it was her but she didn't really look at her. It just felt like something he wanted to hold in his pocket for now.

Then he told her about his conversation with Hanzel's boss.

"Didn't you say he was sort of an exuberant guy, kind of loud?" she asked. "Is it possible that's a well-honed defense mechanism? Act confident and like you're a winner and people will think you are. It's a little like Chief Faster."

That made sense. Both Steven Hanzel and Faster set his teeth on edge.

Talking to Rena made him remember that he had yet to order flowers for Tess. "I've got to go," he said.

"I'll call once I've talked to Melissa Wayne," Rena said.

A.L. hung up the phone and made a quick right-hand turn. Three minutes later, he pulled up in front of Petal Poof.

There was a young woman behind the counter who had probably been hired to take Jane Picus's spot. Five minutes later, he'd purchased a forty-dollar bouquet of fresh flowers with a fall theme. Whatever the hell that was. He'd been assured the bouquet would be delivered today.

"Do you want a special message on the card?" the woman asked.

Maybe *don't pay attention to my crazy ex-wife, I never do.* "No. Just A.L."

"Al?" she asked.

"No. Never mind. Sign it Able."

Rena rolled into Dover at 8:45. She had Melissa Wayne's address plugged into her GPS. The woman's house was a two-story with white siding, green shutters, a brick driveway and well-tended flowers in big pots. *Nice*, she thought. She knocked on the door. A woman wearing scrubs answered the door. She wasn't very tall and Rena could easily look over her shoulder. She didn't see or hear anything that made her think a five-year-old was in the house.

"Melissa Wayne?" Rena asked.

The woman shook her head. "She's not home. Can I help you?"

Rena pulled her badge. "Detective Morgan, Baywood Police Department."

The woman briefly studied her badge. Then lifted her face. "Is something wrong?"

"Can you tell me where I might find Melissa Wayne?" Rena asked.

"She's at her shop."

"Shop?" Rena repeated.

"She owns the Brighter Day Salon on Parke Street," the woman said. "They open at 7:30 on Saturdays."

"May I have your name, please?" Rena said.

"Candiss Lake."

"And your relationship to Ms. Wayne?"

"Personal," Candiss said, her voice edgy.

"Thank you," Rena said. She pulled a business card from her pocket. "If I happen to miss Ms. Wayne, would you give this to her and let her know that I need to talk with her?"

"Of course." Candiss slipped the card into the pocket of her top.

Rena got into her vehicle and pulled up the Brighter Day Salon on Parke Street on her GPS. It was a short drive. She parked just left of the front door. There was a sign in the window advertising services. Cuts, color, facials. The list went on. Rena looked in the rearview mirror. Maybe she should get her eyebrows waxed while she was here. They were looking a little bushy.

When she opened the door, the smell of salon, of every salon ever known, assailed her. A bell tinkled and a small older woman behind the counter looked up. Rena couldn't see anything else because a partition separated the front from the rest of the salon. She looked too old for a *personal relationship* with Candiss Lake but Rena didn't want to assume.

"Melissa Wayne?" Rena asked.

"Oh no, honey. I just work the desk. Melissa is the owner. She's back there."

Rena stepped around the wall. Scanned the oblong space. Swivel chairs. A bunch of tall, thin young girls wearing black aprons. Sinks. A pedicure station. Customers. All female. Wet hair, foiled hair, almost dry hair. Her eyes stopped. There in the back, scissors in one hand, comb in the other, stood Alice Quest.

No. Not Alice Quest. It had to be Melissa Wayne.

But the resemblance was startling. Same face. Same lean body. Same brown hair, although Melissa's had some blond highlights and it was shorter, cut in a stylish asymmetrical bob with one side pushed behind an ear that had at least four gold earrings in it.

Rena started walking toward her. Melissa put down her scissors.

"Melissa Wayne?" Rena asked.

"Yes."

Rena assumed that Candiss Lake had immediately

called or texted Melissa Wayne. So there should be no surprises. Rena passed her a business card. There was no reason to announce to a salon of women that the police were there. Melissa Wayne looked at it briefly.

"I really need to finish this cut," she said. "Can you wait a few minutes?"

Rena looked at the woman in the chair. One side was four inches shorter than the other. "Sure," Rena said.

Melissa pointed to a closed door. "That leads to a break room. There should be coffee. Help yourself."

"Okay."

There was coffee and Rena poured herself a cup. Then she sat at the oblong table and picked up a *People* magazine that was several weeks old. My God, when was everybody going to get over the royal family and their growing brood of royal babies? Still, Rena let her eyes settle on the one closest to the camera. Cute kid. A little red in the hair.

Her child could have red hair.

She owed Gabe an answer about using Shannon as a carrier for their baby. If she said no, they'd have to start the search over. Another delay. Another reason for Gabe to decide that maybe kidless was the way to go.

For one damn minute, can you stop being a cop? That's what Gabe had asked her when she'd expressed concern about Shannon's husband.

No. She didn't think she could. It was who she was.

The door opened and Melissa Wayne walked in. She poured herself a cup of coffee and held the pot in Rena's direction. Rena shook her head. Melissa took a seat on the other side of the table.

"Thank you for letting me finish with my customer," she said.

"No problem," Rena said. "You were expecting me," she said.

"I was. Candiss sent a text."

"More than that," Rena said, taking an educated guess. "After you got Candiss's text, you called Alice."

Melissa stared at her cup. "I did," she said finally looking up. "Woke her up. She hadn't had her coffee yet."

So Alice knew that the police were aware she'd lied about knowing Dover.

"My sister told me about the ridiculous conversation she had at the police station."

"I can't talk to you about that," Rena said. She stared at the woman across the table. "The two of you really look very much alike."

"People used to get us mixed up when we were younger," Melissa said. "And Alice was able to use my ID easily to get into bars when she was still underage. Although I suspect that's not something I should be telling you."

"Not my worry right now," Rena said. "I'm looking for a missing five-year-old."

"It's a terrible thing. But thinking that Alice had anything to do with it is really just a waste of time."

"When did you move to Dover, Ms. Wayne?" Rena asked.

"After college."

"Did Alice ever live in Dover?"

"No."

"You were here ten years ago when Corrine Antler disappeared?"

"I was. Had just started the salon. It was all anyone talked about for weeks, maybe even months."

"Did you know the Antler family?"

"Not before. But some of the local businesses got together to do some fund-raising for them afterwards and we met then. Nice people."

"Did you know Trapper Frogg or his son, Coyote Frogg?"

"No."

"Brenda Owen?"

"No."

"Rosemary Bracken?"

Melissa opened her mouth, closed it. "Actually, I do. I cut her hair, like once every six months."

Rosemary Bracken's hair had been straight to her shoulders with a middle part. Not a hint of style that she saw in Melissa's hair or in the cut she'd been doing earlier. "That's a long time to go between haircuts."

"Rosemary *is* a strange one. She doesn't like to leave her house. But for some reason, she came to me more than five years ago for a haircut. I didn't really want to do it. After all, she's not the best advertisement for my work. But I felt sorry for her. She seemed to have a really lonely existence. Anyway, she continues to come."

A.L. had asked if there was a connection between Alice and Rosemary Bracken. Through Melissa, there was. "Have you and Rosemary ever discussed Corrine Antler?"

"No. She's only been a client for about five years. Long after Corrine went missing."

"Did you know that Rosemary was once considered a person of interest in Corrine Antler's disappearance?"

"Absolutely not."

"Okay. Did you and Alice ever talk about the Antler disappearance?"

"I imagine we did."

"But you don't remember for sure?" Rena asked.

"Detective, it was ten years ago. No, I do not remember every conversation I had with my sister ten years ago."

"You've never talked about it recently?"

"No. I... I don't want to sound crass, but quite frankly I'd sort of forgotten about it. I've had my own shit going on. In the last ten years, I got married, got divorced, started a business and watched Candiss's mother die a slow death from Alzheimer's."

"When's the last time that you saw Alice?"

"Fourth of July. We had a picnic at my house."

Fairly recently. Was that when Alice had remembered the Antler case? Had they talked about it there? "Who was at the picnic?" Rena asked.

"Me. Her. Candiss. A few friends that we've all known for years."

"Their names?" Rena asked.

"Is this really necessary?" Melissa asked.

"I wouldn't ask if it wasn't," Rena said, pen in hand.

"This is just getting ridiculous," Melissa said, shaking her head.

Rena said nothing.

"Maggie Simmons. Patrice Candle. Ben Wallace. Patrice and Ben live next door. Maggie is Patrice's sister."

"Do you have contact information on all of them?"

Melissa pulled it up on her phone and Rena copied

it down. "Thank you," Rena said. She got up and had her hand on the break room door when Melissa suddenly stood up.

"My sister loves those kids. Fuck. Loves them more than their parents do. That's who you should be looking at. Emma's parents. Alice has said stuff about them. Stuff that sure as hell isn't going to get them nominated for parents of the year."

"What stuff?" Rena asked.

Melissa stared at her. "Just pay attention to the parents, okay?" She brushed past Rena. "I have to get back to work. Show yourself out, Detective."

Twenty minutes later, Rena was parked in front of Patrice Candle and Ben Wallace's house. She'd not yet had time to get out of her car when a Honda rounded the corner and pulled into the driveway. A woman was driving. The garage door went up, then down. Rena counted to thirty before opening her door. She knocked and the front door opened.

"Patrice Candle?" Rena asked.

"Yes."

"I'm Detective Morgan from the Baywood Police Department." Rena waited for a hint of recognition. After all, she figured Melissa Wayne had called her friend and neighbor. Rena flipped out her badge.

Patrice studied it, then looked up at Rena. "What can I do for you, Officer?"

"I want to ask you a few questions about your neighbor, Melissa Wayne?"

"Oh my God. Is she okay? Did something happen?"

"You haven't talked to her or heard from her today?" Rena asked.

"No. I...well, maybe she tried to call but I've sworn off my cell phone for thirty days. To prove a point to my husband."

Rena resisted the urge to smile. "May I come in?" She really didn't want to have this conversation on the sidewalk.

"Of course," Patrice said. She opened the door.

"Your husband isn't home?" Rena asked.

"He coaches fall soccer. They practice on Saturday mornings. It's a pain but he loves it."

She'd have preferred to talk to both of them but she didn't feel inclined to wait around for Ben Wallace to come home. "How long have you lived in this house?"

"Six years last May."

After the Antler kidnapping. "Did you have another home in Dover before that?"

"No. We moved here from Billings, Montana, when Ben got his teaching job."

"Are you aware that a child disappeared in Dover about ten years ago? Her name was Corrine Antler."

"Ben had one of the Antler boys in his social studies class last year. He's...well, I guess you could say that he's got some issues. Acts up in class. Disturbs other kids. Ben works with a team of teachers and when they were discussing the kid's performance, one of the other teachers told him the story. It doesn't excuse how the kid is acting but that's a hell of a thing to happen to a family."

"I understand that you attended a party hosted by Melissa Wayne in July. Do you recall who was there?"

"Sure. It wasn't a big thing, just a cookout. It was Ben and me. And Melissa and Candiss. My sister, Maggie. Oh, and I think Melissa's sister Alice was also there."

Matched exactly what Melissa Wayne had told her. "Do you recall, was there any discussion at this cookout about Corrine Antler or the Antler family in general?"

Patrice shook her head. "I don't think so," she said. "Ben doesn't discuss the kids in his school with anybody but me. He got burned years ago when he did that and somebody in the group was the kid's uncle. It got ugly." She stopped. Gave Rena a smile.

This was going nowhere fast. She should probably just admit defeat and go back to Baywood. "Thank you for your—"

"We might have talked about the foundation," Patrice said.

"Foundation?" Rena repeated.

"The Corrine Antler Foundation. I guess when Corrine went missing, donations poured in. The family set up a foundation with the money. On the fifth year of Corrine's disappearance, they paid for a new playground at the local park. Just recently, when it was the tenth anniversary, they donated money so that ten high school kids, kids who were in Corrine's kindergarten class, could go on a field trip to Washington, DC."

Rena could almost feel her blood pressure go up. "And you think this was discussed at Melissa Wayne's cookout."

"I think so. I can't remember the specifics but it was a pretty impressive thing for the Antler family to do."

"Can you recall anything specifically that Alice Quest might have said?"

"Somebody said that it was a cool thing for the family to do in that nobody would have known if they'd taken the money for a nice long family vacation. That might have been Alice." She shrugged apologetically. "We had some wine. Things can get a little fuzzy."

It was enough to know that Alice Quest had been in Dover in July and that there had been some conversation about Corrine Antler. Rena had her hand on the door when she turned.

"Does your husband like teaching?" she asked.

"Uh…yeah. I think so. I mean, it's all he's ever done."

"My husband is going back to school to become a teacher," Rena said, feeling as if she owed the woman an explanation. "After fifteen years in another career. That he didn't hate," she added.

"Then he must really want to do it." She paused. "But you're not as enthusiastic about the change."

"Oh no. It's fine." She couldn't very well voice to this woman, this stranger, her greatest fear. That this career switch was a symptom of a bigger thing. That Gabe would suddenly decide he was in a marriage he didn't hate, but why not shake it up for the hell of it? She couldn't tell this woman that she was a little freaked out because he was growing his hair long and he'd started reading dystopian fiction. She'd sound like a nut. She pulled the door open. "I intend to visit with your sister, Maggie. I'd appreciate it if you didn't tell her about our conversation." She wanted Maggie's own recollection of the evening and all conversations, not one that had been influenced by Patrice saying, *here's what I told her.*

"Maggie is out of the country. Three weeks in France."

Rena wanted to *be* Maggie. "When is she expected back?"

"Monday of next week."

If they hadn't found Emma Whitman by then, it was going to be pretty grim. "Thank you," she said.

Rena walked to her car, started it and called A.L. She got his voice mail. She waited for the beep. "I have confirmation that there was conversation about Corrine Antler at the cookout that Alice Quest attended in July. Call me." She hung up.

Sixteen

A.L. saw Rena's call come in but let it go to voice mail.

He was in the process of dialing Devin Raine, Leah's boss at the law firm who had failed to call him back after he'd left a second message late last night. If the guy didn't answer this time, A.L. was going to be pissed.

It was answered on the second ring. Lucky for Mr. Raine.

"This is Devin," he said.

"Mr. Raine, this is Detective McKittridge with the Baywood Police Department. I've left a couple messages."

"Yeah, I'm sorry about that."

"I'd like to have a minute of your time so that I could ask you some questions."

"About?"

Mr. Raine was definitely an attorney. He wasn't going to agree to anything until he had more information. "About Leah Whitman. I understand that you're her supervising attorney at Bailey Shepherd."

"I am. I would…uh…be happy to chat with you, Detective. I'd prefer to do it in person and I have to admit that I'm a bit rank right now. I've been part of the search team and it's been a hot few hours. If you can give me time for a quick shower, I'd be happy to meet you at the coffee shop on the corner of White Avenue and Mercy Street."

A.L. knew the place. A lot of cops stopped there for a cup of joe. "Fine. Shall we say forty-five minutes?"

"I'll wear a blue shirt," Devin said.

"Don't worry. I'll find you."

He'd already had one cup of coffee before Devin Raine walked in. He waved at the man. Got a nod in return. Devin didn't head for the table. Instead he stepped into line. It was another seven minutes before he made his way over, with some sort of iced coffee. He extended his free hand. "Detective McKittridge?" he said.

"Yes." A.L. passed him over a business card. "Thanks for seeing me. How was the search today?"

"Warm," Devin said. "And pretty depressing if you want the truth," he added. "We're miles away from the day care at this point."

A.L. had been reading the daily updates. The numbers of volunteers were dwindling. Today they'd had forty-two. Still a respectable number but by next week, they'd likely be in the twenties. People had to go back to their lives.

Every day that Emma remained missing it became less and less likely that she'd be found alive. Those were the hard facts. Maybe nobody was saying it but every cop knew it. He suspected by now that Leah and Troy Whitman had also stumbled across the statistics online.

In a few days, they'd even change out the canine unit. Would definitely add more dogs that were specifically trained to find human remains. "I stopped by your office yesterday, spent a little time with Ms. Pistolle. She told me you'd be the best person to talk to if I had questions specific to Leah Whitman."

Devin said nothing.

"What can you tell me about her work?" A.L. asked.

"It's good. She's very talented. Asks the right questions. Works hard. Stays late when we need her to."

"Speaking of work hours, can you tell me what time she got in this past Wednesday?"

"The day Emma went missing?"

"Yes."

"I can't say exactly but I know that she was there by 10:00. We were both in the conference room on a call. I remember that night, when I heard the news, I couldn't get it out of my head that she'd been sitting there, helping me negotiate communal property, in a contentious divorce, when her own child was at risk. It just felt surreal in retrospect."

By ten. That pretty much matched what Leah had said and what the video at the casino had confirmed. "She get along with her coworkers?"

"Leah is a nice person. She's easy to get along with."

"So there's nobody at work that she's had any issues with?" A.L. asked.

"There were words, recently, between her and my other paralegal. Martha has been there longer and was upset that Leah got promoted to a senior paralegal. She seemed to believe the promotion should have gone to her."

"But you didn't think so."

"I don't think you award tenure. You award performance and attitude."

"What's Martha's last name?" A.L. asked.

"I'm not sure why that's important," Devin said.

"I'm going to want to follow up with Martha. Right now we're looking at anybody who might have a beef with either Leah or her husband, Troy, and want to take it out on their kid."

"Martha wouldn't do that. She was angry, maybe a little hurt, and she said some things she should not have said. Leah didn't even bring it to my attention. It was overheard by someone else who told their boss who came to me. I addressed it with Martha and it's over. I want it to be over. I don't like dissension on my team."

He was probably a good guy who liked it when everybody played nice. Unfortunately, that wasn't how the real world worked. "Martha?" A.L. asked again, pen in hand.

"Martha Johnston."

"Contact information?"

Devin thumbed through his phone. "I've only got a phone, no address."

"I'll take it."

He rattled it off and A.L. copied it down.

"Does Leah have any client contact?" A.L. asked.

"Of course. Lots of routine requests go to her and she handles them."

"Bailey Shepherd does family law, right?"

"That's correct."

"Maybe some acrimonious divorces or ugly child-custody cases."

Devin nodded. "We've had some."

"Any that you can recall where Leah was the point person, that somebody might have construed that she was calling the shots either for or against somebody?"

"When the issues are hot, we don't expect our paralegals to field those calls. I would handle those."

A.L. suspected the paralegals handled plenty of dicey issues. But it didn't look like he was going to get anywhere with these questions. "Thank you for your time, Mr. Raine."

"Happy to do it. What I want most is for Leah to have her little girl back."

He used a reverse lookup to find Martha Johnston's address. She lived in a condo, close enough to Bailey Shepherd that she probably walked to work. He drove to her apartment, hoping that she was there.

The building was old but it had been extensively remodeled with high-end finishes. There were eight condos in the building. He pressed the buzzer next to her name and looked directly into the camera.

"Yes," she said.

"Detective McKittridge, Baywood Police Department. I'd like to speak with you."

"Why?"

She wasn't a lawyer but she definitely had learned something from them. "A few questions about your coworker, Leah Whitman."

She didn't say anything but the buzzer sounded and

he grabbed for the door. Then he walked up a flight of stairs and knocked on 202.

A woman opened the door. She was early forties, about his age. She wore pajama pants and an Arizona State T-shirt. "Martha Johnston?" he asked.

"Yes," she said.

He opened his badge and held it steady. She studied it for a minute, then stepped back to let him in. Her condo had glossy wood floors and bay windows, and the kitchen, dining room and living room were all sort of the same big space. She pulled out one of the stools that was pushed up to the kitchen counter. She sat and pointed to the other one. He took it and got out his notebook and pen.

"I wanted to talk with you about your relationship with Leah Whitman."

"Leah and I don't have a relationship. We're both paralegals working under the same supervising attorney at Bailey Shepherd. But I suspect you already know that."

She didn't say it with an attitude, just very matter-of-fact. He decided to get more direct. "How do you and Leah get along?"

"For the most part, it's fine. She's a very competent paralegal and I don't generally have to pick up much of her slack."

"For the most part, you say. What about the other part?"

She smiled. "Mostly everyone loves Leah but she isn't as nice as she wants everyone to believe."

He wondered if Martha knew about Leah videotaping her mother at the casino. "Can you give me some examples?"

"I've seen her take credit for other people's work. Not mine. She knows that I'd call her out on it. But other people. I've heard her on the phone with her husband. Quite frankly, I'm not sure how they're still married. But when the partners are around, she is sweet. Yeah, Sweet Leah."

"I understand that Leah was recently promoted at work to a senior paralegal. How did you feel about that?"

"Not great. It should have gone to me. But I'm not as good as Leah in managing people's perception. That leaves me the choice of voting with my feet. But I like the work and I really like being able to walk to work. So for now, I'll stay."

"Where were you last Wednesday, at about 7:15 a.m.?"

"Just finishing my workout. I run on the treadmill every morning for thirty minutes."

"Anybody be able to verify that?" he asked.

"There's never usually anybody else in the gym but everything is on camera, like most of this building. Behind our doors is about the only privacy we get."

He was pretty confident that this was her way of telling him that she hadn't snuck a five-year-old up the back stairs.

"Thank you for your time, Ms. Johnston."

"You're welcome. I feel badly for Leah and her husband. A missing child is something that no parent should have to go through. But my only advice is, don't be fooled. There's more to Leah than you'll first think."

* * *

Ten minutes later, as he dialed Rena, A.L. couldn't seem to get those words out of his head. *Don't be fooled. There's more to Leah than you'll first think.* When Rena answered, he repeated them to her. "What the hell do you make of that?" he asked.

"I don't know. Melissa Wayne said we should be looking harder at the parents, that Alice had told her stuff. I sort of shoved that aside at the time because I was having a hard time getting my head around the fact that Alice Quest lied both about knowing Dover and also knowing anything about Corrine Antler. Why would she do that?"

"I think we've got a couple things to talk to Alice about. I'll meet you at her house."

"Are we going to call first?" Rena asked.

"Hell, no. We're done being polite."

"She wants us to talk to her attorney."

"She can call her and have her join us. I don't mind," A.L. said.

Twenty minutes later, when he and Rena stood in Alice's foyer, he told her the same thing. "You're not under arrest, Alice. We're just asking questions, trying to clarify information. But if you want your lawyer here, by all means, call her up."

"It's late on a Saturday afternoon. I'm sure she's not in the office."

"You don't have her home number?" A.L. asked. "If not, if it's any kind of law firm, I'm sure they have somebody on call, just for this sort of emergency."

Alice stared at A.L. "I may regret this but I really

don't think you're the enemy. Let's sit in the family room."

Rena sat and didn't waste any time. "Why did you lie about knowing Dover, Wisconsin? Your sister lives there. You've visited there multiple times."

"I don't know why I lied. You said you'd been to Dover—it caught me off guard, and suddenly, I didn't want there to be anything that tied me to the area or to Corrine Antler. I swear to you, I didn't even think of Corrine Antler until I called my sister on Thursday to tell her what had happened. I didn't want her to hear it on the news. She was the one who reminded me about Corrine."

"Wasn't there discussion at your sister's Fourth of July party about the Corrine Antler Foundation?" Rena asked.

"If there was, I wasn't paying attention. I spent the night at my sister's so I wasn't driving. As a result, I was hitting the margaritas pretty hard."

"Still, once your sister reminds you, you don't think that you should have picked up the phone and called us? You had no way of knowing that we were going to stumble upon the connection," A.L. said.

"You're right," Alice said. "I think I got scared. It really dawned on me when Brenda Owen called and told me this thing was going to hang over my head for the rest of my life. People were going to blame me." She paused. "I got freaked out. I'm not proud of that and I'm sorry I lied."

"Did you lie about Emma Whitman being in your backyard?" Rena asked.

"She has never been in my backyard," Alice said.

They were at a stalemate.

"Your sister seemed to believe that you might not consider the Whitmans to be very good parents," Rena said. "What can you tell us about that?"

"It was months ago. Maybe even six months ago. Leah and Troy both ended up at the day care late one afternoon to pick up Emma. There'd been some miscommunication about who was doing what. I've seen it happen before with many parents. They usually laugh about it and that's the end of it."

"But it was different with the Whitmans?" Rena asked.

"Yes. Leah had arrived first and she and Emma were just about to walk out. Then Troy arrived. And Leah got so angry. Said that she'd had to leave work in the middle of an important meeting and that Troy was inconsiderate as usual in not calling her to tell her that he was going to be free to get Emma. It was ugly. They were flinging accusations back and forth. It actually reminded me of how my sister used to fight with her husband. I think that's why I told her. I shouldn't have. It was bad enough that I saw it."

"Nobody else around?" A.L. asked.

"I don't think so. I think I might have mentioned that Emma is generally one of the last to be picked up. It's possible that a couple of the teachers might have seen it. I remember that we were having a staff meeting that night. We do that once a quarter. But we didn't talk about it. It's very uncomfortable to witness someone fighting like that. I think the saddest part for me is that Emma didn't seem all that bothered by it. It made me think that she'd heard similar arguments in the past. And she really is a very sweet little girl."

"You didn't say anything about this before," A.L. said.

"If I had any reason to believe that the Whitmans mistreated Emma in any way, I would have said something. But I don't think that's the case. I think they both love Emma very much. I'm just not certain how much they love each other."

A.L. could relate. It had been that way with him and Jacqui. Both had loved Traci fiercely but knew the marriage wasn't going to make it.

"It's been more than three days," Alice said, sounding hopeless. "They're not going to find her, are they?"

"Nobody is giving up," A.L. said.

"At some point, we'll have to, though," Alice said.

"That point is a long ways away," A.L. said. "I think we're done here now."

Alice stood. "I appreciate everything you're doing to find out who is responsible for this. I really do. And I'm sorry if I impeded that effort."

A.L. could almost see the wheels churning in Rena's head. *Is Alice truly sorry? Or is she simply acting contrite but continuing to be less than forthcoming with the whole truth?*

"Thank you, Alice," he said.

When they were back in the car, Rena sighed. Loudly. "Every time I'm ready to be really pissed at her, she claws her way back."

"Into your heart?" A.L. asked.

"Not my heart. But into some quasi acceptance zone."

"You *accept* her explanations?"

"I *accept* her logic."

A.L. nodded. "Yeah. Me, too. We need to keep looking. Who haven't we talked to yet? Let's go through the list one more time."

"Can I do that with a cup of coffee in my hand?" Rena asked.

"Christ, Morgan. Do you do everything with a cup of coffee in your hand?"

"Just about. Some things are more awkward, though."

That got her a quick smile. And he did drive directly to one of her favorite coffee shops. Which was surprisingly busy even though it was early evening. "Guess this proves that lots of people drink coffee at all times of the day," she said as they stood in line.

A.L. looked around at the relatively young crowd. "Most of these people were having Bloody Marys for breakfast with beer chasers."

"It is Wisconsin and lots of them are probably students."

"That reminds me, how is Gabe doing with his classes? Is he happy to be a student again?"

"I think he loves it," she said. "I heard him say the other day that everybody should go back to school in their forties, that our minds are so much more open to learning."

A.L. thanked the young man who handed him two coffees. He carried the cups to a small table in the corner. At the next table were two men, both wearing light blue scrubs. He suspected they were from the hospital three blocks east.

"You know, we never actually talked to Kara Wiese's husband," he said.

"Right. We did get verification that he was working on Wednesday."

"We did. But I think I'd feel better if we actually spoke to him," A.L. said. "If he's working today, he'd be just finishing up his shift. Want to take a quick run down to the hospital, see if we can get lucky?"

"We desperately need to get lucky," Rena said. "Emma needs us to get lucky."

A.L. shoved his chair back, so fast that it scraped the floor and made a noise. "Sometimes you got to make your own luck."

Baywood Memorial was a level-two trauma center, an accredited chest pain center and a certified stroke center. All that meant that they could treat almost any emergency from a sore throat to a heart attack or stroke to a gunshot wound. The most serious traumas or any burn victims generally got airlifted to Madison.

There was a marked police vehicle in the lot. Parked and empty. That probably wasn't unusual. Sometimes there were disruptive people who required a police response. Sometimes, officers accompanied inmates from the county jail.

They entered through the emergency room doors that opened as they approached. There were at least ten people in the waiting area, one with a service dog sitting quietly at his feet.

A.L. and Rena stepped up to the glass window. A.L. suspected it was bulletproof. "We're looking for Sam Wiese. Is he working tonight?"

"Are you a patient?" she asked, not answering the question.

"No."

She looked at him as if expecting him to offer up more. When he didn't, she pointed to the chairs in the lobby. "Have a seat. I'll see if he's able to take a break."

"He must be working," Rena murmured.

It was almost ten minutes before a man wearing blue scrubs and tennis shoes came through a door from the back. He glanced around the waiting room. A.L. stood up. "Mr. Wiese?"

"Yes."

A.L. passed him a business card. "Could we maybe step outside for a minute?"

"Okay," he said. He didn't sound too concerned. It was hard to rile an emergency department nurse. They'd seen it all.

Once outside, Rena also passed him a card. "Thanks for talking with us. Did we catch you at the end of a shift?"

"Yeah." He ran a hand across his short hair. "Long day."

"We'll try not to keep you long," A.L. said. "We are the detectives who are investigating the disappearance of Emma Whitman."

He nodded. "I recognized your names. Kara mentioned it. She's torn up about this."

"We understand that you were working this past Wednesday?" Rena said.

"Yeah. I do three or four twelve-hour shifts a week. And I'm going to grad school to be a nurse practitioner."

"Had you ever met the missing child, Emma Whitman?"

"No. I've never been to Kara's work."

"So you don't know anyone from there?"

"I know Claire Potter. She's been at the house a couple times."

"She and Kara are friends?"

"Yeah. She's cool."

That reminded A.L. that it had been Claire Potter who had originally mentioned that Kara had been interested in buying a house. Kara had later said that she was talking to the bank about refinancing.

"With working and going to school, that doesn't leave time for much of anything else," A.L. said.

"Not really."

"Kara mentioned that you were recently looking at refinancing your house but decided not to pursue it. That can be a pretty time-consuming process," A.L. said.

Sam shook his head. "We're not refinancing." He didn't sound concerned. Probably just thought A.L. had his facts mixed up.

"Really? I thought for sure that it was Kara who'd mentioned that. But we have talked to a lot of people."

"Yeah. Not us. We just bought our house a couple years ago when we got married. We got a really good rate. We'd be fools to refinance so soon."

"Okay." A.L. looked at Rena.

She smiled at Sam. "Thanks for your time. Good night."

Once they were back in their car, Rena turned to A.L. "What are the chances that Kara was pursuing a refinance without her husband's knowledge?"

"Possible but not likely. Couples talk about things like that. Maybe one person does all the work to gather the documents but it's with the other person's knowledge."

"Agree. What's the likelihood that Sam is going to tell Kara that we came to see him tonight?"

"Pretty high. He knew our names. Maybe Kara had warned him that we might want to talk to him. He'll tell her we came to his work. She'll want to know what we asked him and he'll tell her about the refinancing questions."

"I think so, too. So she's going to know that we now have doubts about what she told us."

"Yeah."

They sat in silence, both pondering what the next best step would be.

"Did you see the yellow ribbons?" Rena asked.

Up and down the main street around the trees. They'd gone up this morning. "Yeah."

More silence.

"You know who I want to talk to?" Rena said.

"Claire Potter," he said.

"How did you know?"

"She's the right one."

"Okay. Tonight?" Rena asked.

"No time like the present." He didn't need to add that tomorrow was Sunday and it would be four days since Emma had been seen.

It was past eight when they arrived at Claire's door, getting dark. Lights were on in the back of her house. They rang the bell.

Then A.L.'s cell phone rang. "McKittridge," he answered.

"Are you at my door?"

He recognized her voice. "Yes, Claire. It's me and Detective Morgan. Can we have just a few minutes of your time?"

"Sure. Hang on." Then she disconnected. In fifteen seconds, the door was opening. She smiled at them. "I thought it was you but I scratched one of my contacts and so my vision in that eye isn't good. I didn't want to open the door to a stranger."

"Good thinking to call first," A.L. said.

"A week ago I might not have," she said. "But this whole thing with Emma has me second-guessing everything. How the hell does a five-year-old just disappear?"

"We share your frustration," said Rena. "We're continuing to follow every lead, which has brought us back to your door."

"Okay."

"On Thursday, when we were here, you said that one of the reasons a teacher might leave the room is to make or receive a phone call. Specifically, you said that you thought Kara was buying a new house because you thought she was talking to her banker or her lawyer."

Claire said nothing.

"Did Kara tell you that she was buying a new house?" A.L. asked.

"No."

"Perhaps refinancing a house?" A.L. followed up.

"No."

Rena leaned forward in her chair. "Did those conversations occur in the classroom?"

"No."

Claire was clearly uncomfortable and that was making the back of A.L.'s neck itch. "We need a little help here, Claire. Why did you think she was talking to her banker or her lawyer?"

"I'm reluctant to say," Claire said.

Now his neck was not only itchy, it felt hot. But he told himself not to push, that Claire would come to the right decision on her own. Rena settled back against her chair, as if she, too, was prepared to wait as long as it took.

"I really like Kara and I know she didn't have anything to do with Emma's disappearance. She was in the classroom when it happened. And then I taught with her all day. And I would have known if something was wrong. But there wasn't. She was fine. We were all fine until we heard the news."

A.L. and Rena said nothing. It was so quiet in the little house that they could hear the pump in the fish tank in the corner of the room.

"Twice when her phone rang, I saw the name of the caller flash across the screen before she answered it. I recognized the name."

"Who was it?" A.L. asked.

"Steven Hanzel. He's a loan officer at the Baywood Bank."

Neither Rena nor A.L. indicated that they already knew the man. "How is it that you know Mr. Hanzel?" Rena asked.

"His kids come to the learning center. And his ex-wife goes to the same place I do for yoga. She's told me a few things about…their marriage. Both before and after the divorce."

"So not great things," Rena said. "But yet, you chose

to believe that any reason Steven Hanzel was calling Kara had to be business-related and not personal?"

A.L. was grateful that Rena had asked the hard question. He wasn't sure how he'd have phrased it and she'd done a good job.

"I told you that Kara and I are friends. We go to dinner sometimes. We've talked about what Steven Hanzel's wife had told me, for goodness' sakes."

There it was. She didn't want to think that her friend had been stupid by taking up with a sleazebag. "You never asked Kara about the calls from Mr. Hanzel?" A.L. asked.

"No. I just couldn't. Maybe I didn't really want to know. But I have to admit that sometimes I was pissed off. He'd call and she'd leave the room immediately and sometimes we'd be in the middle of some activity that really needed two teachers. It seemed…neglectful."

"Can you give a time period that these calls were occurring?" Rena asked.

"A few months ago it was the worst. But recently, it's been better. Maybe they're talking outside of work hours because she doesn't leave the room nearly as much."

"Better but still occurring?" Rena drilled. "Like how often in one week?"

"Like I said, months ago it would have been several times a week. Now it's maybe one every couple of weeks."

"Claire, you've been very helpful," Rena said.

"Really? Because I feel sort of shitty, to be honest. She's my friend and I basically just told you that I think she's having an extramarital affair."

"Trust us on this, Claire. We're not concerned right now with what anybody is doing within or outside of their marriage unless it has some direct relation to our investigation into Emma's disappearance."

"Do you think this does?" Claire asked.

"We have no idea," A.L. said honestly. "But I'm glad we know it."

They sat in their car outside of Claire's house. "Are you surprised?" Rena asked.

"About Steven Hanzel?" A.L. asked.

"About either of them."

"Not about Hanzel. He seemed like a goofball when I met him. His boss thinks he's a loser and Chuck Hayes implied that he played around on business trips. Kara, maybe. She seems pretty bright so I guess I'd expect her to be smarter than to fall for the goofball."

"Love and/or lust makes people stupid," Rena said.

"Which one of them do you want to talk to first?" A.L. said.

"Kara. But wait a minute. Let's think about this. She said that the calls had diminished but not stopped. We checked Kara's cell phone. There'd been no calls between her and Baywood Bank for more than two months."

"We didn't look at calls specifically between her and Steven Hanzel, say, to his personal cell. We have to do that," A.L. said.

"You're right. I'll get somebody started on that." She picked up her cell phone. Typed. Looked up. "You should take Washington Street," she said offhandedly. "That's the fastest way to her house."

"We're not going to her. She's coming to us."

Rena stopped typing. "Trying to make a point?"

"Yeah. Don't fuck with us."

Seventeen

Kara Wiese said she was in her pajamas and asked if she could come to the police station the following day. A.L. said no. She said it would take her an hour to get there. A.L. said, "Do your best."

The good news was that the extra time gave them an opportunity to verify that there had been no telephone calls between Steven Hanzel's cell phone and Kara Wiese's cell phone. Neither of them had home phones.

"You think Claire was wrong?" A.L. asked. "Or they've both got a second phone?"

"Hard to know. I'll get somebody to do a search for another number under her name. Plus, we'll ask her about it. If she ever gets here," she added.

"I'm five minutes away from sending squad cars with lights and sirens to her house." He leaned back in his chair so far that the legs came off the floor. When there was a knock on the door, the legs hit the floor hard.

"She's here," said the officer working the front desk.

"Excellent. Be right back," A.L. said to Rena. He walked to the front entrance. "Evening, Kara."

"Evening, Detective," she said.

"Let's walk back this direction," he said pointing. "Detective Morgan is going to be joining us."

"Everyone's working late, then," she said.

"We've got a missing child," he said.

"Of course. That's why I'm here."

A.L. opened the door.

"Detective Morgan," Kara said.

"Thank you for coming in," Rena said. "We have a few questions about a previous statement that you gave us. In specific, you said that a few months back, you made several calls to the Baywood Bank because you were interested in refinancing your current home. Is there any part of that statement that you'd like to amend?"

"No. Listen, I understand the confusion. I spoke with Sam. Who was also a little confused." She offered up a smile. "My husband is a great guy. Works hard. Is going to school to get ahead. But he's not good with details or quite frankly, anything financial. I pay all the bills in my family. So those discussions I had with the bank about refinancing were done without him even being aware. It didn't go anywhere so there really wasn't a need to tell him after the fact."

Again, Rena thought, *such a fucking reasonable explanation.*

"I guess I'm having trouble with your earlier explanation that you don't recall who you spoke to at the bank. You see, I've refinanced," A.L. said. "And it's sort of a process. And I can't help but think that it would have been unnecessarily complicated if you were talking to several different people."

"Not really," she said. "But truthfully, I never got very far in the process. My questions were mostly the exploratory variety. And a couple times, I know I just slipped them into conversations I was already having with Steven."

"Steven?" A.L. asked. He was, quite frankly, surprised that she'd offered up the connection.

"Steven Hanzel. He's a loan officer at the bank and was my cochair for the Fourth of July Activities Committee. So we were going back and forth on that."

He had some familiarity with Baywood's Activities Committee. If they'd been cochairs, there would be some public record of that. "That was convenient for you," he said.

"Very."

She was one of the best liars he'd ever interviewed or she was telling the truth. He just didn't know. He decided to poke her with a stick.

"Do you happen to know Shana Federer?"

"I know that she has a child at the learning center. But not in my class."

"But you'd recognize her if you saw her."

"I think so."

"And she'd recognize you."

"I don't know, Detective. I really don't understand the question."

"No question," he said easily. "Just conversation. Let's go back to the Activities Committee work that you were doing with Steven. Most of your communication done on the phone?"

"Yes."

"All of it?" A.L. asked.

"Well, no. We met in person sometimes. Our whole committee did."

"Oh, sure. That makes sense," A.L. said. "Probably some emails, too."

"I guess. I don't really recall."

"Texts?" A.L. asked.

"I… I don't really know. I do text a lot. Everybody does, right?"

"Phones, an extension of our hands. You have just the one cell phone, Kara?" A.L. asked.

"Yes," she said. Then she yawned. "I really am sorry," she said. "It's just that I'm so tired. Is there anything else?"

Rena shook her head. A.L. stood. "I'll walk you out."

When he got back to the conference room, Rena was on the phone. Listening intently. All the color had drained from her face. And her hand was shaking. "Thank you," she said. "Appreciate the call." She carefully put her cell phone on the table.

"Fuck," A.L. said. "They found her and she's dead."

"No. No," she said. "It's not about Emma. It's…"

"Gabe? One of the Morgans?"

"No."

"Tell me what the hell is going on, Rena. You look as if you're about to slip out of that chair." He wasn't exaggerating.

"Remember that I told you that we had selected somebody to be our carrier for the pregnancy? And that she lived with a lowlife?"

"Yeah."

"I put a tag on the lowlife, so that I'd get notified if something came in on him."

Cops did that, especially on people of interest in on-going investigations. It wasn't quite kosher that she'd done it for personal reasons but nobody was going to get too upset about that. Privilege of the job in a job where there weren't that many privileges. "What showed up?"

"He got arrested last night. Narcotics. Unlicensed firearms and other explosives." She looked up. "Felony charges. He's has a previous record."

"So he's pond scum. It's not his sperm making the baby."

"I have to tell Gabe."

"Info probably isn't in the public record yet," A.L. said gently. Until then, she had a responsibility to only share it on a need-to-know basis.

"I don't care. Listen, I need a half hour."

"Go."

"I knew something like this was going to happen. I just knew it." She laughed shakily. "Maybe I'm the psychic." She got four steps. Turned. "We need to verify Kara's story, that she was working as a cochair with Steven Hanzel."

"We will. Now shut it off. Go talk to Gabe."

Ten minutes later, she wasn't sure if she was grateful or not that Gabe's car was in the driveway. It might have been good to have a little more time to compose herself, to think of the best way to offer up the information.

To come up with a plan, a solution.

But then again, it couldn't be her plan. It had to be their plan. Just like it was their baby.

She opened the door and was surprised to see him sitting at the kitchen table. Dressed. In dark jeans and a button-down shirt. His hair, which hadn't been cut for months, was pushed behind his ears. Another month or two and it would touch his shoulders. It was too long but he looked good. Always had. Probably always would.

"What's going on?" she asked. She'd talked to him two hours ago, told him that she'd be working late. He'd said not to worry about it, that he was on his way to bed.

"Just getting ready to go out with some friends," he said. "It just came up. I was going to text you."

Right. "Who?"

"Tom and Rick. You don't know them."

"From school."

"Yeah. Did you get done early?"

"Something came up." She pulled out a chair. "I needed to talk to you."

He stared at her. "Are you okay? Did something happen at work? Is it A.L.?"

She held up a hand. "It's Matthew Stahl."

"Shannon's husband."

"He's been arrested," she said.

"*You* arrested him?" Gabe asked.

"No. Another officer. But it's serious. Charges are getting filed. Drugs. Guns and other explosives. He already has a felony record. If he's convicted, he's going to prison."

"Did Shannon call you?" Gabe asked. "Did she want your help?"

"No. I just found out." She paused. "I had a tag on his name. So that if anything came in on him, the arresting officer would know to contact me."

"You were watching him."

She threw up her hands. "Gabe, you're missing the point. We have chosen these people to shepherd our child into the world."

"The last I knew he didn't have a uterus," Gabe said. "Shannon is probably going to want to do this more than ever. They'll have some legal expenses."

"We can't use Shannon," she said. "That's out of the question."

"The paperwork, all fucking nineteen pages of the contract, have been reviewed and initialed. We can't stop now, Rena."

"Our unborn child will be going on visits to the state penitentiary. Is that what you want? Is that what you'd be satisfied with? Happy with?" She got up, too agitated to sit. "People talk and have long memories. Years from now, it'll get thrown in our kid's face. People will say, oh, you were *that baby.*"

"Rena," Gabe said, his voice low, his tone even. "Is it possible that you're overreacting?"

She didn't know. The idea that their child would ever be considered less than…perfect. Or that he or she might actually be less than perfect. After all, who knew exactly how much a fetus absorbed from the outside world while in the womb? She just couldn't take that chance. Not on something so important. "This breaks the morals clause in the contract."

"Is that what you want?" he asked again.

She didn't know what the fuck she wanted. "We'll find someone else," she said.

He shrugged. "We'll see."

"We will," she insisted.

"We've already spent a lot of money on this. And with me being back in school for a job that's going to pay less than what I was making, it maybe wasn't a good idea to begin with."

It was what she'd been afraid of. He was going to back out. She felt sick. All their planning, all their hoping. It would fall apart.

She would fall apart.

"I have to go back to work." She picked up her keys. They felt heavy in her hand. "We can talk later."

"Seems as if you've made up your mind," he said. "I've got to go, too. I'll be home late."

He walked out the door, leaving her in her silent kitchen. Her phone buzzed. It was A.L. Are you coming back tonight? No problem if you're not.

On my way, she texted back.

We've got bus video of Coyote Frogg was his response.

Eighteen

"Everything okay?" A.L. asked.

Hardly, thought Rena. "Yeah, fine." She couldn't even remember the drive back to work.

A.L. studied her. He likely didn't believe her but he also understood that sometimes it really was better to compartmentalize. To give your full attention to something else besides what was troubling you. And right now, it was almost 11:00 at night and she'd been up since 5:00. She should be tired. But the thought that they'd found Coyote Frogg was exhilarating.

The door of the conference room opened and in walked an analyst who often helped them with video evidence. "Hey, Louisa, thanks for hanging out with us tonight."

"No problem. My thirteen-year-old son is having a friend over tonight. Lots of yelling and screaming at the video games. My husband is better suited to dealing with that."

"I get it." Would Gabe be that kind of dad? If she backed out of this deal, would he ever be any kind of dad? Damn. Compartmentalize. "What are we look-ing at?"

"We worked with the city to get video of bus 13, which runs along Clayton Avenue. The stop you were specifically interested in was Wake Street. And we're pretty sure we got your boys jumping on there once but got them another time a little farther down the line on Poke Street." She was pulling up video as she talked.

It was gray and a little grainy but there they were, about halfway back, slouched in a seat. "That's Coy-ote," A.L. said.

He looked as if he was sleeping. The guy next to him was awake but barely. He was just staring ahead. "Date and time, Louisa?"

The woman pointed to the bottom of the screen. That's last Monday, about 16:20 hours."

The kid had said that he'd seen them between 4:00 and 4:30. He was proving to be a good little witness.

"I'm going to fast-forward to where they get off," Louisa said. "Here we are twenty minutes later and they're getting off at the corner of Willow and Spring."

"What's at Willow and Spring?" Rena asked. She had a rough idea. There was a three- or four-block radius of manufacturing companies that had many decades back strategically located near the rail line. Trains no longer ran, however, and many of the busi-nesses were closed up. A few had been turned into cool loft apartments, but it was a work in progress. The homeless liked to hang out there, especially under the Oaken Bridge.

"We picked them up on street cameras heading

north," Louisa said. "We lost them when they turned the corner, but perhaps they were headed here."

Here was an old three-story brick factory. It was a long rectangular shape with a row of very small windows across the front. It would not have caught the eye of a developer looking to turn the property into upscale housing. Some of the glass appeared to have been knocked out. "Nice," Rena said sarcastically.

"Yeah. The city is working to get this one torn down."

"We need to search that building," A.L. said.

"Already done," Louisa said. "I showed my boss this information before I came to you and he greased the wheels. They found some homeless. They did not find these two guys or a five-year-old girl."

"You said that you had them jumping on the bus at another point. Can we see that?" A.L. asked.

"Yeah. This is Wednesday night. About 20:00 hours."

"The night of Emma's disappearance," A.L. said.

"They're at a bus stop on Poke Street, about eight blocks east of Clayton and Wake." She pushed some buttons and the images on the screen flickered. "Here we go."

Sure enough. Getting on the bus was Coyote Frogg and his friend, both looking as ill-kempt as ever. They took a seat but instead of sleeping, they were in an animated conversation. But not a happy one. Coyote looked especially pissed off.

"I wish I could tell what he was saying," Rena said.

"Yeah. No audio and he's not at a good angle to read his lips," Louisa said.

Rena leaned forward. "What's with their clothes?"

"Fuck," A.L. said.

Both men were wearing exactly the same thing. Bib overalls over a long-sleeved red T-shirt with the word *Wisconsin* in white running down both sleeves. "Those look brand-new."

"Brand-new clothes? Matching?" she said. "I don't like it."

"Why?" Louisa asked.

"Unless these two are secretly twins, and we're pretty confident they're not, it's weird to dress alike. They weren't dressed alike in the Monday video and their clothes weren't new. So it seems as if these may have very recently been purchased from somewhere where there wasn't much choice. Who does that? Purchases a whole outfit at one time?"

"Somebody who has to get rid of their clothes quickly," A.L. said, his voice heavy. "Like somebody who had a kid's DNA on them."

No one said anything for a long minute.

Finally, A.L. motioned with his hand. "Let's keep going. Where do they go?"

"Same place. But this time we got lucky. Well, sort of lucky." The video continued, filming them getting off the bus and walking up the street.

"Definitely new clothes," Rena said, pointing. Just barely visible was a tag hanging from the back of Coyote's friend's bibs.

Less than a half a block later, they approached a white Jeep, the kind the sides came off of, and got into the back seat. The car drove away.

The video stopped.

"That's the vehicle that Gi-Gi and Barrett Thompson described. Do we pick it up later? Do we know where it went?" A.L. asked.

Louisa nodded. "We got a nice shot of the plates." She opened the notebook that she carried and handed them a piece of paper. "Belongs to Pierce Dowl, who lives in Madison. We already passed his address along to our friends there and officers have checked his house. Vehicle is there. No sign of anybody in the house or that anybody has been there for several days. No milk in the fridge. No dirty dishes in the sink." She stopped. "No odd men with matching clothes."

"Where does this leave us?" Rena asked.

"I don't know," Louisa said. "I've looked at video of this same route for Thursday, Friday and today. They never ride that bus again."

They were gone. Just like Emma. "Thank you, Louisa," A.L. said. "This has been very helpful. Do you know if somebody is watching this house, seeing if Pierce Dowl returns?"

"They are. Normally, I guess it would be hard to get the resources to do that. But they know what we're working on here. Everybody is willing to help."

Rena waited until Louisa was packed up and out of the room before saying, "We don't need help. We need a miracle."

"We keep working the case," A.L. said. "And it's time to make this official." He typed on his computer keyboard for several minutes. "Coyote Frogg and his unnamed associate are now identified as Persons of Interest in the disappearance of Emma Whitman. We know that Coyote Frogg was in Baywood on both Monday and Wednesday of this past week. He's living nearby. We need to get everybody looking and run him to ground."

"There may not be much more we can do tonight," Rena said.

"Two more things." A.L. picked up his smart phone and started pressing keys. "Here it is," he said. He held his phone out to Rena.

It was a web page for the city of Baywood.

"Look in the middle—there's a section about the Activities Committee." She looked and sure enough, it listed the cochairs of the group as Steven Hanzel and Kara Wiese.

"Kara was telling the truth," she said.

"Looks like it," A.L. agreed. "No affair, just innocent fun and community service." He turned to his computer and started typing. Finally looked up. "That was the second thing. I just sent a message that will get distributed to every one of our officers, county and state, about the bib overalls and the red Wisconsin T-shirts. Somebody will know where those are sold."

"Red Wisconsin T-shirts are sold everywhere," Rena said.

"Yeah, but not with bib overalls, and we're specifically looking for a place with limited choices. I put all that in the message."

He leaned back in his chair and rubbed a hand over his face. "Let's call it a night," he said. "I'll see you tomorrow." It didn't matter that it was Sunday. Nobody was taking any days off now.

A.L. drove home and parked in the lot outside his apartment. By habit, he scanned the area first, then opened his door. It was a clear night and the temperature was a comfortable fifty-six. He glanced at his phone, to check one final search update for the night.

Volunteers led by the FBI had searched the Harborview and Olive Grove subdivisions tonight. Both were on the eastern outskirts of Baywood. Every day they widened their circle, ticking off more and more of Baywood. Every day it became less and less likely that a five-year-old could have covered the distance without anybody seeing her. They'd ended the evening with thirty-two volunteers.

He opened the door of his apartment building and walked down the hall. Stopped when he was four feet from his door. There was a square box, maybe twelve inches wide, on the floor. There was an envelope taped to the top. He took one more step.

Smiled. It was Tess's writing.

He pulled off the envelope and opened it. Inside was a card, with a silly-looking photo of a cat hanging from some draperies, looking really happy. No words. But inside, Tess had written a note.

Able: Thank you for the flowers, they are beautiful. You continue to surprise me. I'm sorry for barging in to your work. I'll try not to make a habit of it. I'm especially sorry that I insinuated that my daughter was more important to me than Traci is to you. That was ridiculous and I'm glad you called me out on it. I know you're working hard. Perhaps this will come in handy as a late night snack. Tess.

He opened the box. Cherry pie. His favorite. Maybe he'd mentioned that a time or two to her when they'd gone to the county fair in August.

He unlocked his door, then carefully picked up the box. He set it down on the counter, grabbed a plate from the cupboard and a knife and fork from the drawer. Then he cut himself a big slab and sat down in his favorite recliner to enjoy a piece.

He did all this before he ever turned on a light.

There was something very nice about eating a surprise piece of cherry pie in the dark. He picked up his cell. It was now almost midnight. Too late to call or text.

He finished his piece and closed his eyes. Leaned back in his chair.

Went to sleep thinking about Tess.

Gabe wasn't home when Rena got there. She washed her face and brushed her teeth and put on a T-shirt to sleep in. Then she crawled into bed.

She was still awake when Gabe got home an hour later but pretended to be asleep. He was quiet as he got ready for bed. When he sat down and swung his legs in, she opened her eyes. They were both lying on their backs. "Oh, hey," she said.

"I'm sorry, I didn't mean to wake you."

"No problem. Have fun?"

"Yeah, it was okay," he said with no real enthusiasm. There was a long moment of silence.

"Listen, Rena," Gabe said. "I get where you were coming from earlier. I do. And I'm not happy about Shannon's husband. It just seems to me that ever since we agreed to go down this path and selected Shannon, you've been looking for a reason to get out of it."

The bedroom was dark and she was grateful for that. She'd never had a great poker face and now she was confident that he'd know that he'd hit close to home. Gabe had always known her best. And right now, he deserved honesty.

"You might be right," she said. "I'm sorry about that. Because it's taken time and money. But the closer we got, it just…didn't seem right. Not for us."

"I don't care about the time or the money. You know that, right?"

"I do."

"Not everybody has to have a child," Gabe said, his voice gentle. "We will be happy still."

He was right. Of course. But under the covers, she slid her hand so that it rested on her abdomen. The emptiness seemed to radiate through her entire body.

"What do you say that we wait, put this discussion on hold for at least six months?" Gabe suggested.

It wasn't forever. But her eggs would be six months older.

Why couldn't this be easy for them? It was for so many people.

But those thoughts swamped her with guilt. Life wasn't easy for Troy and Leah Whitman right now. Or Elaine Broadstreet. Or Alice Quest. Or anybody even remotely connected to Emma Whitman.

Life was just hard sometimes. And feeling sorry for yourself wasn't helpful.

She turned on her side to face him. Could feel him shift, too. And when she was in his arms, knew there was no place she'd rather be. "We'll be okay," she said, her mouth close to his ear. They would be. Could be.

"Damn straight," he said as he bent his head to kiss her.

By seven on Sunday morning, A.L. and Rena were at their desks. Blithe and Ferguson were also in. Faster's office was empty. The chief was likely on the golf course.

"I got the list of all other abductions or attempted abductions at or near day care centers from across the United States for the last twenty years," A.L. said. He tossed it across the desk.

"That's a lot," she said. "More than I expected."

"Yeah. Here's the list if we filter out those that were known to be committed by biological or adoptive parents," A.L. said.

Less than half a page. She tossed it back to him. He left it on his desk where it landed. "Wow. So we were right to give Troy and Leah Whitman a close look."

"Speaking of close looks, I'm meeting Troy at Garage on Division at 8:00 to look at his service scheduling records. Getting a technical assist from Shawn." Everybody in the Baywood Police Department knew Shawn. Data forensics was becoming a bigger part of every investigation and Shawn Moby was a fucking magician when it came to ferreting out information that lived in the cloud.

"What are you looking for?" Rena asked.

"Troy says that he was at work early on Wednesday, contrary to what Pete and Cory said."

"Not a very big place," Rena said. "You think they'd run into each other if they were all there."

"Yeah. He said he was in the office area and they were working in the bays. That sort of matches up to what Cory Prider said. He got to work first and then finished up a brake job that had been started on Tuesday. Pete Seoul said he got to work at 7:30 and I guess it's safe to assume that he started working on a vehicle."

"Why don't we just ask them whose vehicles they were working on?" Rena asked.

"Because I don't really want to talk to those two idiots again and I don't trust their memory or their intent. Remember how Pete sent us scurrying to Alcamay Corners? I think it's better to review the records. Plus I wanted to send a message to Troy. That any unexplained absence on Wednesday was going to get critically reviewed."

"Depending on when the brake job got finished, you're assuming that maybe that customer would have seen Troy? Or maybe the driver of the vehicle that Pete Seoul was working on."

"Bunch of maybes but then again, maybe we'll get lucky. I'd better get going." His cell phone buzzed. He picked it up. Read the message, then tossed his phone aside.

"What?" Rena asked.

"That's Troy. Said he couldn't be at the garage at 8:00. There's something he has to do."

"What could be more important that cooperating with the detective who is investigating his daughter's disappearance?" Rena asked. "I think he needs to—"

She saw Ferguson, who was across the room at his

desk, lean back in his chair and point the remote control in the direction of the television that was mounted on the wall. "Hey, guys," the detective said. "You got to see this."

This was *At Seven on Seven,* a one-hour news show on Sunday mornings on the local CBS affiliate out of Madison. It was hosted by Caroline Jensen, who was tall, thin, blond and blue-eyed. Made for television, one might say. She was also articulate and smart, which had helped attract readers to the program.

The show was coming back from a commercial break and it took A.L. and Rena just seconds to realize what had been more important to Troy Whitman. To both the Whitmans, who sat opposite Caroline.

"Who the fuck thought this was a good idea?" A.L. said.

"Shush," Rena said.

"...being here," Caroline said. "As I mentioned in the lead-up, Emma has now been missing for four days. Please, help us understand what that's like."

"It's the most terrifying experience of our lives," Leah said. "A nightmare. But we haven't given up hope that our little girl will be returned to us."

"Truly every parent's worst nightmare. *At Seven on Seven* attempted to talk with Alice Quest, the director of Lakeside Learning Center, where Emma disappeared from, but she declined our invitation for an interview."

"One sane person," A.L. muttered.

"We are aware that both she and the rest of the staff have been questioned by the police," Leah said. "This is something that a parent doesn't expect to happen in a place that is supposed to be safe." With a quick swipe, she wiped at the corner of her eye.

"There's been no ransom demand?" Caroline asked.

"No," Troy said.

"And have the police shared with you any information that might suggest that they have a suspect?"

"No," Leah said. "We understand it's difficult for the police to share much, but the not knowing doesn't help."

Caroline looked into the camera. "Searchers continue to examine the area east of town this morning, focusing on the land between Kissimee Road and Portage Creek. FBI at the scene were unavailable to provide comment but did confirm that this continues to be a search effort and not a recovery effort."

Caroline turned back to Leah and Troy. "What is it you'd like our viewers to know this morning?"

"Just that we appreciate all the help people have given, all the time. And that we need everyone to keep looking, to not stop," Troy said. "To call if you see anything."

"I understand there is a fund-raising site that concerned viewers can go to," Caroline said.

"Yes," Leah said. She rattled off the website and repeated it just as it flashed across the bottom of the screen. "We're incredibly grateful to Steven Hanzel from the Baywood Bank for assisting with that."

"Thank you, Leah and Troy. I know the whole community joins you in hoping that Emma is found safe and sound. And now, *At Seven on Seven* looks at how recycling is becoming big business in western Wisconsin."

Ferguson flipped off the television. "Could have been worse," he said before turning to look at his computer.

"He's right," Rena said. "They didn't say we were a bunch of clowns."

"Leah threw Alice and the rest of the staff under the bus," A.L. said.

"She's hurting," Rena said. "Her child is gone."

"She sounded as if she was a fan of Steven Hanzel. I didn't get that impression before."

"Did she say something about him?" Rena asked.

"No. But there was something in her tone when she told me that Troy and his friend Steven were in the garage. Anyway, that probably doesn't matter. What matters is that Hanzel's supervisor is going to blow a gasket because it really made it sound as if Baywood Bank was behind the fund-raising idea."

"Yeah, gave it real legitimacy. I suspect people who might have been on the fence about contributing will be opening their checkbooks."

"Maybe that was the point," A.L. said.

Nineteen

It was after ten before A.L. and Shawn Moby entered Garage on Division. Troy was standing behind the counter. A.L. made the introductions and then asked Troy to show Shawn the basics of their computer system.

The flow seemed pretty straightforward. A customer contact led to a work order. Work was dated and timed. Parts and services were billed separately and taxed differently. Monies were received in various forms—cash, check, credit card—and applied to the work order. Notes could be entered at any part of the process. It wasn't a full financial review, but merely a medium dive into a subset of the business. But it gave A.L. what he was looking for. And if Troy had been bothered by the request initially, he seemed fine with it now.

Maybe he was busy thinking of other things. At no point did either A.L. or Troy mention the television interview.

Once Shawn was able to download the data, they left. When they got back to their office, it took Shawn six minutes to find what A.L. was specifically looking for. There it was. Harvey Pointe's 2018 Chrysler Pacifica had come in on Tuesday and was finished at 8:22 on Wednesday by Prider. Then he'd moved on to J.A. Shepherd's 2012 Ford Focus that was serviced between 8:36 and 10:03.

Peitra Jonet's 2017 Honda Pilot had been serviced between 7:42 and 9:24 by Pete Seoul. No doubt she'd been charged for the fifteen minutes for Pete's 9:00 break.

The work order had a spot for customer name, address and phone. Very helpful.

He looked around for Rena but didn't see her. He might as well get to it. He dialed Harvey Pointe.

"Hello."

"Is this Harvey Pointe?"

"I'm not interested."

"Wait," A.L. said quickly. "This is Detective McKittridge of the Baywood Police Department."

"I don't give donations over the phone."

"Sir, I'm not looking for a donation. I'm calling because you had your vehicle serviced at Garage on Division this past week. Is that correct?"

"Yeah."

"According to the records I've reviewed, sir, I believe you took your car in some time on Tuesday and then it was finished on Wednesday."

"Yeah. I wasn't crazy about that."

"What time did you pick up your vehicle on Wednesday, sir?"

"Shortly after they called me. My wife dropped me off."

"Do you recall the time?" A.L. asked.

"It was shortly before 9:00 because I heard the nine o'clock news on my way home. I remember because I had to change the station back to the one I always listen to. Don't know why they have to change your radio station when you're getting a brake job."

"Do you recall, sir, who was in the office area when you paid for your vehicle?"

"I didn't go to the office. When Cory called me and told me the vehicle was done, I asked for the total. Told him that I would bring him a check. Then I wrote my check and drove to the garage. Cory was working in one of the bays. I gave the check to him. He marked Paid on the invoice and gave me a copy of it."

"Do you recall seeing anybody else at the garage?"

"I saw that Pete guy but I don't care for him so I cut a wide path around him."

"No one else? Not Troy Whitman, the owner?"

"Nope. Didn't see Troy. I like Troy. I'd have chatted with him a few minutes if he'd have been there."

But Harvey Pointe had not gone to the office.

"Thank you, sir, you've been very helpful," A.L. said.

"Guess it's a good thing I didn't hang up on you."

A.L. dialed J.A. Shepherd, not knowing if it was a male or female. But a woman answered. She sounded young.

"Hello."

"Ms. Shepherd?"

"Yes."

"This is Detective McKittridge with the Baywood Police Department. I was hoping to ask you a few questions about a visit you made to Garage on Division this past week."

"Uh…okay. I'm at work, though. I just have a few minutes."

"Where do you work?"

"Baywood Memorial," she said. "I'm a nurse in the emergency department."

Kara's Wiese's husband was a nurse in that same emergency room. "I'll be brief," he said. "I have information that says your vehicle was serviced on Wednesday. Is that correct?"

"Yes."

"Do you recall what time you dropped off your vehicle?"

"Before my shift started. So probably about 6:30."

"Was there anyone at Garage on Division at that time?" A.L. asked, already getting a bad feeling that J.A. Shepherd wasn't going to be any help.

"No. They have a lock box for your keys."

"What time did you pick it up?"

"Probably about 7:30 that night. No one was there then. But by then we'd all heard the Amber Alert and knew that the father ran Garage on Division. I wasn't expecting to see anyone. Fortunately, I'd had them put my keys under my floor mat."

Christ, this was one big bust. "Thank you for your time, Ms. Shepherd."

"Sure." She hung up.

Was this why Troy had seemed more relaxed about the request this morning? Had he realized that A.L. was going to run into a dead end?

There was one more person to call. Peitra Jonet. He

dialed the number. It rang four times and went to voice mail. He left a brief message, asking for a return call. Then he sat at his desk, drumming his fingers on the scarred wood.

"Any luck?" Rena asked, coming back to her desk.

"Got the information off the computer system easily enough but didn't get anything helpful from two of the three customers I needed to talk to. Waiting to hear from the third."

"Okay. I managed to connect with the beat cops who cover the area where Coyote Frogg and his friend got off the bus. They told me that Frogg first showed up about a month ago. He's peddling for sure. They're watching him, trying to figure out if he's an independent operator or part of an established network."

From his early days on the force, he knew that was a fairly common approach. The opportunity to catch a bigger fish was not one to be squandered. "We definitely need to talk to Coyote's mother in Vegas. Ferguson tracked down her number for me. She's still in Las Vegas. I may just be spinning my wheels."

"Is that anything like getting your tires rotated?"

A.L. rolled his eyes. "Garage humor? Really, Morgan. That's the best you can do on a Sunday morning?"

"I didn't get breakfast. Let's go to Pancake Magic. Maybe Traci is working?"

It was always a good day when he could see his kid and surprise her with a twenty under his plate as an extraspecial gratuity. "Let me call Dusty first."

"It's still early in Las Vegas."

"Maybe she's an early riser," he said. He looked up the number on the email that Ferguson had sent. He dialed. Like with Peitra Jonet, the line rang four times before it went to voice mail. "Getting to be old shit," A.L. murmured.

"You've reached Dusty. Leave a message or don't. It's all good." The beep sounded. He left his name and number and asked for a call back.

"She sounds chipper," Rena said.

"I do love chipper," A.L. said. "Let's go."

They decided to walk since it was an especially nice fall morning. The sun was bright but the air was still cool, the temperature hovering around sixty-eight degrees. When they got there, A.L. opened the door and motioned for Rena to go first.

She was two steps ahead of him when she turned abruptly. She had a lousy poker face and he could tell that something was very wrong. "I want you to remember that you're in a public place," she said, very fast.

What the fuck. He looked around her. It wasn't hard. He was six inches taller. And there at the counter was his daughter, smiling, chatting, looking like the beautiful girl she was. And then he realized that she was talking to the boy—no, the man—he'd told her to stay away from. Golf Course John. She'd not yet seen him or Rena. She was too busy.

He stepped around Rena and shook off the hand that tried to grab his arm. Then he swung his body onto the open stool next to Golf Course John. He heard his daughter gasp.

"Better hang on to that coffeepot," he said. "Be a nasty burn if you drop it."

"Dad," she said, her voice sounding squeezed. "What are you doing here?"

"Oh no, that's not the right question, Traci. What the hell are *you* doing here?"

Golf Course John had turned on his stool and was staring at A.L. "Mr. McKittridge," he said. "I—"

A.L. held up a hand to stop him. "Right now I'm talking to my daughter."

And his sweet little girl, bless her feisty heart, pulled in a breath of air, stood straight and said, "It's nice to see you, Dad. Regardless of how awkward the circumstances. I'm assuming you'd like some coffee." She looked past him. "Hi, Rena. Coffee for you, too?"

"Hey, Traci. Yeah, coffee sounds great."

Rena's voice sounded far away but he was pretty sure it was only distorted by the head of steam he had going.

Traci turned to get two cups. Rena took the open stool to his left and Traci slid coffee in front of them. The restaurant was at least half full. There were other employees moving around, carrying food, dirty dishes. Customers were chatting. Laughing. All the normal activities of a restaurant.

Why the hell did he feel so damn abnormal? As if nothing was right?

"I thought *this*—" he waved his hand between Golf Course John and Traci "—was over."

"Dad, can we talk about this later?" she asked. "I'm working."

"You should tell him the truth, Tam," Golf Course John said.

"Tam?" A.L. repeated.

"Traci Anne McKittridge," Traci said.

Great. It had been going on long enough that they

had their own secret shorthand. He turned to face Golf Course John. "You know this is not what I want," he said, in his best hard-assed hiss.

To his credit, the man didn't flinch. "With all due respect, sir. I'm more concerned with what your daughter wants."

Traci put her hand on the counter, slid it forward so that her long fingers touched A.L.'s hand. "Dad, John has been the one telling me that I needed to tell you what was going on. I… I just couldn't do it." The buzzer on Traci's hip sounded. "I've got food to carry out," she said, turning fast.

That was good. He needed a minute. His daughter… his little girl who really wasn't a little girl anymore… hadn't felt as if she could come to him. Hadn't thought it was safe to tell him the truth.

Kids lied. Told half truths. Evaded questions. It was part of the growing-up process. And Traci had been no different. But those had been mostly little things, things that didn't matter. *This* mattered. Maybe not eventually but for right now, this thing with Golf Course John mattered to Traci. And how he handled it was going to affect their relationship for a long time.

Golf Course John had pushed away his half eaten breakfast and was gripping his coffee cup with both hands. He was staring straight ahead, as if the pie case was the most interesting thing he'd ever seen.

Rena was sipping her coffee. He was ignoring his because he wasn't sure his throat would work.

It took Traci five long minutes to return to the counter. When she did, she had the same look on her face that she'd had when he'd shown her how to clean her first fish. She was going to get through this, no matter how painful. "Dad, I'm sorry but—"

"Stop, honey. You're right. This is not the time or place. When do you get off?"

"I work until 2:00."

"Okay." He turned to the young man on the stool next to him. "Will you be available at 2:00?"

"I can be," he said.

"Good. I'll meet the two of you at my apartment at 2:30." He reached into his pocket and pulled out a ten dollar bill. "For the coffees," he said.

Then he turned and walked out the door. He wasn't sure Rena was behind him until he got twenty feet down the sidewalk.

"Good job, A.L.," she said conversationally. "I didn't want to be the primary witness for the prosecution on a murder charge."

"She's been lying to me for months. It was never over."

"That's what it looks like," Rena said. "I have to give John credit, he didn't fall off the stool when you glared at him."

John, not Golf Course John. It was probably time for A.L. to call him by his name. "You think they're sleeping together?"

"They might be," Rena said. "She's seventeen. I know what I was doing at seventeen."

"That's just great," he said. For once, maybe Rena should have shielded the truth.

"Are you going to ask her?" Rena asked.

"That would be fucking uncomfortable," he said.

"No pun intended," Rena murmured.

A.L. sighed. "This is a mess, isn't it?"

"Messy but not a mess. There's a difference. Life is messy. But you did the right thing in stepping back from the conversation, not saying something that you'd be sorry for later. By 2:30, I'll have locked up all the weapons in your apartment and it will be fine."

"You're making jokes at a time like this."

"I'm not joking."

"I won't shoot him. I won't strangle him. I don't even know his last name." They took another ten steps. "I should probably know that. Christ, I don't want her to have to lie to me."

"That's right. You don't," Rena said. "Maybe you should call Tess. Get some advice from her."

"She'd say something like, 'The best things happen when people listen with their hearts.'"

"That's nice," Rena said.

"Maybe. Anyway, I don't need to call her. This is between Traci and me."

Rena put her hand on his arm. "You're wrong, A.L. This is between you, Traci and John."

"I'm not ready for somebody else to be part of the equation."

"Yeah, but it looks as if your daughter is."

Twenty

He had more than four hours before he had to talk to his daughter. And he very much needed to get his mind off that conversation. He was grateful when his cell rang and he saw that it was Dusty Frogg's number. "It's her," he said, motioning for Rena to listen. "Detective McKittridge," he answered.

"This is Dusty. Returning your call."

"Thank you. I appreciate it. As I mentioned in my message, I'm a detective with the Baywood Police Department. Also on the line is Detective Morgan. We have an interest in talking with your son about an ongoing police investigation and wondered if you'd be able to assist me."

"Coyote?" she asked.

The file had indicated only one child of Trapper and Dusty Frogg. But perhaps she'd had other children after she'd left Trapper. "Yes, Coyote Frogg."

"Coyote and I aren't close," she said.

"When's the last time you were in contact?" A.L. asked.

"It's always been off and on. I'd hear from Coyote once in a while when his dad was still alive. I don't think Coyote ever told his dad. Then after his dad died, he called me a few times."

"So that would have been in the last couple of years."

"Yes, that's right."

"When he called after his dad died, do you recall where he was living?"

"He was in North Dakota. Fargo, North Dakota. I remember because I really liked that movie. He told me to visit but…I never did. He said he might come here but that never happened, either. It's complicated."

No shit, he thought. Parenting was very complicated but he sure as hell didn't want to be on the receiving end of sporadic phone calls from Traci or have a wedge between the two of them that was so wide it couldn't be bridged.

"Dusty, did he give you his address in Fargo?"

"No. I think he was living outside of town. In a farmhouse. He said they were raising chickens."

"They?" A.L. repeated.

"His roommate. Some guy. I don't think I ever heard his name."

"Do you have a phone number for Coyote?"

"No. He always called me. But like I said, it wasn't often. Is he in trouble?"

"We need to talk to him about an ongoing investigation. If he would happen to call you in the next few days, would you please give him my name and telephone number and ask him to call me?"

"I can do that."

"Thank you," he said. "Goodbye."

Rena waited to make sure the call was disconnected before asking, "Do you believe her?"

"I don't know."

"Think he's still living outside of Fargo?"

"I don't know. When Dawson Ladle bought the Frogg house, he said that Coyote acted as if it was a hassle to come back to Dover. Without looking at a map, I'd estimate that Fargo and Dover are at least four hours apart."

"There and back takes a day. Could be a hassle."

"Right. But we're even farther away here in Baywood. I'm betting…" A.L. stopped. "Fuck," he said. He scrambled through the papers on his desk and finally saw what he wanted. The list of abductions or potential abductions by non-family members. He scanned the list. It was what he remembered. "Fargo," he said. He ran his index finger across the line. "Two years ago this past July. Four-year-old female. Attempted abduction. Suspect not apprehended."

"By a red-haired man?" Rena said weakly.

"I hope not," A.L. said. "We need more information on this case and we need it now."

It took them fifteen minutes to wade through the bullshit and find the person they needed to talk to. Detective Ron Baker was at home, getting ready to fire up the barbecue, but once A.L. filled him in on their case, he said that he definitely had time to talk.

"What can I help you with, Detectives?" he asked.

"The information we're looking at said it was an attempted abduction and that no suspect was apprehended. What can you add to that?" A.L. asked.

"Not much, I'm afraid. The victim was a four-year-old and she was able to tell us that it was a man and he was wearing a baseball cap. The mom, who literally chased the car and hung on to the driver's side window until she was able to attract enough attention that the guy stopped and pushed the kid out of his car before speeding away, wasn't able to give us much more. Perp was twenties or thirties, white and thin-faced."

"Red hair?" A.L. asked. "Maybe bushy or long."

"Nope. Neither could describe hair. In the sketch that we had rendered from the mom's description, the hair was close-cropped, hardly visible under the base-ball cap."

Hair was easy to cut. Easy to grow. "Was he driving a white Jeep, the kind where the sides come off?"

"No. Four-door sedan. I think it was a Ford. My guy was pretty brazen," Detective Baker said. "Lured the kid to his car with the mom no more than fifteen feet away. She had her back turned, looking at some flowers in her neighbor's yard. If she hadn't turned when she did, he might have made it out of there with the kid."

Brazen. Like somebody who would take a kid from a day care in broad daylight.

"That's all very helpful," A.L. said. "Thank you for your time."

"Good luck."

A.L. hung up. Tapped his index finger on his desk. "That didn't get us much."

"No, it didn't," Rena agreed. "You've got a lot on your mind," she added gently. "Focus on that."

Before he talked with Traci, he wanted to make sure that he and Jacqui were on the same page. Given that the temperature between the two of them had been downright frosty the other night, he wasn't looking forward to it. But this was too important. He picked up his phone.

"Hey," he said when she answered. "Do you have a minute?"

"Yes."

"Good. I...found out something just this morning. I stumbled upon it when I went to breakfast at Pancake Magic. Traci and the guy from the golf course are still together."

"No way," she said. "That little shit."

"She admitted it. Listen, Jacqui, I think we need to rethink our approach on this. We told them to end it but they didn't. I think we could tell them that again and we're going to get the same result."

"So we just give in? Is that the kind of parenting we do now? Is that the kind of parenting that *Tess* does?"

He let it go. "Traci told me that she was afraid to tell me the truth. Afraid. We cannot put her in a position where she feels compelled to lie to us. That's when bad things happen to kids. That's when kids dig themselves into holes that are too deep to get out of. That's when parents lose their kids."

Jacqui was silent for a very long time. Finally, she said, "She disobeyed us. Both of us."

"I know. And we know our kid, Jacqui. She's a good one. But this is that important to her. That she was willing to lie to both of us."

Jacqui sighed. "I remember being seventeen and being absolutely in love with my boyfriend. It fizzled out after senior year but...yeah... I get that this could be important."

"I've arranged for them to come to my apartment at 2:30. I'd like to be able to tell them that the secrecy ends. That they need to bring this relationship into the light of day. If John is going to be a part of Traci's life, even if it's not forever, I want us to get to know him better. Maybe we could all go out to dinner sometime."

"Just the four of us?"

"Absolutely." No way would he subject Tess to that.

"I guess it could be worse. You could be calling to tell me that she came to you because she was pregnant."

"That would be worse. Which brings up the issue. You want to talk to her about that or do you want me to?"

"She's going on birth control tomorrow," Jacqui said. "I'll handle it."

"They may not be—"

"Don't be a fool, A.L. She's *your* little girl but she's not really a little girl."

Jacqui wasn't saying anything that Rena hadn't already said. "Okay, then. After I get done talking to them, I'm sending both of them in your direction."

"Fine. I'm…" She stopped.

"Yeah."

"I'm glad you called. Really. The one thing I've never doubted is how much you love Traci."

It was a bit of a backhanded compliment but he was okay with that. "We both love her. We need to tell her that. But we also need her to know that the lies stop now."

It was 2:28 when he heard the knock on his apartment door. A.L. stood, took a deep breath and answered it.

Traci was still wearing her Pancake Magic uniform

of dark pants and a white shirt. John had changed from his shorts and T-shirt that he'd been wearing that morning into dress pants and a button-down shirt.

A.L. couldn't help but appreciate the effort.

"Let's sit," he said, motioning to his small living room.

He looked at his daughter. "I don't want you to ever, ever feel that you can't come to me with the truth. Regardless of how ugly it might be. Regardless of how unhappy it might make me. Regardless of whether you're at fault or not." He paused. "That's the most important part of this discussion, which is why I'm saying it first."

Traci nodded. She'd learned a few things over the years. It generally worked out better for her if she listened first before she talked.

"The two of you have continued dating since spring?" he asked.

"Yes," Traci said.

"So this boy that you're going to homecoming with, you are continuing to use him as a convenient date for a school event?"

"He knows all about John. He wants to go to homecoming. He doesn't have another date so he asked me. I talked to John before I said yes."

He turned to John. "I thought you were in college."

"I am, sir. Milwaukee School of Engineering. Home for the weekend."

"What's your last name, John?"

"Stanley. My parents live on Circle Drive."

Traci Anne Stanley. He'd call her Tas. Wow. He needed to slow his head the fuck down. "My daughter seems to think that you're an okay guy."

John said nothing. He likely figured this was going somewhere.

"And I think my daughter generally has good instincts about people. But if you give me any reason to think that you're not an okay guy, then I'm going to hunt you down. There will be no place that you can hide."

"Daddy," Traci cried.

John put his hand on Traci's arm. "It's okay. I get where your dad is coming from. I've got two younger sisters." He turned and looked A.L. in the eye. "You're not going to have any reason to hunt me down."

"Excellent," A.L. said. He looked at Traci. "From now on, whatever dating you two do will be with the full knowledge of your mother and me."

"Mom knows?" Traci asked.

"Oh yeah. You're going to her house immediately after we finish here."

"How mad is she?" Traci asked.

"I don't think she's mad. Concerned, yes. The thing your mom and I need you to know is that we love you. We know that we can't protect you from every hurt that is coming your way. But we've all got a better chance if we're honest with each other."

"I'm sorry, Dad." With that she sort of threw herself into his arms, the way she might have done when she was eight or nine. When she really was a little girl.

"I love you, Traci. Very much," he said.

He went back to work after Traci and John left his apartment, not knowing if he and Jacqui had done the right thing. It felt like they had but that was the thing about parenting. You never really knew.

Rena's desk was empty. He did not expect her to be there. She'd sent a text that she'd heard from a county cop who'd spotted a store that sold bib overalls and red Wisconsin T-shirts. Rena was on her way to check it out.

He sat down, pulled out the investigation file. Started with the list of people they'd talked to. They were missing something, he could feel it. Got to Shana Federer's name. She'd been fairly confident that she'd seen Kara Wiese in the bathroom prior to 7:30. But multiple parents had confirmed that Kara had been in the room. When he'd asked Kara about Shana Federer, she'd had no real reaction. Maybe some irritation because she didn't understand the relevance of the question but nothing beyond that.

Claire Potter hadn't arrived until close to seven thirty and nobody was going to get Claire and Kara mixed up. According to Ferguson's interview with Tanya Knight, she'd been in the building shortly after seven. It was possible that she'd stopped in the restroom. But surely Shana wouldn't have gotten Tanya and Kara mixed up. Her child was in Tanya Knight and Olivia Blow's classroom.

So if there had been someone in the bathroom, and he was pretty confident there had been because she had clearly been embarrassed by the fact, it had to be a parent or the person who'd taken Emma.

In either event, it was somebody who looked very much like Kara Wiese.

But she had no sisters and her mother was dead. Looking further, there were no maternal aunts and only one fraternal aunt in Utah, who looked nothing like her. That information had been verified.

Dead end. Keep looking.

His cell phone buzzed. He picked it up. Holy fuck. Coyote Frogg and his buddy had been located and were currently being transported to the Baywood Police Station for questioning.

He sent a text to Rena, letting her know.

His phone rang in response. "Hey," he said.

"Good news," she said.

"Yeah. Where are you?" he asked.

"On my way back."

"Did you find the store?"

"Yes. And the proprietress, a lovely English woman who married a Wisconsin farmer and opened the store to save her sanity, or so she said, did remember Coyote Frogg and his friend. Her recollection is that they were in a bit of a hurry and only interested in purchasing something to wear. Her selection was limited and they took what fit. It's the type of store that writes their receipts by hand and she was able to find her copy of the transaction. They paid cash and purchased the clothes the afternoon of Emma's disappearance." She stopped. "Do not start without me."

"You better hurry," A.L. said.

"Ten minutes."

It would take him that long to get things set up. "I'll meet you in Interrogation Room 1."

Coyote's friend's name was Peyton Dowl. A.L. was willing to bet his left nut that he was some relation to Pierce Dowl, the owner of the white Jeep. He was, however, more interested in Coyote so he left Peyton twiddling his thumbs in a conference room while he ushered Coyote into the interrogation room. Rena introduced herself and passed over a card. Coyote was already cradling A.L.'s card in one closed fist. He'd been advised that he'd been picked up for questioning in an ongoing investigation. He was not yet under arrest.

"Mr. Frogg, can you tell us where you were this past Wednesday morning between 7:00 and 8:00 a.m.?"

"I imagine I was sleeping."

"Don't want you to imagine. Want you to think. Where were you?" A.L. asked in his best *I don't tolerate bullshit* tone.

"Okay, man. No need to flip out. I was at my house. Pey and I are renting a place east of Highway 94, north of Walnut Road."

That would be north of the spot they'd intersected with Gi-Gi Thompson, which matched the Thompsons' statement that the Jeep had headed north.

"Pey is Peyton Dowl?" A.L. asked.

"Yes."

"Address of your house?" Rena asked.

"Sprint Trail. I have no idea what the house number is. It's not like I'm having my mail forwarded. But there are only three houses on the road. Ours is the yellow one."

It was enough. A.L. sent a quick text to get officers on the way. He didn't hold out much hope. If Emma was there, or even had been there, it was unlikely that Coyote would have offered it up so quickly.

"Anybody be able to verify that you were at that address on Wednesday morning?" A.L. asked.

"Pey."

"Anybody else?" A.L. asked.

"Ain't nobody else living there."

"Mr. Frogg, where were you on Monday of this past week?"

"Pey and me were in Baywood. We were able to pick up some hours at the Go and Glow."

The Go and Glow was a full-service car wash, the kind where you got out of your car and waited while it went through the automated wash process and was then vacuumed and wiped off by real people. The work was heavily dependent on weather, and A.L. was aware that they hired lots of day labor. They literally doled out wages at the end of every day. "How long have you been working there?"

"Just a few weeks. Pey's girlfriend lives in Baywood and she lets us stay at her house, especially if it looks like the weather is going to be good for business. Otherwise, we can't get there very easily. No wheels right now."

Rena leaned forward. "Let me make sure I understand, Mr. Frogg. You and your roommate, Peyton Dowl, were working at Go and Glow on Monday. Did you work there any other day this past week?"

"Yeah, we worked Tuesday. And I wanted to work on Wednesday but Pey and his old lady got into it and she didn't want us staying at her place. We caught a ride back to our place with another guy who works at Go and Glow. Which was bullshit because three hours later, she ended up driving there anyway all apologetic and stuff." Coyote looked up as if something brilliant had just occurred to him. "You can ask her about

Wednesday morning. Because she had breakfast at our place. I don't remember what time it was but I know it was Wednesday because that afternoon she drove us back into Baywood so that we could get to Madison."

"Slow down," A.L. said. "You were in Baywood Wednesday afternoon and then you went to Madison?"

"Yeah."

"How did you get to Madison on Wednesday afternoon, Mr. Frogg?"

"Pierce drove us."

"Who is Pierce?"

"Pierce Dowl. Pey's brother. He drove from Madison where he lives and we met him in Baywood. He drove us back to Madison and dropped us at the train station. We barely made the train."

"What kind of vehicle does Pierce Dowl drive?"

"He's got a white Jeep."

"You took a train on Wednesday from Madison to where?"

"Denver. We went to a concert at the Red Rocks. We just got back today. And I'm minding my own business, walking down the street and a cop picks me up and tells me that I'm wanted for questioning. I don't know what you think I've done but I wasn't here, man."

"Do you know Emma Whitman?"

Coyote shook his head.

"Is that a no?" A.L. asked, his eyes going to the tape recorder.

"Yeah. I don't know any Emma Whitman. I know an Emily White. I went to high school with her."

A.L.'s gut was churning. He was starting to get a

bad feeling that they were way off base here. "Emma Whitman is five years old."

Now Coyote was frowning at him. "I don't hang around with five-year-old girls," he said. He looked first at A.L. and then Rena. "This is just like what happened to my dad. Just like it. Christ, what is it with you cops?"

"Have you read a newspaper or heard the news lately, Mr. Frogg?" Rena asked.

"No. I've been gone. I told you that."

"Mr. Frogg, we have a report of you and Peyton Dowl driving a white Jeep last week and stopping to… help a woman and her two children on the side of the road. Is that correct?"

"Is that what this is about? That woman was a bitch. All we were trying to do was offer a helping hand. Pierce had let us borrow his ride to move some things."

"Mr. Frogg, we have some video of you on Wednesday afternoon," Rena said. "You and Peyton Dowl are wearing exactly the same outfit that was purchased that day from a store outside of Baywood. What can you tell me about that?"

"I don't want to say anything about that."

"Why is that, Mr. Frogg?"

"Because I don't think it's any of your business and it would not be in my best interest."

Twenty-One

"Mr. Frogg, it is definitely in your best interest to give me a reason why you purchased those clothes on Wednesday," Rena said.

"Somebody told me that they got drug-sniffing dogs at the train stations. Now, I'm not admitting to anything along those lines, but let's just say that I felt better if Pey and me were wearing something new."

A.L. pushed back his chair. "Will you excuse us for a minute, Mr. Frogg?"

"I got nothing but time, I guess."

When they were both in the hall, A.L. said, "We're wrong. We're chasing a damn dead end." He stopped. "You don't disagree?" he grilled Rena.

"No."

"We need to get statements from Peyton Dowl, Pierce Dowl and whoever Peyton's girlfriend is. If those match up, we need to admit defeat," A.L. said. "We got nothing here."

"I know. The train station will have video. We can take a look at that, too."

"Probably should," A.L. said. "Can you believe it? Drug-sniffing dogs. No DNA. I really don't think he has a clue who Emma Whitman is." He slammed his hand against the wall in frustration.

"I'll finish this up, A.L. Take a walk. Get a cup of coffee," Rena said.

"No, I'll…" He stopped. "Yeah, that'd be good. We'll catch up later."

She found him more than ninety minutes later. It was dark outside. He was sitting on a bench outside the building, staring at a lighted water fountain that some charitable organization had decided would be just the thing to beautify downtown Baywood.

"The story checks out. They're gone," she said.

"Thank you."

"We're just mere mortals, A.L. Don't beat yourself up. And by the way, no other cell phone in Kara Wiese's name."

He nodded. They sat silently for a few minutes. Finally, he turned to her. "Early on, we asked *why Emma Whitman*?"

"I don't think we ever answered that," Rena said gently.

"But we need to. We aren't going to find her until we figure out *why* Emma. We need to look at Troy and Leah harder."

"You really think it's possible that they're responsible?"

"I'm not saying they did it. But I think whoever took Emma did it because of them."

"To make them suffer?" Rena asked. "Who are the candidates?"

"For Leah, her coworker who didn't get the promotion. But that doesn't feel right. She was pissed but more pissed at the system that rewards people who suck up."

"Okay. Who else for Leah?"

"Elaine Broadstreet. I think you and I both think she's pretty sharp. What if she figured out that Leah had been modifying her work to make her look bad? Remember when we went to Elaine's house that first time. She said something along the lines that Leah was determined to find fault with her and to have others find fault also."

"You're right. We need to ask her," Rena said.

"Yeah. And the other grandparents, what if they secretly do blame Leah for the poor relationship they have with Troy?" A.L. said.

"Nope. Don't buy that. They only got choked up when they were talking about their relationship with Troy. And they love him."

"Loved him enough to try to prevent him from making a bad financial decision. Even at the risk of alienating him. Okay, they're off the list. For both Leah and Troy."

"Speaking of Troy. Who wants to hurt him? Maybe any of the three guys at Garage on Division?"

"All possibilities. But all of them genuinely seemed to like working at the garage. Hurting Troy might hurt them ultimately. Pete and Cory are definitely pragmatic enough to see that. I think Davy is, too."

"Angry customers? The Thompsons?" Rena asked.

"Not angry enough. Gi-Gi was freaked out but I

don't think Barrett thought it was as big a deal as he was letting on."

"We didn't find a spurned ex-girlfriend," Rena mused.

"Only an exuberant friend," A.L. said.

"Back to square one," Rena said. "Tomorrow is five days."

"Long time to keep a child hidden." If she was still alive. He didn't add that part. Rena knew the odds were getting slimmer and slimmer with each passing day.

His cell phone buzzed. He looked at the number of the incoming call. It seemed vaguely familiar. "McKittridge," he answered.

"This is Peitra Jonet returning your call. I'm sorry to be calling so late but you said it was important."

"This is fine and I won't take up too much of your time. I have reviewed some information that indicated you had your vehicle serviced at Garage on Division on Wednesday morning. Does that ring a bell with you?"

"Of course. I came in for an oil change. But then they convinced me that my transmission fluid also needed changing so I was there for longer than I expected, sitting in a dark waiting room reading six-month-old magazines," she said.

"What time would that have been?"

"I got there after 8:00 and was gone by 9:30."

"Did you see Troy Whitman, the owner?"

"Yeah, he came into the office area about 9:00. I think I surprised him. But we chatted for a few minutes. He's a nice guy. That night when I heard the news about that little girl, it seemed so odd that I'd been talking to Troy just that morning. I need to talk to him again but there's no way I'm doing it now. Not until this thing is over."

He had so many questions he didn't know which one to ask first. "Do you know if Troy was just arriving at work at 9:00?"

"I think so. I mean, I didn't see him drive in. And when he saw me he made some comment about being out back. But they've got a little fridge under the counter and I think I saw him put his lunch away. That's usually the first thing I do when I get to work."

"Okay, thank you. Now you said that you need to talk to Troy again but it would have to wait. What's that about?"

"Well… I'm not sure I should say. I should give Troy a chance to explain."

"I respect that but it's hard to know if it will help us in any way unless we know what it is."

"I don't think it will but since you're the police, I guess it's okay. After I left Garage on Division, I ran to get a cup of coffee. Unfortunately, the lid came off while I was driving and I ended up spilling most of it. The receipt I'd gotten was ruined. My car is a company car. Without a receipt, I wasn't going to get reimbursed for the expense. I was going to go back right away but needed to get to work. I stopped in Thursday morning and asked Davy if he could help me. It took him a little while because for some odd reason, it wasn't with the other receipts. Anyway, he finally found the right file in the drawer and made me a copy. It was only after I got back out to my car that I realized that something was very wrong. My bill was for $89. But the receipt I was looking at was for $389."

"Davy gave you the wrong receipt?"

"Oh no. Same exact receipt as I'd gotten the day before except somebody had added a three to the total. I don't know what the heck is going on but I sure can't turn in a receipt for $389 for an oil change and a transmission flush."

"Do you have that receipt?" A.L. asked.

"Of course," she said.

"I'm going to need to see it," he said.

Twenty minutes later, he and Rena pulled up to Peitra Jonet's house. She met them at the door with receipt in hand. Both he and Rena glanced at it. "We're going to need to take this with us," he said.

She shrugged. "I guess that's okay. It's not like I can turn it in anyway."

They walked back to their vehicle and backed down her driveway. However, two blocks away, A.L. pulled off. He studied the receipt. "This is the opposite of skimming."

"Skimming?" Rena asked.

"Yeah. Restaurants, dry cleaners, dog walkers, hair stylists. Hell, I don't know, probably just about any small business and probably some large ones, too, underreport sales. Then they don't have to claim income or subsequently pay taxes on their real revenue, but rather on some reduced amount. But it looks like Troy is overstating his revenue. Why do that?"

"To make his financials look better. So he could qualify for more financing," Rena said. "From his friend Steven Hanzel."

"I'm a simple guy but overstating your revenue

doesn't do anything to improve your actual financial position. You don't end up with more cash on hand. In fact, wouldn't it make you look worse? Like you're making all these sales but where's the money?"

"We need a better look at his financial records. Or should we say, his cooked books?" Rena said. "It's already pretty late on a Sunday night. We're going to need a warrant and some resources to help us if we're going to do this right. Maybe we wait until morning."

"Absolutely not," A.L. said. "I want those records and I want them now."

At 1:13 on Monday morning, they knocked on Troy and Leah Whitman's door. It was opened promptly since they'd called ahead. The young FBI agent motioned them in. They found both Leah and Troy in the living room. She was standing by the bay window that looked out into the dark backyard. He was sitting in the chair. They didn't appear to have been talking.

A.L. handed him the signed warrant. "You can ride with us down to the garage. A technician will be meeting us there. We will take custody of your computer and any other electronic or paper records that are deemed financial in nature."

"This makes no sense," Leah said.

"Are you ready?" A.L. asked, looking at Troy.

"Yeah," the man said. He looked at his wife but didn't say anything to her. Didn't say anything to anybody for the next hour as a force of seven, three from the FBI and four from the Baywood Police Department, descended upon his business. Simply stood to the side and unlocked things that were locked and pointed to other things when asked a direct question.

"Did you think that was odd?" Rena asked later, when they were back at their desks. It was 3:30 in the morning.

"I don't know. If he's innocent of wrongdoing, then he was in shock. You know, how had it come to this when he and his family were the wronged party? If he's not innocent, then he might have assumed that anything he said now would come back to haunt him later."

"Leah seemed pretty confused," Rena said.

"Yeah." He was staring at the screen.

"How can you still see?" she asked. "We've been awake for almost twenty-four hours."

He didn't answer.

Seeing no choice, Rena pushed back her chair and walked around the desk to stand behind him. She looked at his screen. It was some kind of spreadsheet with multiple columns and rows. She looked at the column headings. Date. Work Order Number. Last Name. First Name. Phone Number. Quote Amount. Sale Amount.

July 1 through July 31. Bunch of different work order numbers. Bunch of names and phone numbers. The columns for the quote amount and sale amount were sometimes the same, sometimes different. She understood that. The quote was given before the mechanic really got into the guts of the problem. He found something else wrong and the price went up.

"I need to find the spreadsheet where these numbers

tie into the money he's taking in," A.L. said. "Damn. I should have studied harder in accounting class."

"You *took* an accounting class?"

"Yeah. I was going to get a business degree before I switched over to criminal justice."

"You'd have hated being a businessman."

"Yeah, probably." He was opening new tabs on the worksheet. "Bingo," he said after a minute. "Here it is."

"What?" she demanded. She was tired and hungry and not in the mood to be kept in the dark.

"Do you remember when I told you that I met Troy's neighbor, who delights in his dog shitting in Troy's yard?"

"Yes."

"He told me that the catalyst to that was an outrageous quote for $1,000 in July that he'd given to his wife. Her name was Lois Martin." He flipped back to the original tab he'd been on. "Here it is. Lois Martin. Quote was $1,080. Final sale was $1,080. And here," he said, flipping back to the second tab, "is where he shows it in his daily deposit as a collected payment."

"But she never had the work done. There was no money exchanged."

"Exactly. This is another form of what we saw with Peitra Jonet. In that case, he padded the amount of the invoice. Here, he made it look as if work he quoted was completed and paid for. Christ, Rena. This is not good. I think he's laundering money."

"Laundering money," she repeated. Running illegally obtained money through a legitimate business to *clean* it. "Drugs? Prostitution? Porn. Oh God, please don't let it be adolescent porn."

"Sick fucks," he said in agreement. "I don't know. I think the only thing we can do is ask him."

"Now?"

"Yeah. My guess is he's not sleeping anyway."

It was a fast drive back to the Whitmans'. Not a lot of traffic on the roads at four in the morning. They were just blocks away when Rena's cell buzzed. "Who is texting me *now*?" she said, pulling her phone from her bag.

She read the message. Read it a second time to make sure that her tired eyes weren't playing tricks on her. "It's from Corrine Antler's mom. Remember how she said that she'd been to Baywood once, to a wedding shower for her sister. It was hosted by a bridesmaid."

"Yeah."

"The bridesmaid was Kara Hamilton. Now Kara Wiese."

A.L. turned to look at her. "Kara Wiese hosted a bridal shower for Patsy Antler's sister. I'm guessing if she was a bridesmaid, then she was a pretty close friend of the sister. What do you think the chances are that she didn't know that her friend's niece had disappeared from her day care when she was five?"

Rena had opened her notebook and was reviewing the notes they'd taken that day. "Sister's name is Toni Krider. Lives in Denver. Bridesmaid who hosted was her sister's college roommate." She closed her notebook. "Kara knew. There's no way she didn't know. But I guess we ask the sister to make sure."

"Yeah. See if you can get the sister's contact information from Patsy."

Rena sent the text to Patsy Antler.

"What the hell does this mean?" A.L. asked. "Kara never mentioned it to us. Never said that what happened with Emma Whitman was eerie because it had happened before to someone she knew. You know how earlier you were pissed because everything had a reasonable explanation. Well, that's the reasonable thing she should have said to us. But she didn't."

A.L. was right. "I think we need to be watching her," Rena said.

"Agree. Get Faster to approve," he said.

Rena picked up her phone again. She was getting a lot of people up early this morning.

Twenty-Two

When A.L. pulled up in front of the Whitman house, there were lights on inside, maybe proving his theory that Troy wasn't sleeping. They hadn't called ahead this time because they hadn't wanted to give Troy any time to prepare a story.

They knocked and the door was opened by the same FBI agent who'd opened it just hours earlier. "Making a habit of this?" he asked.

A.L. took a minute to fill him in. Then they walked downstairs and found Troy sitting in what must have been his favorite chair. He didn't look particularly surprised to see them.

"Troy, we have some questions for you."

He gave no sign that he even heard them. Nevertheless, A.L. forged ahead.

"We've looked at your financial records. And we're confident that you're inflating customer invoices and recording sales where the work was never completed." A.L. stopped. Let that sink in. "I need you to tell me why we're seeing that. I need you to tell me the truth. And I need to know if it has anything to do with Emma's disappearance."

Troy glanced at the stairway leading upstairs. "Listen, you cannot tell Leah this. I have loan payments due at the bank that I can't make. I owe money to suppliers. Money has always been tight but I'm in real trouble."

"Get an extension. Make small payments," A.L. said.

"I've already done some of that. Steven Hanzel told me that the next time I went to the bank, his boss would probably want to see my financials."

That made sense given what the VP at the bank had told him. "None of that explains what we're seeing," A.L. said.

"Yes, it does," Troy said. "Months ago my brother told me about somebody else who would loan me money. But he's a fucking CPA and he warned me that I couldn't just dump the money into my account, I had to dribble it in because any big cash deposit would be scrutinized. If the Baywood Bank found out that I had debt elsewhere, I wouldn't have any hope of working with them."

"So you were going to trick your friend, Steven Hanzel?"

"I was going to do what I had to do to keep my family from losing their house, to keep my wife from realizing that she'd married a damn fool."

"Leah knows nothing about this?" Rena asked.

"Leah knows about the initial loans from Baywood Bank. She knows business has been slow. But she doesn't ask a whole lot of questions. She trusts me to handle it. If she were to find this out right now, fuck, it could kill her. I love my wife. I don't want to lose her."

"So you borrowed the money and for months you've been using it to keep the garage afloat. What now?" A.L. asked.

"I was sure I'd be in better shape, but it was a bad summer. I don't have the money to pay these people back."

"People?" A.L. clarified.

"Yeah, people," Troy said, his tone now belligerent. "If you don't want to go to a bank, there are people who do this."

"Have the *people*," A.L. emphasized the word, "that you borrowed from made any threats toward you or your family? I'm just guessing, of course, but I assume they're not licensed lenders."

Troy ignored the last part. "No, there's been no reason to. The loan was set up so that I make regular installments with a big payment at the end. I've been able to make the regular installments. That's where I was on Wednesday morning, before I went to the shop. I met them at a restaurant over on Lawrence Street. Most times I meet them late at night but a couple times it was early morning, like that Wednesday."

"When is the balance, the big payment, due?" Rena asked.

"Two weeks."

"Or?"

Troy said nothing. Then finally, "My brother said these are not the people to disappoint. This house is almost paid for. I inherited some money from my grandparents. But I put it up as equity against the loan."

Rena and A.L. exchanged glances. "How are you going to meet the loan demand if you don't have the money?" Rena asked.

"I'm probably going to have to ask my parents."

That surprised him. "Do they have the money to give you?" A.L. asked.

"I don't know. They own their house, too. Maybe they'll be willing to take a mortgage. I'll pay them back."

A.L. felt sick. Troy's dad was going to fucking dialysis three mornings a week.

Cops didn't make big money but he'd been a good saver. Even had gone to a guy who'd run the numbers and told him that he'd be okay at retirement. What the hell would he do in twenty years when he was ready to live the good life and Traci came crawling home asking him to take out a fucking mortgage?

Ask for his damn job back.

"I need your lenders' names," he said.

"No," Troy said.

"I think you want us to do everything we can to get your daughter back. What are their names?"

"They had nothing to do with this. Don't you think that I already thought of that? First of all, I saw one of the people just that morning. He gave me no indication that anything was wrong. But just in case, I called my brother right away. Let's just say that he's got several clients who work with these people. He knows them well enough to call them. They swore that they weren't involved."

A.L. remembered that Troy had been talking to his brother when he and Rena had first entered the classroom that Wednesday evening. But not so that his brother would break the news to Troy's parents. No, Troy had had to do that later.

He really wanted to rip into Troy and he forced himself to speak calmly. "Let me get this straight, Troy. You're taking the word of a loan shark on your child's life?"

"They don't have Emma. I'm not late yet. They don't know that I don't have the money."

A.L. stared at him.

Troy wiped his mouth with the back of his hand. "Oh, Christ. You got to make sure that they know that I don't think they had anything to do with this."

It wasn't his job to protect idiots who got involved with loan sharks. But A.L. tried to remember that this man's daughter was missing. "I'll do what I can. Names?"

"Marco and Silva Savayanah. Brothers."

A.L. didn't think they were local. He'd have heard of them if they were. Maybe they worked out of Milwaukee or Chicago. "You got a contact number?"

"For Marco. He's the one I always talk to." Troy pushed some buttons on his cell phone and then held it out for A.L. to see. "He's the one I met on Wednesday morning."

He copied down the number. "These guys got an office?"

"If they do, I don't know where it is. When we set the loan up, they came to my shop."

"Do your employees know that you're in trouble?" A.L. asked.

"No. I mean, they know the money is tight. But I haven't told anybody about this."

"How much are you in to them?" A.L. asked.

"Eighty grand."

He didn't think Troy's parents would make that as Walmart greeters. "And what do you need to satisfy your loan payments to the bank?"

"Another fifty grand."

"That's a lot of money, Troy. And now, suddenly, there is a lot of money coming in your direction in the form of contributions to the fund-raising site that Steven Hanzel set up."

Troy stood up in outrage. "I wouldn't touch a dime of that money for this. What kind of father do you think I am?" Now he was waving his arms around. "I'll spend every cent of that and borrow from anybody if I need more. I want my daughter back. I want her back more than anything. Jesus, I can't even look into Leah's eyes anymore. They're like a goddamn black hole."

He sucked in a breath of air and then sat again, as if the sudden burst of denial had taken every bit of his energy. His eyes looked bleak. "My fucking world is falling apart. And I can't do anything to stop it."

When A.L. and Rena got back to their desks, A.L. emailed the loan sharks' names to the FBI and requested some assistance. He didn't want to call the number Troy had given him without having a little more information about the pair.

"Do you believe him?" Rena asked.

"He's a pretty good actor if he knows where Emma is," A.L. said. "It was stupid to borrow money from

Marco and Silva Savayanah. But he was desperate. And if you think about it, it's sort of consistent with what we've seen all along. Troy doesn't seem to see things as they really are. His relationship with his employees. His relationship with his parents. Hell, even his relationship with his wife. He's overly optimistic. I can see him thinking that if he could just get some quick cash, surely in six months he'd be in a better financial position."

"Insanity," Leah said. "Doing the same thing over and over and expecting different results."

Their old boss Toby used to have a sign with that saying on his desk.

"Do you think the Savayanah brothers have anything to do with Emma's disappearance?" Rena asked.

"I really don't. Like he said, he's not late."

"He's not too smart, either. I'm no business major and I never took an accounting class, but common sense tells me they set the loan up that way anticipating that he'd fail. They get to keep all the installment payments he's made along the way and then at the end, when he can't make the final payment, they now own a modest house that can be flipped quickly for a nice tidy profit. They probably are scary enough that most people this happens to don't take the chance of turning them in to the police."

"Do you think it's possible that Leah might know more than she's letting on? Maybe that's the basis of her anger?" A.L. asked.

"Maybe. That reminds me that we never followed up on whether Elaine knows that Leah changed her work."

A.L. looked at his watch. "Elaine said she was an early riser."

They arrived at Elaine's house shortly after six o'clock. A.L. knocked on the door. Elaine opened it, looking as if she was dressed for work.

"What? What's happened?" she asked immediately.

"No news," Rena said quickly. "May we talk with you for just a minute?"

"Of course," she said, stepping aside. "Would you like coffee? It'll just take a minute?"

"That would be great," A.L. said. It had now been more than twenty-four hours since he'd slept.

Elaine led them into her kitchen and they took a seat at the table while she started a pot of coffee. Once she'd sat down, A.L. wasn't sure how to start. Leah and Elaine had some bad history. Were he and Rena going to open new wounds?

"Going to the casino this morning?" he asked, for lack of something to say.

Elaine smiled. "Interestingly enough, I've sort of lost my interest in gambling. Every time I think about going I think about dropping Emma off at the day care. Was I distracted because I was excited about the gambling? Was I more interested in that than the safety of my own grandchild? You know, Leah is taking medication just to get through the day and then again at night, to sleep. I've caused my daughter so much pain. When does it end?"

Her spirit truly seemed broken. "I spoke to your boss at work, Elaine. He said that there's been some mistakes in your work lately. Mistakes that might have been costly to the company."

"I'm aware of them. I don't think Milo has to worry about that anymore."

"Why do you say that?"

"No reason," she said.

A.L. took a breath. "I think the reason you say that is that you know that it was Leah who modified some of the files on your computer."

"None of that matters now," Elaine said.

"How long have you known?" Rena asked.

"For several weeks."

"That must have made you pretty angry?"

She shrugged. "Angry. Sad. It's taken me some years to realize that Leah has more pain from her childhood than I ever imagined. I regret that because it is largely my doing. Our sins really do catch up with us."

"'Our sins really do catch up with us,'" Rena repeated as they drove away from Elaine's house. "Once this is over, Elaine and Leah have a lot to talk about."

A.L. pointed at the time on his dashboard clock. It was 7:14. "Five days," he said. "Five long days."

"Missing people have been found months, sometimes years, after the event. You can't give up hope until…well, until you find a body," Rena said.

"Tell that to the Antler family," A.L. said. "Listen, we both better grab a few hours of sleep. I'm probably a danger on the road right now."

"Okay," Rena said. Her cell buzzed. She read the screen. "We're not going home," she said. "The tail on Kara Wiese has something. They were in place for less than fifteen minutes when Kara left her house this morning."

"She went to work," A.L. said. "She starts at 6:30."

"Yeah, she ultimately went to work. But first she drove to a park on the south side of town."

"To jog?" A.L. said.

"To meet a man. They want us to see the video."

A.L. and Rena went straight to the conference room where two FBI agents and Chief Faster were already seated. There was a laptop in front of Faster and they had a big screen pulled down at the far end of the room. "We've watched it once," Faster said. "But don't recognize the man." He pushed a button on the keyboard and the screen lit up.

It was definitely Kara Wiese. The tail had started filming when Kara stopped her car near the park entrance. There was only one other car in the lot. She didn't walk toward it. However, she went to sit on a bench. But she wasn't sitting quietly. She was looking around, as if waiting for someone.

And four minutes later, a man walked into view. A.L. sat up a little straighter in his chair.

He watched as the man sat next to her. Then as he put his arms around her and kissed her. Not a *nice to see you again* kiss but more of a *I might consume you whole* kind of thing.

"What?" Rena asked, looking at him.

He looked around the room. "Allow me the pleasure of introducing you to Steven Hanzel."

Twenty-Three

They debated whether to pick up Kara Wiese for questioning first, or Steven Hanzel. In the end, A.L. convinced them to start with Hanzel. "He's going to crack first."

What they expected him to "crack" about was yet to be determined. But the fact that Kara Wiese had lied about the relationship and that both she and Steven Hanzel were significant players in Emma's disappearance was enough.

They'd watched Steven and Kara talk for several minutes, kiss a few more times, and finally part, each taking off in separate vehicles. The tail on Kara had continued and ended when she arrived at the Lakeside Learning Center.

"Hanzel was dressed for work," he said. The man's suit had been all neat and tidy. "I'm betting we find him there." In his notes, he found the telephone number for Tamara Federer. He dialed. When she answered, he didn't waste any time.

"This is Detective McKittridge. I am calling because my partner and I are going to want to have a discussion with Steven Hanzel. Can you verify for me if he's at work?"

"Hold for just a moment, Detective."

She was back within thirty seconds. "He's here. I'll reserve the first floor conference room for your use. If you're coming now, the front door won't be open yet. However, we have a guard posted and I'll give him your names and authorize entry. Once inside, any discretion you can use when you're in the bank around other employees would be appreciated."

He got it. She didn't want a scene. "Will do. Thanks."

A.L. ended the call and pushed back his chair. "You drive," he said to Rena. "I've got one more call to make."

When they arrived at the bank, they saw the security guard at the front door. They showed badges and he said that he'd been expecting them. He didn't ask why they were there; he just opened the door and looked the other way.

They walked through the lobby, past the empty teller windows, and back toward the area where the loan officers called home. A couple desks were empty but there were five people already working. Steven Hanzel was one of them. They approached from an angle that allowed A.L. to see that Hanzel was reading the sports page on his computer.

"Good morning, Mr. Hanzel," A.L. said. "Not sure if you remember me. I'm Detective McKittridge and this is my partner, Detective Morgan."

Steven minimized his screen. "Of course, what can I do for you, Detectives?"

"We need a few minutes of your time. The first floor conference room has been reserved for us."

That seemed to get Hanzel's attention. "Okay. Uh… let me just get a pen and paper."

Had probably been drilled into his head—never go to a meeting without pen and paper. They waited while he found a yellow legal pad and a nice-looking pen. They motioned for him to lead the way.

When they got there, A.L. realized that somebody had already put a carafe of hot coffee and cups in the center of the table. Tamara Federer got things done. He liked that. He poured a cup for himself and Rena. Offered one to Steven but the man shook his head.

"Steven, with your permission, I'd like to record this conversation." A.L. set his cell phone between him and Hanzel. "Is that okay?"

"I guess."

He switched on the record function. "This is Detective McKittridge and Detective Morgan speaking with Steven Hanzel. Today's date is Monday, September 14, and we are speaking in the first floor conference room of the Baywood Bank. Mr. Hanzel has agreed to have this conversation recorded." A.L. picked up his pen.

"Steven," A.L. said, "I want to talk to you about the personal relationship you have with Kara Wiese."

"Um…who said that we have a personal relationship?" Steven tapped his own pen against his paper.

"We have you on video this morning at the park. Meeting Kara. It looked rather personal."

Hanzel scratched his head. "We're good friends. Okay, more than friends. No law against that, right?"

"She's married," A.L. said.

"Well, that's not going to last."

"How long has the relationship been going on?" Rena asked.

"Five, six months," Hanzel said.

"You're good friends with Troy Whitman, right?" A.L. asked.

He looked surprised at the quick change in topic. "You know I am."

"You're also his loan officer?"

"I'm a loan officer who has helped a lot of people secure financing."

Not according to his supervisor. "But you took a special interest in helping Troy. He's your friend and when he needed financing and his numbers didn't quite hit the mark, you went ahead and made sure he got the financing. Because that's what friends do. And then when his daughter suddenly went missing, you didn't miss a beat. You got a fund-raising page set up so quickly. In fact, once we look at your search history on your computer, I'll bet you researched how to set up a site even before Emma Whitman disappeared."

It was a wild-ass guess but A.L. was pretty confident he wasn't far off when Hanzel seemed to sway in his seat.

"I don't understand your point, Detective," Hanzel said. He pulled at the collar of his nice white shirt.

"My point is, your job is on the line here. You know it. You've received multiple warnings about your job performance. If you were to have another big loan default, it might look bad for you."

A.L. took a drink of his coffee and set the cup down hard. "I think that you know that your friend Troy Whitman is close to defaulting on his loan. I think you and Kara Wiese figured out a way to have his daughter disappear and get an influx of cash for Troy."

"How would I know that his business is about to go under? Troy always tells me that everything is fine. That's what he tells everybody."

"Because I just talked to Travis Whitman, Troy's older brother. The two of you are friends. Maybe even better friends than you and Troy. He confirmed with me that you did know, that he told you that Troy was borrowing money from the Savayanah brothers." A.L. pushed his coffee cup aside. "Steven, you are under arrest in connection with the disappearance of Emma Whitman." A.L. then read him his rights. He didn't want the guy to lawyer up but he didn't want anything to derail a conviction, either.

When Steven Hanzel didn't immediately ask for representation, A.L. decided it was time to hit him hard. "Where is Emma Whitman?"

"I don't know. I didn't want to know," he said. "I had nothing to do with taking Emma. Nothing. Kara took care of all of that. But it's going to be fine. Emma is coming home today. This is all going to be over."

Kara had likely acted to help her lover save his job. Now said lover was throwing her under the bus.

Rena reached for her phone. Texted a message to Chief Faster. By the time she and A.L. got back to their desks, Kara Wiese would be there, ready for questioning.

"How do you know that?" A.L. demanded.

"That's what Kara and I were talking about this morning."

"Who has Emma?" A.L. yelled.

"Kara's sister," Steven said.

"She doesn't have a sister," Rena said.

"She does," Steven said. "Listen, I want a lawyer. I'm done talking to you."

Kara Wiese had been read her rights and she'd immediately requested an attorney. One was coming. And A.L. was about to climb the walls. He'd had numerous cups of coffee, no food and no sleep. And they were so fucking close.

Emma was alive. Or at least had been when Steven had talked to Kara Wiese this morning. And supposedly the plan was to return Emma. All that was good, but things like this could go south in a hurry when people got nervous. And with the arrests of both Steven Hanzel and Kara Wiese, there was no telling what the *sister*, whoever that was, might do. If they lost Emma now, it would break people.

Kara's attorney arrived. He didn't recognize the woman. Salina St. John. It sounded like a made-up name. He quite frankly didn't even care if she was a real attorney. He gave Ms. St. John five minutes with her client. Then he and Rena knocked on the door.

"Time is of the essence here, Counselor," he said.

"I understand," she said. "My client has had an opportunity to reflect on previous conversations that she may have had with you and recognizes that she might not have been absolutely forthcoming. Should she provide a more detailed and accurate statement, would there be consideration of that when charges are filed?"

"If we are able to locate Emma and she's safe, then I will tell whoever is interested that there was no further delay. That's the best I can do right now."

Attorney and client exchanged a glance. Kara leaned forward. "There was never any intention for Emma to be hurt. She has not been hurt. She's been cared for and comforted."

"Where is she?" A.L. asked, his voice hard. "I want an address."

"317 Brookline Drive. It's a house that my sister rented a month ago. That's who she's with."

He sent the address to the task force members. Felt his chest ease up a little.

"You don't have a sister," he said. "We checked."

"My parents were boyfriend and girlfriend in high school. My mom got pregnant her junior year in high school. She gave away the baby for adoption. My parents went their own ways but seven years later, reconciled and married. I was born two years later. I was never told that there had been another child. I don't believe they ever tried to find her. My parents were killed in a car accident almost four years ago. Two years ago, my sister, who had always been told she was adopted, had DNA testing done. My first cousin had also had DNA testing done. Long story short, ultimately my sister and I got connected, the story got sorted out, and we had some further testing to verify the results. But it was really unnecessary because it was like looking in a mirror. She's a couple inches taller and there are a few other minute differences, but we look almost like twins."

"What's her name?"

"Catherine Wood. I let her in the back door of the day care before we opened on Wednesday. She was to hide in a stall in the hall bathroom."

She'd been careless and stood in front of the mirror. It was Catherine Wood that Shana Federer had seen and spoken to.

"How did Catherine know when to go to the front door?" Rena asked.

"I can see the street from a window in my classroom," Kara said. "When I saw Elaine Broadstreet coming, I texted Catherine so that she could be by the front door."

"Not on your cell phone," A.L. said. There had been no activity on her phone that Wednesday morning.

"A few months ago, I got a second phone. It's in my sister's name. Everybody knows that cops check phone records."

She'd been ready for their questions about the phone calls between her and Steven Hanzel. She'd had time to prepare her perfectly reasonable answers to all their questions. There was little doubt that down the line they'd find a second phone for Steven Hanzel, too

"You knew about Corrine Antler. You were college roommates with her aunt."

"I was," she said. "And I thought if Emma disappeared in a similar way, people might think that it was related."

"We found out about Dover from a totally unrelated source," Rena said.

"I know. But if you hadn't, Steven or I would have made sure you knew about it. It was much better that we didn't have to. We weren't worried about Emma telling people that she'd gone with me. I had an alibi. She's a child. People would think she was confused. Elaine Broadstreet signed Emma in but Catherine took the sheet with her. I had already placed a second one with Wednesday's date underneath."

It seemed as if Kara had anticipated most everything. But there was something that still needed an explanation. "Scent-trained dogs picked up Emma in Alice Quest's yard. Is she involved?"

"No. Absolutely not. Catherine does not have much experience with children. Evidently Emma was happy enough to get in her car but quickly became restless. I had driven by Alice's house with Catherine. She remembered that there was playground equipment. She promised Emma that she could play if she would stop crying. It was a bad decision. I don't know her well enough to know if it was a lapse or whether her judgment is always a bit off."

"Alice didn't know about your sister?"

"No, but oddly enough, I know Alice's sister. I met Melissa Wayne at the time of my roommate's wedding. She did our hair and makeup. Years later, when I applied at Lakeside Learning Center, I was amazed at the resemblance. And when my own sister appeared and there was such a strong resemblance, I was tempted to tell Alice but I never did."

"Your plan was dependent upon Alice not being in the office. How did you manage that?"

"Olivia Blow eats yogurt every afternoon. I added some stuff to her yogurt to make her sick. Nothing that would hurt her but enough to keep her in the bathroom for a long time. If she was ill, then Alice would be in a classroom."

Kara Wiese was a piece of work. "What's in this for Catherine?"

"Twenty thousand dollars. That's the amount of bonus that Steven will get if he reaches his ten-year anniversary with the bank in December and has a certain amount of loans in his portfolio."

He was pretty confident she had no idea how close Steven really was to losing his job. Steven wasn't ever going to see that money. If A.L. had anything to do with it, he was going to be in jail.

"You did all this for a man that you're not married to," Rena said.

"I love him," Kara said. "He was very concerned about losing his job. Had made some threats that scared me."

"What kinds of threats?" Rena asked.

"Threats that he was going to harm himself. I couldn't take that chance."

"Troy Whitman has said that he never would have used the money in the fund-raising account to pay off his debts."

Kara shrugged. "He would have. Steven would have convinced him."

There was a quick knock on the door. It opened and Chief Faster motioned for A.L. and Rena to come into the hallway. "They're at the house. Emma isn't there. She was there. Dogs verified that. But both she and her kidnapper are gone."

"Fuck," A.L. said.

"Let's have Kara call her sister," Rena said.

"Do whatever you need to do. I want to find this kid," Chief Faster said as he walked away.

A.L. and Rena walked back in. "317 Brookline Drive has been searched. Emma isn't there. Neither is your sister. I need you to call her and find out where the hell they are."

He could tell the news shook Kara. Her hands fumbled with her phone.

"Put it on Speaker," he said. "And don't warn her about the police."

It rang three times. "Hey, sis," a woman answered. "I was just about to text you."

"Why?"

"I just dropped the kid off like we discussed. She should be walking out of the cornfield in ten minutes."

"You were supposed to do this at noon."

"I know, but she was getting cranky and crying and I just couldn't stand it a minute longer. So she gets back a couple hours earlier. People will be happy. I'm heading home."

A.L. motioned for her to end the call.

"Okay, Catherine. I'll talk to you later." Kara hung up before her sister could respond.

"What was the fucking plan, Kara? Where was she getting dropped off? What cornfield?" A.L. demanded.

"The cornfield that backs up to the learning center playground. Catherine was to get her started on a row and tell her to keep walking in a straight line. My job was to make sure somebody saw her when she emerged."

A five-year-old was alone in a ready-to-harvest field, where the corn easily stretched a foot or more above her head. It would be very easy for her to get disoriented. To lose her way.

They'd pick up the sister later. She'd said she was heading home. Now the priority had to be finding Emma. He'd get another officer to babysit these two. "You stay here," he said, looking at Kara and her lawyer. Then he focused solely on Kara. "You better hope we find Emma and that nothing bad has happened to her."

Twenty-Four

He pushed back from the table and was out the door. Rena was on his heels. They ran to the parking lot and got in his SUV. Then he drove fast. While he did that, Rena was on the phone, giving updates, getting officers mobilized to search the immediate area of the learning center.

"Do Troy and Leah know?" A.L. asked when she finished.

"Yeah. They're aware that 317 Brookline was searched and found empty and that Emma may be walking on her own. I suspect we'll see them at the learning center."

He didn't want to have to look at them if they lost Emma at this point. He knew there was no guarantee that she was still in that field. Two minutes after Catherine had left her, she might have gotten scared and backtracked and could now be wandering anywhere.

Five minutes later, they pulled into the lot. There were six or seven other police cars already there. Somebody was handing out water bottles. "For Emma," they said. "If she's out for any length of time, she could be dehydrated."

It was a hot September day. Close to ninety degrees. A.L. and Rena both took off their suit coats. He grabbed two water bottles—one for Emma and one for himself. He wasn't coming out of that field until somebody found her. Rena did the same. And when one of the FBI agents pointed and said, "We need more bodies over here," the two of them headed in that direction.

"Stay in one row. Look left and right as you go, to cover three rows at a time," the agent instructed. He pointed for A.L. to start in one spot with Rena a few rows over.

It was hot. And the drying leaves of the corn stalks slapped them in their faces. The vegetation produced a dense cloying smell that made A.L. want to throw up. "Come on, Emma. Come on, honey," he said. He walked at a fast pace but not so fast that he couldn't carefully scan right and left. A curled up five-year-old could get very small. Within minutes he had sweat running down the back of his neck. Ten minutes later, he emerged from the end of the row. Rena was seconds behind him.

There was another FBI agent at that end. He pointed at two more rows and A.L. and Rena started a return route. They did it four more fucking times. By that point, they'd both emptied their water bottles and grabbed two more from one of the cases that somebody had left on the ground for just that purpose.

Nobody was stopping for more than a few seconds at the end of the row before plunging back into the dense field. A.L. spent the time mentally kicking his own ass. If they'd been a half hour earlier, maybe they'd have stopped Catherine before she'd left her house. If they'd have somehow ferreted out that Kara had a biological sister. If they'd have realized that Claire Potter wasn't off in her suggestion that Kara and Steven had something going.

Should have. Would have. Could have. And now a five-year-old's life hung in the balance.

He picked up the pace, almost jogging. His heart was beating noisily in his chest, reverberating in his ears. Maybe from exertion. Maybe from fear. That combined with the thrashing of other officers working their way through the field almost made him miss it.

But there it was.

"Help."

A small voice.

And there she was. Dressed in the same outfit that had been described in a thousand posters and email posts. Sitting on the ground. Looking up. Streaks of dried tears on her dirty face.

He knelt down. "Emma, I'm a police officer. You're safe. I'm going to take you back to your mom and dad."

She said nothing. But she did look at the water bottle in his hand.

"Are you thirsty, honey? You want a drink?"

She nodded.

He twisted the lid off the water bottle and put it on the ground halfway between the two of them. She picked it up and took a big drink. She did not give it back to him.

He held out a hand. "Will you take my hand and let me lead you out of this field? Will you let me take you back to your mommy and your daddy?"

"Yes," she said, her voice very faint. But when she

stuck out her hand, it was steady. And she didn't flinch when he gently engulfed it in his own.

And together, A.L. and Emma walked out of the cornfield.

It was many hours later, just before 5:00 in the afternoon, when normal people were just leaving their day jobs, that he finally crawled into bed. He'd been up for more than thirty-five hours but he wasn't that sleepy. He suspected, though, that once the adrenaline wore off, he'd sleep like the dead.

Troy and Leah Whitman had been waiting together and had gathered Emma in their arms. After a long and tearful hug, Leah had stepped back, looked for her mother and motioned for her to step in. Then the four of them had held each other tight.

The little girl had been checked at the scene and then later transported to the hospital but had already been released. Physically, she was fine. Emotionally, time would tell, but the experts had said that she was likely going to be okay. While it had been a despicable act to take her, Emma had food and shelter and had not realized the peril she was in.

None of that mitigated law enforcement's anger with Kara Wiese, Steven Hanzel and Catherine Wood, who'd been picked up at her house without incident. Catherine and Kara were being charged with kidnapping and other assorted lesser charges and Steven Hanzel as an accessory.

Troy and Leah had listened to the story with a stunned look on their faces. "I'm sorry, Leah," Troy had said, his voice thick with tears. "This was my fault."

After just a moment of hesitation, she'd reached for

his hand. "No. Not your fault. Their fault. Three crazy people who thought it would be easy to fool a five-year-old."

A.L. sort of thought the Whitmans might have a chance.

A.L. smiled at the woman next to him. Tess had hurried home from the title company when he'd finally been able to call her and tell her it was over. Now she was naked in his arms.

He kissed her. "You know, I recently met a psychic. She says it's important to have all your energy centered, not spread too thin."

She moved his hand to a spot where he liked to put his hand. She was warm and wet. "Feel my energy?" she whispered.

It was going straight to his head. Making him want to say things and make big promises. "Tess," he said. "I—"

She kissed him. Drew him in. "Focus, A.L. What was that you said about spread?"

He moved between her legs. Slipped inside. "I'm doing my best work here," he said, his lips hovering at her collarbone.

"Plenty good," she murmured, moving against him. "Plenty good for right now."

* * * * *

Don't miss Beverly Long's previous book featuring A.L. McKittridge, Ten Days Gone, *available now from MIRA Books!*

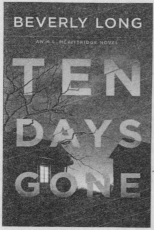

SPECIAL EXCERPT FROM

(H) HARLEQUIN
ROMANTIC SUSPENSE

*Carrie French is escaping an abusive husband when
she seeks refuge at the Double M Ranch—and forms
a friendship with ranch hand Luke Wright. When they
end up stranded in the Rocky Mountains, Carrie's past
threatens their future—and Luke must ensure they
make it out alive.*

Read on for a sneak preview of
In the Rancher's Protection,
the next book in The McCall Adventure Ranch *series
by Beth Cornelison.*

What could she tell him? Her situation was horrid.
Frightening. Desperate. And that was why she had to
keep Luke out of it. She had to protect him from the
ugliness that her life had become and the danger Joseph
posed.

But he was standing there, all devastatingly handsome,
earnest and worried about her. She had to tell him
something. The lies she'd told friends for years to hide
the truth tasted all the more sour as they formed on her
tongue, so she discarded them for one that was more
palatable.

"A few years back I made some…poor choices," she
began slowly, picking her words carefully. "And I'm

trying to correct those mistakes. Until I get my life back on track, my finances are going to be tight. But I can't make the fresh start I need if I accept money from you or anyone else. I need to do this by myself. To be truly independent and self-sufficient."

"Poor choices, huh?" A hum rumbled from his throat, and he twisted his lips. "We all make those at some point in our lives, don't we?"

With his gaze still locked on her, he inched his palms from her shoulders to her neck, and his thumbs now reached the bottom edge of her chin. His work-roughened hands were paradoxically gentle. The skimming strokes of his calloused fingers against her skin pooled a honeyed lethargy inside her. Reason told her to pull away, but some competing force inside her rooted her to the spot to bask in the tenderness she'd had far too little of in her adult life.

Luke is the kind of man you should be with, the kind of man you deserve.

Don't miss
In the Rancher's Protection *by Beth Cornelison,*
available July 2020 wherever
Harlequin Romantic Suspense
books and ebooks are sold.

Harlequin.com